ideal love

Alice Burnett

Legend Press Ltd, 107-111 Fleet Street, London, EC4A 2AB
info@legend-paperbooks.co.uk | www.legendpress.co.uk

 British Library Cataloguing in Publication Data available.

Print ISBN 978-1-7871998-9-7
Ebook ISBN 978-1-7871998-8-0
Set in Times. Printed by Opolgraf SA
Cover design by Anna Morrison www.annamorrison.com

For DB

‘Fair house of joy and bliss,
Where truest pleasure is,
I do adore thee.
I know thee what thou art
I serve thee with my heart
And fall before thee.’

Anonymous

I

‘The charm about you
Will carry me through
To heaven’

Irving Berlin

1

'Cheek To Cheek' by Irving Berlin

It was 25 September 1997, I was twenty-six and I had no idea the evening ahead of me would change my life.

'*Gilles* – ' Tim Woodward was whispering at my office door.

'Ah thank God, let's go.'

We exchanged nods with my principal and I steered Wood out of the building.

He was slightly less miserable than when I'd first suggested tonight's party. We had a laugh about a keen fellow trainee on our way to the tube and I got a glimpse of the Wood of old. But whatever else happened that night, one mission had been accomplished – Wood was neither at his desk nor at home listening to Mozart's Requiem.

He'd been single for a year, I'd only had six days of it, but I was the one who couldn't sit still.

We went down the escalators and squeezed on to a carriage. He'd gone too far into the darkness.

I hadn't expected my girlfriend to call it off either, I'd been upset. But the two of us were like travellers who'd teamed up only to realise we'd arrived, nothing was keeping us together. She'd just bothered to understand that and take action. And with enough notice for me to hear about this party, get Tim invited and coax him into showing up.

We stepped out of Covent Garden tube and I told him to prepare himself. It was going to be a beautiful night.

'So it's all over with Anna then?' he asked bleakly.

'Yup,' I said, walking on.

'Sorry to hear that.'

'No, she did us both a favour.'

'She seemed genuine to me.'

'Yeh, she was, the spark just went out.'

Tim sighed. 'Gilles, I hate to break this to you, but at some point you've got to stop thinking with your dick and grow up.'

A group of girls paraded past, like an erotic pat on the back. I could sense them with my eyes closed.

'Tim,' I said as they walked away, 'twenty quid says I leave with a woman and you don't.'

Tim raised his eyes and went quiet. I didn't speak.

'All right, all right,' he said as if I hadn't stopped talking. 'Done.'

We walked into the club entrance and down the stairs, pulled under by the waves of sound and body heat, until we reached a kind of massive volcanic cave which my friend's sister's twenty-first had filled beyond imagining. The DJ was charging it up with seventies funk – there must have been over a hundred women on the dance floor alone – not only that, the men were all at the bar, dutifully perpetuating that great English ritual of refusing to dance with the women. What was this if not the promised land?

It didn't take long before I was mesmerised. I pointed out the blond woman with the incredible figure to Tim. Tim said she looked aloof, but that on the plus side, this would help her shake off lust-crazed French bastards like me. I brought his attention to a sweet-looking, dark-haired girl I thought he might like, but he wasn't convinced. I finally got Tim to concede that the blond one was 'superficially attractive yes, but nice, no', and went over and bought her a drink.

Her face wasn't quite so pretty close up, but then again I clearly hadn't made her day. She wasn't interested in conversation and when I asked her to dance she looked at me like I'd told her a bad joke.

Did I still smell of rejection? Surely not, it had been nearly a week.

Then I got lucky. She liked lawyers, especially city lawyers. She made a remark about my hair, and I said it was straight before I saw her. She laughed, and looked at me and carried on laughing, beyond the time allotted.

I went from trainee solicitor to cash-laden hotshot in five minutes. She became a stream of gazes, a sweetshop of breasts, waist and thighs, drinking with me, dancing with me, not objecting to the feel of my hands.

At least an hour must have gone by. One of her friends interrupted to complain about a girl they both knew. I went to get drinks and came back into focus.

I couldn't see Tim anywhere and wondered if he'd left. He didn't get it. You just had to throw yourself and see where you landed.

But waiting in the crush at the bar, I glanced over at the one I'd been with as she dished it out, her expression as cold and dismissive as when I'd first asked her to dance.

Nice no, I thought.

Back together, we found a quiet spot on the other side of the dance floor, and she was all hospitality, the sweetshop door open, the jars within reach.

We left the club. Cooling off on the pavement, I found myself asking her to dinner the following Thursday. Did people do that? But within a minute, she'd accepted, I'd hailed her a cab, kissed her goodnight and lost myself twenty quid.

I went back in to look for Tim. He couldn't have needed

me less. He was deep in conversation with a girl. Not the dark-haired one, another.

A guy I knew from law school blared into my ear like a trumpet. 'Gilles you old tosser! I knew you'd be here!'

We had a drink and discussed rugby for ten minutes, which was educational but not what I'd come for.

I scanned the dance floor one last time. It had gone down a gear, mainly smooching couples and people too out of it to know what else to do.

I thanked my friend's sister – I was going to Paris the next day – and went to the cloakroom to get my jacket. It was soundproofed and organised. I put my jacket back on, not half as pleased with myself as when I'd taken it off.

'Hi Gilles.' Tim was following me up the stairs, arm in arm with the girl he'd been talking to. She was pretty and sensitive-looking and I could see the pride in his face.

We chatted on the street. Her name was Elaine.

'He's a great guy,' I said to Elaine, 'I've known him for years, you couldn't meet a nicer person, really fantastic guy – '

'Thanks Gilles.' He was smiling like a light. 'Elaine and I were actually at university together.'

'Right,' I realised I was slightly drunk and neither of them were at all. 'Well then you already know,' I smiled back.

Self-consciously, they wished me goodnight.

Wood had turned it around.

Give it a year or two, I thought, and me and the Trumpet would be handing out the orders of service at their wedding.

I started walking towards Soho Square. I didn't know what I wanted, but I wanted it, whatever it was. Police sirens came and went, beer cans and cocaine packets flowered in the bushes – the place was like a dark mouth, salivating over every human urge. I thought about another me being reincarnated as a prostitute. She'd be good at it. And then I-me could meet this charming woman-me who'd know exactly what I wanted.

It was eleven thirty. The plane left at nine the next morning. Get up when, six?

I had to accept that I hadn't got into the cab with the blond woman, and that this was for the best given I was going away the next day. I headed to Leicester Square tube.

Women weren't ice cream, I told myself, they could wait and melt later. Sometimes it was better to get some distance and re-evaluate.

I strolled down the escalator and caught up with a couple standing side by side. They stayed put until the last moment, let themselves be delivered by the bottom stair and walked off giggling.

I followed signs to the Piccadilly Line, passing an angled mirror in a blind corner of the passageway – a relic, surely, from the days when Victorian lawyers roller-skated through the station. God was I slick. Billowing cape for attracting attention, untouched Victorian women gasping, sweating at my exceptional roller-skating skill. Careful, shy eyes. Beating breasts. And though my feet are strangely shod, my mode of expression oddly modern, they can see that I am strong and tall, passionate yet practical, wild yet sensitive –

A train rattled off into the dark.

In its wake I heard someone singing. Someone who knew what they were doing. A woman, mellow-voiced, light.

It went away.

I needed a cab for 6.30. I had to take a second shirt for the evening. Two ties. Business cards. Pick up some cash at the airport.

I heard the voice again. Faint but not weak.

… I could take the red tie. Or no… dark red, less showy.

You didn't often hear a voice like that on the tube. Or a woman on her own, which took courage. I locked my ears onto it as it faded.

I walked along the passageway, listening out for the voice, wondering if I was getting warmer or colder, until it stopped being a game and listening was all I was doing. Had I heard it? I thought I had, I was almost certain of it – I was taking off, separating from myself, listening with every cell. And although I realised I hadn't, I felt that time had slowed down, that it was only me listening that made the link from one moment to the next.

Then the voice came in from nowhere and I was set back on the ground, the music so tender with sadness that at first I could hardly bear to listen. I hadn't known how much I'd needed to hear it. I'd had no idea.

As I stood there, the sense grew in me that I'd been an invalid, on the way out – for months, years – that I'd been given the right medicine in the nick of time, a shot of emotion calibrated precisely for the way I was feeling, combining inside me, making me cry in my head, making the night fall away like nothing.

The song was an aria, I wasn't sure which, and normally I couldn't stand opera, but there was nothing operatic in it, her feelings were real. A voice as light as sun on the water, barely caught in the physical, and yet this close, this full of love.

It was ending, but there was another.

I laughed in delight. 'Dancing Cheek to Cheek'. Oh perfect choice. I had its pattern in my head, I couldn't have heard it better.

I felt my ears drink in the sound. How wonderful that I was here, that I hadn't got into the taxi, for one moment of this – a woman's voice, simple, smooth, entirely on the note, no tricks, no catches, relaxed, effortless, but with the greatest depth of emotion.

And while I listened, I let something happen to me without me realising it. Something I couldn't explain and for a long time kept to myself, because this feeling didn't usually happen to me, I made it happen. The person singing was you, the passion, the honesty in your voice were yours, and I was falling for you, distantly as if I'd separated from myself again, and the me that was there listening was too ecstatic to know it.

'Heaven,' you sang, 'I'm in heaven.'

I rounded the bend and caught sight of you, standing where the passageway met the stairs. The beauty of your face, the ease of your expression, the grace in your bearing – I took it all in, but it made sense and didn't surprise me. It was dream-like. I could feel and see and hear, but not act. And you were still singing, and I was still listening.

I noticed I wasn't the only one. Other people, women and men, young and old, they stopped. Like me, they walked on eventually, shy of how they felt. Perhaps like me they listened for a while on the platform. 'Fly Me To The Moon' – Piccadilly to Uxbridge. 'Lullaby of Birdland' – Heathrow Airport. 'Sophisticated Lady' – Rayners Lane. Then, like me, their feet took them on to a train.

Sitting in the carriage, it occurred to me that I could have spoken to you. I could get out at the next stop, go back, find you. Of course, I thought, I must, why not?

But I told myself it would be awkward, an interruption to you, an embarrassment to me. Later that night, alone in my room, having gone over my failure to act as if I could have worn it away, I swore I'd never litter my life with excuses like that again. I'd make up for it.

I'd search everywhere, somehow find you. And once I'd found you, I thought as I lay awake, anything was possible. We'd fall in love. For myself, I knew it. For you, I'd do all I could to convince you.

It wasn't that I was totally deluded. I knew I wasn't much. But time seemed suddenly shortened, with an end as well as a beginning, and highs and lows that might never come again. That night in the tube station, I'd been to heaven. I wanted to go back. And if nothing short of insane optimism would get me there, what was the point in being realistic? This was love. And love was all there was, I knew it for sure. And pity the old me – pity anyone who didn't.

2

'Sitting On A Fence'
by Mick Jagger and Keith Richards

Venus parked the car, took the key out of the ignition and didn't move. The lack of sleep had hit her and having just arrived at Charlotte's house, she'd started to feel nervous.

She glanced at her phone. *9:58 Thu 21-09-2006*. Two minutes to go.

'Mum – EE! Get out get out get out!'

She found her purse. '… Look, stay here while I get a ticket.'

She walked along the quiet Chelsea square to the machine. Gilles wouldn't hear her message until he got off the tube. The sound of them fighting would be trapped in her head until then.

'Vee, come on, I'd been at work for thirty hours straight.'

'*You think I want to live with someone who works for thirty hours straight?*'

'Oh so who the hell do you want to live with? Why say that kind of shit?'

'*Don't tell me you never think about other people –* '

'NO I DON'T.'

'*What utter crap*.'

She slotted the coins in. One by one they sank. She pressed a button and the machine made a digesting noise.

'You know Vee, you don't realise that the fact that you never believe a word I say is what totally corrodes us.'

'I tell you what corrodes us. You live in a dreamworld where you can work your soul away, fuck off to a casino, then come home and fool yourself we love each other. Well this is real life. This is where I live. Your choice.'

She opened the driver's door and put the ticket in the windscreen. She'd call him after the interview.

Why was she even feeling guilty?

'Come on Leo.' She lifted Leonie onto the pavement, took out a bag of recording equipment and a bag of toys, carried everything to the pillared house where Charlotte lived and rang the doorbell.

The entryphone stirred into life. 'Vee, Max thinks I've hidden his Blackberry,' Charlotte said conspiratorially. 'He's terribly cross... Max, you're very annoyed, aren't you darling?'

The door was still closed.

Venus leant closer to the speaker. 'Charl?'

'... Oh don't be ridiculous.' Charlotte's voice had come from further away. Max shouted angrily in the background.

'Darling sorry, two minutes.'

Charlotte hung up. It was contagious.

The stone steps were pristine. Max's house, not Charlotte's house. Venus put down her bags, sat on the top step and lifted Leonie onto her knee.

She bobbed Leonie up and down. She was making a radio programme about hedonism in long-term relationships, having spent all night fighting her husband, by interviewing a woman who was fighting her boyfriend. Keeping Leonie away from the microphone no longer seemed to matter.

It was a clear September morning, the air like cold water.

There was a rustle in the branches of a cherry tree.

'Birdie, Leo!' she pointed at the pigeon. 'See it?'

'Yeh!' Leonie said. 'Buhdie!'

They laughed.

Venus jumped at the noise of the buzzer. She pushed at the door, gathered her things and walked with Leonie into the flat.

Max was combing his hair in front of the hall mirror. He looked like a man from a watch advert.

'Hi,' Venus smiled. 'Sorry to interrupt.'

He picked up his case and walked past. 'I'll be working late,' he shouted.

'I'll be out,' Charlotte called.

'Fine by me.' He slammed the door behind him.

Charlotte stretched her arms out to Venus.

'Hi darling.' They kissed one cheek. 'Take no notice.' And then the other.

Venus felt awkward. 'Are you all right?'

'Yes, very,' she smiled mysticly. 'Don't worry, Max needs to be baited, gets his circulation going. Now let me take your things.' She took Venus's bags off her shoulders, then crouched down to Leonie's height. 'How's the Prime Minister today, hm?' She tickled Leonie who burrowed into Venus squeaking with laughter.

Charlotte had the knack of swan-like elegance without self-consciousness and Venus bathed in her presence as she and Leonie followed her down the hall.

They arrived in a large, white-walled room, decorated with refined anonymity.

Charlotte put Venus's bags next to the sofa and Venus sat down lifting Leonie beside her.

Charlotte had walked into the kitchen. '... I heard the ice-skating programme – hilarious old Yorkshire woman – '

Venus laughed. 'We could have done the whole thing about her.' She took a few dolls and animals out of the toy bag.

'Mummy,' Leonie whispered in her ear. 'Bikit.'

Venus reached back into the toy bag.

'So,' Charlotte called, 'it's going well, no regrets?'

Leonie ate it immediately.

'Yeh really well, they're talking about a second series.'

'Same passions theme presumably?'

'Yeh, exactly.'

'Here darling.' Charlotte handed Venus a glass of water with ice and lemon in it and went to the window. 'Well I'm glad.'

Venus watched her move a strange multi-coloured glass clock from the middle of the desk under the window to one side, slip off her shoes and, using the chair as a step, get up onto the desk.

Paper and crayons. Gardens for the dolls, she could try that...

Charlotte closed the top sash. She looked radiant.

Venus put the water down on the table in front of her and lowered Leonie on to the floor with the toys.

'You've caught the sun.'

'Mmm, Barbados, just a last minute thing.' Charlotte winked as she curled her legs up next to Venus. 'That's why Max was still here.'

'You should have told me, we could have rearranged it.'

'God no darling, I wouldn't have dreamt of it.'

They were quiet for a second.

'So,' Venus said, 'how was it?'

'Barbados? Wooo, wonderful. Off season, not too crowded.'

'Good homework.'

Charlotte looked vague.

'I mean I know you've just had a row but you must have both enjoyed it.' Still vague. 'In terms of this hedonism in relationships thing – '

'Aah, of course. Darling listen, I can do hedonism till the cows come home, but you'll have to get creative about the relationship side. Where's your recorder?'

Venus found it. 'What d'you mean, keep Max anonymous?'

'Not exactly.' Charlotte picked it up. 'You know I've always had a thing about West Indian men?'

'Right, sorry when was this?'

'This was yesterday.'

'But Max is Swiss.'

'Through and through.'

'So, what are we talking about?'

'Hedonism as requested. But not with Max.'

Venus's brain clenched. 'But – I thought with you moving in – '

Charlotte shook her head like Snow White.

Venus closed her eyes, her naivety a veil she'd forgotten to remove. Well, but maybe it was nothing too shocking.

Charlotte sighed deeply. 'Work is my life blood,' she stretched like a lioness, 'but you absolutely cannot beat a full throttle fuck.'

Venus adapted her world view. Programme aside, she'd banked on monogamy, as if Charlotte were joining her club.

Then things started to make sense. 'That's why you were arguing.'

'No no, it wouldn't bother Max in the slightest.'

Venus was bewildered. 'You mean he doesn't know?'

'Vee you needn't feel sorry for him, his concession to being on holiday is tennis before breakfast and dinner in the evening. Fine by me, his work is his mistress. Look at those gadgets. Bilgeberry – pure phallus, made to be cosseted. That sweet little mouse button, unquestionably female. Talking of which… ' She pointed at the recorder lying idle on the table.

Venus went through the motions, setting up the microphone and checking the room noise, unsure what she was going to do with the actual recording. Leonie seemed content at least, lining up the dolls and animals on the polished wood floor.

Charlotte yawned. 'Uh, sorry darling, terrible shag lag – '

Venus put her head in her hands. This woman made her laugh, made her envious and annoyed her all at once.

'… So,' Venus took a breath, 'a stunning blond walks into the bar, every man falls to his knees…' She pressed record.

'To be honest, I'm not into bars. What a boozed up man gains in instinct, he lacks in *point*.' Charlotte looked discerning. 'And no question, he was the stunning one. Late afternoon, quiet beach, ultra attractive and double it. I mean *un*missable. And we both knew the score. Out for a laugh, lust strikes, feed the flame. God he had some life in him.'

For a moment Venus lay paralysed on the sand, sun melting, tide lapping.

'So,' she said, 'this was all yesterday, on the beach?'

'No, the day before. We met twice. And we didn't stay on the beach.'

'But isn't it better to be out in the open?'

'You'd probably get thrown in jail over there. But no darling, I'm not really an exhibitionist.'

'But I mean weren't you worried he'd be violent?'

'Good God no. You can spot that a mile off, and it's to be avoided no matter how beautiful the body, one of the most valuable lessons my mother ever taught me.'

She paused as if coming to an emotional admission.

'And obviously get on top. It's like driving – could be anything from a Land Rover to a Bentley. I'd far sooner change gear.' She pursed her lips. 'Darling, remind me to write a book. When I'm sixty and hitching up the stallion like poor Catherine the Great.' She sighed learnedly. 'Of course Catherine made the mistake of letting the horse do the driving…You know ironically he was on call the first time we met, had to go back to the hospital. I'm cursed with conscientious men. At least this one had his priorities straight, switched the thing off for ten minutes.'

'He was a doctor?'

'Might have been. Certainly a cricket fanatic. Could only make love with the radio on. You see that I find adorable... Honestly, the appetite, I frighten myself.' She was putting her shoes back on. 'It's nature telling me to reproduce.

Incredibly sweet of her.' Then she whispered. 'Fuck, that's what I say. Fuck fuck fuck. And often.' She got up. 'Right, let's have some tea.'

She went out into the kitchen and put the kettle on.

Venus felt herself relax. 'How the hell do you get away with it?'

'I come in peace darling,' Charlotte said above the noise.

Chuckling, Venus looked around her at Max's ordered sitting room. She wondered how this cricket guy felt about Charlotte, and how on earth Charlotte could have left him. Or whether when you were Charlotte, the question just didn't arise.

A deep rummaging sound came from the kitchen. Max had divided the flat into his rooms and Charlotte's rooms to cope with the chaos of Charlotte moving in. The kitchen, which was Charlotte's, couldn't be tidied unless Max got food poisoning.

'Arab, Jew, Catholic, Protestant… ' Charlotte was musing. 'I must get hold of a Hindu – '

There was a loud clatter.

'Arse.'

'Everything okay?'

'Yes darling thanks, you stay there.'

Venus sat back in the sofa. Leonie was totally absorbed by her dolls – she hadn't even noticed they were alone together.

She'd ring Gilles when she got home. She'd been harsh. Well of course she had, he'd been infuriating.

Fight, that's what I say. Fight fight fight. And often.

He might have left a message on the landline.

She checked the clock on the desk against the time on her phone.

The glass case must have had a hole in it, for the coloured beads to have been put inside, but she couldn't see any trace of how it had been done. It looked beautiful, standing out in the white room, the beads illuminated by the morning sun.

'Tea,' Charlotte announced from the kitchen, 'is ready…

Now I think we need some contrast. I suggest an adolescent girl-crush.'

Venus swallowed. She switched off the recorder.

Charlotte came in with a teapot and cups just as her phone rang. She groaned and picked it up.

She looked at Venus and raised her eyes in exasperation. 'Mariah,' she mouthed.

'Mariah sweet, how are you?' She walked back into the kitchen. '… Yes I know, two o'clock, Richmond Theatre… Yes of course I know where it is… '

Rationally, Venus didn't feel jealous of Charlotte's career. She told herself that it was acting not singing and therefore not comparable.

She massaged the tightness out of her jaw. What did Charlotte mean, her crush as an adolescent on a girl? … Perhaps she could scrap the relationships aspect, make the programme about a woman's desire in any context.

Find a recording of Sappho in Greek. Merge the Greek with the English. Background of little waves. What was Greek?

Oregano? Not on the radio. What was that smell? Rosemary? Drying in the sun.

Goat bells echoing in the valley, but faintly, so that you couldn't tell where the goats were.

Goats. Gi you… Summer, walking through the woods to the beach, Gilles running like a lunatic, trying to catch a goat. The goatherd, puzzled, rushing, thinking they wanted to steal his animals. Gilles trying to explain that his name meant goat, their hapless joy in the justification. And then staying on the beach into the evening. Laughing, talking, finally getting quiet.

Could they get that back?

'You're being a very – ' she bent down to kiss Leonie, ' – very good girl.'

Leonie carried on with her colouring, barely acknowledging her. Each doll had a garden to sit in but needed another garden to play in. This was a phenomenon of concentration, not to be interfered with.

Restless, Venus walked over to the shelves by the fireplace. She noticed a black and white photo of Charlotte sitting in an old Mercedes convertible looking like Grace Kelly.

'*Quel* pain. Sorry darling.'

Venus put the photo back, went to the table and poured the tea.

'Thanks Vee.' Charlotte took a cup. 'She loves telling me off, it's a ritual. Do you mind camomile? Max has infested the flat with the stuff.' Charlotte looked at the tea. 'Leo won't want this, looks like pee doesn't it?'

She went back to the kitchen. 'Elderflower okay?'

'Fine, thanks,' said Venus, sitting down.

They'd have to start it after this.

Leonie was entranced by the coloured clock.

'Here.'

Venus put the glass on the table, the clink sound like a signal.

Setting the recorder, she moved the microphone a little nearer to Charlotte and nodded.

Charlotte sat back in the sofa and began.

She'd met a student teacher when she was at school and broken the rules one evening to go to her flat and borrow a tape.

'I'd thought of her as tame, but not totally straightforward. She'd played us a song in a lesson which I couldn't get out of my head.

'I remember the look on her face when she answered the door. Part shock, part pleasure. She was wearing a shirt which fastened close to the neck, but with a teardrop-shaped hole below the button. It showed the curve of her breasts. She never normally wore anything like that. I think I must have caught her trying things on, you know, slightly sexed up.

'I went through her tapes and books while we talked, picking things up without asking, not putting them back. I knew it annoyed her, but she didn't react.

'So I started reading her post. 'Don't do that,' she whispered. I looked her right in the eye and carried on reading.

'She walked over to me. I thought she'd explode, but she didn't. She moved my hair to one side. Her fingers touched my neck. And then she slowly unfolded my collar and folded it back down, and put my hair back in place.

'I asked her to do it again. We were alone, we could do anything we wanted. And she did it. But more slowly than I could imagine. I couldn't have craved anything more.'

Venus felt her blood rise.

'We started to kiss. It was like walking up spiral stairs, continually climbing, not wanting to look down.' Charlotte paused. 'There's a cruelty in being a virginal woman. You're aware of sex but you don't know what to do. If you've got some nous you can teach yourself. Or a man can teach. But the sheer glory of the female body, the immense potential for pleasure, that's something very few men understand – '

'God.' Charlotte jumped.

The crash came from the floor by the window. Venus turned and ran towards the noise. Scattered and bouncing on the wooden floor like a rush of hail were hundreds of different coloured glass beads. The sun lit them as they flew, points of colour diving madly in the white room, demanding attention, elasticating time. And still there was the sound of them, against the wood, the glass, the white walls and one against the other, bouncing back, rolling, slowing and coming to a stop.

Leonie wore an expression of shocked delight.

Eyes, eyes first. Hands. Ask her. But no blood, nothing. She wasn't hurt.

God look at it.

' – Leo, it's broken, will you say sorry?'

Seriously, quietly, she said sorry.

'Oh darling, don't worry,' Charlotte said.

Leonie started to cry as Venus held her on the sofa.

'Max'll be livid, silly fool.' Venus caught the sting in Charlotte's voice.

'I saw her looking at it, I should have moved it – '

'Vee come on, it was an accident.'

'No, I should have put it higher up.'

'Oh for God's sake, some things are out of your control and that's that.'

They sat on the sofa, Venus cuddling Leonie as she cried, the tension in Charlotte's voice strangely cathartic.

Venus took a breath. 'Look at these beautiful gardens,' she whispered once Leonie had quietened down. 'How did they get here?'

'Gah-dun,' Leonie sniffed, then started to cry again.

Charlotte went to get Leonie something to distract her.

'Everything's okay. All right my love?' Venus held her more tightly. 'Everything's okay.'

Charlotte came back with a book and a small handbag.

'Look, Leo. – Thanks,' said Venus.

Charlotte sat down, next to the two of them. Venus put her arm out to her, pulling her closer, and as she felt Charlotte cuddle up, it occurred to her that Max might not do that, that Charlotte had chosen one of the few people alive capable of ignoring her.

Venus looked down. '… You're okay, with Max?' she asked tentatively.

'Yes,' Charlotte said. 'It may not seem like it from your point of view, but I am.'

Then something about Charlotte struck her in a way it never had before. It wasn't as if she'd searched for some romantic ideal and failed to find it. She'd never wanted it in the first place. She couldn't take being confined at any cost.

'And you? Is everything okay with Gilles?'

She thought for a moment. 'We had an argument last night. But yes, I think so.'

Neither of them spoke, Venus surprised by her honesty.

Whereas to be in love was what she wanted. And what Gilles wanted. Like a fire in the dark, life seemed clear. They both knew that. So of course they'd get it back.

Leonie was climbing down from the sofa. There was glass everywhere.

'Leo, no.' Venus grabbed her. 'You'll cut yourself. Just stay here.'

She and Charlotte tidied up. As Charlotte dealt with the last of the glass, Venus looked at the clock face. Broken glass stuck out from it. The second hand was twitching between the nine and the ten like an insect chopped in half. She undid the back cover and took the batteries out. She turned the little wheel, hid the second hand underneath the long minute hand and lay the clock on the table.

She saw Charlotte watching her and felt she'd been in a trance. 'Thanks for everything… ' She pushed her hair out of her face. '… God I feel so tired.'

Charlotte squeezed her shoulder.

Venus gathered the toys. 'Tell me how much I owe you.'

'Oh, nonsense Vee.'

'No, I'll pay for it.'

She realised she'd left the recorder on. She clicked it off. Leonie and Charlotte looked up at the noise. Time to go home.

3

'Who Wants To Live Forever' by Brian May

You know Vee, we often have an argument only because something else has gone wrong, but for some reason it still lasts twenty-four hours. You called just as Wednesday began, a few minutes after midnight, I was at work, casinos couldn't have been further from my mind, but you took just my being at work as self-indulgence and we were thwarted from then on.

And it was true I hadn't been hard at it. I'd been monitoring the corridor – a guy from projects was zinging back and forth like a hare on a wire, I couldn't miss out on that – and when the action stopped, my bulldog clip model of the Taj Mahal was waiting for me on my desk. But despite what it looked like, I hadn't entirely been wasting my time. I'd been meditating on the state of my deal. And I'd concluded that it was falling apart.

Kenny was the client's name, a Glaswegian in New York, a decisive if unpredictable sadist. We were supposed to be working through the night to keep the timetable on track, but what kind of freak would flog eight people overnight only to tell them the deal was off in the morning?

Sniffing out my failing purpose, Anthony Stretch knocked on the door, keen as a hard-on. Why they made me a partner over him I'll never understand.

He tried to panic me about some pensions point, his shining blood-filled head looming over my desk, riddled with overactive synapses. I don't know whether he'd noticed what time it was, but if he had it would only have strengthened his resolve: the documents would be turned around for the morning, no question about it.

I suggested he get some sleep and went round telling everyone else to do the same. They vanished like field mice.

'Gilles,' Stretch was back in my office before I was, 'we can't let everyone go, this is madness.'

'I've just told you Anthony, Kenny's going to pull the deal.'

'A, that's pure conjecture and B, it hasn't happened yet.'

'Listen I'll note your objections on the file and I'll check the pensions point, now if I were you, I'd go home.'

I woke up with my head on my desk at quarter to three. Reading pensions law is like taking antihistamine, you can't operate machinery for twelve hours afterwards. I slunk into one of the office bedrooms, texted you apologies and fell asleep.

Back at my desk at nine that morning, still Wednesday, I felt weirdly sick. I couldn't concentrate, every problem seemed insuperable. And when I stopped making the effort, the old doubt itched at my brain – the years galloping, the days limping, why was I wasting my life with this shit? And I thought about the thousand other things I could have done, I could still do if only I could just do them, and it was like scratching, it felt good for a while.

I went to a lunch meeting with Kenny's UK minions, the pointlessness of which allowed me five minutes' sleep. Back in the office, New York was awake. I played my messages.

'JILLS, KENNY. DEAL'S DEAD – RHODA, GET OVER HERE. I WANT ANDY FLOWERS, I DO NOT WANT FUCKING VEGETATION – YEAH, JILLS, NO NEED TO RETURN MY CALL.'

I should have been elated. Stretch was dumbfounded but

he'd find something else to do. I told the team to take the rest of the week off.

I sat at my desk, the evidence of my work, good, bad, all of it useless. Well, I thought, I'd seen it coming. I'd still get some cash out of it. I'd learnt an obscure point of pensions law. I'd known all along Kenny was a pellet of rat shit. None of that got to me. What got to me was that somehow over the three months in which this deal had loomed over my life, I'd become involved.

So Vee, in this rancorous mood I met you for the dinner I'd been about to cancel to get some more work done. And I realise it was a frustrating occasion, a meeting of people who used to be friends, who in their knackered day to day existence believe they still are. I could tell you were waiting for it to end. And that pissed me off even more.

Someone suggested going on to a casino. My deal was dead, what did I care it was a Wednesday? I said good idea. Well can't you see what a depressing prospect leaving then would have been? We had a look-don't-speak session, excused ourselves and went out of the restaurant.

People were milling around outside the pub opposite, drinking and laughing.

You sighed. 'Let's walk down – '

'What are you so cross about?'

'What kind of way is that to start a conversation?' You turned away. 'I can't believe you're even thinking of prolonging this crap.'

'I want to have some fun, it's not illegal.'

'What? At a casino?'

A van pushed through the street, crowding the pavement.

'I thought it was me who never did anything.'

You stared. 'Has it even occurred to you to think about the babysitter?'

'That's what we're paying her for. Vee, look I've got to relax, I've just spent thirty hours at my desk – '

'You selfish shit.'

'What's wrong with you? You think I work day and night for pleasure?'

Your eyes closed in dismissal. 'It doesn't please me.'

'Vee, come on – '

'I've had enough, I'm going home.'

A cab drove up, as if at your bidding. You left and I went back into the restaurant.

An hour later, there were no cabs. The five of us found a guy with a Cortina and a taste for zither music. I felt sick. The top of my back pounded. The guy turned right at a red light and hit one of those BMWs with tinted windows. We left them to it, and like desperados, walked to South Kensington. When we found the place, they told us they had a dress code and wouldn't let half of us in. I bribed the doorman, then bailed out after half an hour.

I got home at eleven fifty-five. Not even midnight. Still Wednesday. At least, I thought, we wouldn't argue.

You put down your book, looked at me in disgust and said you were disappointed in me.

Vee, I hate that. I hate it. What had I done? I'd had a waste of a day. The evening had been disappointing, not me.

Calmly you told me that all I did was work, that this wasn't the life you wanted.

I agreed with you, it wasn't the life I wanted.

You said that if I genuinely agreed with you I'd change the way I lived.

I said that I was tired, couldn't we talk about it another time.

You said I never had time.

'Mum's back on Friday,' you said, 'I'm thinking of staying with her this weekend, she'll look after Leo, that'll give you some time.'

'No – ' Sick with shock, I couldn't understand it. 'Please don't do that, for God's sake, I love you more than anything – '

'You're full of words, but without acts it's bullshit, it's all fucking bullshit.'

'How can you say that? It tears me in two when you say that. If you never believe in me, what have we got?'

'DON'T – *DON'T* – BLAME ME.'

We started shouting, Leonie came in crying, you took her back to bed and we went on, making up for in spite what we couldn't convey in sound until exhaustion ended it.

My alarm rang at half past seven the next morning. I reached out, turned it off and opened my eyes. I remembered I was cross with you. I was about to collect my thoughts and remember why. But I looked at you, lying facing me, asleep, and everything got diluted. And while you wouldn't approve of my fantasist's reasoning, I could persuade myself that maybe we hadn't argued, because either way I'd have woken up the next morning and loved you the same.

My old trainee, *Lapin*, told me about a bird theory of knowledge. Socrates invented it, something about everyone having a birdhouse full of different birds. As if anyone that's important in your life roosts in you.

Well here they were. The rhythm of your breathing as you lay next to me, your black-brown eyes closed, your cascades of soft dark hair still – *l'oiseau chanteur*, *l'oiseau de nuit*, *l'oiseau de paradis*. And across the corridor, the delectable *chouette*. A tawny owl, a snowy owl and, at four in the morning, a screech owl. High forehead, long nose, curls that tightened with each act of wilfulness – these were mine – but your DNA had crept in and made her mouth generous and her eyes bewitching as the night sky. Judging by the quiet, still closed thank God.

But here was contentment, well within our grasp.

All you wanted was for us to be together like we had before life had got serious – a dose of that easy intimacy we'd taken for granted. It was all I wanted too.

Vee, this is what love is, this is how it lasts. If you love someone, you'll always discover your love for them again. At the beginning discoveries rampage at you, you're Vasco da Gama. And people think that when that time's over, there's nothing left to find. But they're so wrong. It's only then that the faraway lands come within reach.

And I can hear you putting it down to early morning lust – it wasn't that – but even if it was, sex doesn't rule out love.

There are kinds of love I couldn't have foreseen. Leo newly born and already I'd have fought to the death for her, yet the minute before, I'd contemplated having to make an effort. You singing her to sleep, me crying with happiness, the skin of my childless self long shed. The re-living of my parents' lives and my own, the serenity of a happy family, the dimensions of even this one kind of love are infinite.

But our love was the origin of everything, it encompassed everything, it was the pattern for my life. There was nothing I took more seriously.

I became more and more fervent as I looked at you. I wanted to tell you exactly how I felt, but you were asleep and I wasn't sure how you'd take it.

I'd do something today.

I got up, shaved. It was true I'd let work get to me. I'd put in the hours to become a partner, then having been made up, far from losing the habit I'd gone into overdrive.

I planned it out in the shower. I'd leave at 4.30, bring back supper, take charge of Leo – I'd have to time it right, be home just after you left to get her. It wasn't much, a change in the weather. But if the swell was kind and the breeze billowed the canvas, who knew, maybe the faraway lands would turn out closer than we thought.

I got dressed in the spare room. Closing the front door as quietly as I could, I walked out of the house and down the hill to the tube. The air on my way was sweet. It was a perfect September morning.

I stepped onto the train and sat down. I felt a surge of rightness. What actually mattered in life? What was anything compared to this? We were lucky. We'd been unlucky before, both of us, but even the bad luck had brought us closer, even that had come good.

The District line caters for this kind of contemplation. Time means nothing, trains wait on bridges, in stations, pausing in thought themselves. The watch-checkers, the pacers, they must do the decent thing and move house.

Around Gloucester Road I checked my diary. I'd had a feeling I'd forgotten something. A nine o'clock meeting – a senior partner, a potential client. I looked at my watch. Ten to nine. I couldn't believe it. Phone? 8.50, clear as day. I asked the guy next to me. 8.51.

I was in southwest London, the meeting was in the City. I'd be late. Not irretrievably, but it didn't inspire confidence.

The train was full of people. I looked at the map of the line behind me. Nine stops to Mansion House.

Nine? I counted again. There were nine.

I could run the three-quarters of a mile from Mansion House to the office. That would take five minutes. Maybe ten.

Or get a cab? No, running would be faster.

Or get off now and get a cab? No, I'd be in traffic for hours.

I looked at my watch again. I'd be at least twenty minutes late. I put my phone back in my pocket.

The train came to a halt. For fuck's sake, what kind of transport system was this? Why did I sit here taking it? Why didn't I revolt?

My shoulders felt like lead. Tiredness, being crunched up at my desk, the last few weeks of this god-forsaken deal.

I wondered if I was hungover. Some kind of delayed reaction. I had that indigestion that wouldn't ease off. My shirt was sticking to my back, everything was uncomfortable.

I felt sick again which infuriated me. If I was off form as well as late, the meeting would be fucked to hell.

I'd have to have an impregnable excuse, something to do with work. I'd have time to think of one at least.

Then – and this is something I shouldn't have done, but I didn't mean to do it – I got too aware of breathing. I was so aware of it, I started to think I couldn't do it, until I actually couldn't. It was as if a metal plate had attached itself to my chest and was squeezing my lungs out. I wondered if it was the air but no one else seemed to feel it.

A man was standing in front of me. He asked me if I was all right. I couldn't speak, I just looked at him.

When our eyes met, I saw his thoughts take over his face. He started shouting, 'Pull the cord! Someone pull the cord!' But I felt less pain. And the guy next to me spoke, but I don't know what he said.

Then the pain disappeared completely. I hadn't realised how bad it had been.

Thank God, I thought.

4

'Landslide'
by Stevie Nicks

Venus changed gear. The engine loosened. She anticipated telling Gilles Charlotte's holiday gossip and sang to herself.

'Mumma?'

'Yeh?'

She'd drop Leo off, ring Gilles then decide on the programme.

'Mum-eee? Want Pansus.'

'We'll find him after playgroup.'

'NO. No go playgroup.'

'Ssh, come on.'

'… Mum-eee?'

That singer her mother had accompanied – who'd married the opera fanatic. The two of them devoted. It was possible. No children though.

'Pansus.'

Not that Leo hadn't brought them closer. They adored her, they adored the way the other adored.

'PANSUS.'

'Leo, stop kicking the seat.'

'PANSUS. PANSUS. PANSUS.'

Venus turned left down a side street and stopped the car.

'Leo listen, we'll see him when we get home from playgroup.'

'Mum-eee,' she was using her cute voice, 'want see him now.'

Venus looked at her watch. It was already quarter to twelve, they'd be late anyway.

She drove back home, quickly made them cheese on toast, found the stuffed toy cat Gilles called Agapanthus and took Leonie to playgroup.

Had that been something to do with their argument?

She got back into the car, opened the window, pushed a CD into the slot and drove off. She'd get Gilles to come home early. Leo would go to bed early. They'd work it out.

Returning home, she went straight into the sitting room and picked the phone up. The dialling tone was broken. She smiled with relief – so he had called.

'Message received today at 10:06am.'

It wasn't him. A man's voice. Measured, soft. Ian Spence, nurse. Accident and Emergency Department, Chelsea and Westminster Hospital.

She took down the number.

'Repeat?'

She wondered what it could be. Her mother? But not in London.

He'd called her Mrs Matheson. Gilles' mother?

'Remove?'

She rang the number. A woman answered with a rush in her voice.

'Casualty?'

'Hi. It's Mrs Matheson. I got a message from Ian Spence – '

'Just transferring you now, Mrs Matheson.'

She seemed to be expecting her. Wordless panic sounded in Venus's head. Then the nurse's voice.

'Hello Mrs Matheson. It's Ian here.'

'Oh hi.'

'Hi. I'm looking after your husband. I'm afraid he was brought into hospital earlier this morning feeling very unwell.'

'Oh.' Venus paused. 'But he's all right?'

'No, I'm afraid not.'

'But he was fine. Sorry… What's happened?'

'He's not at all well, so it would be a good idea if you could come in and see him as soon as you can.'

There's a thudding in her head.

'But he was here, just this morning he was here. He's fine. Sorry, I think you must have the wrong person. It's Gilles… with a G – '

'I'm afraid there's no mistake. I'm sorry Mrs Matheson.'

The thudding surrounds her.

'If there isn't anyone nearby who can drive you, you might want to phone for a taxi. Say you need to get to Chelsea and Westminster Hospital, it's three hundred and sixty-nine Fulham Road, they'll know where it is.'

'… Mrs Matheson?'

'Yes.' Her voice sounds blank.

'When you arrive, come to Accident and Emergency reception. It's to the right of the main hospital entrance. Say you're here to see me. I'll come and meet you, okay?'

'Okay.'

'I'll see you here soon.'

'Yes.'

'Goodbye then.'

She follows the red signs around the corner of the hospital building. The woman behind the desk says take a seat, Ian won't be long. Venus sits down. She looks through the blue metal mesh of the seat next to hers.

If she loves him enough, he'll be all right. She tries to picture him but she can only see his face from the night before. She repeats in her head that she loves him, aggressively repeating it.

Someone calls her name. A kind-looking, grey-haired

man. It's the nurse. They walk along. He takes her into a small room with chairs and a sofa and asks her to sit down. He offers her tea. She says no.

He asks her to wait, he won't be a second, he'll just get the doctor.

He returns quickly with a tall man. She stands up.

The man says he's Doctor Laakkonen. He's been looking after her husband. He asks her to sit down. He pulls up a chair close to hers. She shifts back. He looks at her. He says he is afraid he has some very bad news.

She asks what's happened.

He says her husband was travelling on the underground this morning. He had a heart attack and fell unconscious. He was taken into hospital. He could not be brought back to life.

He says he is so sorry. They did everything they could. But the heart attack was extremely severe.

Almost to herself she says that can't be right, she heard him close the door.

He says he knows it must be a terrible shock.

But she says he's not even ill – he's only thirty-five –

He says even young people can have heart problems.

She says but he's healthy.

He says sometimes it's not obvious. The heart attack was so big, no one would have survived it.

She is quiet.

She says so he is dead.

Yes, he says.

She asks what happens, what happens now.

He says there are lots of people who will be able to help her. He suggests that she might want to ring her family or a friend.

She says nothing.

She hears him speak.

He says Ian will look after her. Ian will take her through everything. Is there anything she'd like to ask him?

She says no, no, thank you.

He says his name is Erik Laakkonen. If she thinks of anything else, Ian can find him. She mustn't hesitate to ask.

He gets up.

She almost speaks, but doesn't. He looks at her, gentleness on his face.

He asks her if there's anything else.

She says no, no thank you.

He says how sorry he is and closes the door behind him.

The nurse pulls the doctor's chair back and sits down.

He's so sorry, he says. Everyone did everything they could.

She asks what happens now.

He says that it's up to her. He asks whether she would like him to phone anyone for her.

She says but who.

Maybe her parents, a brother or sister.

No, she says. No, thank you.

He says she can see her husband if she likes. Most people find that it helps. She can stay with him for as much or as little time as she wants. It's up to her.

She asks what will he look like.

He says like he's sleeping.

The nurse walks with her through the corridor. He says they'll go into a room and see her husband and if she wants him to stay, he will, but otherwise he'll be back in the other room. Of course she can touch him, if she wants to. And she can see him again after this. It needn't be the last time.

Venus becomes aware of the nurse's speech. But already they are at the door.

She goes into a room with white walls and no windows. She doesn't look at the person on the bed. She feels the thudding, the draining of saliva from her throat.

The nurse tells her that he'll be in the other room, where they were before, down the corridor. Quietly he closes the door behind him.

There is a sheet over the body, folded back to uncover the

head. She summons herself and looks properly at him. Then she can't take her eyes away. It's him and not him at the same time. It's indisputably him, but he's still. She screams inside, silent. His eyes are closed. His lips are dry, blue around the edges, his face set.

She should take him home.

She puts her fingers on his forehead. The skin is cold.

She loves him. She loves him so much. Does he know?

She feels over the sheet for his hand, puts her own underneath, bears its weight.

She repeats and repeats that she loves him so much, that she will love him forever.

She loves him. Does he know? Does he?

She looks from ceiling to floor, wall to wall. She touches the palm of her hand on his forehead. Her husband is lying on a bed in a white room.

She holds his shoulder through the sheet, puts her head against his. She whispers to him, Gi, please.

She sits down on the chair next to the bed. The minutes don't pass. Her connection with reality is as broken as his. They are two puppets in a room. And while her inner voice reiterates that he is dead, while every one of her senses shows her he is dead, the knowledge of it is as beyond her as if it were her own death.

She stands up. For a second she puts her lips on his. She tells him she'll come back. But as soon as she's heard the thought aloud, she knows she won't.

She grits her teeth. And it's as if a door that has been clamped shut has loosened.

Leo. How will she – ? Oh God.

A low howl sounds from the back of her throat. The whole of her body feels sucked out and hollow. Then it fills with tears.

Venus sits in the room with the nurse.

She asks would he have felt the heart attack, the pain –

Not for long, says the nurse. In a way he was lucky – he probably didn't have time to realise what was happening.

The nurse begins to speak. '… If there's anything at all you'd like to ask the doctor, I can easily call him – '

'No,' she says. 'It's okay.'

'How about a cup of tea? That might help.'

'Okay,' she says. 'Thank you.'

When he's gone her thoughts go back to Leonie. Her stomach seems to shuffle. She looks at the carpet, concentrates on the pattern.

The nurse comes back carrying two white plastic cups. Sitting beside her, he puts the cups on the low table.

He says don't worry, she doesn't have to drink it.

She thanks him, blows her nose.

He asks her what his first name was.

Gilles, she says.

Sounds French, he says.

She says his mother's French.

Sorry, she says. She blows her nose twice more.

He asks her if she needs a hug.

She leans against him. He says he was there when Gilles first came in.

She is crying again.

He says some things don't stop. Not completely. He promises her that.

She breaks down.

They sit together, she crying, trying to stop herself and crying again.

He asks her if she's sure she wouldn't like him to get in touch with anyone, ask them to come in.

She says her mother's on holiday, her brother lives in Cornwall –

Sorry, she says. Sorry –

As Venus cries the nurse's voice is calm. He says he's here to help her. Anything she wants to ask, it's okay.

He speaks to her steadily. 'It's the realisation of it over

and over again, just when you think you've got it, it comes back again.' He pauses. 'I lost someone three years ago. You don't think you'll ever recover, you don't want to recover, sometimes it still feels like yesterday, but sometimes you surprise yourself. It only needs to happen once for you to know it's possible.'

She takes a breath. They stay quiet for a while.

He says maybe she'd like to go through the practical side? It might help.

She says yes, the practical side. What does she have to do? She doesn't know. She just can't – it's not –

Sorry.

She blows her nose.

He asks will there be any other visitors to the hospital in the next few hours.

She says no.

He says the body will be taken to the mortuary. If anyone wants to see him later on, that's fine, just give him a call. There'll be a postmortem, because it's unexpected, and her husband's GP will talk her through the report –

That'll explain everything, she asks.

Yes, he says, that's right. Then, when the postmortem's over, the funeral director will collect the body.

But, she asks, it will stay here until the funeral.

He says if that's what she wants, yes.

She says yes, she'd like it to stay here.

He says that's fine. He tells her not to worry, she doesn't have to decide anything now.

She doesn't reply.

Well, he says, it's probably best if she talks about it with her family.

She looks at the floor.

She wonders how she's come to be here. It's as if there's another her. The her who went home and phoned him, who made up with him for the night before, who said come back early tonight. She wonders how she took the wrong branch. Was it arguing with him? Seeing Charlotte? Taking Leo home for lunch? What should she have done? Because she could still do it. If she could work out the correct route –

'I'll get you some information, I won't be long.'

He closes the door.

She listens to his footsteps going down the corridor.

Widow. Her heart thumps.

Widow, *vide*, empty.

No. It's too basic, it would come from old English. And it's *veuve* in French.

Oh, stop for God's sake.

But if you don't think, then what? She tries to breathe slowly, think slowly.

She could imagine him, as if he were next to her. He's the one she would tell. She knows him completely – someone that real doesn't turn into nothing.

The nurse gives her a handful of papers. Her head is aching. She's got to get Leo.

She asks him for some water.

He returns with a full glass and she drinks it.

'Thank you,' she says, hearing her voice aloud.

She wants to ask him about Leo. 'I don't know how to tell my daughter.'

'How old is she?'

'Two.'

'Tell her as straight as you can.'

'But she adores him – ' her breath shakes, ' – how do you say it?'

'You'll do it,' he looks at her with total faith. 'You have to say you've got something very sad to tell her. Then say, Daddy's body stopped working, the doctors couldn't fix it. Tell her he's dead. She won't understand, but it's good to say it. She'll ask lots of questions. The thing to do is to be honest.' He pauses. 'She'll take everything literally. If you say he's gone to sleep, she'll be scared a monster will get her if she goes to bed.'

'Yes,' she says, smiling with recognition.

'You'll be all right,' he says, as if it's a fact.

'You've been kind to me.'

He meets her eyes, sending compassion towards her.

At the door, he asks her what she'll do when she leaves the hospital.

She says she has to collect her daughter.

Okay, he says.

He asks her whether she wants to take his things. They had to cut his clothes. It's up to her if she wants to take them. There's also his briefcase. She can take it all today or come back later.

The shock is slower, heavier. She hadn't even thought.

She says she'll take everything now.

He returns with two carrier bags and Gilles' briefcase. He says just call him if she thinks of anything else. She mustn't hesitate.

He puts a box of tissues into one of the bags.

He says he'll get her a cab.

Outside things look different. The noises and the living and the present twist about each other in a tight plait. She moves, blown wispy as a ghost, undone.

II

‘The philosophy I cultivate is not so savage or grim as to outlaw the operation of the passions; on the contrary, it is here, in my view, that the entire sweetness and joy of life is to be found.’

René Descartes

5

'Strawberry Fields Forever'
by John Lennon and Paul McCartney

Vee, this habit of thinking of you must have started a while ago because I can't remember a time when I didn't. As if I was climbing a building hoping you were inside, trying to reach you before I even knew you. And I can recast that as the noblest thing there is. What would have been nobler? Fighting baddies. Freeing slaves. I didn't know any. I was blind and ignorant. I was standing on a window ledge, tapping at the glass.

When I was seventeen, my aunt Christelle invited me to spend the summer at her house near Antibes. My mother couldn't stand her or her depraved parties, but it would be a convenient month's entertainment. To me, it was manna from heaven.

Apart from her self-assurance, Christelle was my mother's opposite. Free-thinking, full-figured, keen on life. It was a relief to be related to her.

The first party was given the night I arrived. It was a hot evening and there were good-looking women everywhere. You think you want to be twenty-one when you're older, you forget how much you want it when you're seventeen.

There was a large tiled terrace, balmy and darker. The

women's shoes on the tiles – I sweated at the sound. Strange-smelling smoke wafting in the bougainvillea, the music from inside more distant.

I'd noticed a blond girl with a sweet smile. I took her to be younger than me, and tried to think of something to say to her. Deep in debate with myself, I got accosted by a middle-aged psychologist.

The man was one of those talkers who select their prey carefully. He'd have preferred the blond girl, but an awkward youth would do. He told me in detail about his experiments. He was, he said, profoundly interested in perceptual isolation. He'd been paying students to lie on a bed blindfolded, in a soundproofed room, in the dark. I told him I couldn't think of anything worse – I didn't really think that, I thought it would be money for nothing but I wanted to get away. He told me my comment interested him. The students thought they'd be able to handle it, but in fact I was right, it turned out that most of them were screaming and having hallucinations within two days.

So, he said, it was interesting wasn't it, most of us really cannot live inside our heads for very long. *Tu vois?* We talk of *les sens*, *les organes des sens*; we think it is only biology, we think it is innocent, we think it has no other implication. But without sense, where are we? We say *cela n'a pas de sens*! *C'est un non-sens*! Sense is reason. How can we escape the conclusion? We are designed to experience the world. We go mad without it.

He watches me now, that man. He's trained his binoculars right at me, finally caught up with me here on the window ledge. I keep going higher you see.

He's intrigued, he can't help it. Experimental conditions have come a long way since those early years, but to find a subject with no sensory inputs whatsoever – perhaps nothing except thoughts and feelings? He should have tried tall, sentimental lawyers before.

…It won't be long now. Such a polite form of annihilation.

But as he continues to watch, he grows restless. Why, he wonders, is the lawyer not yet mad? Why is he not falling into the void? Can he really be hanging on?

…In defiance of his central hypothesis. Not helpful.

He climbs into a little hot air balloon, lights the flame, pops up to join me. He sighs at human nature, his eternal mistress. He might have guessed it. There I am, clinging to the tower block of my past, a perverse look in my eyes, angling my head at the glass like a window cleaner gone rogue; no doubt – his dirty Freudian mind is in overdrive – no doubt trying to catch myself at it inside.

6

'Love Of My Life'
by Freddie Mercury

'Sorry Mum, I think I can hear footsteps, Leo must have got out of her cot – '

'Oh,' Patricia said, 'Okay darling.'

Leaving the phone on the bed, Venus walked into the dimly lit corridor looking for Leonie. She checked her bedroom. Leonie was right there inside her cot, sleeping peacefully, her duvet in place. Venus went back to her room and picked up the phone.

'She's fine, she's in her cot, I don't know what it was.'

'Try to get some sleep, Vee. You know I really think I should come back.'

'It's only one day, I'll be fine.'

'Are you sure?'

'Yes. I'll go for a walk.'

'A walk?' Patricia paused. 'What about Leo?'

'The monitor's got enough range if I walk up and down the street.'

'Why don't you ask that nice woman next door? I'm sure she'd come over.'

'Mum, I won't get any sleep unless I get out of here and the last thing I want is chat. I've got everything crashing into my head like a tank every five seconds.'

'Okay,' Patricia swallowed. 'I know, sorry – ' Patricia paused again. 'Is it one moment in particular you keep thinking about, or just everything together?'

'I don't know. I just keep going over what I said, what he said – what would have happened if I'd got up earlier – '

'You argue because you love someone, you've got to remember that Vee, because you care enough to want to put things right.'

'But the fact remains – we didn't remotely make up. I just can't stop wanting to make it better. I know it sounds weird Mum, but somehow I've got to get through to him.'

'Imagine it from his point of view, he must have gone through the same thing.'

'He was having a heart attack, what could he do – '

'But before he got on the tube, when he woke up that morning, he would have wanted to make sure you were friends again.'

'I'd left him a message. I was literally about to call him when I got the message from the hospital. I should never have seen Charlotte. If I hadn't been distracted by that, I'd have caught him before he got on the train.'

'Vee, I know it's no comfort, but it would have happened regardless.'

'But, we would have had a chance. There must be a way. There must. Just to get a connection with him – ' She took a breath, trying to calm down. 'What I mean is he's constantly in my head. So in that sense, he's still alive.'

Patricia didn't speak.

'He could just be in Paris, working on some deal, we wouldn't need a phone, we'd just talk in my head.'

'Darling, have you had supper?'

'I know it wouldn't be a real conversation, but it wouldn't be far off. You don't need to be with someone for them to exist.'

'Vee?'

'What?'

'Have you eaten?'

'Of course.' Venus wondered why her mother didn't ask her straight out if she'd gone mad. 'I'm being pragmatic Mum, you don't have to worry. I'm just trying to work things out.'

7

'Writing To Reach You'
by Fran Healy

I found Alex sitting in my office in August 2005. I'd been on a roll at work, you'd started this excellent radio job, Leo was happiness itself – I didn't think I needed anything else. But you can never have too many guides in life, or too many real friends.

I'd taken on a file for a colleague while he was away – Project Cronus, aptly named after the castrator. The client was like sand in the wind, topography shifting moment by moment, going everywhere and nowhere. It dawned on me that he thought he'd get sacked after the deal, so we polished up his employment contract and his wonderland of issues evaporated in the desert sun. I spent the evening with the finance director knocking the agreements back into shape, slept for a few hours, then assuaged the other side. Pleased with myself, I strode into the office just before lunch and deposited my brand new handmade calfskin briefcase on my desk.

I'd forgotten I was getting a new trainee. And I might not have noticed him sitting in the corner had he not tried to hide what he was reading. And I probably wouldn't have noticed that had he not blushed.

He was like a deer leaping through trees, strikingly

good-looking but shy, when he could so easily have been insufferable, which for six months would have blighted my life. In my gratitude, I took to him instantly.

I told him my name. He said his was Alexander Todd.

Ten to twelve, I thought, we had some time.

This was his second seat. When I asked him which other departments he wanted to try, he said he was keen to work in the Paris office. I explained that I knew a few people in the Paris office and I could sort that out for him – if he wanted me to.

I asked him what he was reading, but the phone rang before he could answer. It was Janice telling me that Sergio was on the line, a good client, I'd ring him back.

He hadn't met her, so I took him down to the secretaries. She smiled maternally at him. She'd have known who he was for the whole morning but wouldn't have introduced herself.

Then there was Esther, standing at the photocopier. Her eyes lingered over him. She told him in her smoker's voice that he looked like a good boy and he wasn't to pick up any of my bad habits. I explained to Alexander that I often made Janice a cup of tea and that Esther was so jealous she would do anything to work for me. Esther told me not to flatter myself and pointed at Alexander and said she'd far sooner work for him thank you and that I was just going to have to buck up my ideas from now on.

By this time Irene had taken the earphones out of her ears. Irene exerts a hold on me. A master of economy of speech, lawyers lost all verbal dexterity in her presence. If you could keep your nerve and break through the sonic wall of Dolly Parton, her work was impeccable. The rest – her former life as a bareback rider at a Hungarian Circus, her stint as an authorised markswoman – I'd constructed for myself.

She shook Alexander's hand, gave him her fire and ice look and replaced her earphones.

Back in the office I told Alexander that Janice was fantastic, very reliable. Esther was fine. Irene, I hesitated, was extremely competent. Something about him had activated my bullshit filter.

We sat down at our desks. I studied the back of his head. He had dark hair that came over his collar as if he didn't often think about cutting it.

He must have been older but he looked nineteen. Perhaps he had an Italian mother, possibly still quite young, probably breathtaking.

He seemed unaffected and gentle. Had I seen him on a train I'd have taken him for a student or some kind of artist. I wondered why on earth he wanted to be a lawyer.

I asked if I could make him a cup of tea.

He turned around, surprised and said yes.

I collected the tins I had on my desk and opened them. Earl Grey, *Vanille des Iles* and Darjeeling, the best that Berry Brothers and Mariage Frères could find. The smells of Chinese and Indian tea leaves swirled into my tired office like genies.

He looked up, polite exoticism briefly turning us into conspirators.

I made us both tea, dealt with my case and watched him pick up a slab of a book on VAT legislation that I'd happened to leave on the window sill beside his chair.

'You're welcome to read what you were reading before,' I said.

He looked around.

'You hid it, so it must be interesting.'

He blushed again. 'Sorry.'

'No, read whatever you like.'

'Well – it's not legal – '

'Can I ask what it is?'

'It's just a paper. Someone asked me to read it over.'

'Ah, okay.' He was engagingly unforthcoming. 'What's it about?'

He looked apologetic. 'Descartes,' he said.

'Oh right,' I feigned familiarity. 'Any good?'

'Yes – yes it is.'

How did law firms manage to con these idealistic types into working for them?

I sat back in my chair and put my feet up on the pile of Halsbury's Laws under my desk.

'Well I'll let you know when I need your help, but otherwise I'd advise you not to do anything unless you want to do it, particularly when I'm not around. You needn't get in until nine-thirty – '

I had his attention.

' – and if you haven't got anything to do at four then I'd leave discreetly. It's not life and death, whatever the client says. It's only money. You may be here to work but you're also here to live. The two needn't be mutually exclusive.'

There was a look of disbelief in his eyes.

'You don't have to take my calls unless I ask you to. If you want to make a call in private, bear in mind there are phone booths on the first floor. Free international calls and no one knows they exist.

'The food in the canteen's hopeless.'

That made him sit up.

'Go out of the office, turn right, you'll see a good sandwich place on your left. If you need a restaurant, ask me. I've got a deal with a decent French one and a reasonable Japanese. Tell them I sent you and they'll look after you. If you find a good one, let me know.

'If you're feeling sleepy – it hits me after lunch – there are bedrooms in the basement. Michael, the security guard, he's got the keys. I did him a favour with his conveyancing once and he understands the importance of a siesta. Otherwise it's the library, but that's uncomfortable.'

I love to watch trainees when I give them this spiel. They think they've arrived in heaven.

'Now, remind me to give you a massive piece of work

which you don't actually have to do. If someone tries to dump something on you, get that out and tell them it's urgent.'

The phone was ringing. It was you. I excused myself to Alexander and, probably because he was in the room, assumed the personality of one of those unruffled American detectives.

'Miss de Milo.'

You said hello quite affectionately.

Alexander had turned back to his desk.

I smiled. 'You sound well.'

'I *am* well.'

I leant back in my chair.

'So,' you asked, 'how did the meeting go?'

'Big success,' I said, 'all patched up.'

'Well done.'

'Yeh, thanks… Leo get off all right?'

'Yeh, fine. Gi?'

'Mm – ?'

You paused. 'You don't feel like coming home early do you?'

That sounded inordinately nice.

'It's just they're broadcasting the programme today.'

'What?' It was tremendous news. 'Vee, that's fantastic.'

We were both in good moods, independently of each other and together. These times do happen Vee, you mustn't forget them.

'Yeh thanks, thing is it's at quarter past four.'

'Oh. Why did they do that?'

'I don't know. Cancelled something else at short notice. It's fine, I don't mind. Can you make it?'

I looked at my diary. 'Ugh. I've got a meeting at five – could be internal – God,' I lowered my voice, 'I don't believe it… '

'What?' You whispered back to me.

'He's just popped out and closed the door, like a little rabbit.'

'Who has?'

'My new trainee.'

'*Un petit lapin?*'

'Yeh.'

'Maybe he's having lunch with his girlfriend.'

'Mm. Don't know. He's good-looking all right, just other worldly. Delicate. Hard to describe.'

'Uh huh.'

'*Un chaud lapin,*' I whispered ardently.

You were laughing.

'Come home now,' you whispered.

'Vee.' I was taken aback.

'It's okay, I know you can't.'

'I want to.'

'…I don't feel like working.'

'Why don't you come here?'

'No, no. Who is he anyway?'

'Why not? …Don't know, still formulating.'

'So very good-looking?'

'Mm. Slightly serious, intellectual. An artist maybe.'

'A famous artist traps him at an exhibition.'

'Vee, come here.'

'I'd have to turn back as soon as I arrived.'

There had to be a way.

'What's his colouring?'

'Dark. Boyish.'

'Like you?'

'No no. Mediterranean. Smaller, shorter.'

'Perhaps the artist takes him back to his studio.'

I glanced at the closed door. 'Listen if we each got a cab, right now, we could be together in half an hour, less – '

'I've got to get Leo in forty minutes.'

'Ugh.'

'Well don't blame me.'

'Of course I'm not, why say that?'

'Your tone, sex machine.'

'Tonight. Without fail. I'll say I have an academic commitment.'

'*Bene Dottore*, don't be late.'

Then I realised quite how perfect it was that you'd rung. Alexander gone, you on the phone, the planets were aligned. '*Professoressa*, permit me, I have una questione molto importante, molto academico, non jocare – '

Then I saw him. 'Shit,' I whispered. 'He's back.'

'Who?'

'*Lapin*. Oh no, wait, hang on.' I could see him through the glass, walking past the office. 'No, he's gone again.'

'He was letting us talk privately.'

'Yeh. Vee listen, what do you know about Descartes?'

'What?' you laughed. 'Why?'

'*Lapin*-related. Anything at all.'

'Well, 'I think therefore I am' obviously.'

'Right,' I said, convincingly.

'And Cartesian coordinates, but that's maths… Hang on, I'll look it up.'

You were walking with the phone. 'The I think therefore I am thing – you know it's called the *Cogito*? From *Cogito ergo sum*. Hang on a sec.'

I waited for you to pick up the phone again. 'So you can refer to it as the *Cogito*?'

'Yup.'

'Perfect.'

You started reading. '… *greatest work the* Meditations (1641). *'Once in a lifetime,' Descartes said, 'anyone who seeks truth must call in doubt whatever can be doubted.' Asking 'How and what do I know?' he arrived by a process of reduction at his famous statement* 'Cogito ergo sum'. *From this core of certainty he proceeded to prove to his own satisfaction God's existence – he was a sincere and lifelong Roman Catholic – and hence the existence of everything else*.' You paused. 'I have a feeling he liked to get up late – '

'Descartes did?'

'Yeh.'

'Sensible guy.' I thought for a second. 'How on earth do you know that?'

'Ha I don't believe it! Listen to this: *Queen Christina invited him to Sweden. Here the cold climate and* predawn tutorials *with the queen caused a fatal attack of pneumonia.*'

'How awful.'

'I was right.'

I smiled. '… But *Professoressa*,' I said, 'surely we must ask, what was he really doing alone with this queen in the half-light?'

'You know *Dottore* it's possible he was teaching.'

'Yes.' It was a gentle reproach. 'Teaching at the same time – ' I was impressed. 'Sating both body and mind, the consummate man.'

And your sigh was like a spring breeze. 'Then you have a competitor, *Dottore*.'

I smiled broadly.

Out of the corner of my eye, I saw *Lapin* walk past my office again. Life hummed with potential.

'*Grazie mille, Professoressa.*'

'*Prego, Dottore. A presto.*'

I opened the door and looked down the corridor. There he was.

'Alexander!' I called.

He turned around.

'Oh hi,' he said, walking towards me.

We went back into my office, and I told him about you. How brilliant, marvellous, etc. you were. Your programme was about mimics this week – you had some hilarious contributors – quarter past four, if he was interested.

'Oh right,' he said, seeing the implication about departure time, daring to believe that he really had found nirvana.

'What a great job,' he said.

Sergio. Phone call.

'Yeh. It is.'

Sergio. Sergio. I found the latest file.

But *Lapin* had got his paper out again, and I couldn't hold it in. As long as I took it gently. I didn't want to fire all my bullets at once.

'Back to Descartes?' I ventured.

'Yeh.'

I browsed through the papers at the top of the file. '... Philosophical is it, rather than mathematical?' Nice and slow. 'I'm pretty ignorant, but he was an accomplished mathematician, wasn't he? Coordinates and so on?'

'Well,' he said humbly, 'I don't know much about maths.'

'No, well that makes two of us.' I tried to look thoughtful. 'I suppose Descartes' work tends to be rather – ' I shrugged *Sorbonne* style, ' – dominated by the *Cogito*?'

His eyes lit up. 'Yeh, exactly. That's what everyone knows him for but his method was at least as important as his result.'

'Mm. But quite a result.'

'Yeh, it's compelling.'

'And then from that, the existence of God and everything else.' I furrowed my brow, thinking I was spinning the shit. 'I suppose we're all after some form of certainty – you know, that something exists outside ourselves. It's that fear of being alone.'

'Yeh,' he looked shocked. 'I was just thinking about that.'

'Really?'

'Not knowing what it's like to be someone else. All you've got to go on is their behaviour. You can't know what happens inside them.' His eyes shone with calm interest. 'So much of what people do seems to be motivated by that. The fear that no one else is like you, looking for reassurance. I suppose that's why people read novels, given they're not factually true.'

I smiled. 'Or papers on philosophy?'

'Well, I don't know...' he hesitated. 'To me philosophy is

a bit like going down an empty gold mine. Even when you think you've got something, you come out empty-handed.'

'Maybe you learn to see in the dark.'

He smiled, relieved that in this daringly thoughtful exchange I'd adopted his mental picture.

'Did you do philosophy at university?' he asked.

'No,' I said, 'law, I'm a masochist. But I went to the philosophy library once. The room was small, the books were thin, and the titles were quite promising. So it didn't seem like an empty mine at all. More like a plate of cakes when all you've eaten so far is mashed potato.'

He looked at me, compassionate as a priest.

'Well when we've got time, you can tell me what I missed,' I said rashly. 'As long as you don't mind.'

'No. No, I'd love to.'

I found Sergio's number. '…The deal I've been working on should close soon – you've been saved the worst of it. We'll talk about it after lunch.'

And he turned back to face his desk. A semblance of normality drew itself like a theatre curtain. You wouldn't have known we'd had a conversation.

I didn't think he'd take it seriously. I certainly didn't think I would. But late that afternoon when he left he gave me the agreement he'd proofread and said he'd bring in a book the next day. Descartes.

Bloody hell.

After he'd gone I got up and closed the door. I looked at my watch – two minutes to five. Within ten minutes I was out of my meeting and on my way to my academic commitment. I felt like a repressed intellectual, coming out of the closet.

Talking to him was like getting out of city streets into open fields.

He played down philosophy at first, I did the same with law, each of us admiring the other's subject. But the truth was that most of the time I enjoyed being a lawyer, and he loved philosophy. As we got to know each other we revealed the sides of ourselves we'd condemned. Perhaps we both saw the lure in the other's argument. Forming a friendship by reciprocal congratulation and self-deprecation, a very English dance.

But there was more to it than that. I was interested in him. I was glad he existed.

We were walking back to the office one evening when he brought up his personal life, which was unusual. I wondered whether something had happened to him that he wasn't letting on. He asked me about my childhood and I told him my father had died when I was six. He said that his parents were divorced. He clearly loved his mother, which made me think I'd been neglecting mine. But Vee, like you and me, he needed a father, and maybe because theoretically he had one, I thought not many people had noticed that in reality he didn't.

Then, seemingly unconnected to his family, he said he'd become too critical of people, that he found it difficult to like them; that he was so exacting he worried he'd be alone forever.

There wasn't desperation in his voice, just a haunting acceptance.

'But,' I said, afraid of his answer, 'you like me?'

'Yes,' he whispered. 'Of course.'

We walked on and I felt like I had to make something of it.

'Well, I'm a pretty poor specimen. If you can like me, I'd say that's cause for hope.'

He smiled, and the balance tipped my way again. I told him he wouldn't have to compromise, that there was more in the world than he thought, that when you underestimated it, it surprised you.

'My friends – ' he said, ' – can't understand…'

'But they're not you. They're only speaking to have something to say.' I paused. 'You know,' I said, 'life is full of tossers who think love's an admission of defeat. All they do is cripple themselves. I tell you what defeat is. Aiming for anything less.'

8

'Blackbird'
by John Lennon and Paul McCartney

The notice in the paper had said *Thursday, 28 September 2006 at 6pm*. The minute hand at twelve precisely, the hour hand pointing directly opposite, the two hands making a straight line.

A sixty-seven year old man pulled the sleeve of his jacket over his watch and turned the round handle of the back door of the church. He wouldn't stay long, he thought. No one would ask him anything, no one would notice.

He saw the people. Panic struck him. He could step back over the threshold, disappear. He closed his eyes. He would calm down if he waited. He wouldn't leave yet.

From the shadow of the transept he watched them. Women and men and children.

He noticed that some were holding a light, a long thin candle with white paper shaped like a tulip around it, so that the candle looked like the stem of the tulip, and the paper, the flower.

He understood how it worked. The paper was for catching the melted wax. But it also turned the point of candle light into a diffused whole. It sent his mind back thirty years, to the time when he lived with his wife, how she'd play the tune on the piano with her right hand, then flesh the music out with her left.

All around the church, which would have been empty and dark, there were people holding lights.

He made up his mind. He went to a table and picked up a candle and lantern. He pushed the candle through the small hole in the base of the lantern and straightened the wick.

There was a middle-aged man at the end of a pew whose candle was lit.

He walked to the man. He pointed to the candle. It was clear.

He went three paces with his light. Then, still in the transept, he stopped. There were six men walking up the aisle and on their shoulders was a coffin.

He wanted to leave at once. But he knew that if he did it would be impolite. Yet the fact that he was in the church was impolite. He decided to stay, but not for long.

Then he was distracted again.

A young woman, singing. He knows it. Schubert, a setting of a poem. He knows it so well that the hearing of it assaults him.

The song evokes the past in him until he has to shut his eyes. But he can't stop hearing the young woman. She sings it with grace. There's no edge, no twisted expression. Her voice is deep and clear like a pool in a cave. It springs from far inside her and fills every recess. It engulfs and loses the congregation. It fills the church, fills it with the pressure of her passion. And the lanterns might as well have been extinguished.

Du bist die Ruh,
Der Friede mild,
Die Sehnsucht du,
Und was sie stillt.

Ich weihe dir
Voll Lust und Schmerz
Zur Wohnung hier
Mein Aug und Herz.

Kehr ein bei mir,
Und schließe du
Still hinter dir
Die Pforten zu.

Treib andern Schmerz
Aus dieser Brust,
Voll sei dies Herz
Von deiner Lust.

Dies Augenzelt,
Von deinem Glanz
Allein erhellt,
O füll es ganz![1]

The song comes to an end. The young woman is standing still.

No one gives anything back. It's an outrage. They must give something.

There is a blond woman near the front. She goes up to the young woman and embraces her. The accompanist embraces her. The old man turns away until the women have returned to their seats.

The priest starts his patter. The old man doesn't listen. Instead he looks for a while at the side of the young woman's face. He wonders that nature took a flame from

---

1

'You are my rest, and gentle peace; you are my longing, and yet you still it.
Full of joy and grief, I consecrate my eyes and heart to you as a dwelling place.
Come in to me, and silently close the doors behind you.
Drive all other cares from my breast. Let my heart be filled with your joy.
The temple of my eyes is lit only by your radiance. O, fill it wholly!'

Poem by Friedrich Rückert. Translation by Norma Deane and Celia Larner, from The Schubert Song Companion by John Reed

his voice and lit the voice in that young woman. He doesn't look at his wife.

He notices that there's a spot on his lantern where the wax fell. It makes the paper translucent. He walks back to the door he came in by. Still carrying the lit candle, he leaves.

Venus heard the muffled shut of the back door of the church in the silence. It sounded like Gilles coming in from parking the car. But whoever it was had gone.

Next to her in the pew at the front were Leonie and Patricia on one side and Gilles' mother, Hélène, on the other. Patricia's husband had disappeared, Hélène's had died, Venus sat between the two.

She'd argued with her mother several times over the previous week. First about the preparation of the body.

'I'm not having any fiddling around. People can see him *dead* dead or not at all.'

'But Vee what about everyone else? It looks so neglectful.'

'Screw them.'

Then there was the question of Venus singing. Her mother had said Venus was crazy to consider the idea.

'Why don't you ask one of your friends? Charlotte would do it beautifully. I can't understand it, it's as if you want to break down in the middle of it all.'

'What if I did? What is this pretend we don't have emotions *shit*? I'll sing, you'll accompany. It's the right thing to do and that's *that*.'

Then again there was Leonie.

'She's far too young. It's just not fair to expect her to keep quiet.'

'How do we know what it means to her? If she makes a noise, fine. She can run riot through the whole FUCKING thing.'

There was a space between Venus and her neighbour on

the right. Hélène kept a respectable distance. Venus's arguments with Hélène took place unspoken and underground, using others as intermediaries. The bats perhaps could hear them.

Hélène was an elegant woman. She wore her sense of superiority lightly but unmistakably, a sugar-dusted plum amid the plain. She'd moved back to Paris after Gilles' twenty-second birthday, declaring that the time had come for her to turn her attention to her mother. But it was the end of an affair, and an argument with Gilles about his future, that had prompted her to go.

She'd been silent on the phone. It had made Venus sadder than tears would have. When Venus had spoken to her again a few days later, she was oddly composed, still tearless but no longer withdrawn, as if Gilles had been a distant cousin.

In the pew behind Venus were her brother Matthew, his wife Isobel and their two children, Sam aged seven and Lucy aged four. Isobel was five months pregnant. They lived in Cornwall where they ran a hotel and restaurant. Isobel liked to make wholemeal pasta for the children. She had a very supple body, which she attributed to regular yoga. It seemed to Venus that over the years the angry part of Matthew, the part that got touched by life, had withered.

Isobel had, through Matthew, agreed with Patricia over the question of the children attending the funeral. But this issue had been cast aside when Venus had asked Matthew to come up to London early to help her arrange everything.

'Vee we're desperately short-staffed, I'll have to check with Issie. Maybe Mum can – '

'WHAT,' she'd shouted, 'WHAT is wrong with you?'

'Don't shout.'

'SHOUT? I'm beginning to think you've forgotten how to make any FUCKING NOISE at all.'

He'd said nothing.

'… Sorry,' she'd taken a breath. 'Sorry – I just need someone – '

'No it's my fault – '

'I'll never ask this of you again.'

'Forget what I said, I should never have said it. I'll be there, we'll get everything done the way you want it. Vee? I'll be there, I promise.'

Gilles' best man Tim sat with his wife Elaine on the other side of the church. He and Gilles had got on more through jokes than conversation, so that it was difficult to tell how close they were. Venus had been reassured as soon as he'd answered the phone, exultant when he wanted to make a speech, galvanised by his energy.

Two pews from the back of the church sat Steven, a softly-spoken American guitarist. An old friend of Venus, Gilles had been suspicious of him from the start, and once Steven had realised that, there was nothing she could do to get them to like each other. It had made her determined. She wanted the song, Gilles loved it, he'd carry it off best. She knew, she said, she was asking a lot. No, he said, of course, he'd be honoured.

Father Kevin had known Gilles, but had only met Venus once. She'd thought church a ritualistic waste of time, a fact that hadn't escaped Hélène's comment, but Gilles had taken Leonie every Sunday from birth and she'd gone with them once to see what Leonie was being subjected to.

She concentrated when the Kevin guy talked. It didn't take him long. He'd always been struck by Gilles' great warmth and humour. Above all Gilles was a man whose love for other people, for his wife Venus and his daughter Leonie, for his family and friends, shone out. All true human love had in it something of the infinite and eternal. Gilles would be with God, and God is love.

Charlotte's mother sat beside Charlotte, keeping her sunglasses on throughout. She and Gilles had met at one of Charlotte's parties. Wearing only a cocktail dress, she'd opened the front door to go to her car. He'd grabbed her waist, taken off his jacket and hung it over her shoulders. She'd pressed his hand in hers, told him how delightful that was in a young man. He'd kissed her hands and elevated himself to enchanting.

From then on, they acted out a courtly flirtation whenever they met.

'Darling,' she'd confided to Venus as they'd left that evening, 'you don't know how lucky you are.'

Behind Matthew and Isobel sat Mary, a talkative, middle-aged woman whose lively eyes were stung with crying. Originally from London, she'd moved to Paris when she was young and got a job as Hélène's mother's housekeeper. Over the years she'd been a companion, a nanny when Gilles visited and a nurse. When Hélène's mother died, Hélène had asked Mary to live with her.

Gilles would reminisce about sitting in the kitchen while she was cooking, first at Mémé's, then at Hélène's flat. He loved to hear her London accent. They'd talk in English about his girlfriends, about Venus and Leo; about how London had changed and the men she'd kept at arm's length.

Mary rang Venus the day after Gilles died. Venus had been relieved, she hadn't known how to talk to her without speaking to Hélène again. There was something calming about her voice. She'd offered to organise the food and drink after the funeral. It would help, she said, to take her mind off it.

The sound of the back door again. Isobel, coming in with Lucy. Returning to their pew, Isobel smiled supportively, then took up singing the hymn.

With a chill Venus became aware. All the people in Gilles' address book she'd phoned, people he'd worked with, traced by his secretary shocked and quiet, people he'd been at school with, been at university with, travelled with, people from the paper shop at the end of the street, people from further away than she'd ever gone, all of them here, all singing that schoolish, fragile hymn *My Song Is Love Unknown*.

The tune of it was like the tide going out. The world seemed to be pulling back, dissolving her as it went. All that making of a life. When the whole thing could be stripped away, what was it for? The tears massed in her eyes, then in the shock of it, didn't fall.

Her brother took her arm and they followed the coffin out of the church.

They had to get back into the car for the reception. Venus felt Hélène squeeze her hand.

Her mother pulled her tight, Venus heard the sob caught in her throat. 'Exactly right,' she whispered.

People came up to her and said kind things. How sorry they were, how young he was, how beautifully she'd sung, how wonderful it had been. She wasn't ready for their compassion, their genuine regret. It seemed as if she, the widow, was the one making parlour talk.

Yes, Mary made the food; no, the burial is tomorrow morning; yes, Steven came from Colorado; yes, we thought the service would be better at night; thank you, thank you for coming.

An hour in, Venus felt someone tap her shoulder.

'I'm so sorry, my dear.' It was an older woman with a strange, constant smile. Venus couldn't place her immediately. 'We don't know one another well, but you must feel you can talk to me.'

It was Jane, she realised. Venus hadn't seen her since the wedding. Jane had married Frank, Gilles' uncle, and they'd settled in Africa as missionaries until Frank had become ill and they'd had to return to England.

'I really do understand – the suddenness, the dreadful loss. As does Hélène of course, but sometimes it can be helpful to speak to someone, well, outside the direct family. I do think – given the three of us have been so terribly affected – I know

Hélène isn't keen, but I feel sure this can be a beginning. When a tragedy like this cuts across the generations, with the same sorrow striking us yet again, so much is taken away it's difficult to see that God may actually be offering us the most precious of gifts: the opportunity to heal one another.'

Venus's mind lifted out of the fog.

'Now my dear you do know that I lead a bereavement support group up in Hertfordshire don't you? It isn't so very far once you're on the motorway – '

'Jane,' Venus stopped her. 'Sorry, what do you mean, the same sorrow?'

Jane looked unsteadily at her for a moment, as if trying to understand Venus's point.

'How thoughtless of me, we're here for you and Gilles – and Leonie of course. Each bereavement must be honoured in its difference, goodness knows I felt that way. You see that's a perfect illustration, it's the *sharing* of experience that's so vital. Ah, here's Father Kevin. Hello Father!' The priest joined them. 'What a marvellous sermon, wasn't it my dear?'

'Yes.' Venus smiled at Father Kevin. 'Thank you.'

'Not at all, I think it's you we should be thanking,' he said calmly. 'Venus has been an inspiration to me these last few days. She and her brother Matthew, they're miracle workers, the both of them.'

'Yes, aren't they,' Jane smiled. 'Now Father, I was talking to Venus about my bereavement group up in Berkhamsted. I wonder do you have that sort of thing here? The parishioners have certainly found it useful. If you need help in getting one up and running, you must let me know, it's so very important…'

Venus excused herself. She went to the lavatory and washed her face.

The question that had sprung into her head began to drift along with everything else. She sat down for a minute and checked her watch. People would go soon, surely.

Back in the crowd, she absolved her comforters. For not

being him, for not being able to bring him back, for the pity in their eyes and the sadness on their lips. With smiles and thanks, she said everything and nothing, performing until exhaustion overtook her.

The next morning, creaking-eyed, she stared at herself in the mirror. She hadn't expected to be there.

Into the car again, the chemical-clean smell, the driver whose face she hadn't seen.

Maybe doing the whole thing in one go would have been better. It was something else her mother had said. But she'd been right to have the funeral at night. Night was when people felt things.

She saw an old woman in the street cross herself as they went by. She wondered whether that was for Gilles' soul or for the woman's own.

They turned onto a dual carriageway, but kept to their stately pace. People overtook slowly.

Hélène put her hand on Venus's coat. 'This is the worst time *chérie*, and tonight when it is all over you'll think, but I lived through it! We'll have these times when we think this must be the worst, but if we think back to today we will take courage. Don't you think, Patricia?'

'Yes,' Patricia said. 'Vee, how are you feeling? Shall I open the window?'

Hélène's hand went to her coiffed hair. 'Surely it is nearly winter Patricia... But if *Vénus* would like the window open, would you *chérie*?'

'No, thank you.'

Patricia coughed.

The cemetery was cold. The bearers walked with the priest, the coffin on their shoulders, paired like oarsmen. Venus and Matthew followed with Patricia, Leonie and Hélène. A small group processed behind. They came to the rectangular hole in the ground.

The priest spoke. The coffin was lowered. The priest spoke. Venus couldn't stop crying, and gave up the attempt.

As each person filed past, they were to pick up some earth and let it fall onto the wooden top of the coffin. Venus saw the priest bend down, pick up a small handful and let go of it. The sound was like large drops of water hitting the sink all of a sudden, long after the tap had been turned off. It was her turn. She scooped up the earth in both hands. It was the colour of dried blood. Her tears dropped into the mass of it.

But as she let it go, the thought burst back into her head like sunlight behind clouds.

This wasn't the end. Everyone thought it was. They were wrong. They had no idea.

9

'There Ain't Half Been Some Clever Bastards' by Ian Dury and Chaz Jankel

Alex had been with me for a few weeks when I won a summer deal like no other. I'd spoken to a woman in the tax department and we'd found a way around crystallising a massive capital gain. It would mean restructuring the whole agreement, but it would also mean more fees, embarrassed accountants and the client telling several carefully selected partners that I was shit hot.

One evening as I was heading back to the office, it occurred to me that *Lapin* had been short-changed. The gentleman's hours I'd promised him were no more. Eight-thirty and he was still at his desk, the drafting I'd charged him up with on my chair, the proofreading in progress.

'Alex, sorry to interrupt. Do you want to have dinner? I'm waiting for comments, but I'm damned if I'm working in the meantime. Only if you want, don't let me keep you.'

His expression lightened. I showed him the menu of the faultless French restaurant round the corner.

'They'll bring it over. Decent bottle of wine. Proper plates, no plastic. I think we've earned it.'

He was convinced.

So we sat at my desk, he in the chair opposite with his Dover sole, me with my steak medium/rare, and shared a bottle, which worked out well because he didn't drink fast.

I didn't ask him about women. The girl trainees had already tracked him down, secretaries stayed late for him, female colleagues renounced the phone and came to my office with questions. He had the looks without the arrogance. You felt a sort of grace when you were with him. I could understand the attraction. What mystified me was that he didn't seem to liquidate his positions.

I was pretty sure he didn't have a girlfriend. I didn't think he was gay, or wholly innocent, or strictly religious. He just didn't seem to be firing on all cylinders.

I topped up his glass, wondering how I could get him going.

'How's the Descartes?' I asked.

'The paper?'

'Yeh.'

'Good thanks. I've finished with it now.'

'Ah.' I nodded.

He ate well. It wasn't as if he didn't like food.

'... So what's your theory of life?' I asked.

'Oh... well I don't know,' he said embarrassed.

'You know that book you gave me, I'm afraid I haven't read it all yet.'

'No that's okay, it's for pleasure.'

I dolloped the rest of the *béarnaise* onto my steak. 'I like it, I like the style.'

'What have you read so far?'

I regretted bringing it up. 'Only the first one.'

'Do you think it's convincing?'

I'd barely read a word. I put more salt on my chips. 'It's better than I thought it would be,' I said, 'but I can't see where he's going with it.'

Then I had him. His eyes focused and he replied in a flash. 'He's trying to work out what people can know for sure. You think you're sitting here talking to me, but maybe you're all there is. You could be caught in an incredibly sophisticated virtual reality machine – like a flight simulator but for the whole of life.'

I finished the wine in my glass, topped us both up and wondered what kind of anaemic know-all had persuaded Alex to take this drivel seriously. He was sensitive. I was convinced this nothing-is-real attitude was holding him back.

'Okay,' I said. 'What if someone punches you in the face? You're immediately proved wrong.'

'But someone punching you could be an illusion as much as anything else.'

'But even if you thought the guy didn't exist, you'd still fight him back or make a run for it, so you'd contradict yourself. It's denying the obvious. Life is hard enough, why plague yourself with doubts?'

'The point of the doubts isn't to make you worry, it's to make you work out why you're sure of your beliefs.'

This was too second order. 'But why not just go for it and say it's all balls?' I gave my desk a crueller slap than I'd intended. 'Of course I'm here talking to you. I exist, you exist, this is as real as it gets.'

'That's just how it feels to you. It doesn't prove anything. On that basis anything anyone thought existed would exist. Aliens, ghosts, God – '

'I believe in God,' I said.

'Okay, but you can't know that God exists with the certainty that you know that 2 + 2 = 4 or even that I'm sitting in front of you.'

'No, it's about faith.'

'Right, that's the point. You also, even if you don't realise it, have faith that a devil isn't deceiving you about the world and that it actually exists. The certainty you thought you had is faith.'

I paused. 'And no one's come up with a better theory than that?'

'Descartes tried to,' he said. 'He was like you, he hated the doubt, he wanted to eliminate it.'

I poured more wine. I couldn't understand why Alex accepted this doubt idea. 'So what d'you mean he tried to?'

'Well, imagine making an unassailable base of everything you're sure exists. It can't include the world or other people, or even your body because you could just be some kind of spirit, being fooled into thinking you have a body. So the question is, what can you be sure of?'

'God knows. Nothing.'

'No. There's one thing. No matter what you're being deceived about, there's still a you, whatever that is, that's being deceived.'

I thought about it. That sounded right. 'Okay.'

'You're thinking, even though you might be thinking something unreal. And if you're thinking, there must be a you that thinks. So *you* are real, *you* exist. And that's for certain.'

I realised what he was saying. 'This is I think therefore I am?'

'Yeh,' he smiled, 'exactly.'

Nice. Intelligent.

'And,' he went on, 'if you can't be sure about your body – this is one argument – then the you that you are sure about might be something different from your body. So maybe *that* you is actually your soul, or some part of you that's spiritual rather than physical.'

'Okay. Yeh.' I would have preferred a body, but it sounded plausible.

'Which fits in with what you want to believe. Take your desk.' We looked at the desk. 'It's just a load of atoms. You can feel happy, fall in love, desks can't do that.'

I wondered if it was a trick. But he was right. I could fall in love, desks couldn't.

'And if the body and soul are different, it might be possible for the soul to survive the death of the body.'

'Right, exactly,' I said. 'That's exactly right.'

'So if you died, what do you think would survive?'

I shrugged. 'Thoughts, feelings – '

'But don't you need a brain to have thoughts and feelings?'

I paused, I wasn't a biologist. 'No idea, I've never been dead.'

He smiled. 'But if you damage your brain, it can change who you are. And if your brain dies, that seems to be it – no one genuinely communicates with the dead. So maybe the soul's just one of those hoax answers people adopted for lack of anything better.'

'Can I just say something?' I said. 'I don't care for one moment how the afterlife works. I just think something lives on. I don't even care whether it's true. I'm saying for me believing in it is psychologically necessary.'

He looked at me as if he hadn't heard that argument before.

'You're in a corner by the way,' I added. 'If souls are a hoax, and you can't be sure about brains because bodies aren't in the unassailable base, you've got nothing at all.'

He nodded. 'Exactly.'

'But then the whole I think therefore I am thing goes up in smoke.'

'Yeh. That's the problem.'

He wasn't as disappointed as me. Why didn't these academic types fight? Why did they take it lying down?

I sat back in my chair. All this needed was five minutes' concentration.

My soul was in the base, but it was there at the expense of everything else, including my body, Alex's potential girlfriends, their bodies and my desk. Not only that, my soul was a dubious concept.

Descartes' theory was crap, it had to be. It worked by setting the standard too high. How could you be as sure about everything else as you were about yourself? What did I think about most of the time? Certainly not everything else.

Maybe life was one long fantasy session. I could waste a

day at it, why not years? Maybe I was the devil, deceiving myself.

'The problem,' I announced, 'is with the I think therefore I am.'

'Okay,' Alex smiled. 'Why?'

I was about to spout some random bullshit, but I stopped. It had dawned on me. 'You know what the answer to life is don't you?'

'What?'

I gave the desk an affectionate pat. 'Descartes got it totally wrong.'

'What?'

'It's that thing you said. Desks don't fall in love.'

'What d'you mean?'

'That's it, that's the cure for the doubt,' I smiled. 'If you love another person, you know they exist. There's no doubt about it. And you know you exist, like never before. And when it develops, it's as if you understand each other so well you can speak each others' thoughts. Not all the time, but you only need to experience that for a moment to know for the rest of your life.' I paused. 'Have you ever been in love?'

He didn't meet my eye.

'No don't worry, it's private. But that's it. I used to think it was poetic types getting over-inflated. I promise you it isn't. That's what life's about. I mean it doesn't have to be romantic love, it could be a Christ-like thing, or love of music, my wife's got that, or even philosophy like you – anything that connects you to something outside yourself.'

He was looking at me fondly.

'You think I'm wrong?'

'It's inspiring to hear someone say that.'

He was softening me up for demolition. 'That's because it's one hundred percent irrefutable.'

He was confident. But so was I. 'Go on,' I said.

'Okay. Even when you doubt you're thinking, you're still thinking. That's what makes you sure you exist. But the problem with making it come down to loving instead of thinking, is that you can doubt that you love – '

'Wait, wait. I don't doubt that I love. That's what I'm saying, there's no doubt about it. I mean we argue now and then. But whatever happens, I'll always love my wife. I can tell you that cast iron guaranteed.'

He didn't speak for a moment. Most human beings are more easily swayed by passion than reason, but he was unusual.

'The point is it's possible to doubt it.' He paused. 'And a lot of loving someone is really thinking.'

'No. No Alex it isn't. It really isn't. It's visceral. You're engaged with the world – not just your brain – that's why it cures the doubt.'

'But any part of loving that's sensory is open to doubt.'

I saw someone pacing in the corridor out of the corner of my eye and got up to have a look. 'Well just because I'm convinced I exist doesn't mean I have to doubt everything else.'

'You're retreating.'

'I'm reaffirming my position.' Whoever it was had gone into hiding. 'No one actually doubts like that, it's not consistent with life.'

I went to open the window, my torch newly kindled. 'What I'm saying is forget the doubt, that's theoretical crap, ask yourself what it means to live.' The night air streamed in. 'I know I'm alive when I'm in love. Wherever I am, whatever I'm doing – you don't have to be with someone to love them – you have this fire in you, you feel it in the other person, you feel it burn brighter in you when it burns in them – '

I caught the expression on Alex's face. He longed to believe me.

We'd dusted off Descartes – it was only fitting that another great mind would follow. A cursory knock on the office door and the pacer had given himself away. Anthony Stretch, the supercharged assistant, the top of his head glowing red, was on a torpedo mission. No other human being's arrival could have chimed so perfectly with my mood and although it was late, I welcomed him with open arms.

'Ah, Gilles – '

'Anthony, thank God you're here. We've had some exceptional news. Love,' I stared at him, 'is the answer. To life, the universe and everything.'

There was a look of exasperation on his face.

'We've solved every problem. We must all leave at once.' I shooed Stretch out of my office and – he occasionally had this effect on me – strode down the corridor, yelling as I went. 'Everyone out! Stop work this instant!'

Howard's head popped cautiously out of his door.

'Go home to Maureen, man!' I urged him, Stretch at my heels. 'Senior partner's orders!'

'Gilles, for God's sake – ' Stretch was apoplectic. ' – this is gross misrepresentation – '

Peter's light was on. I flung open the door. A couple of pubescent trainees glanced up from their clinch.

'Outstanding work you two! I shall inform the senior partner immediately.'

I rounded the secretarial bay and charged into my office to get my jacket. *Lapin* looked up. Stretch almost bumped into the back of me.

'No Anthony, no. We must leave this place! Get out and love!'

'Gilles, please!' He stared at me, his face twitching. 'I must insist you stop this nonsense.'

'It's the opposite of nonsense Anthony, it's the meaning of life.'

'I'm sorry, I simply don't have time for this.' He looked about him, then lowered his voice. 'I've got to bring you into the loop on Project Beaver.'

I stopped still. But his furtive glance was being replaced

by the usual expression of blank solemnity. I looked at Alex. Alex looked down with a hint of a smile.

Surely Stretch had at some point in life appreciated the subtler nuances of this word… but it seemed he hadn't. My office was silent with the unsung potency of this new gift.

Stretch checked his watch. 'I'm on a call at eleven thirty with EGG.' He paused for the initials of Edward Gordon Gunn, head of the corporate department. 'He's with the client in New York, hence the timing. So, uh… ' he looked sideways at Alex, 'can we have a word?'

He meant ditch the trainee. I told Alex to stay put and pulled up another chair which Stretch sat in. As I watched Stretch clear a space on my desk for his pad of yellow A4, my destiny revealed itself.

'Actually Anthony before we begin, I must put in a call to Tim Woodward.'

Stretch dismissed the interruption with a sweep of his hand.

Poor Wood, I knew he'd be there. He'd come up earlier in the day to moan about some monumental banking deal he'd taken on. What with all his other syndicated revolvers, his only option was to defy physics and put in five hundred hours a week. I loved the guy but he couldn't say no.

I withheld my number and pressed the speaker button.

'Tim Woodward.' He sounded half dead.

I adopted EGG's gin-soaked old colonel voice. 'Aaah Woodward, Gunn here. Got a moment?'

Stretch, engrossed in a diagram of two group structures, wasn't listening. Tim, unused to being called by the head of the corporate department, was at a loss for words.

'Ya, glad I caught you. Got capacity? Good, good. Banking's always quiet as the grave isn't it?' I caught *Lapin*'s eye. 'Can't see how you buggers make any money at all.'

'Right,' Wood reached for the Arctic but found the Orkneys. 'Actually we're quite busy at the moment.'

'Oh good, good Tim good. In that case, you won't mind if I throw something else at you. Eh?'

'Well – ' Northumberland.

'Come on Tim, if you're busy, you won't even *notice* it.'

'I don't think… sorry, I just – '

'No problem at all, Tim. Now, I'd like you to take this down. You won't regret it. Preliminary instructions as follows. Ready?'

He sighed. 'Go on.'

'I want you to *vacate* the building ASAP, that's V. A. C. A. T. E. the building A. S. A. P. Got that?'

'… Right…'

'Now, immediately following departure, as a matter of the utmost urgency. You concentrating Tim?'

'… Yeh…' His nose was on the scent.

'Immediately following departure, instructions are to commence M. A. K. I. N. G. L. O. V. E. in the manner you, and naturally Elaine, see fit – '

'*Matheson*?' he whispered. 'Okay, that's it. This is war.'

'Tim you'll be pleased to know I've got ANTHONY STRETCH here with me.'

'You fucked-up shit – ' Tim was cut short.

Stretch looked up. He was drawing his own group structure diagram in pencil on his yellow pad. I moved the phone towards him.

'Anthony, would you like a word with Tim?'

'Sorry Gilles, I don't follow – '

'About *Project Beaver*.'

Anthony's face contorted as he mouthed the word confidential.

Wood cried out as if he'd been stabbed. 'What are you on? I'm putting the phone down, be fucking afraid.'

'Wait Tim, please wait, this is important. Anthony is here with me, aren't you Anthony?'

'Right. Yes.' Stretch frowned at me.

'Tim, we're working on a fascinating deal called *Project Beaver*. We were wondering whether you'd like to be involved.'

Stretch was frantically mouthing the words no no no.

'… Right,' Tim said uncertainly. I looked at *Lapin*. He was laughing, quietly but unquestionably.

'Mm,' Tim spoke lightly, 'the codename… '

Stretch took the baton. 'Tim, I do apologise, Beaver is absolutely not a banking deal. Obviously if in due course we do require banking input, I'd be happy to bear you in mind, but I'm afraid with the way things stand currently, it's unlikely.'

'No – no problem Anthony,' Tim coughed. '… I'm up to my eyeballs.'

'Yes of course. Well so are we all.'

'… Yes,' I said. 'Well I imagine you want to get stuck in, Anthony?'

Tim cleared his throat.

'If you don't mind Gilles, yes.'

'Okay Tim,' I said. 'I'm just sorry we couldn't get you any penetration… you know. At this time.'

Poor Tim was prone to minor asthma attacks.

'It's unfortunate Anthony, isn't it?'

Stretch looked up. 'What?'

'Well you know, that we couldn't get Wood in.'

'Yes yes. I do apologise, next time Tim.'

I picked up the receiver. 'Okay Tim, thanks for that.'

'… beaver?'

'Yes,' I said, grave as a swami. 'Yes, well that's right. I've done my best at this end, but the Torpedo's slightly off course.'

'Oh man… ' he was getting his breath, 'God… that bloke, what's his name, Randy Cock?'

I coughed like a man possessed. '… Yes, a stroke of genius. Let me check that with Anthony. Anthony?' He looked up. I had to clear my throat. 'Is Randolf Dick on the deal? Tim tells me he's extraordinarily gifted.'

Tim whimpered.

Stretch looked at me like I was a halfwit. 'Gilles, Randy's been on secondment since May.'

'Aah, what a shame. Tim, Randy's otherwise engaged.' I

took a deep breath. 'Doesn't surprise me actually, they say he gets through briefs like a shot. Incredible instinct.'

'Who told you that?' Stretch asked.

Tim let out a snort. I was beginning to lose it.

I looked at the window, but Stretch's head was reflected in it; moreover, as I performed a few quick breathing exercises, it seemed to undergo a violent spasm.

'Gilles,' Stretch hissed, pointing at his watch repeatedly.

'Tim, I think we need a meeting on this tomorrow.'

Once I'd hung up, Stretch talked us through the transaction, which, he whispered, 'might involve a dam', then came to the point.

'Working with EGG of course, and myself. Angela North's in, very bright girl. Had to get the Paris office on board,' he paused and smiled, 'so obviously I thought your name ought to go into the hat.'

I sat back in my chair and savoured Stretch's attempt at a put-down.

'Who've you spoken to in Paris?'

'Well I was thinking Cecil Pitt. Best not to ask a frog in the first instance. No offence, obviously.'

'Yes,' I said, 'Cecil's an excellent front man.'

'Worked with him?'

'Does a lot of marketing.'

'Right.'

'Spontaneous guy, quite seat of the pants.'

'Aah.'

'Always lends a – a certain *je ne sais quoi* – to the transaction.'

'Right, right.'

'I wouldn't quite say unpredictable.'

'Mm.'

'Speaks very good French.'

'Dual-qualified is he?'

'I don't believe so no. I suppose if you really needed a dual-qualified, Georges Costel's very capable.'

'Right.'

'Over conscientious possibly, a bit of a stickler.'

'Well we don't want too many bodies in the tent at this stage… Costel did you say?'

'Mm.' I wrote the name on his yellow paper. 'Well-organised, reliable.'

'Right, I'll have a think. Yes. Gilles, thanks for that. Discuss bright and early tomorrow?'

'Great… – Oh God.' I put my hand to my forehead.

'What?' Anthony looked worried.

'I've got a meeting at nine.'

'Ah.'

'Shall we say ten thirty?'

'Fine.'

'See you then.'

'Good good.'

He left the room.

I looked at *Lapin*, waiting for the coast to clear. He looked back expectantly.

'Whatever you do,' I said quietly, 'never work with Cecil Pitt.'

'Why not?'

'He's an incompetent, lying arsehole.'

'Okay.' He tilted his head at the door. 'What about that guy?'

'Stretch? Punishes his trainees, otherwise harmless.' I smiled. 'He's an eager beaver.'

We started to laugh.

'I can't believe they're calling it that.'

'Ah, God.' I was rubbing my eyes. 'Poor Wood.'

I turned to the phone. 'I've got to ring my wife. Sorry Alex, I shouldn't have kept you.'

'No, that's okay.' He put on his jacket.

'Come in late tomorrow if you want. I won't be in before ten thirty.'

He looked confused. 'What about your meeting?'

'Ah. Nine o'clock meeting, early morning avoidance strategy. You teach me truth, I teach you bullshit.'

'Okay,' he smiled. 'Thanks.'

On his way out, he stopped. 'Thank you,' he looked me in the eye, 'for dinner and everything.'

I looked back at him. 'Project Love-Is-The-Answer. Don't forget.'

10

'Fever Breaks'
by Michelle Shocked

Venus held Leonie on her lap. Having offered condolences, the doctor looked over his glasses and apologised, one of his receptionists was away, there was no Mrs Matheson on the system.

It's Venus Rees, she said. She hadn't changed her name when she got married.

Ah, he'd found her.

They'd begin with the cause of her husband's death. As she knew, he had had a severe heart attack, which for a man of his age and apparent health was unusual. The practice had no medical records for him – presumably he had not felt unwell.

'However,' his voice tightened, 'the body does not always provide warning signs. A heart attack tends to arise when a blood clot obstructs the flow of blood to the heart. The clot typically forms on the surface of ruptured cholesterol plaque, rupture itself being caused by various factors – high adrenaline, high blood pressure, oddly even certain types of cholesterol... '

Venus listened, the importance of the words vying with her unwillingness to process them. The argument she could have done something about. Exaggerated insults staked on sure odds of reconciliation, waking up to the sound of the front door closing, not even calling from the bedroom window –

'... a tendency to high levels of cholesterol and low density lipoprotein in particular, hence the increased likelihood that plaques will form and eventually rupture. Diet is a factor, but the primary problem is the inherited inability of the body to clear cholesterol efficiently.'

The doctor took some papers from the side of his desk. 'The postmortem indicates a high-risk lipid profile, along with external manifestations of hypercholesterolaemia. The white ring of cholesterol around the iris for example is rarely seen in the under fifties.' He set the papers down in front of him. 'I assume there's a family history of premature death?'

Venus hesitated. 'Sorry, this is all new to me.'

'Yes, it can seem complex. Is there anything you'd like me to explain again?'

'No, no.' Venus held Leonie. 'His father died young. In his thirties I think.' She tried to remember whether she knew his father's exact age. 'He was six, so his father must have been young. I'm sure it was a heart attack. His uncle died fairly young as well.'

He nodded. 'Now I'm afraid there are likely to be implications for anyone related to your husband.' He glanced at Leonie. 'Did your husband have any other children?'

The thudding had started in her head. 'No.'

The doctor turned to his computer screen. 'And this is Leonie?'

'Yes.' She hadn't allowed the thought, the direct phrasing of it.

He read for a moment, then looked at her. 'Well unfortunately we must consider the possibility that your daughter may have inherited the condition. There won't be any need for medical intervention at this stage – '

'But... ' Venus interrupted him, then stopped.

His eyes darted for a moment. 'There's a one in two chance, unless by a quirk of fate – ' He paused. 'That would be most unlikely, but I assume you'll want to have a cholesterol test yourself. Now, if your daughter does have the condition, there are several effective cholesterol-lowering drugs available for when the time comes. Managed properly, it needn't be a serious worry.'

Her face felt almost see-through, an imperfectly wiped windscreen.

'… My husband's death could have been prevented?'

He looked at her, then nodded. 'Yes, had he been diagnosed, it's very likely that his blood lipids would have been reduced to more acceptable levels.'

She looked steadily at him. 'He would have lived. I mean, had he known.'

'Had he been treated, yes, he might well have lived an average lifespan. Now as far as your daughter is concerned, there's little point in carrying out a cholesterol test until age eight at the earliest. How old is she now?'

'Two,' she said. 'Sorry, you mean we can't find out now?'

'There's no need for your daughter to be treated at this stage.'

'But couldn't she have the test anyway?'

The doctor gave a short sigh. 'If she has inherited the gene, her cholesterol levels are unlikely to be dangerous until adolescence at the earliest.'

'But couldn't she have a genetic test?'

'As I said, there would be no need for treatment.'

'Yes, I understand that,' Venus spoke slowly, 'but I'd like to know one way or the other.'

The doctor cleared his throat. 'Should a reliable DNA test come into existence, you must ask yourself whether the rigmarole could leave you with any positive benefit. Besides which, the cholesterol test is perfectly adequate.'

'But the result might be negative.'

'And it might be falsely negative.'

'But this kind of science is progressing daily, surely… ' She was speaking from ignorance. 'What I mean is I'd like to know now. One way or the other, I've got to know.'

'Mrs Matheson, we must also take into account whether your daughter has got to know. The most important thing you can do at this stage is to ensure she eats healthily.' The doctor took some brightly-coloured leaflets from the side of his desk and passed them to her. 'These should give you all the information you need. Now, we mustn't forget your husband's other blood relatives.'

The doctor's phone rang.

Within a minute, Venus was carrying Leonie out of the surgery.

Over the previous few days, Leonie had asked Venus questions in bursts. Where was Daddy, when was he going to stop being dead, why was he dead, what was dead. Venus had told her it was like when the phone broke that time Daddy threw it on the floor. But she'd regretted saying it. There was too much cause in it.

It was lunchtime when they got home from the doctor's. Venus cooked some pasta, cut some butter to stir into it and then stopped herself. She looked at the label on the jar of tomato sauce and mixed some in. She wrote *low fat cheese* on a piece of paper. What a slop of a meal.

Half way through eating, Leonie said, 'Want Leo dead now.'

'*No*.' Venus wondered whether Leonie had understood everything the doctor had said.

'Want go with Daddy.'

'Listen Leo. If you were dead I'd never see you again, and I don't want that to happen.'

Once Leonie had started watching television, she took Gilles' address book up to the phone in their bedroom.

Jane answered with her surname. She said how nice it

was to hear from Venus and how was Venus coping and wasn't the funeral wonderful, if one can say that about such occasions, one thinks one can, and was Venus ringing about the bereavement group.

Venus took a breath. 'Jane, there's something I've got to ask you.'

'Of course dear. What is it?'

'At the reception, you said this tragedy had cut across the generations, that the same sorrow had struck yet again.'

'Oh goodness yes, that was insensitive, I do apologise.'

'But you knew Gilles had a genetic condition?'

'… Well of course I was never absolutely sure. But Hélène asked me not to bring it up – you know, she said she and Gilles had agreed to live as if nothing had happened, Gilles wanted to get on with the life he had – well I assumed he'd tested positive and there wasn't anything anyone could do. Drugs can only achieve so much. And Hélène is awfully sensitive about these things, understandably of course. That's why I so admired you my dear. Your wedding day was such an inspiration to me. Two young people so in love and so joyful, despite all this dreadful business. *Carpe diem*, I thought.'

Venus's eyes closed. 'Jane – I knew nothing about this.'

There was silence.

'… But you must have discussed it with Gilles? Surely, I mean he wouldn't have kept it to himself?'

'No.' Venus wiped her face. 'No, he never said a thing.'

'Oh my dear.' Jane's voice faltered.

'So I need to know exactly what happened. When you found out about Frank, what Gilles said when you told him, *everything*.'

'Of course, of course. Gosh… I'm so sorry.'

'Please, just tell me what happened.'

'Yes. Well I have to tell you I – I never spoke about it to Gilles directly.'

'What?'

'No, it was all through Hélène, I mean I wrote to Gilles of course, but – '

'You mean you never once *talked* about it with Gilles?'

'No. No, I didn't, but – '

'Why the *hell* not?'

'Please Venus, let me explain. It was just after Frank died. Gilles would have been… well, let's see.' She paused. 'Twenty-one. Yes, that's right. I saw the doctor and he told me that Frank had had the high cholesterol condition, and that it was inherited and that everyone should be tested – our two, thank God both in the clear, and Gilles, and Aunt Elisabeth, and so on. So I wrote to Gilles and Hélène, separate letters, at home in London. It wasn't the sort of thing one could just announce over the phone, and Frank and I had only been back in England for a matter of months. We really didn't have much contact with Hélène.'

'But the letters could have got lost, stolen, anything – '

'No, please wait dear. Of course I would have telephoned after a week or so, but in the end that wasn't necessary because Hélène telephoned me. She said that Gilles had seen the doctor straight away. And she begged me not to mention it again. She said she and Gilles had agreed to live as normally as possible. And I promised her I would say no more about it.

'I understood completely. No one wants to face death at any age, let alone twenty-one. The repetition of the whole business must have been more than either of them could bear. She said how lucky I was to have a daughter, possibly she thought girls were safe which of course they're not. But the fact was that neither of my children were affected, so it was particularly hard on her and all the more difficult for me to mention.'

Venus was quiet.

'I didn't see Hélène or Gilles for years. Frank and I had been in Africa for so long, and then of course Hélène moved to Paris. I suppose the next time must have been at your wedding, and that was far too nice an occasion to spoil. And then nothing until, well, until last Thursday.'

Venus had screwed her eyes shut. 'He wasn't taking any medicine. I never saw him take a pill – he didn't do it. He never went to the doctor.'

She stopped, and it hit her fully that he could have known and not told her, barely even told himself, literally pretended everything was fine.

'You don't know, do you, for certain… ' Her voice trailed away. She started again. 'You don't know that he actually knew, do you?'

'No dear, I don't.' Jane paused. 'But I know that Hélène knew, and that the instinct a mother has to protect her child is one of the strongest on earth.'

Venus dialled the Paris number. The answering machine kicked in. Venus started to speak and Hélène picked up the phone. Her voice sounded over buoyant.

'I was going to phone *chérie*. How are you? I hope you are taking care. Maybe you would like to come to Paris soon?'

'No, thank you Hélène, I have to be here at the moment. I was ringing to ask you something.'

'Please.'

'I've just spoken to Jane. She said she wrote to you and Gilles after Frank died to say that Gilles should have a cholesterol test. You told her he'd been to see the doctor and you didn't want to discuss it again.'

There was no sound on the other end of the line.

'Hélène?'

'*Vénus*, this was a long time ago.'

'Yes I know.'

'You must understand it is difficult for me.'

'It's difficult for everyone.'

'It is as she says. She wrote to me and I became very anxious, of course. And then Gilles went to the doctor – to have the test. It was just a blood test, not complicated. And when the result came, well, we decided not to speak about it. I told him, it was for him to decide what to do, he knew what I wanted, but I would never speak of it again. I could not… But Gilles must have told you this. You know all of this? Is there anything else?'

Venus's jaw set. 'No, there's nothing else. I – I just wanted to check. Well, I'd better go. Leonie is hungry.'

'*Bon*. My kisses to Leonie and to you, naturally. We will speak soon.'

She put the phone down, gripped with silent convulsions.

Seizing one possibility after another, she ran through its implications, its plausibility. He couldn't have known, he couldn't have lived like that. Hélène was mad, lying, protecting herself.

But however hard she tried to banish it, the thought came back. Perhaps he really hadn't told her. Let it happen, kept it quiet. Some insane form of sacrifice.

Lived a lie but at least he hid the pain. '*Don't* make me doubt you.' She grabbed the photo of them from the table by the bed. '*Don't do that*.' She flung it on the bed. '*DON'T DO THAT*.' She shoved the clutter from the table to the floor. Light, books, radio, photographs, crashing. Receipts floating down like leaves. And dust that hung and didn't fall.

But it was too quiet, too lacking in consequence. She felt the sinew in her fists, the blood in her brain. You could snap yourself apart.

She had told him everything, from the unforgettable to the half-forgotten. But there was always something he kept back. Gaps, bits of delusion. The truth, all she wanted. More than bloody love.

Was it her blindness, was that what had seen them through?

But it hadn't, had it?

He was dead.

Her mind shrank from the thought. He is dead. Crunched in on itself. He is dead. She'd just spoken to his mother. Just pushed his things to the floor. Leo downstairs. Dead dead dead.

The house was dim when Venus heard the brush of the door against the carpet. She saw the look on Leonie's face.

Overcome, she stood up too quickly and felt faint. She couldn't understand how it had got dark.

Leonie was walking with her head bent down.

Venus took her in her arms and hugged her.

When they separated, Leonie looked at her as if she were a sick animal. 'You cry Mummy?'

She breathed out. 'Only because I'm so pleased to see you.'

'Catty in garden.'

'Yes… ' And she wept that the means of comfort she used on her child was being offered back.

She took a breath, blew her nose. It was late, they needed to eat.

'Aren't you hungry?'

'No. Had bikit.'

'Oh clever you,' she blinked as she smiled.

She picked Leonie up. 'Come on my love,' she carried her out of the room, 'let's have supper.' She turned the hall light on and they went downstairs.

Later that evening when Leonie was in bed, she went back to their room. She pulled out the radio trapped between the bed and the wall by its long aerial, picked up the books from the floor, the crucifix with the zigzag body hanging from the rosary, the photograph of them smiling which he'd taken with his arm outstretched.

She checked the other photographs – Hélène, Gilles' father, her mother. They were all intact. She put them on the table beside the shrine that she'd spared, the picture of her father standing alone. As Leonie would no doubt in time spare a picture of Gilles.

Everything back in its place.

She sat against the bed, stretching her fingers then closing them tightly.

To love until death do us part? That was not what she'd meant. She'd meant that she'd love him eternally, beyond life and time. Forever.

Was it supposed to be impossible? Were people too defeated to try?

Oh poor Mrs Matheson. Did you hear? Her husband died. What? But he was so young. Heart attack, apparently.

Had he been treated, yes.

Some genetic thing. God, poor woman. And the daughter – so young.

Managed properly, it needn't be a serious worry.

Death, the patient waiter, his spiral of coils, his cosy snake nest. Waiting for the mother to drop her guard. Unable to believe his luck when the mother showed him the way.

She washed her face. The house had gone cold. She went downstairs for a glass of water.

She came back up, opened the window, breathed the air and closed it. Each moment, each act was too defined.

She crept across the corridor to Leonie's room. She watched her chest rise minutely with her infrequent breath, her brushed hair around her resting face. She put the duvet back over her legs. The spare bed was right beside hers, ready for Gilles when Leonie woke up in the night. Still dressed, she went to it.

11

'I Want It Back'
by Shawn Colvin and John Leventhal

You struggled to pick up the phone.

'Oh, hi Gi.' You sounded sleepy. 'God what's the time?'

'11.15, sorry my love, were you asleep?'

'Yeh. Where are you?'

'Sorry, sorry. I'm still here. I was waiting for comments, but then Stretch came in full of this hilarious deal.'

'Right.'

'I know you're tired, I've just got to tell you I made a great discovery this evening Vee, you'll love it, I was talking to *Lapin* about Descartes – '

'Gi, I'm worn out, Leo's been sick three times, everything's in a state.'

'Oh God, sorry.' I felt like an idiot. 'Is she okay?'

'Well she's asleep, she's probably fine. I feel weird, I think I'm getting it.'

'I'll come back right now. Sorry Vee… I'm going in late tomorrow, I'll look after her if she wakes up, go back to sleep.'

I should have got out and loved.

… Darling? Let me tell you something. Remembering it will be like walking into cool woods.

When I was little, my mother often went out for the day. It didn't seem strange to me. My grandparents lived next door and I went out all the time myself.

One afternoon, I came home before her. She never threw anything away but put it all neatly into cupboards, and having eaten everything my grandmother had given me, but with no one telling me to go to bed, it was nice to have a look around.

There was my DB5, kept in a special cupboard in the hall so I wouldn't lose it. It had an incredible ejector seat, just like the one in *Goldfinger*, the roof actually flipped up. And in the same cupboard, a stash of other things I'd forgotten about: a wooden box full of little metal soldiers, medals on silk ribbons wrapped in velvet, jars of odd coins, tennis rackets in presses, spanners in cases, puzzles in boxes. I freed all these things from their prisons.

I went into the cupboard under the stairs with a torch, found my way past the stacked up chairs, shone the torch at a pile of large books, recognised one with a red leather cover and took it down.

I sat on the floor in the hall, opened it up and felt with a dizzying sensation that I was a trespasser. It was an album of photographs. My father as a young man. My mother. My father and mother and me, my mother's parents, my mother and me, my father and me, everyone together.

I looked more slowly. My grandparents' holiday house, my father's mother holding me when I was a baby, my father and mother and me by the sea. I began taking out the pictures with my father in, to see him more clearly.

I knew he was dead. I'd understood that he'd gone away forever. It had made me cry. Certainly I'd sensed the enormity of the event. But it seemed that I'd been an onlooker rather than a participant. I hadn't, I'd been a six-year-old boy. And later it would come at me again, and again I'd feel that I'd never truly appreciated it before. It's the same with anything momentous in life, tragic or glorious. So much of learning is learning what you already know. But that day the lesson hit me hard, perhaps because I'd see my mother learning it as well.

'*Gilles!*'

I hadn't heard her get back. The mess I'd made announced itself like a bomb.

I rammed stuff into cupboards.

'*Gilles…?*'

What could I do? There were things all over the place. I forgot about the photographs.

I heard her heels tapping and ran upstairs to my bedroom. She sped up, following me. I shut my door and crawled under a table wedged between the wall and the wardrobe.

I listened for her, but there was no sound. Only the most complete silence, sad and heavy, drowning the house, my mother and me.

When I crept downstairs, it was dark outside and none of the lights were on which made the house seem foreign. But my mother was there. I could see the photographs shining on the floor around her. She stretched out her arms and I ran to her. I'd never seen her cry openly before, nor have I since. But that evening we were so close we reached a perfect intimacy.

12

'Walk On By'
by Burt Bacharach and Hal David

The boy was back. Walking up the street towards the morning sun.

A man stood on the balcony of his Paris flat, so happy to catch sight of the boy he forgot to smoke.

The outline of his body was apparent through his shirt, holding his jacket over his shoulder.

Perhaps he'd been on holiday, the man thought, his skin was darker. He'd really only been away a few weeks.

The boy was walking past the laundrette when someone in the street called out.

'*Eh! Adonis!*'

He didn't turn his head.

The man smiled. He went in, rested his cigarette on a plate, set the needle on his record player, picked up his cigarette and walked back onto the balcony.

First the brooding introduction, keeping time with the boy's purposeful steps, passing in front of his block now, heading for the *métro*, and then Dionne Warwick's light touch: *If you see me walking down the street, and I start to cry each time we meet, walk on by, walk on by*.

The receptionist on the first floor overlooking the escalators saw him come in at ground level. Alex, that was his name. He didn't really enjoy his looks. Like all English. But she continued to look at him nevertheless, as he came up towards her.

He was a trainee, he'd only be around for a few more months.

Actually he was sexy. A bit slim. Quite tall. Tall enough. He was tanned, he looked Spanish.

He was humming something. And then as he came closer he started singing it, quietly in English, 'Walk on by'. She didn't know what it was.

'*Bonjour Alex*!' She smiled, her breasts stretching the button holes of her shirt.

He looked at her and smiled back.

She crossed her legs.

Alex took the lift up to the fourth floor, walked down the corridor and went into the men's loos. Cecil Pitt came in after him.

'Mr Todd,' Pitt stood unnecessarily close. '… Look like an Eyetie, been away?'

'Yeh.'

'Where?'

'Tenerife.'

'What the hell d'you go there for?'

'My brother-in-law rented a house.'

Alex was washing his hands.

Smiling to himself, Cecil leant his shoulders back and hitched his trousers high.

Alex was about to go.

'Hold it.' He watched Alex's face. 'There's a client of mine I want you to meet. We've got a little project for you. My office at eleven.'

He smiled and patted Alex on the back. 'Not in Tenerife now.'

At his desk, Alex was looking through his emails.

Swedish women. Ray was having a party in Camden this Saturday. He replied saying he'd come and booked the Eurostar ticket.

Hi from Rebecca. Great to meet you on the mountain – let me know when you're in town & we'll go for a drink. Weird timing. He replied: *You too. How about this Sunday?*

Philosophy newsletter. He unsubscribed from the list, deleted the message, then deleted an entire file of philosophy messages.

Gilles Matheson. He sat up. He opened the message, skimming the words. *Gilles Matheson… funeral… please contact Janice Steer…*

'Shh – '

He reread the message.

Gilles Matheson's funeral will be held at 6pm on Thursday, 28 September at the Sacred Heart Church…

Hurriedly he scrolled back, flitting through the earlier subjects, looking for the pattern the letters made.

…with great sadness … yesterday morning at Chelsea and Westminster… severe heart attack …partnership in May this year…

There was a short account of his life.

Alex read the message again. He sat in his chair, gazing at the screen. The words blurred.

He got up, walked out of the office and into the street.

Ten minutes later, he returned. He reread the message about the funeral. He'd missed it. It had happened while he'd been away.

He thought about ringing Janice but it was only half past seven there.

He rang his mother.

'Hi,' she said brightly. It sounded like she'd been outside.

'Hi – '

'Al?' But her voice died down. 'What's wrong?'

'Gilles… the guy at work… '

'What?'

'He's dead.'

'What?'

'He had a heart attack.'

'Oh God.'

'I can't believe it.'

They talked for a few minutes.

When he put the phone down, he felt like he'd used a life too early in the game.

He rang Ray's number. Ray didn't hold back about personal subjects.

'Ray, it's Alex.'

There was coughing on the other end of the phone.

'... Who is this?' He was sleepy.

'It's Alex.'

'God, Alex. Thanks a million. What's the time?' His accent was broader than usual, he must have been hungover.

'Eight forty... Sorry.'

He groaned. 'Look, your time, eight anything is unthinkable, nine anything is poignant, as in always shit, only practical *if* I've got an early lesson which I pretty much *never* have because teaching is a profession I have adopted *entirely* for the slack hours, okay?' He took a breath. 'If it's a woman I don't want to hear it, I haven't had a shag in two weeks, Eve went back to Ireland.'

'It's not.'

'Okay so what in hell is it?'

'You know that guy I worked with last year? In corporate in London – the one who was interested in philosophy?'

Ray didn't reply.

'I told you I couldn't believe they made him a partner.'

'Alex, you are seriously obsessed with that bloke.'

'He's dead.'

'What?'

'He died. While I was away. He had a heart attack.'

Ray paused. 'Shit.'

'Yeh.'

'Sorry mate. How old was he?'

'Thirty-five.'

'And he had a heart attack?'

'Yeh.'

'Jesus.'

They were both quiet.

'Okay,' Alex said. 'Well I'd better go.'

'Yeah. Look... Will you be coming over for the funeral?'

'No. It's already happened.'

'Okay... Did you get my email about Saturday?'

'Yeh, I'll be over for that.'

'Grand. Kip here if you like, Eve's not around now.'

'Yeh thanks, I'll probably stay with my sister.'

' – Sorry I was a bitch about the time and that.'

'Yeh, no problem.'

'Take care mate.'

Alex looked at his watch again. It came to him what to do. He'd write a letter to Gilles' wife. Janice would have the address.

He tried to remember her name. Gilles always called her 'V'.

No, he'd do it now. Mrs Matheson, that was right anyway.

He walked out of the office again. He came back with writing paper and envelopes. Sitting at his desk, he took out the paper and found a pen with black ink. He wrote:

Dear Mrs Matheson,

I was so sorry to hear about your husband's death. I've been away and I only got the news this morning, so unfortunately I didn't come to the funeral.

I met Gilles through work. I was his trainee from August to December last year.

He was a very generous and inspiring person. It was always refreshing talking to him and I'll miss the conversations we had. It's rare to meet someone you can talk freely with. I feel lucky to have known him, and close to him beyond the short time I spent with him.

I should say that I asked him once to tell me the secret of his happiness and he replied, 'My wife'.

With regards and sympathy,

Yours sincerely,

Alexander Todd.

13

'Love And Affection'
by Joan Armatrading

… Darling? We were wandering around Valladolid in Mexico when suddenly you weren't there. You'd gone to get orange juice and then there was no sign of you. After thirty seconds, I was a panic-stricken version of my twenty-six-year-old self, pulling out of Leicester Square tube again, knowing the happiness I'd left behind.

It took me ten minutes to find you. When I did, and you saw how breathless I was, you looked straight at me.

'Hey,' you whispered, 'I'll never leave you.'

The weight in my lungs turned straight into oxygen.

We walked to the park in the town square and lay down together, my hand on your arm, your head on my rejoicing chest.

'… You know,' I said after a minute, 'I've been here before.'

'Really?' you asked.

'Back when I was papal legate, looking for the love of my life.'

'God man shut up, I believed you.' But a moment later, you said, 'Why would the Pope have let you do that anyway? That's not even crap, it's crap crap.'

'Yes,' I loved it when you took me seriously, 'the

resurgence of Mayan idols in the Yucatan came at a helpful time… There's a convent near here, with nuns in it. One in particular, extremely beautiful. Her name was Sister Venus.'

'… Oh,' you lay back, 'I see.'

I let the story out like bleeding a defective radiator. Sister Venus had been adopted at birth – the nuns were her family, the convent her home. Jealously protected by her mother superior for the singing voice that had won the order innumerable accolades, the two holy women had travelled to Rome, the old nun's ambitions having reached their zenith: Sister Venus was now twenty-one years old, eligible for Liturgical Singer of the Year. Meanwhile I, Father Gilles, imprisoned by my conscience into a Vatican career, had developed an astonishing aptitude for the organ, solitary practice twice daily being the only pleasure I allowed myself.

The day of the competition dawned. As deputy vice accompanist, I waited backstage with my missal, peeping occasionally from behind the curtain. According to the Vatican's subsequent statement, it was unseasonal heat that made the senior and vice accompanists collapse. Lies. They'd never seen a woman like her. The judges were desperate. They couldn't sacrifice another seminarian surely? Finally they called me to the organ. 'For God's sake, don't look!' the old mother superior hissed. Of course I looked. And no one knew, while I accompanied her exquisite voice, that my heart was lit with passion. No one knew, from that moment on, that I was consumed.

However I did nothing and you returned to Mexico.

'No!' I thought later in my cell, 'why, why, why?'

You settled your head into the crook of my arm. '*And back in Mexico*,' your velvet voice continued, '*she thought of his delicate touch on the keys for one so handsome, tall and passionate…* '

'I wrote her letters, I couldn't restrain myself, I would have exploded otherwise.'

'She slipped his letters into the bodice of her habit, reading them by moonlight, writing replies on the back of psalm sheets.'

'I devoured her subtle reciprocation, squeezing every drop of ardour into my pen, defying that inner voice that turned all sensuality into sin.'

'Until the dark day came when one of his letters fell out of her bodice and onto the mother superior's breakfast table. All correspondence was confiscated, and Sister Venus was condemned to work in the convent's stables.'

'Her letters stopped, the sapling of their passion cruelly felled. Had she forgotten me?'

The park had grown quiet, the smell of orange blossom dense on the warm air.

'… Mérida, the bishop's palace, forty degrees and I, now papal legate, toss restlessly in my hammock. For, no matter if an eternity passes, I will not forget her.'

'She strokes the Arab mare and thinks of Father Gilles, yearns for some sign of his passion. Still she remembers his fingers' caress – envies the keys of his organ, the beads of his rosary, the pages of his Bible. Is there nothing she can do?'

'Enough! I rush to the garage and seize the episcopal Harley-Davidson. It is time God's gladiator took off into the swelter of destiny, roared through the littered streets of chaos, coasted along the open road of chance.'

'Daring to voice her secret to a kindly old nun, Sister Venus at last learns the truth. 'Venus,' the nun whispers, 'this life of religious confinement was chosen for you as an infant. If you wish, you may leave it with good conscience. But I tell you this against our mother superior's wishes. You will have to be brave.' Stunned, Sister Venus distracts one of the grooms with a large chocolate pudding, hides the stable key in her bodice and plans her escape.'

'After a long night astride the bishop's machinery, the torrent of devotional visions to which I've been yielding my parched soul has led to enlightenment: I must defrock myself.

'I pull up beside the entrance to a local *cenote*, a deep underground pool revered by the ancient Mayan people. Once in the cave, I leave my silken robes on a rock in clear sight of some local ragamuffins. Wearing only Vatican diving trunks, I enter the pool. Yikes. A relief to be out of the sun, but this is a glacial refuge.

'I look back at the rock. Why don't those urchins get on with it?

'I swim to the centre of the pool, its limitless icy fathoms beneath me, and again look back. But this is ridiculous, how long can it take to pinch a few vestments? Chilled to the bone, I plunge under the freezing water. A giant silvery eel is writhing inches from my head. I race to the edge of the pool and push myself out, my well-developed right bicep permitting welcome alacrity.

'Hosanna! The bundle has been stolen! But wait, is that laughter I hear? Sweetly the children scamper towards me, throwing my robes to one another, their faces lit with smiles, their joyous folk melodies resounding in the rocky chamber as they try to tempt me with a game of piggy in the middle.

'I sprint out of the cave to my motorcycle, the youths' urgent calls of '*Padre*' echoing behind me. Thanks be to God, the engine starts first time. I feel for my Vatican Amex nestling in the inside pocket of my trunks. I will make haste to the nearest town to acquire a selection of linen shirts, lightweight trousers and perhaps the odd tie.'

Vee, you softly clear your throat. '*Lunch is over and the nuns sit at their needlework, with the exception of Sister Venus who as usual makes for the stable yard. No one is there. Delving in the hayrick, she finds her carefully hidden backpack of supplies. Still no one. She runs to the tack room, seizes the saddle. Everything is in place. Taking the key from her bodice, she throws open the stable door. It is time. She gallops across the threshold to the outside world, clasping the hot animal musculature between her thighs.*'

I can feel your waist. 'Finally released from the trappings

of priesthood,' I close my eyes, '… I become gripped with desire, gripped with sating your desire. I ride harder, picture the two of us riding together, the midnight wind blowing through the curls on your naked head, the desert sand moulding to the shape of your voluptuous body, the ocean wave lapping at your tender, awakening lips.'

'*Urgently she makes for the nearest town. With a wardrobe consisting only of nun's habits, she could do with some underwear.*'

' – Hey – ' Vee I'm scandalised. 'At last,' I hurry, 'I see the sign to Valladolid, peppered with bullet holes according to the local custom.'

'*But wait,*' you say, '*who is that man parking his bike?*'

'My God,' I say, 'who is that heavenly woman tying her horse?'

I sit up, looking at you there with me, everything swimming into the present.

'*Si,*' you smile.

'But Sister,' I touch your cheek, breathless with wonder, 'are you not a nun of the Holy Order of Eternal Fantasy?'

You free your hair from its ponytail, your dark curls tumbling around your flashing eyes, your burning lips.

'*I am sister no more,*' you stare at me with Spanish fire, '*I am woman.*'

I kiss you, only just believing you're real. And you kiss me. And then all I want is you.

And I still do, Vee. I still do.

I want to be there under the trees, with our lips on each other and our hands in each other's pants. I want to hear you sigh when I touch you. I want to feel the softness of your breasts and the heat between your legs. I want to hear you say, 'Let's go back to the room' in that urgent voice, then see you walk properly through the lobby and take the stairs two at a time. I want to feel the roof of my mouth dry with anticipation and your fingers struggling with my clothes. I want to make you so desperate for us to fuck you'd kill me if we didn't. And I want to lie with you afterwards and in the whispers of intimacy wonder that life could be so generous.

... *Gi?*

I wake up, a god in a cloud. Lying on the bed, your hand in mine, our lives like distant stars, as if we'd already lived them but their light was still ahead of us.

You wipe the tears from my face. My fingers and yours, my lips and yours.

Turn over. Gi let me... Oh God. Ah it's strong as fuck.

Sun through the open window and we're gently back at it, you above me, the silhouettes of us on the white wall, your shy breath as you see them, the beauty of them, moving together.

Oh God. Oh my love. *Slow, slow*. Ah fuck.

I love you so much. *Oh my love*. I love you –

Months later, back in London, you tell me something.

... You mean? *Yes, no question*. Shit. *I know, it didn't fucking work. I've done three tests*. Vee wait. Vee? Come here.

A few weeks pass and we get used to it. And then it becomes natural and obvious, an inseparable part of us.

Winter, the heating's broken, you're pregnant, it's too cold, we're about to leave, I've booked a hotel. I'm standing in the kitchen while you get ready, looking out of the window. And like a miracle, as I watch, it starts to snow. I look at a single snowflake, hypnotised by its drifting, the silent, accidental beauty. It melts when it touches the pavement, but there are more coming.

And then you come downstairs, your love and excitement as you smile, knowing what I know, this huge sweep of the future ahead of us, and I hold you, I can't believe you're here with me, and we open the front door and step outside. Oh my love. What an air there is. How we'll thrive on the breathing of it.

14

'Good Morning Heartache'
by Irene Higginbotham, Ervin Drake and Dan Fisher

Venus put Alexander Todd's letter in a different place from the others. She kept it beside the bed for a while, then in her handbag. It was something she needed, like an amnesic might need a passport, as much for remembering where she'd come from as for travelling on. And although she was grateful for the written evidence, her gratitude laid bare her doubt.

And he replied, 'My wife': the secret of his happiness. The secret of my happiness is my wife. My wife, the secret. The secret happiness.

Two weeks after Gilles' death, she came to a decision. She couldn't carry on making radio programmes. She couldn't fake being interested. And when she told them that she'd be back after six months, that she'd be in touch, they understood.

The day afterwards, she decided she'd made the wrong decision. She needed a regular source of income. There was no point changing things unnecessarily.

A week later, she noticed an advert for a job as a French and Italian teacher. She sent her application, hoping that the private school wouldn't make a fuss about her lack of teaching qualifications.

It turned out that one of the school's music teachers had recently announced her pregnancy. After several interviews, Venus was offered a job as a music teacher, with the possibility of five lessons of pure maths a week to help cover for someone who was sick. She accepted the offer and felt invulnerable for half a day.

By the following morning she'd become anxious about working at all. She had to look after Leonie – she couldn't leave her with someone else, not this soon. She had to convince the specialist to test her, she had to get their diet organised. She needed more information – from the people at the heart charity, from wherever she could find it. Once all that was in train, she had to go to Paris to find Gilles' medical records, get Mary to go through everything she remembered, talk to Hélène.

Learning not to trust herself, she left ringing the school until the next day, by which time it was obvious she needed the money. Leonie could manage a few more hours at nursery school, she could forget the maths if it was too much. Her mother would step in if it came to it. It was a good job, she was lucky to have the offer.

Friends asked her if she was all right, if they could do anything to help. Yes, she was okay, she said; no, she could cope; her mother had gone through a similar thing. Oh, they said, how awful. At least her mother would understand.

Cautiously, Venus began to think it wasn't as bad as all that. The solution was to do things, always to have something else to go on to. Of course there were times, when Leonie went to bed, when the television was inanimate, the house dead. She'd remember that she hadn't eaten since lunch. She'd make an omelette, it was too late for anything else. And then it would start – every action ringingly prominent, echoing with loneliness. Cracking the eggshell, piercing the membrane, prising the egg open, tipping it out, every breath noted.

She would eat, knife and fork on a plate. There would be

washing up, locking the door, turning the lights off, getting ready for bed, getting into bed.

It was bound to be difficult. Of course she was upset. Of course she cried, like an alcoholic, secretly, on her own, desperate to be caught.

But on the whole, it wasn't dreadful. Better for her in a way, she thought, than the average person. She had a lot to do. Leonie, and the medical implications, and finding out what had really happened, and changing her job. She couldn't just let go.

A month after Gilles' death her worst fear had been, if not removed, allayed. Both hers and Leonie's lipid levels were normal. Leonie was still at risk – the doctor had said the condition didn't usually assert itself until later, she'd have to be tested again when she was six and fourteen, but its most lethal form – inherited from both parents – was ruled out.

By six weeks, Venus had gone to Paris and realised there was no point her going again until Hélène had recovered. Mary knew nothing and they'd found no clues to Gilles' medical past in Hélène's flat. Hélène herself had gone into hospital suffering from some kind of nervous collapse and couldn't be disturbed. There was nothing more she could find out.

She'd wondered whether to take Gilles' things back to London with her, and then decided to leave them. They were mainly childhood possessions in any case, not hers to meddle with.

On the journey home she panicked that Hélène might never get better. She wrote down what she'd previously only gone over in her mind. A list of evidence, every point with its verdict.

– Hélène. If didn't know, she in effect killed him. ⇒ He knew.

– Never saw doctor, never took pills. If knew, completely ignored medical advice. ⇒ He didn't know.

– Complained of indigestion, heartburn, backache. If knew, wouldn't have put it like that. ⇒ He didn't know.

– Life insurance, no disclosure. ⇒ He didn't know.

– Leo. He would have said.

He surely would have said.

He'd been ecstatic when they'd found out Leo was a girl. He'd confessed it to her. He couldn't help how he felt. She'll be free, he'd said, she won't be constrained by crap.

Like a worm, the thought slithered into her head that whatever the truth was, he half knew, he knew the men in his family had died young, he must have had a sense that he was at risk. More than that, it was only the men who'd died. He could have assumed a girl would be fine. From what Jane had said, Hélène thought the same.

But then, given what he must have guessed, why hadn't he done more?

He could swap what he wanted to believe with reality. A trait she'd once loved had become pitiful.

Back in London, she telephoned doctors, surgery receptionists, plagued them about his medical records. She sent search forms to each health authority she could think relevant. It seemed that he'd had no past, never once gone to the doctor. Common among young men it was. Lived abroad? Oh well then, that would be where – No, only until he was about five. (But didn't she know exactly?) And then again when he was twenty-seven. But what if he'd had the test privately? Or actually in Paris?

Every trace of him was falling through her fingers.

She went back to Paris for a long weekend. She and Mary searched the flat. For the name of a doctor, a note, anything. Hélène's room, his room. She rifled through his things, and the fact of his death began to hit her unevenly.

One moment she would dismiss a letter, a photograph, for its lack of medical information. The next she would look at a thing precious only because he'd kept it – a coin, a map, an object without any personal content other than that it had been his – and feel hopeless with sadness.

In the presence of his childhood possessions, she was being dislodged. Spying on a time that shared apartness with this, but unflinchingly contrasted promise.

They found a name. They telephoned. Yes, the French receptionist said, yes. We have his records. Venus should come to the surgery with the following papers. Venus had interrupted. No. It was important. Please, please could she be told over the phone. Then she would go to the surgery, straight away, show all the papers. But couldn't she just be told? She could give his name, date of birth, place of birth, everything. She was his wife. She knew him better than anyone –

The receptionist asked her to wait. A minute later, she came back to the phone. Just a typhoid vaccination Madam, when he was three. That was all.

Again she left Paris thinking Hélène would have to recover before there was any point in her returning. Again she made plans to go back despite herself.

With Leonie settled at the nursery, she worked harder. Having been asked by a pupil's mother, she started to give private singing lessons. She told herself that in this sphere of her life at least, things weren't going badly. She liked teaching, she liked to see the children react, and it was right to go back to music, it was something she could trust.

Then, when she'd finished work for the day, and everything was done at home, she walked. Putting Leonie in the pushchair. On the streets, in the common, in the dark. There was no route to sleep other than mental and physical exhaustion.

One day, her mother rang to ask how she was. Venus replied that she was okay.

'... Darling? Are you sure?'

'Yes, why?'

'Well,' she said, 'there's something I've got to tell you – I thought I should let you know before Christmas so it doesn't come as too much of a shock.'

'Right.'

'Vee, I don't want this to upset you – '

'Okay, just tell me.'

'I've met someone. A man called David. I didn't want to tell you before, but it was during that holiday, in Greece, just… just before Gilles died… '

Her speech slipped like silk rope.

'Vee?'

So four months ago, her mother had met someone. In fact no, not met, she had fallen in love. On a cruise, she had fallen in love, while Venus had held her dead husband.

'Vee?'

'Right, okay.'

Why hadn't she said something immediately? What did she think, that Venus would dissolve? Was that her assessment?

From then on, Venus didn't attempt to confide in her, deemed her too removed from grief to understand.

Gilles was the one she had to talk to. He'd know how she felt. And yet every night, in every blank moment, when she tried to think of him, she couldn't seem to bring him back. She could forget he was dead, but to forget her rage and her doubt – to forget all of these things, at the same time, for long enough to dive into the old life – it was too much.

Charlotte called a week before Christmas. She'd had a show fold, she'd booked the three of them a holiday. She'd checked the school's term dates, there was no way Venus could back out. She'd used Max's air miles, the tickets were free. They'd stay at a house in Anguilla, there was no rent to pay.

No, the owner wouldn't be there – no, he was just a friend – no, in fact Max knew him; no, Venus could consider it a Christmas present; no Max had a deal to sign before January, working through Christmas was a long-held career dream.

The idea was so foreign to Venus's life that she couldn't believe it would come to anything. But, overwhelmed by Charlotte's generosity and by anyone wanting to spend time with her, she found herself following Leonie and Charlotte onto the plane.

She'd taken a bag of maths books with her to prepare for the extra lessons she'd start teaching in January. On the first day of the holiday, she and Leonie came back from the town with the shopping and found that both the books and Charlotte were gone. That evening Venus asked Charlotte if she'd seen her books. Charlotte said maybe the cleaner had moved them.

The next morning, Charlotte told her that her maths books had left the island and were on their way back to England by airmail.

'Darling, don't fight me. Come to the beach, then you'll be home in time to meet Sweet Pea.'

The week was a blip, a strange, outer-space adventure, propelled by Charlotte's unremitting spontaneity. If the boat trip was cancelled, of course, going back to Twenty the boatman's bar was only practical. If the ride along the beach happened to pass Patterson's place, naturally they would all dismount, have a drink, play on the karaoke machine and make a date for later. A neighbour having drinks? We'd love to come. A couple on the beach with a child? Join us for lunch. Waiters, gardeners, the parasol guy, the pool guy, the guy who played calypso, the girl who braided hair, Charlotte knew them, their names, their families, and what got under their skin. She took people like a drug addict, except it was they who wanted more.

The time passed in a haze of half-made excuses and timid attempts to join in, listening to Charlotte pronounce from the Gospel According to St Venus: Mortal Sin no 1, getting dressed after breakfast; Mortal Sin no 2, interacting with any male; Mortal Sin no 3, acknowledging the attractiveness of any male; marvelling at Leonie's full body waves of laughter usually prompted by Charlotte's mimicking, being forbidden to pay for things, and every other evening no matter what else was going on, being massaged to her bones by a belligerent, middle-aged woman called Sweet Pea.

One evening, Venus fell asleep putting Leonie to bed. She came out of the room imbued with gratitude. Charlotte was back, lying on the sofa texting.

'Charl, you've got to let me do something, I mean to thank you.'

'Oh balls, Vee.' She didn't look up.

'Don't disguise how nice you're being.'

'What, riling you all day?' Charlotte chucked her phone into a chair. 'How are you feeling?'

'Better than if I'd been at my mother's.' Venus sat on the rug at the foot of the sofa. 'What made you do it all?'

'To be honest what I thought you needed was an erotic encounter with the opposite sex, but I decided the prospect of you agreeing to that was so remote, I'd organise the next best thing.'

Venus breathed out. 'How sensitive.'

'Mm. I knew you'd agree.'

'What about you man-wise?' Venus asked. 'Patterson seems nice.'

'But very indiscreet – which is why I like him.'

Venus smiled.

'You moomin, are you taking the piss?'

'No.'

'Good,' she smiled, 'it's a serious subject.'

Charlotte took Venus in, recalibrating her tone like a chameleon adopting the pattern of its surroundings. '… You look better Vee, you really do.'

'Thanks.' Venus paused. 'Leo's adored it here.'

'She's a wonderful girl. Brave as anything.'

'Yeh.' Venus rested her back against the base of the sofa. 'She loved Gilles very much.'

'She certainly loves you.'

'Not in the same way.' She hesitated. '… She calls out to him in her sleep, even now.'

'Don't sell me that one, Vee. She adores you, anyone can see that.'

Venus looked down. 'Well, between freaking out at night that she's going to die, and spending the day walking around like a robot, I'm not exactly giving her the best chance.'

'I always think that when parents worry about their children, they're really worrying about themselves.' Charlotte met her eye.

Venus didn't say anything.

'Can I ask Vee, what do you do – I mean when you're on your own?'

'Walk mainly.'

'Do you sing?'

'Only at school.'

'So – any kind of emotional release?'

'Crying.' Venus clenched her teeth. 'And failing to live in the past. It's not like it's a high aim, but I'm so enraged with him I can't even do that.'

'You mean fantasising that he's still there?'

'Yes, but I can't. I thought I could, but I can't seem to.'

'It's not such a bad thing to do, everyone needs an escape.' Charlotte was quiet for a moment. 'Have you tried thinking of when you first met?'

'It's not so much particular memories, more the idea of him.'

'But particular memories help. Go back to when you were having sex five times a day. It'll be easier to magic up, there's less to pretend.'

And while she put this suggestion down to Charlotte's routine sex-mania, just talking about it was incredible.

'You know what I think,' Charlotte went on, 'you've got to do nothing once in a while. Take it in when you're more relaxed. Not on your own – with someone else, that's what people are for.'

Venus wondered who that person could possibly be, if not Gilles.

Yawning, Charlotte stretched. 'And then, who knows?'

'What?'

'Well, you might, one day – not for a billion years, obviously – want to have a shag. Personally, I'd get some new bras.'

'Ugh.' Venus's eyes flashed. 'Shut up.'

Venus sat with Leonie on the tube going home from the airport, planning the three days before school started. She'd have to ask her mother for help, she'd never have time to prepare the lessons otherwise. She'd go to the supermarket tomorrow, get bread and milk tonight, make supper, unpack, put Leo to bed, sort the washing out, check the post.

She opened the front door of the house and felt a weight – everything was just as they'd left it. But her heart lifted when she saw Leonie dancing round the hall.

Venus smiled, watching her leap about like a frog. The holiday really had done her good.

Leonie looked up at Venus, her head tipped to one side.

Venus laughed. 'What is it?"

'Daddy Daddy Daddy!' She jumped up and down.

'Oh darling, no – '

Leonie's whole body clouded over.

Venus grabbed her in her arms, couldn't look at the expression on her face.

In the dark, Venus lies awake. She can hear the birds outside, feel the day begin again. Alone in bed, time stretches limitlessly ahead of her.

The sadness comes on slowly, unpredictably, like an old drunk walking up a hill. She sees him from a long way off, but doesn't expect him when he arrives. He leaves and comes back again too many times to count. He stays for months, but when at last he goes, she can't wait for him to return.

One day she wakes up without giving him a thought. Absorbed in something else, she catches herself and realises her happiness. It betrays her instantly. The knock sounds. The drunk is waiting, his lungs whirring, his hands outstretched in supplication. She'll always be taking the bastard in.

III

'*Je comprends ici ce qu'on appelle gloire: le droit d'aimer sans mesure*.'
'Here I understand what is meant by glory; the right to love without limits.'

Albert Camus

15

'Being for the Benefit of Mister Kite'
by John Lennon and Paul McCartney

It was Saturday 17 July 2010, three years and ten months after Gilles' death. Venus had left the couple she'd been talking to by the back porch of Charlotte's parents' house, walked up the stairs into the bathroom and shut the door.

She went to the window, pushed up the sash and leant out. People were making their way towards the marquee that covered the huge lawn at the front. A striking woman and two long-lost male friends embraced, the evening sun shining on their faces as they tipped their glasses to the Georgian house, the beautiful day, each other.

Beyond the garden, fields sloped down to a tree-lined valley, then rose to the next hill where a church stood in the distance. The land gave a feeling of space without isolation, the hills invited you to look and the valleys to wonder what you couldn't see. Further away was the high moor, the open sky, the sun itself.

Two cows were lumbering up the road from the village with two men strolling behind them. One of the cows broke into a trot as one of the men sprinted up to it, trying to get on its back. The other doubled up with laughter.

'Ladies and uh… gentlemen… ' Charlotte's father's slurred voice over the microphone reached Venus up in the locked room. 'It's my great pleasure, uh… to announce… '

She put her sandals back on. She'd sneak through the small tent at the side.

'Max, what the fuck are you doing?'

Venus popped back to the window.

Dieter, Max's best man, as candid as he was tall, was poking his head out of the marquee. Phone at his ear, Max put his finger to his lips repeatedly.

'What's your ETA? We can delay things here.' Max paused. 'Quite, it's Bobby that counts... That's kind Zane. You've got the GPS of the field?'

Charlotte was walking out of the house towards him, a large black labrador barking at her side.

'No just a dog.' Max motioned vigorously at Charlotte as the dog sniffed his trousers. 'Rest assured it's not that kind of farm, the animals are all off-site… Yes it's alarming, I understand perfectly… Okay Zane, many thanks.'

Disconnecting, Max beckoned Dieter. 'Lose the dog for the duration. Better still for all time.' Max made another call. 'Jack, Max. Bobby's heading our way. Dimente's ours, I guarantee it.' He slid his phone back into his jacket pocket. 'They said it couldn't be done.' He pursed his lips and blew. 'They lied.'

'I cry with excitement,' Charlotte stroked her dog's ears.

'Ugh, fuck you.'

'Sweet offer darling,' she put a collar on the dog, 'traditional too, of course.'

'Do you have to be flippant? After the months of work I've put in, your mother's put in, every bloody member of my team? Without your degenerate friends it would be triple A in there.'

The labrador jumped up on him.

'*Scheißköter*.' Max kicked at it but missed.

Dieter whistled and the dog came galloping towards him. Scowling, Max brushed the dirt off his trousers.

'Now, your move remember darling,' Charlotte watched him. 'Giddy up.'

'For Christ's sake. You expect me to go through some childish charade when I've got half a *trillion* under management in that tent?'

'Max,' Dieter advised, 'that's why they're here.'

Max angled his legs this way and that, performing a thorough check of his trousers.

'I do so want to be on my best behaviour when God arrives.' Charlotte winked at Dieter.

Max sighed hard. 'Who gives a shit.' And with an efficient movement, he picked Charlotte up and carried her towards the marquee.

'… Ladies and gentlemen,' Charlotte's father bellowed lustily, 'the bride and groom!'

Charlotte launched into 'I Wanna Be Loved By You,' in the breathy, Marilyn Monroe style she'd perfected. The applause grew loud. Everyone was thrilled.

Venus came away from the window. She went to the basin, turned on the cold tap and washed her face.

Who didn't live in a counterfeit world?

The trick was not to mind it. To distract yourself from it, with a barrage of events. Eventless, there was no present. There were the 'once's – once she was back from Paris, once her maths class had done their exams, once she'd changed the house around. And when that got too much, there was the cushion of pretence. Looking at herself in the mirror and feeling him behind her, linking the hook and eye at the top of the zip, kissing the back of her neck – just a touch, just the feel of him touching her –

'God, stop,' she whispered.

She looked at her reflection again. Her dress fitted well. The bra was the key, and the lady who'd found it for her a symphony of oohs and aahs which she'd played back a thousand times. She put her fingers under the thin straps of the dress and moved them out a little. The silk felt cool against her skin.

She was alive. It was only a party. Max was right – who gave a shit.

Unlocking the door, she walked out of the bathroom, down the stairs and out of the house.

The air was hot, her dress felt good. She crept along the length of the marquee, listening to the sound of talking and laughing on the other side of the canvas. She turned into the steamy, crowded kitchen tent. Young men and women dodged each other and their armfuls of plates. She slipped between them until she came to the entrance to the main marquee and stopped.

Hundreds of people had shimmered into life in front of her, table after table, faces and voices, the men debonair in their dinner jackets, the women effortless with evening style. She hid out of their sight yet trying to see, like a child who should have been in bed.

The top table was on a stage with a microphone in front of it and a vast TV screen on a stand to the side. Charlotte and Max looked like Greek gods.

A waitress tutted and Venus moved further to the side. Charlotte's mother was talking to one of the waiters. She was wearing a low cut gold dress with a necklace made of linked gold discs.

A waiter hurried past her to one of the smaller round tables, opened a bottle of champagne that had been lodged in the wings of a life-size ice swan and replaced it with two more. In the middle of each large table, pink and white climbing roses twisted round circular canes. And arranged around them, the porcelain, silver, linen and crystal of a lost colonial power. The ceiling was covered with hundreds of tiny glass lights – how had they managed it? And on the floor, a seagrass carpet, finely woven so as not to catch the women's heels, with parquet in the middle for dancing. And there they were, the women with the heels, the men with the women, basking in this oceanic perfection.

The rah rah of conversation died away, and Charlotte's father got up to make his speech. He was experimenting with the microphone like a little boy. He was funny without even talking. She laughed and for a second he seemed to spot her and beam her a message.

Aah, tremendous, come in my love, don't worry about all those arseholes, I'm drunk as a skunk.

Overjoyed, she smiled back. A tap on her bare shoulder made her jump.

'You lost my love?' An older waitress was passing by. 'Us'll show you through d'rectly.'

'Thanks,' Venus whispered.

She scanned the room for empty places, hoping Charlotte's father would speak for a while. But having been kind about his daughter, he was quick to propose the toast.

Venus followed the waitress into the cooler air of the marquee, past another huge TV screen that had been hidden from her view and in and out of tables.

'Her's not comin',' the waitress whispered, pulling out an empty chair. Venus thanked her and sat down. The nameplate said *Madeleine*.

She was on the third row of tables from the front, but in the middle of the marquee, and if she turned her head, in direct line of sight of the stage. She smiled cautiously at the people around her. A few smiled back. Max was speaking.

The man beside her on her right had broad shoulders, a beard and glasses. Early forties, good-looking in a solid way. An older woman sat on his other side with very long hair, less attractive. Both were blond. She felt at ease, they looked like peaceful Scandinavian naturists.

Loudly an English voice said, 'Here here.' A fat man two tables away was nodding.

' – without question a magnificent achievement,' Max said. 'I'd also like to thank Michael Brady who has flown in from Shanghai, architect of the Ventura deal, now running the supremely successful Pan Asia VC fund.'

Venus glanced at the bearded man beside her. He smiled. He, his wife, their two children – perhaps they didn't speak English, she thought. The guy next to her on her left either couldn't be bothered or was asleep, some cousin probably. Then there was an Italian-looking girl with a tall young blond man who would have been interesting if they hadn't been so interested in each other.

' – so I'm truly delighted that Mr Wu could find time to be here this afternoon. Mr Wu, sincerely, a great many thanks.'

The bearded man played with his watch. He would have to take it off, she thought, to be a true naturist. A picture formed in her mind of him naked, his beard relentlessly evoking his pubic hair. And then she was on the beach with him, running through the dunes, sinking into the warmth, his beard and her pubic hair locked in a velcro embrace.

The bearded man smiled. She smiled back, hoping the flicker of her thoughts didn't show.

She gestured towards the sleeper enquiringly. He shrugged and smiled.

' – which brings me to Charlotte. They say work hard, play hard. I work hard. She plays hard.' The audience tittered. 'Ladies and gentlemen,' he looked at Charlotte and she looked provocatively back at him, 'what's not to love? – To Charlotte.'

The bearded man took his champagne glass to get ready for the toast. Together he and Venus stood up, drank and sat down.

They waited for Dieter's speech to begin. Venus pretended to tickle the sleeper's neck. The bearded man chuckled. The Italian girl was laughing. She seemed good fun.

The screens came to life. *Max PLC & the Charlotte Group: expertise meets flair in merger of the year*.

Dieter was operating the screens with his phone, making irreverent comments as he went.

Max PLC: original seed capital. Everyone laughed at a photo of Max, blond hair brushed to one side, meticulously dressed in school uniform.

Max PLC: sophisticated management structure. More laughs at Max as an adolescent, wearing a suit and standing in what looked like a boardroom.

But in the quiet, a phone rang. Max fumbled with his jacket.

'It's for you, Max!' Dieter yelled, to roars from the audience. Max, speaking rapidly on the phone, was walking out of the marquee. Dieter called over to Max in German, then threw up his hands, egging the audience on.

'Bloody cheek!' a dapper old man bellowed, Venus's closest neighbour on the table in front.

'Ladies and gentlemen,' Dieter announced magnanimously, 'we wait for Max PLC to come back to the table.'

Smiling, Venus turned to the bearded man. 'I wonder what was so important.'

He shook his head. 'Excuse… I cannot understand… '

'Do you speak German?' she smiled.

'Ya, I am speaking German.' He spoke in a cheerful voice. 'May I you helping?'

His wife whispered something to him and smiled at Venus.

He spoke again. 'Aah! Excuse. May I help you?' He laughed in a friendly way.

Venus looked at his large beard and smiled while trying to think of something to say. 'That's kind of you. I wondered what Dieter was saying to Max as he left.'

The boy spoke up. 'He tells to Max quickly to return.'

'Ah, I see,' said Venus. 'You speak good English.'

'I learn English in the school,' the boy said.

'He is learning so fast,' the father said. 'It is like water to the duck!' He laughed.

The girl rolled her eyeballs. His wife nudged her husband while continuing to smile.

'And Tova is dancing also, like the duck. It is incredible.' The girl was not appeased.

'A dancer!' Venus had sounded too enthusiastic. 'That's – that's great.'

She drank some water.

Max came back into the marquee, bringing with him a stocky, large-headed man, a second, small man with bouncy footsteps and Charlotte's dog, which he gripped by the collar. Max whispered to Dieter and pointed at the dog, which was doing its best to slide out of its collar to greet the bouncy man. Anxiously, the bouncy man edged away from the dog towards Dieter, a strategy he reversed when Dieter took the dog from Max. Dieter escorted the bouncy man to his seat then carried the dog, yelping, out of the tent.

'Ladies and gentlemen,' Max took the microphone, 'we will hear more from Dieter shortly. I would first like to introduce a man who has been a key figure in my life, and in the lives of so many in the financial world. In the driving seat of a meteoric banking career, he assumed the Chairmanship of the Dimente Group as if it were a natural progression. Epic dealmaker, born global player, the race may change, but the winner stays the same.

'Bobby,' Max addressed the stocky man beside him, 'I grew up dreaming that one day I would meet you in person. That dream came true for me two years ago, and another dream comes true for me today.'

'God help us,' said the dapper old man aloud.

Max registered the old man and resumed.

'Bobby, I know you will add unimaginable value to this event. It's always an immense privilege to work with you, and it is an honour that you have made a window in what I know is an awesomely tight schedule to be here tonight.

'Ladies and gentlemen,' Max paused, 'I give you Chairman, CEO – 'Extraordinary Joe' – Bobby Jones.'

Max, Charlotte's mother and soon most of the tent broke into applause as Bobby took the microphone.

Max, still clapping, was making his way towards the dapper old man's table. He thrust himself between Venus and the old man.

'Listen Payne,' he hissed, 'anything more like that – *anything* – and you're out. Do I make myself clear?'

'*Sieg Heil!*' The old man's arm shot forward.

'I'm Swiss, idiot.' Max left.

'Ladies, gentlemen,' Bobby began in a Manhattan accent, 'two people have today pledged to share their personal wealth. Wish them luck, they'll need it.'

The audience laughed and clapped.

'Seriously,' he continued, 'my faith is important to me, and we rejoice that God has blessed this union. Now, we have several ultra-high-net-worth individuals here tonight, who *may* believe, as I did, that they have been spurned by God due to wealth issues. For those intending to join the circle between this life and the next, particularly elite business people like myself, I advocate a work by Bobby Jones – *God Made Rich Man: The Second Coming*. To access this and other works, please speak with my assistant Zane.'

Bobby indicated the bouncy man sitting at the bank of technology at the back of the tent.

Venus looked around her questioningly.

'He shrinks the camels,' the old man Payne muttered.

'To conclude this preface, for the avoidance of doubt, all fees for tonight's appearance will be waived, this is my wedding gift to the couple.'

Max gave a deep 'thank you'.

'It'll be a director's cut, Max. – So,' he raised his voice, 'people tell me Bobby, you're the best. You've got judgement, foresight, acumen. You've got guts, you've got charisma, you've got the biggest balls in the park.

'Yes, I'll admit I'm a winner. That's a responsibility I

bear. Now when I meet a winner, I ask him two questions. I'll pose these to myself for you right now.'

Vaguely apprehensive, Venus realised that this was God. He'd arrived. Charlotte and her father both had their eyes down, as if corresponding under the table. Venus watched Max's rapt face while Bobby continued to speak. She wondered whether his bank had funded the whole evening.

After a period of monotone, Bobby raised his voice again. '*Whatever I engage in, I must push inordinately.* God, ladies and gentlemen, does not stop. And, let's join up that circle – neither do I.'

'We'll all be dead,' Payne announced in a stage whisper.

'Excuse him ladies and gentlemen,' the woman next to Payne said in a Southern drawl. 'Liquor makes him cruel, doesn't it dear?'

'Nonsense! I'm perfectly beastly when I'm sober!' He guffawed.

'For goodness sake be quiet, this is a man to listen to,' a woman said.

Growling, Payne got out his phone and to Venus's surprise, started rapidly texting. Then, as if the technology hadn't satisfied him, he held his phone up in the air and waved it at Charlotte's father who nodded sagely and lowered his eyes.

But before long Payne had moved on, becoming distracted by a young French woman with an enormous bust and a large cross hanging over it. The bearded man was making an origami shape out of his son's menu. The guy on her left was still asleep. She regretted not going to the table she'd been meant for.

With a feeling of nausea, she realised that Bobby's helper, Zane, was adjusting the height of the TV screens. There would be a presentation.

Venus lifted her glass of water and pretended to pour it over the sleeper's head.

'Ya!' the bearded man laughed. His son let out a caustic cackle.

Bobby was reaching the end of his introduction. Zane was liaising with Dieter over a different set of controls. The lights dimmed then came back on.

The sleeping man's nameplate, pushed towards the middle of the table, said *Al*.

A few drops wouldn't hurt. Giggling herself, she dipped her fingers into her glass and flicked them against her thumb above the sleeper's neck. By the time three drops of water had floated to his skin, the whole table was watching him.

Within a second, the sleeper's hand had gone to the back of his head, the bearded man and his children had laughed unpleasantly and the lights had gone down.

Venus felt crass.

'Sorry,' she whispered in the dark. 'Are you all right?'

' – Mum? – Where are you?' he whispered.

He sighed and yawned. Venus couldn't make out his face.

' – A corporation is an extension of one, maybe two, platinum individuals – '

'Is your mother here?' she asked.

'… No, no sorry,' he said.

He sounded like a polite schoolboy.

'Sorry,' he said. 'I'm so tired.' And in the dark he lay his head back down on the table.

A funny noise came from near the tent entrance, as if someone big and drunk were trying to find their way out. She couldn't see beyond Bobby's spotlight. The noise stopped a moment later, but she couldn't tell what had caused it.

A detailed list of bullet points appeared on Bobby's next slide, entitled *Platinum 1.1* and subtitled *In the beginning was the Word*.

'So,' Bobby continued, 'the famous Platinum 1.1. Remember this, Max?'

'BJ, we have to talk… ' Zane's whisper was picked up by the microphone.

'D'you hear that?' Payne chortled to his neighbour. 'They don't even know what a BJ is – '

'Ed, hush.'

But Payne was lost in subtle movement. '... BJ, I worship thy holy name,' he breathed, '... and thou wilt forever be my God.' Venus couldn't see what he was doing, except that it culminated in him checking how he looked using the camera on his phone.

'BJ,' Zane tried to get Bobby's attention again, 'BJ, I hate to interrupt – '

'Aaagh! BJ *salva-me*!' Payne shouted all of a sudden in a high-pitched zealot's voice. 'BJ is the one!' he strained, about to expire, 'THE MESSIAH HAS COME!'

Confusion was breaking out on Payne's table.

'Ladies and gentlemen,' Max rushed to the microphone, his rage trained on Payne like a laser, 'could I *please* ask for silence.'

' – Max, wait,' Bobby seemed unnerved. 'I cannot overlook this man's conviction.'

'Bobby, I assure you, your presentation takes infinite precedence over the rubbish that spews from this idiot's mouth.'

Bobby angled his spotlight at Payne. The French girl's cross hung resplendent on his chest. 'Are you serious? This is a man of God.'

'And the light shineth in darkness,' Payne cried, 'and the darkness comprehended it not.'

With renewed vigour, Bobby's voice shook. 'He knows something.'

'He knows nothing at all for heaven's sake.'

'Now hold on Max, as my potential *financier*, are you *questioning my judgement*?'

'Of course not, I'm simply saying that this man, who has been awkward and abusive from the start, is an appalling troublemaker.'

'You're drifting Max, Christ was a troublemaker.'

'Well I can tell you categorically that he isn't Christ, he's *Satan*.'

Silence descended on the entire tent. A small crash came from near the entrance and the noise level began to rise again.

Venus turned to the bearded man. 'That was blunt.'

'Aah,' he said and laughed in the dark. He hadn't understood a word.

Venus drank some champagne.

The sleeper seemed to be leaning his head back slowly against his shoulders as if his neck were stiff. Nor probably had he.

'Sorry I woke you up,' Venus whispered.

'No,' he whispered, 'don't worry.' He sounded serious, older than she'd thought.

'I did it deliberately,' she said. 'It was only water.'

'Why?' he whispered.

'Well… ' she half laughed. 'This is an incredibly strange wedding. I suppose I wanted to talk about it with someone.'

'Okay,' he sounded impatient.

She looked down at the table, wanting to justify herself.

Everything was getting louder.

'Sorry,' he whispered, 'I was working all last night.'

'What d'you do?' she asked.

'Oh, well… ' he hesitated, 'it's not that important.'

The bearded man's daughter was shouting. Lights were coming on near the tent entrance.

'To you, or the world, or the conversation?' she whispered.

He turned fully to her. In the dim light her eyes focused on his, and the people and the noise fell away.

'Or all three?'

'All three.'

More lights came on. She caught another glimpse of him, then saw him look down at her nameplate. As if noticing her noticing, he looked away and drank some water.

He wasn't all that young, she thought, but she was older than him, and that wasn't a bad thing to be.

Venus breathed in. 'You have a beautiful face,' she whispered.

He turned back to her.

'Thank you – ' he said, his voice cracking between a talk and a whisper.

She looked down, surprised that the words had come out of her. But, she thought, he must have been told that before.

'Good God.' Payne sounded wonder-struck. 'Ken's hired the circus.'

Venus turned around.

Two cows were stumbling about just inside the marquee entrance.

She touched Al's arm and pointed.

'Uh oh,' he breathed.

They seemed stunned by the lights.

'Oh my God they're coming.' Zane rushed to one of the big screens for protection.

People were getting up, panic in their voices.

Max ran to the microphone. 'Ladies and gentlemen, please keep calm – '

'*The oxen!*' Payne leapt to his feet, electrified. '*They come to worship!*'

Max shot off stage, dodged the rushing guests and flew at Payne, who high on prophetic delirium, was yelling '*MIRACOLO*!' for all he was worth.

'You bastard,' he breathed. 'Admit it, you did this, admit it – '

'Max, control yourself.' Bobby's voice cut the air as he sidled away from Zane and the cows.

'BJ please,' Zane's bounce frequency was increasing, 'we've got to get out of here.'

Seemingly lured by his voice, one of the cows reversed into Zane's screen, which fell like a tree to the floor. Countering the motion, Zane sprang up on to a chair. The cow itself looked strangely peaceful. Then, as if in apology, it let out an ebullience of shit which fell onto the screen with a wet patting sound.

'Bobby, I hate to do this, but I resign!' Zane's voice had gone up an octave. '*Strictly no animals*, I raised it verbally.' His head shook. 'I've been flexible with canines. I CANNOT BE FLEXIBLE WITH BUFFALO.'

'*BUFFALO MIRACOLO*!' the old man sang out.

'*Shut up, you cretinous shit*.'

'That's it Max,' Bobby yelled, edging still further from the cows, 'you've crossed the line. If you think that after your behaviour this evening, we can do any kind of business – '

Venus gasped. With a flourish, Charlotte unclipped her train and jumped down from the top table.

'Max,' she called as she strode through the chaos, 'in the light of God's revelations here tonight, I cannot let this misunderstanding continue.' She took Bobby's arm like a bodyguard.

Venus couldn't hear any more.

Al got up. 'I'll give Charlotte a hand.'

She was about to go with him, then caught sight of Payne processing towards Charlotte, his tie reversed, the large cross hanging solemnly round his neck.

'... Such luck these animals are here Bobby,' Charlotte was quietly talking as Venus got nearer. 'I'd love you and Zane to lead a ceremonial blessing when the rest of the herd arrives.'

'Herd? No. I'd like that, but I can't do it to Zane.'

'Spoken like a true gentleman. I suggest you and Zane slip out first.'

'Damn right,' Bobby whispered.

' – Aah, Bishop.' Charlotte took Bobby's hand in her right and Payne's in her left. 'Join the circle for the blessing, Max.'

Max glared at her. She shot a glance at a group of fleeing fund managers.

Max took Payne's and Bobby's hands, to Charlotte's swift 'Amen.'

'Ladies and gentlemen,' Charlotte's father was calm as a pond. 'Do come and raid my cellar while we get things seen to here.'

People were shoving each other, fighting to get out. Dieter carried Zane on his shoulder.

' – Max sweet,' Charlotte raised her voice, 'what was it you were saying about Bobby's schedule? What a shame it was he couldn't stay longer, and I said not already surely, and you said that I didn't realise the constant activity, Bobby was the chairman of a vast company with a particularly crucial decision to make this very evening if only I'd give the two of you five minutes.'

'*So true*, oh my goodness,' Zane bounced in his eyrie, 'Bobby's beyond busy – '

Bobby's body shuddered slightly. 'Let's get to the chopper Max, I have a corporation to run.'

With that, Charlotte led Bobby, Max, Dieter and Zane out of the marquee.

16

'Only The Lonely'
by Roy Orbison and Joe Melson

After the rush of seeing you in Leicester Square, I got infected with reality. Whatever I did, I couldn't get interested in other women. I'd already made two fruitless pilgrimages to the tube station. I was entering the wilderness, with no prospect of ever finding my way out.

I'd only been working for a month but obeying orders had quickly lost its appeal. What did these fools know? All pink blood and glasses, exciting themselves over mergers and acquisitions like some troupe of ecstatic virgins.

I'd go down to the post room looking for life. They knew how to do it, they knew all about it.

Who put the arse in the Arsenal. Seen the legs on her? Mate, it's the style, I'm not criticising the engine.

But I wasn't made for gangs, however much I wished I was. What I was made for was walking into Leicester Square tube station and getting your number. But I hadn't even done that. Which left me made for nothing except masturbation.

Vee, here is a description of a phenomenon I will call the 3am Eternal, occasionally experienced by the lonely young bachelor.

God man, a renegade neuron mutters in my brain, *don't tell me you're doing this again.*

Ah shut up, fifty billion others shout back.

You're lying on the sofa watching telly. The hand in your trousers is unfortunately yours. And an ancient pulse calls you onward.

Change channels. Women's tennis. Oh nice. Oh lucky man.

But no. Just highlights.

God, not snooker again.

Change channels. Can this be right?

... My television cannot transmit anything except snooker.

But wait, can't a woman play snooker? The stretching the leg over the table thing. *BBC Gilles*. And slowly, seductively, she rubs her finger over the head of the cue, she's having to take that cue in both hands, and now she's bending over, just a little lower in her tennis skirt, and perhaps a demonstration, close behind her, of the finer points, yes, she says, oh yes, and she likes that, and pretty soon you're going to slide that cue into place, and oh, she says, oh God now, then Lord have mercy see how you pocket those balls.

It was a brave attempt.

But the tennis girl's opening her mouth her tongue and her mouth is warm and her tongue is like wet silk and you're seized with new energy and your left hand takes up the rhythm except the pleasure's losing its grip.

... Dinner party, all women, they're nice nice women, you have a problem you say, it won't go away, oh poor sweet baby, but with our treatment, nurses outfits, cure me, black stockings...

Change back, change to the wanking hand, tennis girl she'll take you to the winning post, lipstick secretary she'll take you, blond girl at church, yes blond girl at church – except where the hell is the winning post?

But you won't give up the faith. You'll get a new dawn, you'll get several. Women get never-ending orgasms for Christ's sake. God, is it better as a woman?

And then you'll feel it. Back in the hot seat. And this is it now, you've really got it now, this is sweet deliverance, yes this is right, it's coming good and she's there, and she's looking up and she's going down, oh God release me, and shit if you could suck your own cock, just out of scientific interest –

... No... No, that really won't work.

Vee, I've come to associate the months after seeing you with being in the vortex of a 3am Eternal. I wasn't continuously afflicted, I don't want to give you undue cause for pity, but the metaphorical interpretation always applied: you were my one destination, no matter what I did I couldn't get there and I was plagued by the thought that I might never get there again.

From my chair in the office I could see a building site. The steel frame looked too fragile to support the building, but within a few months it was finished and people were going in and out, oblivious of the thin skeleton underneath. As I watched them, castles of my own would twist and turn into the air, towers of happiness, turrets of bliss.

I'm back in the tube, I tell myself. There's a secret place with a piano, a beautiful, softly lit hall. I take you through the tunnels, leading you to it, and you gasp at its magnificence and the effrontery of its hidden existence. And then I sit at the piano and play with the strength to make every note just right, with such elegance of rhythm, such subtlety of touch that it would be impossible for you not to join me.

I kept a tally. I went back to the station thirty-two times. I went during the week and at the weekend. I took three days off work to vary the time of day. I combined scientific rigour with the infinite hope that only superstition allows. If I wanted you enough, I'd find you. There were people in life you had to meet again.

One of the tube men told me he'd seen you. I went wild: Where? When? What was she doing? Where did she come from? Where did she go? It had been a while ago, but from his description it was definitely you. And then he told me that someone else was after you. I believed him. I gave him a bottle of whiskey and my phone number and asked him to keep me fully informed. He rang a couple of times, mainly to complain about his ex-wife. He told me that what he liked about me was that I was insane.

I was crossing Regent Street on Christmas Eve when I saw a woman. Heading towards the side of the road I'd come from. It made sense – she'd be going to Liberty to get something for her mother. And Chappell's Music was just down the road, all in all it was the height of convenience. But she was on the far edge of a crowd and I could only see her profile. The collar of her coat was turned up. I followed her in and out of the mass of people, keeping my eye on the coat. When I spoke, she looked directly at me. I realised I'd never thought it was you in the first place.

A few months later, I was walking through the Barbican to a meeting. I heard the sound of singing in an operatic style, the beauty of it rendering the city money machine offensive. Of course you'd be singing in the Barbican, didn't it have a school of music? Why hadn't I investigated it before? Already a few paces behind the two lawyers I was with, I stopped and hid behind a pillar. Once I'd lost them, I spent the next hour looking for the practice room. The singer was a man. But I didn't despair. No, I hung around. And then I hung around at the Royal College of Music and the Royal Academy.

And even though a year later I did not always wake up thinking of you, even though I lived the safe life, that tooth-brushing, shirt-ironing, amoeboid life, you were still there. The one I spoke to in my head, the one I had to love. And you may wonder Vee how I could be sick with love for someone after hearing her voice in a tube station, I don't know either, I have no idea, but that was how it was.

17

'Moonshadow'
by Cat Stevens

Venus followed the cow she'd been put in charge of into the hot night air. She rounded the bend in the lane. Charlotte and Al were with the other cow, just before the junction with the main road.

'Sorry,' Al called, 'I thought you were right behind me.'

She looked at him dubiously as she walked towards them. The details – her cow doing an about turn, charging towards her as she dashed away in fear, she and a waitress running around the marquee trying to herd it back out – could wait.

'Sorry,' he said again.

Dieter, who was settling the guests in the house temporarily before getting to grips with the marquee, had begun by building a cow pen. He'd closed off an area where two walls met at right angles with a long gate. Al's cow was waiting inside. As Venus's cow approached, they moved one end of the gate away from the wall and it walked through the gap.

'Brilliant,' Charlotte smiled.'Thank you, both of you.'

Venus touched the cow's forehead, admirable now that it was confined. 'No more?'

'Doubt it,' Charlotte said, 'I'm going to make a few calls. Back in a sec.'

'Poor Charlotte,' Venus said once she'd gone. 'You would have thought someone else could do it.'

'I think she knows who they belong to,' Al said.

A deafening noise came from the field opposite the lane as Bobby's helicopter prepared to take off. The wind from the blades blew their hair, flattening the grass. They watched it lift up and then hang, low in the sky.

The noise was unremitting. Powerless, she held out her hand and he took it.

A few moments later, it rose and found its course. They stayed watching the sky, as if it might turn around and come back. Then Max drove into the lane on the quad buggy and they separated.

Once Max was gone, Venus asked Al about the owner of the cows. A farmer Charlotte knew, he thought.

'Sorry to leave you up there,' he said.

'You were paying me back for waking you up.'

'No,' he said, 'I'm glad you did.'

She looked at him, remembering what she'd said in the marquee.

'We could sit down,' she said.

They sat on the tarmacked lane, warm with the sun it had absorbed during the day. She took in the trees at the edge of the field opposite. It was good to be quiet.

'Do you live near here?'

'I used to,' he said, 'about a mile away. Charlotte and I – our parents were friends – '

He didn't elaborate.

She went back to the owner of the cows, and Al told her his name was Jake.

She smiled. 'Sounds rustic.'

He smiled. 'Yeh.'

She wasn't sure whether to ask him another question or not.

'If you want to sleep – ' she indicated the tarmac behind him, ' – you could just lie down.'

'No, I want to talk to you.'

He seemed tired in a calm way. It was pleasant being with him.

'What were you going to say?' he asked. 'Before?'

She wondered why he thought she was going to say something.

'… Well. So what's the Jake guy like?'

'A bit of a hero I suppose. Or he used to be. A bit like Charlotte.'

'Oh I see,' she said.

'They call it *useful*.' He pronounced the word in a quiet West Country accent.

She looked at him enquiringly.

'I think it's a term for describing bulls.'

She felt an urge to wake him up. 'Good at fucking?'

He flushed, then looked directly at her. 'Everyone's good at that down here.'

Their eyes met and she looked away.

'Sorry,' she said, 'you're tired, I'll stop asking questions.'

'No, you just distracted me.'

She felt her stomach pull in as she looked back at him. His face, his lips…

'Whenever Jake's name came up in conversation, people tried not to change the subject. The smallest thing was enough. Someone told my mum once that he'd made a fruit cake.'

She laughed. 'What did they say?'

'What d'you mean?'

'Go on, do the accent.'

He seemed embarrassed.

'That there Jake,' she said temptingly.

'Ruby up Pretty Top said 'twas a proper job. Reckons ee did it all by eeself.'

She laughed.

'But ee made that cake mind,' she said.

'You'm raight there.'

Smiling, she caught his eye.

'Jake's cake… ' she said slowly.

He was looking at her, but not self-consciously, more as if he were a zoologist studying an animal.

It was unusual, she thought, this being shy and open at the same time.

'… Is he good-looking, Jake?'

'Yeh, I suppose so. But mainly it was, I don't know, his attitude.'

'And… ' she hesitated, '… so he and Charlotte were lovers?'

He stared at her for a second. Perhaps she was going on about sex.

'I think so,' he said. 'I didn't realise it at the time. I was about thirteen so she must have been about seventeen. We were watching *The Go-Between*, you know, the young daughter of the landowner falls in love with the farmer… '

'Yeh,' Venus said. 'With the little boy who takes their messages?'

'You've seen it?' he smiled.

'Well, I've read it. So she's the daughter?'

'Yeh exactly. She was watching it as if it meant more to her than I could possibly imagine. And when it finished she got changed in my mother's room and went off on her bike. I didn't see her for the rest of the summer. And after that she didn't come home for the holidays.'

'What happened?'

'A farmer saw her and Jake somewhere, I don't know. Anyway her mother made her stay with some aunt somewhere. And then Jake crashed his motorbike and everyone stopped talking about him. He lost it, you know, his confidence.'

'That's awful,' she said.

'Yeh,' he paused. 'Yeh it is.'

She was ruffled that Charlotte had never mentioned it.

'Her mother – she's unhappy I suppose, but she's such a hypocrite.'

She looked at his face, his features fine in the low light. His mother wasn't at the wedding. He'd said that when he'd woken up. And if he was anything to go by, his father must have caught Charlotte's mother's attention. Perhaps it was too intimate.

Her mind wandered back to Charlotte and this Jake guy. Charlotte's silence about it was striking.

'So do you think Charlotte really felt something for Jake?'

'Yeh, I think so.' He paused. 'He loved her anyway. And he must still, otherwise he wouldn't have done this.'

'You mean you think he made the cows go into the marquee deliberately?'

'Someone must have. They wouldn't have gone in on their own.'

'But – there must be easier ways.'

'Maybe,' he said. And then he sighed. 'I just don't understand Charlotte. She's done exactly what her mother did and married someone she doesn't love. She doesn't even *think* she loves him.'

He certainly knew how to be serious.

'No, I know what you mean.' She wondered why she hadn't made that point to Charlotte herself. 'I suppose,' she said eventually, 'she decided he was the best person she'd find.'

'But why do people compromise like that? When there's someone else who loves them. It's such a waste, don't you think?'

Venus looked away, a little overwhelmed. 'If they both love each other, yes.'

'The old Jake wouldn't have let it happen. That's the sad thing.'

He'd stopped. She looked round to see Charlotte walking down the lane towards them. They stood up.

'They're Jake Ashley's,' she said.

Al glanced at Venus, his story confirmed.

'He's getting someone to come over with the horse box.' Charlotte laughed. 'You look like a couple of naughty children.'

Before the silence could stretch, she'd put her arms around both of their waists. 'You've been wonderful, thank you.'

'Why don't we wait here for Jake?' Al suggested.

'Yup,' said Venus definitely. 'We'll do it. You go back to the marquee.'

Charlotte looked from Al to Venus, then smiled. 'That would be lovely. He shouldn't be long. But he'll probably have to do two trips.'

'That's fine,' Venus said.

She took a few steps towards the marquee before turning around.

'Al, can you tell Jake I'll give him a call?'

'Okay,' he said.

'Thanks.'

They watched Charlotte walk away.

Venus smiled at him. 'Go-between.'

The moon was rising. Bat wings patted the balmy air. The resiny smell from the pine trees in the field opposite the end of the lane was getting stronger as the night fell.

They sat back down on the tarmac.

'Did you have a crush on her?' Venus asked.

'No, no.' He sounded taken aback. 'She was like an older sister.'

He smiled at her tentatively. 'You're very direct.'

'Sorry,' she said quickly.

'No, it's a relief. I saw her again when I was about eighteen, but we didn't seem to know each other anymore.' He hesitated. 'Or at least that's what I thought. I find her quite… hard to be close to. And I doubt she'd be interested in me.'

She didn't say anything.

'What about you and Charlotte?' he asked.

'Well I think I was sexually attracted to her,' she said, trying to equal his solemnity.

'Really?'

'No,' she laughed. 'I mean, kind of but I'm not like that. She's been a good friend to me.'

He was smiling. 'Do you plan what you're going to say? Or does it come naturally?'

'Why?'

'Would you say anything you thought of?'

'To you? Not yet.'

He looked back at her immediately, but she sat up.

'I've got an idea,' she said. 'You'll probably think it's stupid.'

But before he could reply, a Land Rover arrived with a horsebox behind. They both stood up. A young man got out. He walked towards them with the gait of someone who kept melons between his legs. He nodded at Venus.

'Hi,' Al said.

The man took a look at the cows and then opened the door of the horsebox.

'You're taking one at a time?'

'Can't take more'n one,' he said flatly.

Venus stood in the middle of the lane so that the cows wouldn't go back up to the marquee. The two men herded one of them out and into the horsebox. As she walked back down the lane, she noticed a figure sitting at the wheel.

'Oh,' Al spoke in a by-the-way voice, 'Charlotte said to tell Jake she'll give him a ring.'

The man nodded and the Land Rover's exhaust fumes filled the air and dispersed.

'Who was that?' Venus asked.

'I don't know.'

'So Jake was the one driving?'

'I didn't see. Could have been.' They sat back down. 'What were you going to say?'

He seemed more awake now. It encouraged her.

'You know how when you're at a wedding, people talk about how you know the bride and groom, where you live, what you do, all of that.' She looked at him. 'I thought we should make it up, be whoever we want.'

'Why?' he smiled.

'Just for a laugh,' she smiled back.

'But I've told you a lot already. All I know about you is that your name's Madeleine.'

Suddenly she felt ecstatic, as if fate had endorsed this night.

'… And you secretly think Charlotte's attractive.'

Of course, Madeleine. She would be Madeleine.

She did like him. His shyness, his honesty. She looked at the ground between them, guilty for a moment.

'Okay,' she said. 'You're tired, you don't like your work, and you used to live here, that's it. And your name's Al.'

'That's more than I know about you. And it's Alex. Only Charlotte and my mother call me Al.'

'Well,' she said victoriously, 'that just shows how little I know about you.'

'I suppose it does.'

'Anyway you might be lying to me about everything.'

'But I'm not.'

'All right, but you might live on a Greek island by the sea, and catch fish with your bare hands.'

He looked down smiling and she wondered whether he actually did.

'Why do you want me to make it up?' he asked.

'Because – ' She paused. 'Sometimes the things you imagine can be more real to you – can mean more to you, than reality.'

He didn't say anything. Perhaps she'd sounded mystical.

'… I suppose I had an ulterior motive.' She felt herself tense.

'What?'

'Well it's – ' Her heart raced. 'Just to say that I – I like you.'

His eyes jumped to hers. Neither of them spoke.

But as they looked at each other his expression relaxed. And she felt her own face relax. He gently touched her hand, and she took his hand in hers. Touching him, feeling him touch her, it felt so unexpectedly good, she bent her mouth towards his. But then seeing him with his eyes closed about to kiss her, she kissed his cheek instead. Embarrassed, she drew back.

They sat, not talking. The air was still, the noise from the marquee distant, the day's heat breathing out into the dark.

'Let's lie down,' he whispered.

They lay back on the tarmac, side by side but with enough space between them.

'I've got a place in Greece by the sea,' he began quietly. 'You might like it.'

She smiled.

'I make the food, it's a kind of restaurant,' he said.

'What's it like?' she whispered.

'Well...' He breathed out slowly, and her spine seemed to lengthen at the same time. 'It's in the country, high so there's a breeze, facing west for the sunset... the sun sinks into the sea, it looks like the sea's on fire, you can't believe it.'

She caught her breath.

'And there isn't any jangly music. And it's hard to find so not many people come, but I don't mind that.'

Her smile broadened. 'How would I find it?'

'I'd give you directions, but I don't think you'd need them.'

She turned her head sideways to look at him but his eyes were closed.

'And when you arrived, I'd make you whatever you wanted.'

She reached for his hand, but couldn't feel it.

'As long as it didn't have garlic in it.'

She grinned. 'Why not?'

'Because garlic enters my soul through the pores in my fingers and consumes me with untameable passion.'

'Alex!' She laughed.

He laughed softly. 'I'm so tired, sorry.'

'You're totally at the mercy of this bulb?'

'Well, it depends.'

Was he being flirtatious?

'I've got garlic in my garden,' she said.

'Really?'

'Yeh. I'm not making it up.'

'What else do you grow?'

'Oh.' But she didn't feel like launching off. 'Well nothing, mainly.'

'… It's good with toast and honey.'

She laughed. 'Yeh,' she whispered.

She was lying next to him in the dark. She was with this person at this moment, she did like him, she wasn't deceiving herself, and if she were to turn and look at him, she'd want to do more than like him. And if being her made it difficult, she could be absolutely anyone.

'Alex?'

'Yeh?'

'I'm writing a thesis, shall I tell you the title?'

'Really? Yes, sure.'

'It's called, The Untameable Passion Of Alex.'

'Sssh… ' he laughed.

'I climb up my ivory tower – this only happens at night because it's secret – and I think about how to study my subject.' Perhaps it was too weird, but she continued. 'I've decided to use every sense I can – sight, smell, touch, taste, even listening. People think the true nature of a man's passion is never revealed in speech, but I disagree.'

She heard him breathing. She wondered what she'd say next.

'Then again,' she whispered, 'you can go too far in the

opposite direction. There are some academics who are only interested in talking.'

She turned on to her side slightly to see him, but as soon as she did, her speech came to an end.

They looked at each other for a moment, quite still. And when he touched her fingers, it seemed all of her was in her fingers.

She looked at him again. At his eyes, and how he looked at her.

She was Madeleine. They could do anything, whatever they wanted, nothing else mattered.

She sat up a little, watching his eyes inviting her. She began to undo his tie, the silk loosening fluidly against itself. Heard his intake of breath. Felt her self-consciousness slipping its mooring. Undoing the top button of his shirt. Undoing the next button, bringing her head to his neck and throat, breathing the smell of him in, hearing his pulse quicken, her own so fast it felt suspended.

They were about to kiss. She put her hand between their mouths to stop them and he breathed out with an ache that made her pelvis curl in.

Sitting up, she lay his hands on the ground beside him as he sat, and his legs along the ground in front. Her heart trembling, she knelt over him, her legs outside his, so that she was directly in front of him. Softly she drew her fingers around the edge of his face, then took each little finger from the middle of his lips gently to the corners of his mouth and the top of his jaw.

Looking at his eyes so he wouldn't notice, she undid another button of his shirt, touching the skin of his shoulders, hearing his tight-jawed sigh, his hands suddenly on her waist, pulling her nearer, his mouth kissing her shoulder, her neck, her cheek. But she drew back again.

'Madeleine – '

' – let's stop now,' she whispered.

'What is it?' he whispered.

'Just – it would be awkward – ' She was frustrating both of them. 'Sorry – sorry, I – '

But he traced his finger lightly around the outside of her mouth. Her skin tingled. And then his hand went to the back of her neck, up into her hair. She angled her head to rub against it like a cat.

They heard the Land Rover engine and immediately moved apart. They took the same positions as before, Venus standing further up the lane nearer the marquee and Alex at the makeshift cow pen.

She gazed up into the clear sky. Fainter stars began to reveal themselves so that it seemed they approached.

'What am I doing?' she whispered.

That she could not be her, for one night. That had to be it.

So many points of light, so much nothing in between. She shivered at the small feeling.

The headlights shone against the dark. It was impossible to see. The driver flashed a torch. She blinked in the glare. When she opened her eyes the beam of light was shining on the one remaining cow. The mist of its breath was caught like sprayed silver.

She watched the men moving the gate, heard them calling to the animal, then stood shaken with nerves as it made a break. It came bounding towards her, then equally unexpectedly stopped twenty yards away. With a strange delay, she realised that Alex had got himself between it and her. Gasping for breath, he was turning it round, herding it back down.

Later she tried to thank him. It was nothing, he said, just what normally happened. But his kindness had shocked her into herself. She felt frozen over in comparison.

18

'One Of These Nights'
by Don Henley and Glenn Frey

Vee, I'd found no trace of you. I'd told a few people I was thinking of becoming a priest, to their groans of derision. I didn't mean it, I was just broken-hearted.

I met a woman called Mia. Small breasts, long hair, thin as a wire. She worked at an insurance company across the street from my office. I had a feeling she'd be insatiable, but in fact nothing could compete with her cat. And in any dealings not involving her cat, she was as unpredictable as a cliff in the dark.

In March 1999, eighteen months after I'd seen you, the firm offered me a job in Paris. I was given the weekend to decide. Good boy Peter Reeves had turned it down to go to Hong Kong, I was their second choice.

The sun was brighter, the days were longer, I felt like taking it. My mother didn't think there was a decision to make. It would advance my career, clearly, and I would live with her, of course.

Living with her would have been insupportable, there was no question of that. Being near her was enough to make me hesitate. Her critical powers were wonders of nature. Not only was she adept with the straight sting – which hurt, but after retaliation could at least be cathartic – more subtly, like a mosquito, she'd developed a means of anaesthetising the prick. I felt nothing until a day later when the itching started, and I couldn't understand how something so seemingly inoffensive could have caused such incredible annoyance.

Little did her friends' children know how many of their successes I shared – a lawyer moving to New York, a doctor changing laboratory – still holding on to their balloons of promise, but heading for the golden clouds. Not to mention the exemplary qualities of her stockbroker, his good sense for one so young – state-educated too, all that money she'd paid – his forthcoming marriage, to a charming Belgian girl, and naturally they wanted to have a family as soon as possible.

But as far as going to Paris was concerned, it wasn't my mother who was the problem. I'd seen you in London. Leaving was like giving up.

My mother read my mind. Paris, she said, was the solution: a progression in my life. Forget about London, forget *the girl*, I had cursed myself in that place.

I decided it would be a temporary distraction. Only six months. I'd lost you for longer than that, I'd just be losing you somewhere else. I didn't have to abandon hope. I rang my mother to let her know I was coming.

Mary, she said, had already made up my bed. Ably she recycles her disappointments. I'd told her I'd have my own flat. She hadn't forgotten. On the contrary, she was reminding me of that blasphemy.

When I'd been allocated one of the firm's flats, I called her again. I'd be living in the Marais, a ten minute walk from her flat in Place des Vosges. She was pleased, and I was pleased she was pleased. Like a friendly corpse, my desire for her good opinion had bobbed back to the surface.

She helped me settle in. I refused to give her a copy of the keys. She asked when I was going to come to supper. I said I'd get the hang of the new office and let her know. I'd taken up the firm's offer of a guaranteed five o'clock departure every Thursday to attend French lessons. I knew she'd approve – she picked holes in my written French at every opportunity. I'd probably see her after the first class. Then I could gossip with Mary, eat decently and go out later.

For all its beauty, Paris isn't an easy city to love. But the food was better than in London and the atmosphere more fitting to my ill-tempered state.

Sentimentality began to twitch inside me. The Seine, the Iles, the graffiti on the shuttered shops, the dog shit in the street. Tradition and subversion in long held mutual admiration. The satisfyingly uninterrupted views, the curtained restaurant doors. The irritating little cocks who rode their motorbikes on the pavement. The cleaning men branded *Propreté de Paris*, a slogan that an English eye jumped to misconstrue. All of it presented its cheek like a long lost but aloof sister. There was that feeling of a common bond that, if not manifest, could always be drawn on, and yet a foreignness that dredged up more of me than I'd been living on before.

My flat was on the third floor of a five-storey town house. The house had a wrought iron gate where you'd have expected the front door to be, with a remarkable silhouette of a laughing face sprayed in blue paint beside it on the stone. I had a feeling this joker was on my side.

Beyond the gate, in the hall, were the rubbish bins, and above these a series of pigeon holes with locked doors for letters. Getting through the hall, which always stank, was like an underwater swimming test. Past the rubbish was the door to the staircase. The stairs were narrow, dark and occasionally strewn with dead birds.

The benefit of this dismal entrance was that, once you'd charged up three flights and gone into the flat itself, you did at least feel some relief. Nice would be an extravagant claim, but it got the daylight in the morning.

The sitting room had a small kitchen in the corner. The floor was covered with lino, the plaster largely with paint. A tight sofa lined one wall, a folding table and an electric heater the opposite wall. It was unembellished to the point of fanaticism. If I'd been serious about becoming a priest, this room was what my mind would have looked like.

After the sitting room came the bedroom which at least had a double bed. The winner was the bathroom. The bath was big enough for two and the hot water was limitless. It gave me confidence in the whole place.

Better even than the bathroom was the *quartier*. It was a five minute walk to the *métro*, past chemists, a vet's and a Russian sweet shop. There were magical parts towards the river, places I'd dismissed only because they were on my mother's doorstep which I now discovered like buried treasure. The whole area agreed with me, the developing Marais, the Place du Marché Sainte-Catherine, the Église Saint-Gervais. The church was left open and sometimes at night I'd go inside.

Thursday came. Did I need an umbrella for a French lesson? No.

I walked out of the *métro* station. The rain had stepped up a gear. It made things wet for a while, then like an evil dictator, it went beyond its remit, trying to turn everything into rain.

The lesson was in a desolate *lycée* near République. I was already late and it took me a while to find the building. I walked in dripping water. I wandered through the empty corridors at random, my suit clinging to my skin. Finally I bumped into a cleaner who led me to the room.

I opened the door and apologised.

Everyone turned around except you.

19

'Purple Haze' by Jimi Hendrix

'Aren't you cold?' Alex said suddenly.

They stood near enough that they were breathing the same air, the marquee looming out of the dark in front of them.

She felt him touch her waist, this gentle show of willing which she couldn't quite understand.

He drew her closer. 'Don't leave without telling me.'

'Of course not. Don't you either.'

They stood together for a moment, and then she quickly kissed his cheek.

'We'd better go in,' she said.

Inside the marquee there was a smell of warm shit. Like explorers they tried to find the source. Both giant screens had gone. A couple of rugs lay at odd angles over the matting. Otherwise, perfection had been restored.

'Now you two!' Charlotte's mother waltzed up to them, her tanned breasts like toddlers' heads jostling to peek. Her perfume, though strong, couldn't mask the smell. 'Al, Charlotte tells me you were magnificent.' She put her arms around both of them and steered them further inside. 'There really is nothing more marvellous than a man who knows what he's doing.' She winked at Venus. Alex's face had turned to stone.

'I've arranged everything with the girls in the kitchen so just let them know you're here. Food's delicious, all organised by Caroline Fleet – d'you remember Al? – Emily's mother.' She put her arm around Alex's bottom. 'One of Al's old flames. I bet she wishes she'd held onto him, mmm?! Getting more *gorgeous* by the day – '

' – Don't touch me.' His whole body tensed.

'Oh darling relax… ' Charlotte's mother's voice oozed. 'Let's get you a glass of something.'

'There you are!' Charlotte took Venus by the arm and she and Alex glanced at each other as they separated.

'Now Vee,' Charlotte was leading her towards the top table, 'you're still going to sing aren't you?'

Her heart dropped. She'd completely forgotten. She felt nervous about not having been nervous.

'You look lovely by the way.'

'Sorry I don't think I can.'

'Why on earth not? Anything you like – '

'No, it's to do with Gilles, I don't think – '

'Oh what utter crap. You'll love it, you know you will.'

Before Venus could reply, Charlotte touched her hand. 'See that old prowler with the woman in red?'

'The fake bishop?'

'Exactly. Edward Payne, Cambridge friend of Daddy's – slight tosser but he's got a good ear and he knows people. Jazz, opera, fairly rounded, you'll get him going in a jiffy.'

She turned back to Venus confidently.

Venus imagined a stellar performance, Alex at her feet.

'You've got to start somewhere Vee. Why you stopped in the first place I'll never understand.'

'Caesarean – I totally lost my voice – '

'That was a temporary problem.'

'It wasn't a problem, it was deliverance. Do you think

given all that happened I regret one second I spent with my family?'

'Okay.' Charlotte spoke more quietly. 'Okay.'

They stood apart.

'Alex told me about Jake.' She felt unkind bringing the subject up.

'Oh? What did he say?'

'That you were in love with him, and that he'd arranged for the cows to come in to win you back.'

'God what a romantic.'

'Alex or Jake?'

Charlotte laughed. 'Jake, Vee, keeps his romance in his cock. Covered in it when you're up close but doesn't work at a distance.' She shook her head. 'Listen to you. I make a tiny criticism and you immediately get righteous.'

'Of course not. I want the best for you, I can't help it.'

'What a coincidence, so do I.' Charlotte looked at her.

They didn't speak. Venus asked herself what she could have to lose.

'Listen I'll stop nagging, Mummy wants me to cut the cake.'

'No,' Venus looked down, then ahead. 'No, I'll do it.'

Charlotte bloomed. 'Oh darling!' She squeezed her hand. 'That's it, that's it!'

'On one condition.' The ground seemed to be falling away.

'What? Anything.'

'You introduce me as Madeleine.' She felt dizzy. 'And refer to me as Madeleine for the rest of the evening.'

'How intriguing. So Madeleine Rees?'

'Yes.'

'Singing 'Fly Me To The Moon'?'

Venus nodded. She felt sick.

Charlotte lost no time. She asked a waitress to dim the lights, then stood on a chair.

'Ladies and gentlemen!'

Lit candelabra had been put at either end of the top table. Shaking, Venus got up on to the stage and stood in front of them.

'Ladies and gentlemen!'

Everyone hushed. 'I am delighted to introduce my great friend, Madeleine Rees, who will sing 'Fly Me To The Moon'.'

Charlotte started clapping. Everyone joined her. It was almost dark inside the marquee.

Between the candles, Venus felt like a sacrifice. Outlines of people looked back at her as the clapping was replaced by silent expectation. She became over-aware. Sensing the thud in her head, she waited for it to die down, but it got more intense. She tried to concentrate on the song, find the notes. She knew them, she knew every one of them.

Her jaw froze. The weight of the silence around her seemed to be drilled into each of her teeth. She couldn't open her mouth.

'Come on, get on with it!'

The bishop. It was him.

But she couldn't see, she couldn't really see.

She breathed.

Layers of voices covered her like blankets. She shut her eyes.

Out of breath. Hot, too hot. Falling and falling.

'Vee? Vee, can you hear me?'

'Look, try and drink some water.'

Water.

'Oh blast.'

Water.

'No, it's okay thanks. He knows her. Al?'

'Oh well done. Let's get her outside.'

Venus was sitting on the cold grass.

'... Darling? It's me.'

She put her hands on the ground.

'What happened?' she whispered.

Charlotte's face came into her field of vision.

'You fainted that's all, everything's fine.'

'Here.' Alex gave her a bottle of water.

She drank from the bottle, felt the water run down her throat.

'Thanks,' she said. She looked at him.

'Tell me what happened again.'

'You were about to sing, but you fainted,' Charlotte said.

'God.' She felt hopeless.

'Don't think about it, everything's all right.'

Her hair was wet against her cheek; she pushed it back.

'Sorry darling, only water.'

Her breath was coming more regularly.

'I've ruined it – '

'Nonsense. It was my fault. I shouldn't have pushed you into it.'

'You didn't.'

Then she thought about it, standing up there, collapsing in front of everyone. It was as if she were two people, one humiliated and one strangely invulnerable, and as the invulnerable one, she could run from the shackled footsteps of the other like a sprite.

Charlotte and Alex helped her up and the three of them walked round to the kitchen tent.

The female atmosphere was comforting. Girls and women were cutting slices of cake from a large square slab and putting them on plates, casually lobbing dirty knives and forks into plastic boxes, talking and joking now the end was in sight. Charlotte spoke to the woman who'd helped Venus to her seat earlier. Venus asked if they could sit where they were, in the kitchen. The woman cleared part of a trestle table and brought over two white plastic chairs, carrying them like cats from the neck.

Alex went to get glasses. Venus sat down.

'Better?' Charlotte smiled.

'Fine, thanks. Go on, cut the cake.'

'I'll say goodbye, I'll call when I'm back from the States.'

They kissed cheeks. 'Charl, sorry.'

'Don't be.' Charlotte gave her a hug.

As she was leaving, Alex came back.

'Look after her Al won't you?'

'Of course,' he said.

Charlotte turned to go.

'Charl,' Venus called, 'I'm going to Paris next week after all. I might be there when you get back.'

Charlotte grimaced. 'Good luck.'

She left.

Venus and Alex were quiet, waiting for the food. One of the girls brought bread and water. As he put butter on his bread, Venus felt herself salivate.

She poured them both water and drank.

'Here,' he said. He was handing her his bread.

She looked at him, astonished. He watched her as she ate. And then she buttered her bread, made a show of cutting it into four pieces and gave it to him.

She asked him if he thought she was mad, for fainting.

No, he said, of course not. She was hungry, it was hot.

He made it sound like a simple, biological event.

She wondered whether to tell him about Gilles, singing at the funeral, the whole sorry truth. But it was silly, she hardly knew him.

They were given their starter: carefully positioned mozzarella, avocado and plum tomato with basil, and green and red oil trailed in a fancy pattern around the outside.

It was good, like baby food, but it tasted of something.

As they ate, she caught his eye. 'So do you run a restaurant?'

'No,' he said. He hesitated, and then said, 'My grandmother's Greek.'

'Really?' she smiled.

'Yeh,' he smiled.

'That's unbelievable. I wondered, when I said that thing about catching the fish – '

'I've never done that.'

'Still – ' She smiled. 'How amazing.' She was taken by it.

They ate for a while. Two waitresses were standing by the sink, finding something funny. He looked at them sharply and they went out into the main marquee.

He broke the silence. 'So, you're a singer? That's how you know Charlotte?'

She looked up, surprised. 'Yes, sort of.'

'You've got a lovely voice.'

She smiled. 'You didn't hear it.'

'I mean in speech.'

'Thank you.'

They ate some more. She finished her food and looked about the kitchen. Everything was being put in its place, all to be loaded up and taken away before the morning.

He caught her wandering glance.

'Where do you live?' he asked.

They were asking all the questions now.

'London,' she said. 'What about you?'

'You said you might be going to Paris?'

She thought he'd changed the subject. 'Yes. That's a bit of a long story.'

'Oh, right.'

He poured them more water.

'It's just that's where I live.'

She sat back. 'Really?'

'Yeh.'

'How strange.'

She paused. 'We could meet – '

'Yeh, I'd love to.'

'So – where exactly do you live?'

'Ile Saint Louis.'

'Wow.'

'I was lucky, I got it through work.'

'What do you do?'

'Oh, it's – pretty boring.'

The main course came at the same time as the starter was taken away. It was roast beef, with a round cake of creamy potato and a mixture of thinly sliced vegetables.

They started eating.

'Go on, so what do you do in Paris?'

He shrugged. 'A bit like the French I suppose – eat, have pretentious conversations, sleep – and then go to work.'

'Okay,' she smiled. That was mysterious.

They ate some more.

'Where are you staying?' he asked.

'Probably Place des Vosges, there's a flat I can use. Not mine.'

'Right,' he said. 'Whose is it?'

It was a strange question.

'It belongs to someone who's not there anymore. She had to go into a… a hospital.'

'Is she a relative of yours?'

'Sort of.'

She sighed, felt she was being evasive. 'Sorry,' she said, 'I'm running out of words.'

He looked away.

'Don't be cross,' she touched his arm.

'… Wedding talk?'

'I'm no good at it,' she smiled.

'No,' he looked at her. 'Well nor am I.'

But it was only that she hadn't wanted to go into detail.

'That's one thing about Paris,' he said. 'They're not afraid to talk properly.'

'Mm.' She buttered more bread. But she didn't want to be serious. No small talk, and no big talk. What else was there?

'You have to get the English drunk,' she said. 'Either that or stick them in the dark.'

'Yeh, exactly,' he said. 'You bring up some larger

question in London and everyone feels they have to turn it into a joke. It's all gossip or work.'

'That's where the cabbies come in,' she said. 'The true thinkers of the city.'

'But why are people ashamed of it? Everyone loves talking like that, it makes you feel significant whatever you say.'

She smiled. 'Perhaps that's why Parisians take themselves so seriously.'

'Yeh,' he smiled.

'Maybe it's being in a foreign country,' he said. 'If you're speaking English, it's a bit like talking in the dark.'

She was smiling. 'So you've disdained the French as well?'

He paused, then smiled. 'Well the Parisians are too pompous, the English are too repressed, so perhaps the English in Paris are the perfect mixture.'

The pudding came, a strawberry tart but made with shortbread instead of pastry.

'Do you want some wine? I forgot about it – '

'No thanks. But go ahead.'

'I'll have a look.' He walked off.

She began to think.

Younger than her. Way younger than Gilles. A bit serious.

But he wasn't self-important.

And he seemed to like her.

Shy. But they were both being shy now. Anyway she liked that. It wasn't as if he was unfeeling. She'd put him off.

Very good looking. She only had to look at him…

But he didn't really laugh. Maybe that was shyness.

Thoughtful. All that stuff about not compromising. Naive. Or idealistic.

Kind, good-natured. Honest. Gentle.

Together with him, it could be…

And responsible. More than that. Courageous.

Nervous? No, that was the odd thing. He wasn't nervous. He was quiet but balanced. She was nervous.

There could be a way out with him. If she didn't mess it up. Him and Madeleine. She wouldn't mention Gilles.

He looked a bit like Gilles. Darker skin, darker hair. Silkier hair. Shorter. Slimmer build.

Better looking.

Eyes. Dark brown eyes.

'They've run out of white.' He sat down. He smiled at her. 'They've only got champagne apparently.'

'Oh.' She smiled.

They started to eat.

Surreptitiously she watched him.

The meal would soon be over. There would be the question of what next, how to leave it, whether to leave it.

The music started in the main marquee. It crashed in, too loud, and then diminished.

Venus held the spoon in her hand. Her stretched reflection looked back from the silver handle.

She watched him, cutting into the shortbread case with his spoon. The cream spilled out, the nearest strawberry slumped. He ate, then brought his spoon round for the next mouthful.

She wasn't going to wait for him to ask. And no idiotic prompting, no euphemistic bullshit. It didn't often arise. This kind of chance.

She put down her spoon.

'Alex.'

'Yeh?' He put his napkin down beside his empty plate. She felt her heart in her mouth.

'Shall we go back to my hotel?'

Venus unlocked the door to her room. She turned the light on. Her clothes from the day lay on the bed, ghosts of another self. She picked them up, opened the wardrobe and slung them inside. The click shut of the door jarred in the quiet. As if prompted, she went back to the door of the room and locked it. Again the noise was too loud, an unmistakable broadcast of her intention.

Alex was standing by the bed watching her.

She took off her sandals and thought about other people's feet treading on the carpet. Traces of strangers left behind. The more of them there were, she felt, the better.

She didn't want to fool around. Self-absorbed, she sat down on the bed and slid the straps of her dress off her shoulders. The material fell slowly to her waist, more sensually than she'd intended, gathering on the bed around her making her look like a mermaid.

She heard him breathe in. She glanced up and began to realise that it was actually him there, close to her, watching her. She looked at her breasts in the bra and felt a rush of excitement. Another person, watching her undress, a different person.

But he didn't undress.

She stood up and her dress slipped down to her hips, leaving her so aware of him and his view of her, she felt her will might evaporate. But she continued, her fingers finding the zip, keeping to her plan just to do it.

'Wait – ' he whispered breathlessly.

He bent down and carefully picked up the straps of her dress, then crouching in front of her, his eyes half-closed, he gently put his lips on her waist, her head spinning with the unexpected intimacy, his fingers slowly pulling her dress up around her, brushing her skin as the material went over her stomach, her breasts. He was covering her up. He was holding out the straps for her to put her arms back through.

She didn't understand.

'What?'

'Please – ' he whispered.

She put her arms through the loops and felt small with him for the first time.

'Do I disgust you?' she whispered.

'*God no*.' His fingers touched her cheek. 'The *complete* opposite.'

But she wanted to know. 'What then?'

'I just – I haven't done this kind of thing – '

'Oh God, sorry.' She felt anxious. 'Let's leave it – '

'No,' he seemed embarrassed, 'I mean not like this, this quickly.'

She was overcome with irritation.

'But you wanted to come back?'

'Of course.'

'So what did you think I meant, play monopoly?'

'No,' he said, smiling.

But then he looked at her, openly and lovingly. 'Sorry, I'm not used to liking someone this much.'

She looked directly at him. Oh, but that was a mistake. Saw his beautiful face. Saw his eyes heavy with tenderness. Wished he'd just let her get on with it.

But he touched her with a grace she hadn't anticipated. And for a while there was just the feel of his hand through the material, accentuating the shape of her figure underneath, the pleasure of being touched.

Her sorrow the more acute as she woke up to it, this person, taking it slowly, wanting more than she'd offered, her mind in a skid.

But he kissed her lips so lightly that it was almost nothing. And when she didn't pull back, he smiled with relief. She saw his eyes as he closed them and kissed her mouth, softly but passionately, so that like a clear bell, it was he who was being true and she who wasn't.

She tensed, went back to being her separate self, and found that it appalled her.

'Sorry,' she whispered, breaking away. 'Sorry,' her voice splintered.

And then every force seemed to leave her so that only Gilles was left, trapped in her, his tears inexpressible.

Startled, she heard herself make a broken, hollow noise.

'What? Madeleine?'

She tried to breathe.

'God, what is it?'

' – Sorry – '

She sat on the edge of the mattress, held onto the bed. He sat with her. They didn't speak, waiting until she'd got her breath back.

'I'm so sorry.' She swallowed, not wanting to cry in front of him.

She breathed in, dried her eyes with her hands, the light from the ceiling catching her wedding ring, making it shine out like a child's face.

He went still, next to her.

'I've been so stupid,' she whispered. How had she even thought she could go through with it? 'God how pathetic.'

She met his eye, but he seemed to look past her.

'I've totally misled you,' she said hurriedly.

'Why didn't you tell me?' His expression was broken with incomprehension. 'I thought anything could happen between us – I had no idea – '

He was so distraught she couldn't take it in.

'I should never have suggested it,' she said.

'But – the whole evening, everything – what were you trying to do?'

'I'm sorry what more can I say?'

'So – that's it, no explanation.'

'Alex please, stop it.'

'Stop what?'

'This – interrogating – '

He looked at her as if she were beyond him. 'You're extraordinary.'

Shocked at his tone, she tried to meet his eye. But he didn't look back. He got up and stood, looking around the room.

'What – what are you thinking?' she asked.

He glanced at her, bewildered. 'I thought you'd want me to leave.'

'Of course,' she hesitated. 'You must – feel free to leave.'

'Sorry,' he said, unequivocally, not wanting to be excused. 'I just hate this kind of thing.'

'No.' She breathed in. 'You're right. I was wrong. You're right.'

She didn't know what to do. He was leaving. God what a fiasco.

Her words shot out in bursts.

'I'd like – I mean – could you bear to – give me your phone number? In Paris? Please don't if you… I'll understand.'

He looked down at her. 'What's the point?'

'I don't know,' she sighed. 'Just – to talk to you again. If you don't want to, I'll understand.'

He started looking in the inside pocket of his jacket. He took out a receipt and wrote on the back.

She went to the table in the room and found a paper and pen. She wrote down her number, then beneath it wrote, *I am a coward. Sorry.*

Quickly she folded the paper and gave it to him. He handed her the receipt. She unlocked the door and he closed it behind him.

20

'To Try For The Sun'
by Donovan Leitch

Vee, it could have happened so differently.

I'd thought about catching sight of you at a restaurant, at a concert – in a speedboat, in a villain's lair – driving along the *quai* with you in my DB9, the chase over, the persistent international terrorist outwitted, the idea inexorably gathering momentum in your head that I was extraordinarily accomplished.

But I'd also thought about not finding you. And when I did, everything was normal, as if I'd secretly accepted that would be the outcome.

Neither was how it was.

I was sitting at an old sloping desk in a cold Paris *lycée*, noticing a girl for not noticing me. I stared at her back, her dark hair rippling over her close-fitting navy blue ribbed sweater. When she turned to get something from her bag I could see the shape of her breasts, the way they stretched the straight lines of her sweater into curves.

I kept trying to get a better view. I thought if I couldn't see her eyes, she wouldn't see me looking, but within a minute she'd turned around and caught me in mid-gaze. And that was when I began to wonder.

The teacher had cut the discussion short to ask me to

introduce myself. I could speak French fluently, so I could have shown off. Instead I gave my name, and said that I was working in Paris for six months, training to be an English-qualified lawyer.

'*Très bien*,' she said.

She asked the others to introduce themselves again for my benefit. We were about a dozen altogether. Eventually she came to the girl with the rippling hair.

The room went quiet. All of us turned towards her, as if by looking at her we'd hear her better. And as soon as she started talking, I knew it was you.

Every sense on fire, I listened. I heard your smooth, effortless voice. I heard you say you were studying singing. My heart like a peal of bells, I stole another look at you, and then another. I began to realise that there would be more than the you I remembered – that the miracle wasn't only that I was seeing you again but everything I had yet to find out.

You said your name was Venus Rees. You were studying singing at the Guildhall in London. You loved music. It was your favourite thing in life. You were in Paris over the Easter holidays to improve your French, and to take singing lessons from a teacher who greatly inspired you.

You stopped, and I thought about every word you'd said.

Speaking a foreign language has more to do with playing a part than it does with simple translation. The English tend to speak French with a poetic emotion, available but unvoiced by them in their mother tongue.

The teacher asked us where we were living. I said a flat in the Marais. I said that it was a flat like any other, in a street like any other, but that I could walk from it to some very beautiful places, parts of Paris that were more informal, less grand, more… intimate.

It was catching.

Then to you. You said you were staying at the Hôtel des Jeunes in the fourth *arrondissement*.

But that was close to me – I was in the third – that was close –

It had been converted from an old convent.

See Vee? The singing nun, I didn't make it up.

It was a charming place, near the river, near an old church, on a quiet street with – you'd forgotten the word – little stones –

'*Une rue pavée*?' I suggested.

You turned around and we looked at one another.

'*Oui*,' you said, '*une rue pavée*.'

And Vee I could say, what an amazing coincidence, but breathy exclamation can't do it justice. Of course I wouldn't meet you again – of course I'd accepted that – it demanded death and only the most extravagant heaven. I would learn to bear life, in time I might even forget.

But it was you, and it was me, in this strange classroom. That an improbability is not an impossibility is not an adequate explanation. My mind transforms the statistical unlikelihood into an endorsement from on high.

The teacher passed round a newspaper article which we read and discussed. It was clear that you and I were the best in the class.

I longed for the hour to be over.

At half past six the teacher handed out a homework exercise. You took the sheet of paper, put your things away, put on your coat and walked towards the door.

I stopped you. You looked annoyed.

You might not like me. I'd thought about that in London, but it wasn't conceivable here.

'Hi,' I smiled. 'Are you in a rush?'

You looked at your watch.

'I'm meeting someone at seven.'

A girlfriend, surely.

'I just thought, we live so close, I was wondering whether you were walking that way?'

'Oh,' you said. You were wondering what I meant. 'Thanks, but I'm not going home.'

'Well, to the *métro* then?'

You smiled. I smiled. The room was quiet, everyone had left except the teacher.

'It's the wrong way though, for you,' you said, 'I don't want to – '

'No, no it's perfect,' I said. 'I've got to go to Place des Vosges, so in fact it's ideal. If you don't mind.'

You looked at me, amused at my transparency.

We set off up rue de Turbigo. There was so much I wanted to say, but the words weighed down on me. All possibilities seemed inadequate in such a context.

The rain had stopped but it was windy. Your hair blew lightly and you pushed it back, away from your face. You looked beautiful.

'Your hair… looks lovely in the wind,' I said stumblingly.

You smiled. 'It's nice to feel it move.'

The huge roundabout at République was coming into view. We couldn't have been walking for longer than two minutes. A couple of hundred yards and you'd be gone again. What if you didn't come to the next lesson? What if you moved from the youth hostel? What if you had to go back to England?

There was tonight, I could ask to see you later tonight. But no, for God's sake, you'd think I was obsessive. Tomorrow? The weekend? What about the weekend?

The wind blew the paper and plastic bags on the street.

'Where are you going?'

'Opéra,' you said. 'The Palais Garnier.'

'What are you going to see?'

'A ballet actually. I'm going with someone who doesn't speak any Italian or French – or German – so I thought the ballet would be better. And I've never been before.'

The wind caught your hair again. We walked down the stairs into the *métro*. Time was running out.

'Is your friend here from London?'

You were slotting coins into the ticket machine.

'No,' you said. 'America. He's only here for a few days.'

'Oh, right,' I said.

He. Coming from *America*. Going to a *ballet*. For fuck's sake. He had to be in love with you.

Well of course he was, how could he not be?

But come on, how could a pitiful American compare to me? I spoke more languages than him, I made funnier jokes than him, I had better taste than him. I was a European, I had mastered the art of living.

'Would you like to buy a ticket?' you smiled.

'Oh, thanks.' I used the same machine. 'Sorry, I'm holding you up.'

'No, no. That's okay.' You looped your hair behind your ears.

We stood with our tickets by the machine. People pushed back and forth, muttering at the obstruction. We moved across a bit.

'I was thinking – ' I would spare no one, least of all this ballet-attending creature. 'Have you ever been to the *Musée Rodin*?'

'No.' You looked up at me, the corners of your lips gradually turning up until your mouth opened in a smile.

Then you spoke with a suggestive voice that I will always be able to play back in my mind. 'Maybe we should go there together…?'

I smiled like an imbecile. 'What about Saturday, at eleven? I could meet you at the hostel?'

'Steven, my American friend, he'll still be here. But I could make it on Sunday.'

I breathed in. I would depose him. Oh God. Nonchalance.

'Perfect. Sunday would be perfect.'

'Are you sure?' you asked.

'Yes,' I said. 'Of course.'

We stood looking at each other. I kissed the side of your cheek.

I might have kissed you properly. But you touched my hand, your fingers brushed past mine.

'I should go – ' you said.

I took your hand. 'See you on Sunday.'

You turned to leave. Then you turned back.

'It's 12 rue des Barres,' you were smiling. And you let the machine suck in your ticket, picked it up, walked through the barriers and disappeared.

I stood for a while, then put my ticket in my pocket. I walked out of the *métro* and down the street, the wind breathing into me and the future infinite.

21

'Unchained Melody'
by Alex North and Hy Zaret

Venus's brother had a steady life. He seemed happy with Isobel. Enviously she imagined the two of them with their three children, Sam, Lucy and Josh, and their golden retriever, Noodle, all spending glorious summer afternoons playing in the sea together.

The Rees family lived in the Cornish town of Fowey where their hotel and restaurant had become very successful. Their garden sloped down to the water, overlooking the estuary and the sea beyond. They grew lavender and rosemary and other fragrant plants Venus couldn't identify. In particular, Isobel had planted a camomile lawn just after giving birth to Josh.

Matthew kept his electric guitar in the loft, along with a hydroponic cannabis growing system which was no longer in use.

Matthew and Isobel had suggested that Leonie stay with them while Venus went to Charlotte's wedding, and when Venus knocked on their door at half past one on Sunday, they both let her in, asking her how it had gone in light voices. Matthew said that she looked tired. Isobel said it must have been a good night then.

Leonie ran in breathless from the garden. 'Mummy, can we have a dog like Noodle?'

Venus picked her up and kissed her.

'Mummy?'

Venus said they'd think about it in the car tomorrow.

Isobel excused herself – she had to supervise lunch. Then with a furtive expression, she beckoned Venus out into the hall.

Isobel whispered that Noodle might be having puppies soon. Oh, said Venus. She thanked Isobel but said it wouldn't really be practical at the moment.

She went back into the sitting room.

'Mummy, what were you and Isobel talking about?'

'Dog breeding Leo,' Matthew smiled. 'It's a fascinating subject.'

Leonie stared at Matthew.

'I'm going to play with Noodle!' she said and ran off back into the garden.

Matthew piled the papers on to a low stool and rested his feet on top of them. Venus saw Gilles in the action.

'She's been a pleasure to look after.' Stretching out his arm to her.

'Oh great.'

'It's nice for Lucy to have another girl to play with.'

She came into focus.

'So,' he said, 'Charlotte finally did it?'

She told him briefly about the American businessman, the cows and then Jake.

He laughed. 'I wonder how many men Charlotte's shafted.'

They gossiped a while longer. The conversation came to a pause and she felt the Gilles question hang, about to be asked. But he stood up.

'The children have had their lunch – there's soup, is that okay? It's carrot and something I think. You know Heather left? Went to some place in London to be with her man.' He began to whisper. 'The guy we've got now's awful. Issie's having to do a lot of the routine stuff.' He was leading the way to the kitchen. '... We even asked Heather if she'd come back.'

Matthew put the soup and bread on a tray, she took some water and a beer and they went outside and sat down at a wooden table. Bees buzzed by the lavender. Two guests were sitting on a bench beside the camomile lawn. The air smelt of holidays.

The children were playing at the bottom of the garden. Venus took in the railings, the life buoy and the padlocked gate that shut off the steps down.

Matthew stirred the orange gloop. He let his spoon drop into the bowl and started cleaning his glasses between the buttons of his shirt.

Venus put her soup to one side and cut some bread. She checked on Leonie.

'Matt,' she said anxiously.

'Mm?'

'Can I talk to you about Gilles?'

He looked up at her, putting his glasses down. 'Of course.'

She breathed in, then felt flooded with emotion.

'I really tried at the wedding, I can't tell you.' Her eyes filled. She blew her nose. 'Oh for fuck's sake. I can't THINK about him without this shit.'

'It's okay, you're bound to – '

'It's not okay. Look I'd prefer it if you didn't repeat this to Isobel. I know you will, but I'd like you not to.'

He examined the table. 'She does care about you.'

'Well I've got no one else to tell so do what you want.'

'Oh come on, don't say that.' He paused. 'I don't see why you feel uncomfortable with Issie.'

She blew her nose again. 'Okay, okay, tell her all you like. I absolve you one hundred percent.'

'Vee, don't make me feel guilty, she's my wife.'

She groaned. 'Just shut up and let me tell you.'

He closed his eyes for a second.

She looked at him. 'I hate it when you do that.'

'What? What the hell did I do?'

'Close your eyes, in that exasperated way, as if you're talking to someone completely insane. I CAN'T FUCKING STAND IT.'

He didn't say anything. She blew her nose and drank some water. 'Sorry. I can't seem to have a normal conversation.'

She had another drink of water. 'I was late – I arrived late at the reception.' She wiped some water off her lip. 'So I walked into the marquee through the kitchen tent, but of course I had no idea where I was supposed to be sitting. This woman doing the food led me to an empty seat and the nameplate said *Madeleine*. And whoever she is, I don't know, but I pretended to be her, or at least someone else. It sounds ridiculous. I just wanted to get Gilles out of my head. But of course it came unstuck. Charlotte asked me to sing and I completely dried up. I fainted Matt, I couldn't get a note out.'

He sighed. 'I can't believe she even asked you. She can be such a tactless idiot.'

'No, it wasn't her fault. Anyway, that's not the worst of it.' She took Matthew's glass and drank some of his beer. 'God I'm so stupid.'

'What happened?'

'I met this man.'

'Well that's great.'

'No it isn't.'

He clasped his fingers in front of him. 'Right. Okay. Why not?'

'I mean it was so good, talking to him and everything – and he was exceptionally good looking. And not overt, you know, modest.'

'So?'

She looked at him. 'I asked him back to my hotel.'

'Oh Vee, what's wrong with that? I'm sure Gilles would have wanted – '

'Matt, let me finish. The point is that I couldn't do it. In the best possible context – I suppose it wasn't – but anyway I just couldn't do it. Poor guy, I think he thought I was mad. He seemed so nice, incredibly attractive, sensitive, there was nothing about him I didn't like – and I was in a hotel. Completely anonymous, to the point that he literally didn't know my name. He knew almost nothing about me, no mention of Gilles – '

'Well why didn't you tell him?'

'But how the hell would I have been able to do anything then? … I know, I know I should have told him the whole thing but I wanted to get it over with. I thought if I could just do it, you know, it would get me out of this shit. It was horrible of me. Then suddenly it was as if Gilles was everywhere… ' She stopped and sighed. 'Matt, I really don't know what to do. Nothing's changed. I hate talking to Mum about it, I'm sure she thinks I've made what Hélène said into more than it needs to be. And I often just really miss him.' She tensed her hands. 'But there's this gnawing doubt I absolutely cannot shake. Either he let himself die or she killed him. It's a fact. And I'm never going to know, so how am I ever going to move on?'

Matthew was pointing subtly behind her. Venus looked round. Leonie was standing still, a foot away.

'Oh Leo,' Venus stretched out her arms. 'Come here.' Venus hugged her. 'I was getting cross with Daddy… ' Venus blew her nose, then lifted Leonie on to her lap. 'Mummy's a stupid Mummy,' she whispered.

'No you're not, it's an impossible situation.' Matthew got up. '… You know I think that's the first time you've talked about him without me asking.'

He said something about more bread and walked off.

Venus and Leonie were quiet for a while as the sounds of the garden drifted back to them. Venus kissed her head and Leonie sat on the bench beside her.

The carrot soup was lukewarm.

'Looks like sick,' Leonie said.

Venus offered Leonie some on her spoon.

'Ugh!' Leonie made a being sick face.

Venus started eating the soup.

'So,' she said, 'how's it been?'

Leonie looked serious. 'Josh wouldn't let me play with his dolls. He's got loads of dolls and he wouldn't let me play at all.'

'How annoying.'

'He's such an annoying boy.'

'What about the food?'

'Well Uncle Matthew said they didn't have Sugar Puffs because they were bad for your teeth. But they did! They were in the cupboard by the Aga and we ate them really quickly in case Uncle Matthew came back but then Josh told him and he got cross with Lucy but he didn't get cross with me. Lucy said it was because I was the guest.'

Venus smiled. 'Lucky escape.' She wondered what that had been about.

'Did you go to the beach?' she asked.

Leonie nodded. 'It's actually called Readymoney. Sam found a starfish but Uncle Matthew said it was dead.'

'That's a shame.'

'But he said there were loads of others walking about on the bottom of the sea, because they've got these funny feet underneath. That's how they walk.'

'Yeh?' Venus blew her nose with her wet handkerchief.

'And then me and Lucy did starfish walking.'

She smiled. 'How's it go?'

Leonie got up and lay face down on the grass. 'Mummy?' She pushed herself along on her stomach, moving her legs and arms and making a blobloblob noise.

An hour later, Venus set off with the four children to the beach at Readymoney.

Along the road, they passed a white wall with several

head-sized holes in it. The round view of the town on the other side of the estuary, framed by the white stone, made it look like a model in a glass paperweight. The road began to slope down and the view over the water opened out.

The walkers settled in groups, Venus and Josh ambling at the back, Lucy and Leonie in the middle, and Sam, on the verge of being too old, in front with a football.

A couple came up the hill towards Venus. They said hello and walked past.

'Gosh, what a brood,' Venus heard the woman whisper.

Venus learnt that Josh had fourteen girl dolls and two boy dolls and that his favourite doll was Three Wishes Sindy, ballerina, bride and princess.

They emerged from a canopy of trees and she lifted Josh up so that he could see down to the cove. The cliffs were green with plants, the sea was clear and the air was warm. The algae-covered rock showed below the high water line. It was low tide, just as Isobel had said. 'Should be some space on the sand!'

It was pretty, she thought. She and Gilles had walked past it, on to somewhere where they could be alone together, for miles sometimes. Fooled around in the grass, laughed about everyone except them. God that must have been years ago. Eight, maybe nine years. And then again it felt like days.

Venus and the children marked out their territory. Sam and Lucy ran into the water. She helped Josh to change his clothes, changed herself and walked into the sea with him and Leonie. Their laughter, amplified by the water and the cliffs, bounced into the sky.

The children had supper soon after getting back to the house. Leonie went off to play and Venus decided to go out again before it got dark.

She went up to Josh's room where he and Leonie were fighting over a doll and said she was going to take the dog for a walk. She'd come in and say goodnight when she got back.

'How long will you be?' Leonie looked cross.

'Just a couple of hours.'

She raised her eyes.

'It'll go quickly when you're playing. – Hey Josh,' Venus said, 'where's Sindy?'

Josh pointed to a doll in a ballet dress with a tiara in its hair. He picked up the doll and started to undress it.

'I want to come.' Leonie frowned.

'Leo, I'd love to take you but you'll get too tired. I'll come and read you a story, okay?'

'I *can* read by myself.'

Venus hugged her. 'I know you can,' she whispered. 'I'll be back soon.'

Venus made to go but Josh wanted her to wait. There were Sindy's two other wishes to show her. Painstakingly he was fitting the doll inside its wedding dress. Venus looked at Leonie but she turned away. Staying for him and his stupid Sindy.

Once the dress was on, Venus said she'd go now, but could Josh get the princess ready for when she came back? Leonie flashed her eyes at her mother.

There was a pounding of feet on stairs and Lucy rushed in. Breathlessly she said she and Sam were going to get a DVD and did Leonie and Josh want to come. Absorbed, Josh said no. Leonie said yes, she would come.

In front of the older one, she looked defiantly at Venus. 'See you later.'

Venus smiled. 'Bye darling, be careful.'

Venus sat for a few moments with Josh, watching him balance the doll against a pile of books.

'I like the princess best,' he said.

'Can I still see the princess when I get back?' she asked.

'Yes you can,' he said.

Venus and the dog walked into the open air. The sun hadn't even started to set. She picked up speed.

Widows weren't supposed to like the light. It was a reality avoidance scheme.

Widow Sindy? Now wouldn't that be a seller. Widow Sindy complete with black gloves and veil, and she cries real tears.

A hundred yards down the Esplanade, she took the dog off the lead and watched it sniff and piss and scamper. She put her hands to the back of her head and pulled out the elastic keeping her hair up. It had been wound too tight. She rubbed her scalp, freeing her hair from the position it had been drawn into.

Wasn't everyone afraid of the dark? So the widow who didn't like the light… was she afraid of the dark too? Was she afraid of everything? See, children, how Widow Sindy trembles.

There was a man locking up the public lavatories at Readymoney. He wished her good evening. She smiled, breathed in as she walked on. Even that blurred her up.

Come on Sindy. Keep it together now.

Why was she walking down here anyway? Self-pity is your worst enemy, that's what they said. And then they said don't be too hard on yourself, let it out, give it time.

She climbed up the steep steps from the sand, the dog nosing at tree roots, the air damper. She hardly paused for breath. One thing all this walking had made her was fit.

She passed the sign to St Catherine's Castle. No, only bits of stone.

She thought warmly of Matthew. He'd tried to make her sound rational. Probably worried about her sanity.

This self-examination hadn't arisen before. This thinking about how often you thought about yourself – had she done that before?

It was how madness began. A psychiatric condition, pathological grief. Four years was nothing.

She'd expected books about grief to act as companions, and moments of introspection to comfort her. They'd only decanted her loneliness and allowed it to breathe.

The constant going over it, the same unanswerable question debated as if the answer could change things, when none of it would matter if she could do the one thing that didn't require his presence.

And yet maybe it did. Could you love someone who was dead? Really?

She came to a cove with a lush green valley behind it. No one there. Waves gently bringing in the tide. She sat on a rock. The dog bounded into the sea, happily ripping the quiet. The sun warmed her right side.

But she wanted to move on. The dog followed her. It shook and water sprayed off. A few drops touched her hand.

It was Easter when they sprayed you with water. She remembered the sprightly look on the priest's face as he walked around the church, dousing his flock.

Up she went, over the stile and along the next cliff, due west, the sun full in her face.

There'd been a landslide. Part of the field had been fenced off. Gingerly, she approached and looked over the edge. There were uprooted trees half way down the cliff. She stepped back, then backed away further.

But the dog had poked its head under the wire.

'No!'

She ran up and grabbed its collar, pulling it away. She told the dog how stupid it had been, put its lead back on and walked with it up the field.

It strained to be let off. She bent down and looked into its eyes.

'Why did they call you Noodle? Hmm? What kind of name is that?'

The dog yawned in her face. 'Ugh.' She flinched at the smell of its breath, and let it off the lead again.

'Hali!' she called.

The dog looked back.

'Halitosis it is then.'

They were walking down a steep muddy path, seemingly

away from the sea, trees blocking the view. She had a feeling this was the place, but she'd thought that about the other cove. She started running down the slope, skidding down the shale.

'Hey Hali, what d'you think? Is this it?'

Then at the bottom of the path, she stopped and looked.

It was so hidden, you couldn't see it until you came upon it. She remembered how it had looked back at them as they'd stared, as if they'd dreamt it together, united in their delusion. And from then on it had occupied one of the rooms in her mind reserved for intimates.

There was a flat sweep of grass, raised only a few yards above sea level and bordering the beach. On the left and right, trees and hills flanked the whole cove like cupped hands. In the centre of the lawn was a lake, and at the edge of the lawn, sheltered by the hills with a side view to the sea, was a house. The man-made and the natural enhanced each other, and an artful perfection seemed instinctive.

Venus watched the dog as it ran down to the lake, around and around while the ducks outwitted it, and then off again to the beach, through the seaweed piled up by the tide and on to the clean pale sand. The sun caught the sheets of undrained water that the sea had left behind, soaked again after another wave, then shrinking into the sand as the wave receded.

Between the beach and the next cove were ridges of slate where clumps of sea pink grew. She went to look at them. Each small flower in the round head was held in a tissue-paper-like case. The low sun shone through the cases, creating clusters of pink lights in the green and grey.

She found a flat rock and sat down, felt her legs relax, and looked out at the stretch of sea and sky.

It came to her that there was no one about. No lights in the house, no fishermen on the sand. Just the ducks and the dog.

She took off her shoes and socks, her trousers, the sweatshirt tied around her waist. She looked around her. She pulled her t-shirt over her head. Looked again. Pants, bra, off. And she ran into the sea.

It was cold. No currents of warm piss like at Readymoney. And shallow for a while so that she had to wade out. Losing feeling, numb, nipples like rods. Freezing cold. But when she started to swim, her body moving through the warmer upper layer of water, she felt she could go on forever. She swam out, to the edge of the cove. And still for a second, outside the bay, she was almost part of the sea.

Then back, back fast, powering through the water, the land further away than she thought, up on her feet, running through the shallows, running to her clothes, heart on fire in its ice body.

She grabbed her sweatshirt, rubbed her head, her legs, her back, squeezed the water from her hair. Then sitting on the flat rock in her t-shirt and trousers, brushing the sand off her feet, she felt the kind of warmth that suffuses, after sleep, after the shiver of sex if she could only remember, glorious and thorough, each cell alight and burning.

She looked out at the sea.

Gilles. Could he see her? Wouldn't he look if he could?

The rocks sank into the water like tired crocodiles. Slowly in her bare feet she crossed the sand and stepped onto them, sharp and slimey. The dog joined her, sniffed at crabs and then ran back to the beach. She dipped her finger into a rock pool. The new tide hadn't reached it yet and the water was still warm.

'Hali!' No response.

She returned to her rock and sat a while longer. When the dog came up to her, she put on her socks and shoes and made her way back. Past the seagulls coasting. Past the yellow-flowered bushes that smelt of suntan lotion. Past a boat heading for harbour. Past the ferns coming out of the ground foetally curled.

By the time she got to Readymoney, it was dark. She

gathered her damp hair in her right hand and twisted the elastic around it. Up on the Esplanade, she clipped the lead into the steel ring on the dog's collar. It was Isobel who answered the door.

By half-past ten all the children were in bed. Venus and Matthew were sitting at the kitchen table. Isobel was making herself a cup of coffee.

'Josh's doll phase has caused a bit of a stir hasn't it?'

'Mm,' Matthew said. 'He's quite a character don't you think Vee?'

'Yeh. Seems very sure of himself.'

'You know,' Isobel smiled, 'he asked Matt whether boys could be princesses the other day. Isn't that sweet?'

'Yeh?' Venus said. 'What did you say?'

Matthew had stood up to pump the air out of the wine bottle.

'Yes, what did you say?' Isobel was standing in front of the Aga holding her cup.

'Look at you both, why are you so desperate to know?'

'Pure penis envy,' Venus said seriously.

Matthew glanced at her.

'No thanks,' Isobel laughed.

About to put the bottle in the fridge, Matthew hesitated. 'Issie, this is crazy, we should be putting our stuff in the Cruvinet with the rest – '

'Oh shush.'

'Vee, you know these so-called vacuum pumps are only worth it for one night don't you? I mean we usually just polish off the lot, but if you're on your own – '

Isobel took the bottle of wine from his hand. Matthew took it back and put it down on the table.

'All I said was that princesses were girls, but that a boy could be a prince, of course.'

Venus laughed.

'What's wrong with that for God's sake?'

'Nothing… ' Venus giggled.

Matthew charged at her, tickling her arms.

'Hey, no! … Matt, wait! … Stop!'

Between breaths Venus said, '… Sugar… Puffs.'

'What?!' Isobel was smiling, as if this was a childhood amulet.

'Aah,' said Matthew. 'What did she say?' He sat down.

Venus got her breath back. 'You said you didn't have Sugar Puffs because they were bad for you but actually you did.'

'Yeh, I said bad for your teeth. I suddenly thought she shouldn't eat them. Then I looked at the pack and they've got almost no saturated fat.'

'Oh Matt, honestly!' Isobel looked at him. 'It's a cereal. It's the milk that's got the fat. I got some skimmed specially.'

'Okay, I know now.'

With a pang of guilt, Venus wondered why she underestimated them. 'Thanks for thinking about it.' She looked at them both. 'Really. It really means a lot.'

'It's the least we can do.'

'Well I'm… it's just nice you gave it some thought.'

Isobel sat down. 'She's a great girl.'

'Yeh. I wouldn't have got very far without her.'

'So she knows everything now?'

'Pretty much. The next test is in September, so it's best she knows all about it. It's just hard to explain that it won't be conclusive. We'll have to do one more at least.'

'Thank goodness the last one was normal.' A flicker of a smile died on Isobel's face.

Venus saw their concerned expressions.

'Yeh,' she looked down. 'If it hadn't been, I don't think – ' She stopped herself. They waited for her. 'Well I wouldn't have had the guts to tell her. I mean she was only two, I couldn't have told her then anyway.'

'I suppose,' Matthew said, 'it does make it slightly more understandable that Hélène said nothing.'

Venus stared at him.

'Well you just said you wouldn't have had the guts – '

'Matt, please, *of course* I would have told her later on.'

'Okay, okay.'

'The situation's not even comparable. Gilles was twenty-one. He couldn't have had the test without knowing what he was being tested for. Either they both knew he had it, or they both knew he was at risk but he decided not to have the test – or she never said anything so he didn't know he needed a test. It's more than likely there were no results for anyone to find out about.'

'But in a sense that's more justifiable. Not telling him when she knew for sure would have been awful.'

'Well she knew he had a fifty percent chance – does that mean she's fifty percent less bad than if she'd known for sure? I don't think so.'

'Do you think – ' Isobel furrowed her brows. ' – she just didn't appreciate that there were drugs available? Maybe she closed her mind to it altogether?'

'Yeh maybe, but would you have done that, as a mother?'

'Well no, obviously not, but – '

'She's a nutter Vee,' Matthew looked at Venus. 'You can't judge her like you would a normal mother.'

'So one minute you're saying it was understandable for her not to tell her child, and now you're saying she's not a normal mother. You can't have it both ways.' She paused. 'Anyway, I don't think she's mad.'

They didn't speak for a moment.

Matthew looked up. 'So you're going over there as soon as you get home?'

'Yeh, Tuesday. Not that anything will have changed since January. She sometimes says a few words to Mary but otherwise nothing. It's been so long I think the nurses have given up. The crazy thing is I feel guilty, I don't know why, for being furious with her I suppose.'

'Let us know how you get on,' Isobel said.

'I doubt she'll tell me the secret of the universe.' It sounded too strident. 'Yeh,' Venus said, 'of course I will.'

They sat, separated.

Isobel broke the silence. 'Well, you should sleep well tonight, what with your walk *and* swim!'

Venus nodded and smiled. She said she thought actually she'd go to bed.

She took Isobel's hand briefly. 'Thanks for putting up with me.'

'No, no – '

Matthew followed her out of the kitchen.

'Goodnight,' she said to him, about to go up the stairs.

'Vee, you're feeling better aren't you?'

She stopped.

He put on an old Jamaican accent. 'Venus, she got a lotta argumentation.'

She began to laugh. 'De boy Ma-tchew, ee got a lotta cool.'

'Mum wants you to ring her by the way, about the party.'

She groaned.

'Just give her a call.'

'I know, don't go on about it.'

'I'm not.'

She was standing on the first step, elevated to his height.

'… Come here.' She hugged him.

22

'Stuck In The Middle With You'
by Gerry Rafferty and Joe Egan

Alex poured himself the last of the wine while Ray talked. It had quietened down in the back bar where they were sitting. A girl and two men swept out. Ray's keen blue eyes followed the girl for a second, then caught the barman. He broke off from what he was saying and asked for another bottle, his Irish accent chewing up the French and spitting it into the Paris air. Emptying his pockets, he put a twenty euro note on the table, reinstated the cards, phone and condom packets and turned back to Alex.

'… She's bleeding me white mate, seriously.'

Alex didn't react.

'I'm back from school, working like a dog, domestic scene and all that. She's only under the table – '

The barman came over.

'Great, *merci*.' Ray took the bottle and poured. 'I mean what am I a fucking salami?' Ray drank. '… Monday today. Friday night she's in Brazil. Yeah, what I'm saying is don't let me down Alex, Thursday night, okay? I've got this priest getting back to me with the saints days, poor fella – there's got to be at least two a week.' Ray looked at Alex. 'You know this is interesting stuff.'

Alex glanced up.

'You'll be there Thursday?'

'Yeh, yeh.'

'Holidays, Christ. No holiday for me.' Ray drained his whisky glass and poured the wine into that. He moved it around on the surface of the table for a while, then pointed at it. 'Stay boy.'

Ray flicked a finger at the glass. It pinged and Alex looked up.

'Yeah, this is unreal mate, seriously. She told me she was a seccie, PA whatever, right?'

'Mm.'

'She speaks French, Portuguese, I mean she's lingual, point taken. So I'm nearby the embassy, I'm thinking I'll stop by, you know, she likes surprises. Okay, get this. She's in the reception, talking Chinese. To this fucking Chinese bloke. He's in there lapping it up.'

'She could still be a secretary.'

Ray burped. 'Secret agent. Two to one.'

Alex covered his nose and mouth with his hands. 'So what if she is?'

Ray stared at him. 'I.F.G.'

'What?'

'I'm saying Alex, that I have reason to believe that my girlfriend Lotta is an Insatiable Fucking Genius.' Ray tapped the table. 'It's Sylvie all over again.'

Alex resumed normal breathing. 'She's a mathematician?'

'Christ knows.' He shook his head. 'You know what's going to happen? I'm going to die of sex. It'll be a legend. Ray Cassidy? Died of sex.' Ray laughed.

But Alex was looking at the table.

Ray grunted. Nothing happened.

He made the sound of an owl.

'… What?'

'You're fucking comatose.'

'Sorry.'

Ray looked about him, delaying. Still Alex didn't speak.

'Listen mate,' Ray began, 'just because it's not for me, doesn't mean I'm going to judge you for it, you know. I'm really not that narrow-minded. Just don't become a Rangers fan – '

'I've told you a *hundred* times – '

'This is what I'm saying. Textbook denial. There are never any women in your life. That's the fact of it.'

'So if you don't have a girlfriend begging to give you wall to wall oral sex you're gay, clearly. For God's sake. I mean isn't there *any* other option?'

Ray squealed. 'Yeah, yeah, I'd say there's a few other little bits and bobs.' Ray was laughing, topping up his glass. He put on an American accent. 'You know I should write a book.' Then in a more knowing American accent, he said, 'No, just a pamphlet.'

Alex didn't say anything.

'Classic Murdock line that.'

'… What?'

'Alex, listen, the way you live, okay, is not normal. It's like you're in a waiting room. Why not just admit it? I mean there was that bloke, what was his name? That guy who died, you got all quiet. That lawyer fella.'

'Why is that relevant?'

'It's an explanation. What about that fucker Didier? He was a pederast son of a bitch, remember all that restaurant crap? *Come Aleks, we make beef jerky…* '

'What makes you think they've got *anything* in common?'

Ray looked thoughtful. 'Now you see that is interesting.' Ray pointed. 'What you're telling me, is there was something about that bloke, that totally didn't compare to Didier. Namely, you were *obsessed* with him.'

'I *liked* him.'

'When did all that stuff about finding the right girl start? After that bloke died.'

'No.' Alex looked down. 'No, it was months after that.'

'Exactly. Months. God,' Ray sat back in his chair. 'You know I hate to break it to you Alex, but you are gay.'

'Which would be fine, except I'm not.'

'I'm being sensitive here.' Ray narrowed his eyes. 'When did you last do it?'

Alex shook his head.

'Man you're repressed.'

They sat with their glasses until Alex spoke. 'I… I met a woman.'

'Okay… ' Ray seemed to have stopped listening.

'This weekend.'

'Oh yeah.'

'Mm.'

'Shagged her?' Ray brought his glass to his lips then saw Alex's face and put it back down. 'Okay, okay. That's great, seriously. Progress. So, what happened?'

'It was at a wedding.'

'Nice.' He paused. 'I mean that's a development.' He nodded. 'So, what's wrong with her?'

Alex closed his eyes.

'Mate, come on, you got to see the positive.'

He didn't comment.

'Okay. I'm at this wedding, single man, hot for it. I see this drunk old fella, he's dancing with this young ticklish girl, and I'm thinking for pity's sake darling you and me we could be a thermonuclear explosion… '

'We talked. It was as if we already knew each other.'

'Okay,' Ray said. 'Okay.'

After a few seconds, Alex sighed distractedly.

'So you kissed her and she turned into a snow goose, and off you both flew into the night.' Ray's head was swaying. 'I'm walking in the air,' he sang, feathering his fingers, 'I'm farting in the midnight breeze… '

Alex looked up.

'What's her name?'

'Madeleine.'

'Pretty is she?'

'Yeh.'

'As in?'

'Fine face, mouth, breasts… figure like… I don't know.'

'She has breasts.'

'It's her voice, it's like something you could live off. Just listening to her voice.'

Ray inhaled discerningly. 'Age?'

'Older I think. She had a scar like my mother's caesarean.'

'Okay pause right there.' Ray spoke slowly. 'You're looking at her naked belly?'

'… What?'

'You've left out a stage, I'm missing a stage here.'

'I went back to her hotel.'

'So you're with this woman, she's naked, and you're in a hotel room?'

Alex didn't reply.

'So you're telling me, you met this woman at the wedding, then shagged her? That self same night?'

'I'm not telling you anything.'

Ray looked at him. '… God she must be something. Bloody hell, I mean, so this is the news of the century – '

Ray cut himself short as if something didn't compute. He studied Alex carefully.

'Okay… ' Ray held his tongue between his teeth as he concentrated. 'It's a Dustin Hoffman thing. I'm seeing this tiny figure walking up between her fishnetted legs, standing in the crook of her thighs where it's just bare flesh, and you're looking at her cunt and it's wet like a waterfall and you're just gonna dive in – '

Alex sighed. 'I'd better go.' He reached for his wallet.

'God's sake man, you're such a fucking minimalist.'

They sat in silence for a moment.

Ray picked at his fingernails. 'I need all the material I can get.'

Alex looked appalled. 'If you remotely think about her – '

'Yeah?' Ray was laughing. 'What, you'll arrest me?' He flicked a bit of nail away and began in a low voice. 'D'you reckon there's a finite number of stiffies the body can take? You ever thought about that?' He looked like an anxious reporter. 'You do it ten times a day, you're using up your allocation.'

'All we do is sit here and talk crap.'

'Yeah, well no thanks to you.' Ray bit his thumbnail meditatively and focused on Alex again. 'She's affected you hasn't she, this woman?'

'She made me think. She woke me up. Literally. I've been living this low level life, doing a job I hate. Speaking to her, it made me feel so – '

'Alive?' Ray's eyes darted. 'Like you never felt before?'

Alex looked at him searchingly.

'Overheat when you think of her? Stomach lurch? Sweat?'

'It's hopeless,' he whispered.

'Okay, this is my preliminary diagnosis. You have fallen in love with this woman. Talk to her, eat with her, shag like – '

'I can't.'

'Why not?' Ray frowned. 'Typical English masochism.'

'She's married,' Alex said.

Ray paused. 'Well?'

'She's got a husband. And she's probably got a child, you know, with the scar. I just couldn't believe it.' He sighed. 'It could have been anything. And then... It was just incomprehensible.'

'What did she say about her husband?'

'Nothing.'

'So maybe they're getting a divorce?'

'She was wearing a wedding ring, I saw it, on her left hand. And then she said, 'I've been so stupid."

'Well, Alex mate, she's got to be as dizzy as you because if she wanted to cheat she'd have taken the ring off.'

Alex didn't reply.

Ray hesitated. 'So this episode with the ring, that was after you did it?'

Alex tensed with anger. 'I want to LOVE her. Forget anything less.' His jaw hardened as he whispered. 'Can't you see how *easy* it is? You think I don't feel it?' He stared at Ray. 'It's not enough. It's *nowhere near* enough.'

Ray sat back.

Alex breathed out. '… It was the way she behaved,' he said. 'As if she liked me but there was something wrong. Then I realised she was married and it all made sense. I just can't understand why she didn't tell me.'

They were quiet.

Eventually Ray spoke. 'Did she mention her husband? Did you ask her about him?'

'I thought it was best to leave. It was just obvious.'

'Can you get in touch with this woman?'

'She wrote down her phone number and she put 'I am a coward. Sorry.' underneath.'

'Shoo. Sounds complex. All right, so have you phoned her?'

'Of course not. Her husband might answer. She's got my number, she can phone me. Anyway I can't be with someone like that.'

'Listen Alex, first, you don't know she's being unfaithful. She may be divorced, separated, anything. Maybe her husband's an arsehole, you know? If she says she's being a coward and that. Or she could be wearing a ring for some other entirely different reason.'

Alex raised his eyes.

'It's possible. Okay, let's say she's married and she has a kid. Right? Easy. Ring her. If the husband answers, say you got the wrong number. If the kid answers, say you got the wrong number but you know, keep him on his toes in case he infiltrates my class. Catch him out with seven eights. Or no, eleven twelves is better, everyone knows seven eights. Right, so that's the husband and the kid. Now, if *she* answers, say come to my flat in Ile Saint Louis where we will make mad… No, no.' Ray paused. 'Okay, we will… No. Shit, Alex what are you going to do with her?' Ray drummed his fingers on the table. '… Okay, we will check out the art galleries, take in a ballet. That art and ballet shit, I mean it's bodies and women, basically sex for virgins, shy types, all that crowd that spends too much time in their heads. Well look, I'll leave it to you.

'Oh yeah,' Ray looked sideways, 'ask her to bring over some Marmite would you, I need the minerals, I'm running on empty.' He caught Alex's expression. '… Not if it's awkward. Obviously.'

Alex looked at him. 'You've got no idea what this is about.'

'Alex, the secret of life is simplicity. This is about phoning a woman. And doing it before Thursday. And we'll take it from there.'

23

'I Want You'
by Bob Dylan

'Gilles, you cannot carry on like this, dreaming like a puppy dog.'

My mother and I were walking up rue de Turenne towards the Église St-Denys, her shoes clicking on the early morning pavement.

'I say it for you not for me.'

I'd thought that by getting up at dawn, I'd avoid having an argument with her. I couldn't take her to the eleven o'clock Mass or have lunch with her, but we'd go to the eight o'clock Mass and have breakfast. To me that seemed agile diplomacy.

Instead, a tangle of roots had invaded my mother's system, sending up new shoots of annoyance at the slightest provocation.

Of course she wasn't against women in theory. In practice, she'd found my girlfriends vulgar without exception, but a responsible young woman, capable of taking orders from her and giving them to me, was fundamental to her plan. This woman would marry me, allow me to fertilise her, then set about making children while instructing me to make money. Our children would go to Mass with and have lunch with their grandmother. Jealously trying to win back his mother's attention, their father would by some miracle transform himself into an effective man. After a few decades at the pinnacle of world importance, a discreet priest would hear his dying words, and his soul in the balance, he would leave a large fortune, a percentage of which would, by hurried codicil, be diverted to a Catholic charity of the priest's choosing.

That was the theory. It all started with a good girl. But my debauched private life had hit a new low before I'd even got my first pay cheque. I'd fallen for a girl who didn't exist. I was floating away on a moonriver of delusion. How was I even going to spawn a bastard child like that? This was beyond the self-indulgence of promiscuity and contraception. It was an entirely new evil.

All right, I thought, some scepticism was understandable. Back when you were an apparition in Leicester Square. But now? I'd met you, spoken to you, arranged to meet you again and the day of that meeting had arrived. My mother would surely rejoice. The salmon was heading upstream at last.

In a state of naive awe, I wanted to tell her that although it seemed like I was dreaming, it was only because I was so happy. Finally I'd found you! You were so beautiful, intelligent, spirited. So free, so alive, so attractive. So... well, it was incredible.

But I knew enough to rein it in. I smiled as we walked along, then thought one confidence wouldn't hurt.

'You know I really like her. And I think she likes me.'

She patted my elbow.

'*En français s'il te plaît.*'

Already we're defeated.

We stopped on the pavement outside the front of the church and I took her hand.

Inside, she didn't make small talk. Her acquaintances would go to the eleven o'clock. She walked towards her usual row of chairs – special ones with lower chairs in front of them for kneeling on – crossed herself in front of the altar, hung up her handbag and knelt down to pray. I sat beside her.

Once she'd sat back down, I made another attempt.

'*Elle s'appelle* Venus.' I wasn't going to Frenchify your name.

She looked down her nose. '*Elle est anglaise*?'

'*Elle parle bien le français*.'

'*On l'a baptisée Vénus? Comme le* flytrap?'

The priest had come in.

'*Comme la déesse*,' I whispered.

'*Tu es tombé dans son piège*.'

I smiled beatifically. '*Je suis tombé amoureux*.'

My mother had decided you were a flytrap and I was the fly. I'd decided that I'd fallen in love with a goddess. I'd forgotten it was Palm Sunday. Our difference of opinion infused the entire ninety minutes.

By the time we got back to the flat, Mary had gone to the market. She'd have put me at ease, but she wouldn't be home before eleven.

I made some toast but I wasn't hungry.

I looked at my watch. Twelve minutes past ten.

Rue des Barres. It would take less than ten minutes. Leave at, what, twenty-to? Couldn't be late.

The American was *here* – that's what you'd said. A friend, not a boyfriend. But *here*. In Paris, or in your bedroom?

Perhaps you had several male friends. It was the done thing in Bohemian circles. I was training to be a lawyer. I'd just taken my mother to church. I felt too young and too old at the same time.

Why the fuck was I worrying like this? I'd never worried like this.

I was pacing the kitchen floor when my mother came in with the *Financial Times*. Her investments were like elderly relatives, wheeled out every Sunday to take the air.

I carried on walking.

'Gilles, sit.'

She was marking the share prices with a pencil, preparing to calculate her profits.

'Gilles – '

I kept moving.

'Stop it, for goodness' sake!'

She read the newspaper while speaking. 'Why did you come here?'

I didn't know what she meant.

'Why did you come to Paris? To find your *direction*, to do something with your life. And now look at you. It is absurd. What do you know about this girl? Nothing. Forget the incident of the underground train, I don't give a damn who is who. What I mean is you do not love *this* girl. You love a dream. That is all.'

'What are you talking about? She's *not* a dream. That's exactly what I've been trying to tell you.'

My mother was circling figures.

'My point is that you do not love *her*. You love a fantasy.'

'Well my point is that I do.'

'Listen to you, will you spend your whole life wasting time? Mm? Will you tell me that? *C'est de la folie tu sais*?'

She could tell me I was mad all she liked, in reality she didn't know what she wanted of me.

'Gilles, I am serious.'

'What more can I do?'

She took up her pencil.

'WHAT MORE CAN I DO?'

'Stop it. Shouting like a barbarian… I'm happy about the job. You've taken too long but you have it now. But you must stop dreaming of this girl. I'm saying this for you, only for you. Another year will go by and what will you have to show for it? You cannot waste time like this – '

'IT'S NOT A WASTE, IT'S MY LIFE.'

She sighed like she had the weight of the world's tears on

her back. And I knew what would come next. In that low voice of despair.

'There is so much you don't understand.'

Always the same, you just don't get it, the shit that I've put up with, the shit that is your destiny. As if I'd spent my life a fucking spectator.

I went to the door.

'Don't you *dare* to walk away.'

'Can't you say what you mean?' I mimicked her. 'You're wasting time Gilles, no one has forever Gilles. I can't think about it every second of my life. *I can't live like that*.'

It was as if there was a shroud clinging to us, making us so close we repulsed each other.

'*Sors d'ici*.'

So I left.

Oh Vee. You came out looking so happy. And I so wanted to make you smile. Words fell out of me in confused spaghetti sentences, I was so keen to please you. And if my mother had any effect it was to make me want us to be together above all else.

We arrived at rue de Varenne. I assumed I'd pay for both of us but you were taking out your purse.

I said no, don't worry, I'd pay.

You said no, you'd been busking the last few days on the *métro*.

I said no, I'd pay.

You put your finger on my lips.

You opened your purse. It was stuffed with 200 franc notes. 'We took all the coins to the bank,' you said. 'They won't fit. You'd be doing me a favour.'

I looked into your eyes and they shone at me. You paid.

The Rodin museum is the best museum in Paris. Vee, I haven't been to any others but I like to sound authoritative. The main thing is that it's erotic. There was a small crowd dotted around The Kiss, trying to look as if it appealed to their intellect.

'I suppose,' I said, attempting sophistication, 'it's become a bit of a cliché.'

'What d'you mean?'

'Well in that it's so famous… ' What plasticine crap was I talking? 'It seems a bit trite.'

'Just because people like it doesn't make it bad.'

I looked at it and looked at you and a flicker of current in my brain said 'kiss her' and another said 'that would be trite' and then you turned to the next exhibit.

The wooden floors creaked. There were old mirrors on the walls, dusty chandeliers hanging from the ceiling. It was an eerie, half-dead house. And yet everywhere around us bodies were bending out of the stone, alive but for the breath. Hands and backs and shoulders. A woman's despair, a man's devotion. Love, passionate and sad.

Upstairs, I beckoned you towards me. You'd missed a small bronze statue, a woman stretching up and leaning back. She was drying her hair but at the same time she seemed to want someone to hold her. It was called *La Toilette de Vénus*.

We walked down the steps at the back of the house into the large garden. The sun shone. The white gravel crunched under our feet. We didn't look at the statues.

We agreed that it was a peaceful garden, that you wouldn't know it from the street, that it was nice. Green. Verdant.

We got to the round pond at the far end.

I asked you about singing in the *métro*. It turned out you hadn't been on your own. Steven, your American friend, had been playing the guitar and singing with you.

I imagined a heightened affair between co-performers, loving looks over the microphone. Who did this dogfart of a minstrel think he was?

So Vee, I asked you whether you were in love with him. And you laughed. You said something very generous, you said that if that were the case you wouldn't have agreed to go on your own to the Rodin Museum with a strange man.

I looked at you, at your smile, and then I kissed you. On the lips, longingly, but politely. And you kissed me back, politely. And we looked at each other, and you took my hand.

As we walked back from the pond, we must have appeared almost the same as when we'd walked towards it. But I'd seen a new world in between. It was a world I'd dreamt of with such persistence but so little cause for hope. And it was suddenly so close. I felt like a child, desperate to go there immediately, but walking with you and holding your hand, just the relief that it existed was glorious.

You came alive when you talked about music. Back on the steps by the Rodin house, your confidence in your subject, your lust for it, filled me with excitement. Your surprised smile when I said something knowledgeable, my pleasure at your pleasure. He had a good voice, yes but she had a great voice, but hers was so light, so able to be quiet, so effortless. That songwriter, that composer, that instrument, that note. All of it we wanted to tell each other. My theories, your theories. What did I think of – ? But didn't I think she was – ? But haven't you heard – ? Yes, you're so right.

And it seemed the more we talked, the more potential there was. Breathlessly changing subjects, doubling back, hooked. That ability to tell each other something which opens the door to simultaneous understanding. That constant capacity to surprise. The wanting to know, the learning, and the never-ending proliferation of curiosity and mystery that is so much part of love.

And then you stretched your legs down and leant forward. You were wearing a low-cut, pale pink V-neck sweater. And you knew that that view I had from the side – you knew it would kidnap my attention.

'Why don't we have lunch?' I said.

'The two of us?' you asked.

I smiled. 'Of course.'

But you seemed anxious. I wondered what was wrong.

'It's just, there are some people we should invite.'

I couldn't judge whether you were serious.

You shrugged. 'I was thinking we ought to ask you and me. I mean they're a bit shy.'

Phew. I laughed. 'No, you're right,' I nodded, 'they're decent people.'

We began to kiss again.

'Oh God,' I whispered, 'you know who'll be there?'

'Who?' you whispered.

'What are their names? ... They flirt... ' I was kissing you. 'They're impossible... '

You kissed me harder.

I brought you closer to me, smelt the spring morning in your hair, imagined taking it down, undressing you, touching you...

We sat back.

'You must have a good voice,' I said.

Your eyes sidled. 'Why?'

'The people in the *métro* liked it.'

'It's easy in the *métro*, people want to be reminded they're human.'

'Yeh, but it's easier if you're... ' I looked at you.

You smiled. '... What?' You gave that some topspin.

Our eyes met, parted, met again. The ball was floating over me and I couldn't reach it.

... Charm, sex appeal, all of that. But the rest, how to put it? Perhaps, that if I impressed you, I would know it wouldn't be for nothing.

And then I felt bound to tell you about Leicester Square – how I'd been wishing I'd said something, longing to see you again, ever since. It was a kind of lie, keeping it to myself. But admitting to it wouldn't sound clever.

'So,' you turned to me. 'Who were you meeting at Place des Vosges?'

Lord. I couldn't say my mother.

I smiled. 'My mother,' I said.

'Really?' You looked like you didn't believe me.

'Yes.' You still looked like you didn't believe me. One day I'd realise everyone was less honest than you.

Change the subject. Leicester Square? But no, no.

'So how was the ballet?' I asked.

'Oh, good. Romeo and Juliet.'

'Prokofiev?'

You smiled. 'Yes.'

'There's that bit, I think it's the oboe, in the Montagues and Capulets, just after the heavy dance.'

'Yeh, the way it slides.'

'It's very sad.'

'Yeh, it's beautiful.'

'Venus… ' You turned, tugged out of yourself. 'I've got to tell you something. You'll think it's weird, but I promise you it isn't.'

'What?'

'I saw you singing in Leicester Square, in the tube station, a while ago, about a year and a half ago. I've been looking for you ever since.'

You watched me intently.

'Please, don't think I'm… I wasn't following you or anything. It happened completely by chance. That's why I had to talk to you after the lesson. It sounds pathetic I know. The more I say, the worse it sounds.' But I carried on talking. 'I heard your voice in the tube, and then I saw you. It was all so beautiful. I just wished later that I'd said something. I looked for you, but I couldn't find you. Until Thursday, at the lesson. And I couldn't believe it. I was so happy. I had to tell you, I couldn't keep it from you.'

'No, wait, I – I don't think – '

'I know it sounds strange. But don't let it be that that puts you off.'

'No, no.' You had a look of such sorrow on your face. 'I

would be flattered. I just don't think I'm the one you're looking for – '

'But you are. It's the way you are. All of you, everything.'

'Well that's kind of you – '

'It's just what I think.'

'No listen. I've never sung in Leicester Square.'

I sat, beached.

'I can't be the woman you saw.'

You looked down, and I realised how I'd hurt you.

'Sorry,' you whispered.

24

'Fixing A Hole'
by John Lennon and Paul McCartney

Mary was holding a plastic supermarket bag in her hand. She opened the door to Hélène's bedroom. The curtains were drawn. The air was cloying. She turned on the light, walked to the window and lifted the curtains to check the sill.

'I only do the flies,' she whispered. 'That's the first thing I tell her, puts her mind at rest.'

Venus pushed her hair away from her face. It was stiflingly hot. She hadn't been in here for ages. There were still awkward gaps where furniture had been taken to the hospital. Hélène's sister Christelle had organised the move, but she rarely visited. Perhaps Mary did actually think Hélène would come home.

'How do they get in, eh?' Mary was picking up the insect carcasses and putting them into the bag. Venus went to help.

'Thanks love. If it were down to me, I'd have it opened up, you know, but this is how she wants it, untouched like. Mind you, when the sun gets in… ' She angled her head towards the back of a yellow chair that had been faded by the light.

Venus held a dead bumble bee by its wing and dropped it in.

When they'd finished, Mary shook the bag so that the

carcasses went down to the bottom, then looked around the room making sure everything was where it should be.

'I told her I'd nurse her, right here in her room – course she didn't want it. Well, that's how she is. I'd have done it, mind you.'

She closed the door behind them and they walked towards the kitchen.

'Now Leo'll have fish won't she, how about that for supper?' Mary was holding the bag of dead insects. 'Nice bit of cod, salt and pepper, squeeze of lemon.'

Venus touched Mary's arm. She said she felt bad Mary always doing the cooking.

'Don't be silly love. Once I know what I'm doing, it's as good as done.

'Here!' She held the bag aloft. 'Squashed fly biscuits for afters?!'

Mary cooked well. She felt for Venus and Leonie and their restricted diet and had a knack for making food that Leonie wanted to eat. She also liked to talk, and having been starved of the chance in English, took it gratefully that evening.

Venus put Leonie to bed, then told Mary she needed to make a phone call.

She went into Gilles' bedroom. Alex's number was in her purse on the table by the bed. She sat down, took off her shoes, then gave way and lay down on her front and buried her head in her arms.

They'd come in here. After that first stilted dinner with Hélène, Gilles had led Venus out of the dining room, past one door, through another and into the dark, closing the door behind them, kissing her as if his life depended on it.

She crossed over the memory like a fire-walker, kissing her own hand, mesmerising herself with the feel of it, body wild, heart kaleidoscopic to find its equal.

She turned onto her back and lay still, the ceiling high above her.

In the light, his bedroom was old-fashioned and innocent. Large, rectangular, the tall window opposite the bed overlooking the square, the pattern of exotic birds on the wallpaper that was restfully absorbing. And then when you started looking for them, the childhood possessions that had made her realise that just like her, he'd existed before they'd met.

It was good to think of him like that, alone in here like she was now, a young man she knew nothing about.

The wedding had been on Saturday. Today was Tuesday. Three days, that was fine.

She looked at her watch. 9.45.

Alex might be in. Later would be too late. It was ridiculous to wait any longer.

She took her purse from her bag and unfolded the piece of paper.

She'd explain why she'd acted so strangely, that was the purpose of it. At least then things would be clear.

She typed in the numbers and watched them on the screen for a second before ringing.

A voicemail message started playing. She felt relieved.

'Alex, hi. It's… ' She hesitated.

'It's Venus, Venus Rees. We met on Saturday – at Charlotte's wedding. You think I'm called Madeleine. Sorry, it was stupid of me, it was because of the name on the card – but I didn't correct you, which I should have done. Obviously.

'I'm… I just wanted to say I'm sorry. I really enjoyed talking to you. I shouldn't have suggested you come back with me –

'Sorry, I must seem insane to you. I wanted to tell you a few things, just to explain. It would be good to speak to you. I'm here, in Paris.'

She left her mobile number and heard her voice drain away.

She put the phone down on the bed and thought about what she'd said, then tired of it, tired of herself and got up.

It was still light. She opened the French doors.

The air was hotter outside than in the room. She stood against the railings, tall houses like the one she looked out of on every side of the square. She wanted to find them ugly. Their roofs too steep, their chimneys like food caught between teeth. The trees seemed to hold the line round the perimeter, keeping the square from closing in on itself.

She'd have to get out.

Was Alex listening to the message? Probably not.

She looked at the arrangement of windows in the roofs. Most roofs had windows on two levels, small square ones higher up and more elaborate square and round ones a level down. She stared at the lower windows.

She'd have liked to replay the message. Just to check it didn't sound too... Although it would have done. Incoherent, desperate.

There were three larger windows in the roof of the big *pavillon* in the middle. She tried to find a rule. No round windows in the roofs of the corner houses? No, there was an exception. And one roof was asymmetrical even in itself.

She shouldn't have said all that stuff about her name – he already thought she was weird, why had she said that?

She shouldn't have even left a message. If she hadn't left a message she could have phoned until he'd answered.

She decided to go for a walk. She stepped back and closed one of the French doors. She realised the other one wouldn't close if it wasn't closed first. Before she could open the original door, the phone rang.

She rushed to it.

It was Alex.

'Hi,' she said warmly. 'Thanks for ringing.'

'I got your message.' But he sounded blank. 'I was on the phone.'

'Oh, okay. Sorry it was incoherent.'

He didn't say anything.

'I'm sorry. About the Madeleine thing. I should never have done that.'

'I don't think I understand you at all.'

'No,' she said nervously. 'No, I don't blame you. It was ridiculous of me. I just wanted to be someone different. Sorry, this is all going to sound strange, maybe it would be better if we met – '

'You might as well tell me now.' It was as if he was barely there.

'Tell you what?'

'About your husband.'

She paused. 'How did you know?'

'I can't believe you even asked me to the hotel.'

'No, no – '

'I thought we were in the same situation. I had no idea.'

'But you must understand now why it was difficult.'

'Of course, but I can't see how you could have let me think it was possible.'

She couldn't work out why he was so upset.

'Charlotte – you spoke to her?'

'Charlotte? No I saw your wedding ring. If I'd realised before, I wouldn't have gone with you.'

'Oh Alex.' She sat down on the bed and felt a mixture of relief and anxiety at the misunderstanding. 'You've got it wrong. And right at the same time. I was married, but my husband's dead.'

She heard him take it in, and while he did the time seemed cocooned.

They each took the blame.

'I should have said – '

'No, no.' He sighed. 'God I've been so stupid.'

But she noticed the fact that she'd told him. It began to settle inside her, like sand on a river bed, so that as the particles made their way down, the water above ran clearer.

'Thank you,' he said, 'for ringing.'

'I haven't even spoken to a man like I did with you since he died. Let alone – anything else. I mean, I haven't wanted to. We seemed to get on so well. … I know I shouldn't have made that the important thing. I just – couldn't face explaining.'

He didn't say anything. Perhaps it sounded ignoble.

'I suppose it amounts to the same thing,' she said. 'I thought I was being unfaithful and so did you.'

'But you weren't, in fact.'

'But I felt like I was.' She paused. 'I – I don't think it was just my husband. I mean it was also that I hadn't told you about him.'

'Oh… right.'

She wondered whether he'd understood what she was trying to say.

'… At least,' she said eventually, 'we had a good talk.'

'More than that.'

'It doesn't happen often.'

'No,' he said. 'I know.'

Neither of them spoke.

She began again. 'There's something else. It's – well it's nothing. I last sang at my husband's funeral. You know, in public. So, maybe that was why I fainted. Probably not – '

'Oh right,' he said. 'That must have been tough.'

There was another silence.

'Sorry,' he said, 'I'm still taking it in… I'm so pleased you rang.'

'Yeh – ' she smiled.

She felt contented, as if a wave of calm was carrying her. She'd told him, he knew, that was it. And then the wave pulled back, drawing shifts of possibility.

'I must have seemed,' he hesitated, 'I don't know, detached.'

She was about to speak but he continued.

'I've got so used to being on my own.'

She wasn't sure what he meant. 'You're not going out with anyone?'

'No, no. I wouldn't have – '

'I know. I just… Sorry, what do you mean, detached?'

'As if I wasn't interested. In the hotel. Before – '

'Oh.' A flare lit through her mind.

'No,' she said. 'No, you were right to slow me down.'

She thought about how he'd kissed her. She wanted to say something more but couldn't think how to put it.

'How are you?' he asked. 'Do you still feel faint?'

'No, I'm fine. Thanks.'

They waited.

'… So, do you have children?'

'Yes. A little girl.'

'Oh right. I thought maybe… I saw the scar.'

'Oh – ' He'd noticed that.

He coughed quietly. 'How old is she, your daughter?'

'She's five, nearly six.'

He must have really looked. It wasn't obvious.

'So she can talk?'

Venus laughed. 'Yes, she can definitely talk.'

It hadn't crossed her mind about the wedding ring. Perhaps she should have taken it off.

'I suppose six is quite old.'

She liked his voice, the delay in it.

'Where was she – on Saturday?'

'She was staying with my brother and his family,' she said. 'In Cornwall.'

And this circling around each other.

'Do you – have children?' she asked.

'Me? No – I've never been married.'

'Oh.' She smiled at his delicate answer.

He breathed out minutely.

She laughed quietly.

'What?' he asked. It sounded like he was smiling.

'… Nothing.'

'You sound so… '

'… What?'

'I keep thinking of you as Madeleine.'

'That's okay,' she whispered.

She wondered what to suggest. They could meet. Later this week. Soon.

'Where are you?' he whispered.

'In the flat – in Place des Vosges.' She became uneasy.

'It's so close.'

'I know.'

'Less than five minutes.'

'Not walking – '

'I wouldn't walk.'

It felt like a dart had numbed her stomach. She hadn't heard it in his voice before.

'Where are you?' she whispered. 'I mean, where in your flat?'

'In my bedroom.'

'What's it like?'

'Quiet. The window's open. Sometimes you can hear the *Bateaux Mouches* commentary.'

She smiled. *A gauche, l'appartement d'Alex, qui parle avec Venus…*

She could drift past in a boat. She wanted to do something.

'Is the light… ' she began. 'Do you have the light on?'

'No, but there's light, from the sitting room. And the street lights.'

She looked up. 'It's nearly dark outside… '

'Yeh… '

She got up and walked to the French doors. She opened the one that was still ajar. Looking out, she half thought she might see him. A light breeze blew a rosy smell, caressed her face, and she felt a surge of happiness, physical and mental, to be here, in the beauty of the evening, talking like this.

'Oh Alex, Alex,' she sighed.

'Hi,' he said.

She smiled.

'What are you doing?' he whispered.

'Standing against the railings, looking out at the square. It's a beautiful evening.'

'... I'm so... happy you rang.'

She smiled broadly.

'I liked you so much, I couldn't sleep.'

Her breath disappeared for a moment. Then she thought more consciously about what he'd said.

'Are you there?'

'Yeh, sorry. You... ' She felt the warmth between her legs get more compelling. He was right, it would take less than five minutes. 'I could come to your flat,' she whispered.

'Please,' he whispered back.

He spoke with such urgency. But the real chance of it made her feel the pang of what had happened before.

'I don't know... Perhaps not tonight.'

'... Okay.'

Stepping back into the room, she pushed the open door to. She closed the curtains, closed her eyes, felt such a desire to see him she almost changed her mind. She sat down on the floor against the wall.

'Can I say anything I think of?' she whispered.

'Of course,' he whispered.

'Will you do that?'

'Yes.'

She undid the top button of her trousers.

'What... ' he whispered, and then he paused. 'What do you want?'

The way he asked the question filled her mind. It was as if he knew what she was doing.

'If we talk... '

But she was thinking about how he moved when she touched him.

'... Alex?'

'What?'

She wasn't bold enough to say it.

'Are you lying on your bed?' she asked.

'Yeh, what are you – '

'I – I want to… '

'What?'

' – Hang on.' She stood up. 'Don't go.'

She put the phone on the bed, took off her trousers and then quickly, as if she wasn't really doing it, took off her pants. She picked up the phone. 'Sorry,' she said.

She lay down under the sheets, and unbuttoned the top of her shirt. 'Are you in bed, between the sheets?'

'On it, on the top. What were you doing just then?'

She felt embarrassed, and then wanted to tell him. 'Taking off my clothes,' she whispered.

He sighed. 'I couldn't stop thinking of you, at work, everywhere, I haven't been able to do anything – '

She breathed in. 'Do you think about – ?'

'Yeh. Just – anything with you.'

She opened her mouth as if to kiss him.

'Are you sure you don't want me to – '

'Yeh, it's okay.'

'Okay.'

She waited for a while, listening to him, there but not talking. She felt her hand on the skin of her thighs.

'What are you doing?' he whispered.

'Just,' she said, 'thinking of you.'

'Your voice sounds beautiful.'

'Thank you.'

'I feel I could eat it.'

'Do you?' She smiled, moving her hand between her legs.

'Yeh.'

She felt the glide of her finger, sighing at the pleasure of it. She thought of him outside with her, kissing his mouth, his finger between her legs, he slowly touching her as she kissed him.

Then she could just hear his breathing, the sound of it, like being among high, feathered clouds.

'… Alex?' she whispered.

'… Yeh?'

His attention was so light.

She took a breath. 'Pretend I'm… I'm walking into your room.'

She heard him breathe out.

'What… what am I wearing?'

'The dress at the wedding.'

'And… underneath?'

'Nothing.' He breathed. 'So you feel it… like hands, touching you.'

Her mind seemed to melt and reform.

'You were out in the rain,' she began. 'You're wet, you take off your clothes.' She swallowed. 'You lie on the bed. The air's warm… like breath.'

She imagined him naked, almost asleep, her lips glancing over his cheek.

'You turn your head, and the drops of water from your hair fall on me and wake my skin up where they fall.'

She heard her heart beating.

'I kneel beside you on the bed,' she whispered, 'and take off my dress from the top.'

He breathed out.

'And I lean down, to dry you with the silk – your waist, and your thighs. The silk's hot. You know it's been touching me.'

'God – just – '

'… I kiss the water off your stomach, and your hips – '

He sighed at a higher pitch.

'You're – exquisite,' he whispered. The sound of his breathing was like sea in a shell. '… Uh, if you knew how much I thought of you.'

'What do you think?' she whispered.

'Your dress falling to your waist… your breasts… '

He breathed more heavily.

'… Seeing you undressing. Feeling you… ' He sighed. 'Kissing your breasts – '

She murmured softly, the wet spreading around her cunt as she slid her finger over her clitoris, imagining him lying on the bed watching her, her breasts offering themselves to his mouth.

He groaned. 'God, I wish you were here.'

'What – ' she breathed, 'what would you do – '

'Kiss you, everywhere – taste you – '

'… We'd – make love – ' Her heart thudded.

'Ah – ' His breath cracked.

She sucked at the air as her finger slipped inside. 'You – want that – '

'Yes – God – ' he breathed.

Sighing, she let her finger go in deeper.

'If you want – '

'Yes – ' she whispered. The blood in her seemed to burn up. She was moving her finger faster, her cunt closing in, trying to pull his cock inside.

She gritted her teeth.

He made a beautiful sound, between a sigh and a moan.

'Oh m – ' Her jaw tensed.

'Tell me – Tell me – '

She thought of him sitting against the bed.

'You're sitting on the floor, I come down – ' She swallowed. ' – No one can tell,' she whispered, her breath shaking. 'I could just be sitting down – '

' – Like – in the lane – ?'

'Yeh like that like that – '

There in the lane, his face, his hands on her, his cock sliding into her –

'Oh f – '

'Ah – ' he whimpered.

His mouth on her, his tongue, kissing, licking. 'Shh… '

He breathed in sharply.

'Oh my G – '

Her eyes closed tighter.

'Oh, oh God.'

It was quiet. Her mind felt like it was cased in velvet, soft and smooth and hushing so that there were no echoes.

She was lying on the bed. She closed her eyes again and lay still, the evening sounds of the square percolating through the partly open door.

She heard him make a small sighing noise.

'… Alex,' she breathed.

'I wish I could kiss you,' he whispered.

Against her will she saw herself in the hotel room, dissolving at his attempt.

'I don't want to say goodbye.'

'No,' she blinked.

She pulled the cover over her.

'I'd like to see you.'

'Me too.' She breathed out.

She looked around the darkened room. It had become Gilles' again.

She closed her eyes. 'Sorry, I – '

'I know… it might be difficult,' he said.

But it hadn't been difficult.

She brushed a tear off her cheek. Why was she still this screwed up?

'We can just talk. We don't have to – '

'Yeh,' she sighed. She wondered if that was true. 'Yeh I know.'

He didn't say anything.

How she liked him, how incredibly she liked him. 'I just don't want to make your life impossible. If you don't want to – to be involved – '

'I am involved.'

'But I'm not – free of it.'

'I want to help you.'

'It can't be pity.'

'It isn't that at all.'

'… Then thank you.'

'You don't need to thank me.'

She closed her eyes and breathed more regularly. Perhaps talking about it made it worse. They could just meet, see what happened.

'To me you seem free,' he said. 'Not free of your husband, but free of grief.'

'It's complicated by the fact that I… I'm so susceptible to you.'

'But why's that a complication? I mean if you like me – '

'Of course I like you. I mean as far as my husband's concerned, it pushes me further than I ought to go.'

He was quiet. She'd sounded curt.

'Well look,' she said, 'let's meet – '

'It can be as friends,' he said. 'If you want.'

She paused. But he seemed to be serious.

'Right,' she said uncertainly.

'You don't think it's possible?'

'No, no, I didn't say that – '

'I think it is.'

The tone of his voice was unexpectedly set.

But, she thought, with the Hélène business to come – perhaps once she'd seen her. And for God's sake, they'd only just met, she hardly knew him, what was she thinking?

'Yeh,' she said. 'Yeh, that's best.'

'I want to get to know you.'

She felt uncertain again; that hadn't stopped them a few minutes ago.

But no, he was right. Things were different in reality, of course he was right.

'Okay,' she said, 'how about Thursday evening?'

'Oh, well… '

'Is that difficult?'

'No, not really. I'm having a drink with someone – I can easily change it.'

'When's better?'

'Tomorrow evening?'

'Okay.' She paused for a moment. 'Yeh, okay. Where?'

'Why don't you come to my flat?'

'Are you joking?' She laughed.

'Why not?'

'Alex – '

'It won't be like that. I'll make you supper – you can tell me what you think of my cooking.'

'Oh God.'

'It isn't that bad.'

'I mean it sounds too nice, maybe we should make it a restaurant.'

'No.'

'What d'you mean, no?'

'We'll just have supper.'

'And then I'll leave?'

'Yes.'

She felt dubious.

'We'll just – take it easy. It doesn't have to be – ' He paused. 'There's more to it than that, don't you think?'

'Yes,' she said. And she felt he was trying to help her. 'Yes of course.'

But he was right, there was more to it. That was how it should be. They'd started strangely, she hadn't been herself.

'If you wanted,' he hesitated, 'you could bring your daughter – '

'What?' she snapped. 'No way.'

'Okay, no. Sorry.'

'You don't have to be a saint.'

'I know, I didn't mean – '

'There's someone here who'll look after her.'

'Okay.'

She sighed. 'Sorry.'

'No, no.'

'It was kind of you. To ask.'

They waited. Then she half laughed, half sighed. 'There'll

be lots of conversations like this – ' And she heard herself say it and suddenly thought she was assuming something.

They were both quiet.

'Okay,' Venus said.

Alex gave her his address. She'd arrive at 8.00. It was settled.

25

'Smoke Gets In Your Eyes'
by Otto Harbach and Jerome Kern

We sat on the steps overlooking Rodin's pristine garden like the statues themselves.

Vee, the last thing I wanted was to upset you. I couldn't bear you to feel like a substitute, or see me as someone who'd be willing to accept one. I could tell that mild scepticism was part of your nature. It wouldn't take much to turn that into full blown doubt.

And perhaps you could tell that I was occasionally elaborate with the truth, but the problem here wasn't bullshit, it was the lack of it. The fact is, you were the woman I saw. I'm not mad, I wasn't dreaming. I wasn't going out of my way to be an arsehole, it's just what happened. And it wasn't as if I couldn't grasp the inconsistency, I understood it perfectly, but it was nowhere near enough to change my mind. You say you didn't sing in Leicester Square; I saw you sing in Leicester Square. I love and hate my mother. Sometimes in life you have to settle for contradiction.

But there on the steps we didn't know what to do.

'I'll go,' you said.

'No,' I said, panicked. 'No don't. Please – ' I took your hand.

You pulled it away.

'I'd like you to stay,' I said.

You stared. 'I'm not the person you're looking for.'

'No,' I said. 'You are. I'm absolutely sure of it.'

'I've told you explicitly that I can't be. If you want this woman, you're wasting your time with me.'

But Vee you didn't go quite so soon. You sat still. And then into your voice came a hint of the teacher.

'I have to say, if you were planning on chatting me up, you've gone about it in the most ridiculous way.'

I smiled inwardly. 'Why's that?'

You looked down your nose. 'One, you describe this woman you think is me; two, I tell you this woman can't be me; three, you maintain that although *I* am me, you know where I've been better than I do; four, you assume I'll do whatever stupid thing you like; five, you haven't even said that it doesn't matter that I'm me and not your damn beautiful woman.'

My heart fluttered at this sudden clarification.

'What was this woman singing?' Your voice had taken a professional tone.

'An aria, I think Puccini, then 'Dancing Cheek to Cheek'.'

You pursed your lips. 'And then?'

''Fly Me To The Moon'.'

You raised your eyebrows in surprise, saying nothing.

'So – it *was* you?'

'NO. I sometimes sing that kind of stuff if I'm on my own.'

You looked at me. 'Why would I lie to you?'

'Not lying necessarily, maybe you just forgot.'

'Maybe you're just a fucking headcase.'

'Maybe you're just an uptight princess.'

Silently you stood up.

What was I doing? Losing you over this foolishness?

The doors to the house were ajar, but you were facing the garden.

'The Rodin was good,' I said, getting up.

'I'm glad,' you said.

You could leave either by going through the doors, or by going through the garden, around the side of the building.

'Thank you.'

'Not at all.' You paused. 'So,' you said, 'see you on Thursday. At the lesson.'

'Yes,' I was casual. 'Yes, I hope so.'

It would work either way, but it would be better if you went around the side.

'Bye then.'

'Goodbye.'

And away you went, down the steps, into the garden, turning right to walk around the side of the house, past the café and out towards the street. I knew you wouldn't look back. As soon as you'd got to the bottom of the steps I walked up through the doors and into the museum. I ran straight through the middle, past the striding St John the Baptist, past the tourists and out of the museum's front entrance. Then, without looking behind me, walked so as not to catch your eye, through the crowd in the courtyard at the front and into the street.

There was no sign of you to the left or right. I was in time. I walked a few paces to the left alongside the wall dividing the museum grounds and the pavement and I waited, hidden from your view until you came out.

After about a minute, there you were, turning right down rue de Varenne.

I lowered my voice. '*Mademoiselle! Excusez-moi –* '

You looked around unaware. It was perfect.

And then in French I continued. I was sorry to disturb you, but I'd just seen the most beautiful woman in the Musée Rodin.

You began to smile. It was odd, I said, but you do look extraordinarily like her.

You strolled towards me without making a sound, closer and closer until your breasts touched my chest. I could smell your skin, feel the warmth of your breath, your hard-headed stare on me. And once we'd entered that time warp in which the moment pervades and doesn't pass, you opened your mouth. Your lips began to move. Your tongue played with the word, oozed it out like a sweet.

'Goodbye,' you whispered.

You'd turned around. You'd started walking.

'Venus?' I called, horrified.

Without looking back, you said, 'Eight o'clock, Wednesday night, my place. We'll talk.'

Time passed slowly between Sunday and Wednesday.

Away from the sense of purpose that prevailed in London, office life was farcical enough. But my mind kept returning to you, and I found you everywhere. What were the absurd priorities and petty dramas of the legal profession in comparison?

I spent most of Monday wandering around the office discussing restaurants. You were cross, I needed to get it right. Decent food, a relaxed atmosphere. Not a show-off place, but not just anywhere. At five o'clock, I decided to look at a few, then remembered I'd been asked to translate a lease the week before and ended up working late.

On Tuesday morning, Cecil Pitt stopped me in the corridor. He'd taken on a deal and wanted to expand the team. Five of us sat round a table. The way Pitt pumped it, I thought we were preparing for a moon landing.

I'd been observing Pitt since I'd arrived in Paris. He had style. Nothing worried him. He could build something up or cut it dead as he chose. He was amusing, his suits were well-cut and he had good furniture in his office. By the end of the meeting, I'd made up my mind to impress him.

That afternoon, Pitt called me. The assistant shouldering his deal had a habit of contracting very serious 'French illnesses', the client wanted to discuss the latest version of the agreement, he was busy, no one else was around, would

I take the call. I'd never laid eyes on the agreement and told him so. Pitt said get up here now.

He sat in a high-backed chair behind his desk. The low armchair opposite was the only option.

'If there's one thing I can't stand it's someone who spurns a favour. Now I'll take this call. You'll take notes. And I shan't forget it. Got that Gilles?'

So Pitt graciously delegated to himself, holding forth to the client in cogent if slightly long-winded French. Still Pitt's acolyte, I wrote down everything I heard. But as the in-house lawyer's meticulous questioning continued, and Pitt's answers grew more long-winded and less cogent, it dawned on me that Pitt didn't know any more about the deal than I did. His career of client entertainment hadn't primed him for this particular feast. Slowly, carefully, he was being spit-roasted on the speakerphone, the client's faith in him haemorrhaging between his ineffectual attempts to bind the wounds. That's the thing about Pitt. You almost feel sorry for him.

He phoned London immediately after the call and warned them to expect trouble. He explained that unfortunately there had been a problem with a trainee, Gilles Matheson, due to a linguistic misunderstanding, for which the trainee had been duly disciplined and for which he, Pitt, had of course taken full responsibility.

The linguistic misunderstanding was not pure invention on Pitt's part. Nothing to do with Pitt or the deal, but everything to do with me.

There was something about that Paris office. A devil-call that sounded late at night. A call I was too immature, too 'pathetically unprofessional' to ignore.

A property partner had caught me at my desk earlier that day. Had he been equipped with the right instrument he would certainly have flayed me. In a legal context, the word *jouissance* doesn't mean orgasm, it means possession of land. I knew that very well. And yet grappling with my translation late on Monday night, I'd gone off-piste with every *jouissance* I could find. I'd left it on the property partner's desk, revelling in the laugh we'd have in the morning, joyfully unaware that the firm had classed me as a native French speaker. No one had checked my translation. The lease had been photocopied, bound and delivered to all eleven of the interested parties before anyone had got the joke.

Vee, you were my secret salvation. I would escape this life of toil and injustice. I was seeing you on Wednesday, and Wednesday was tomorrow, soon to be today.

Back home, I put my resolve to the test. Perhaps a hands-on investigation of the meaning of *jouissance* would comfort me – visions of you in your low-cut sweater were already tumbling in my imagination.

I got up, opened the window, paced the floor. A midnight run? The rest of me was exhausted. A shower? Nakedness was the last thing I needed. Telly? Too Pavlovian.

Iron of will, I preserved my continence.

At quarter to eight on Wednesday I left the office. It was warm in the way spring is not meant to be and all the more delectable for it. I ran down rue Royale, heading straight for the sun, then into the *métro* at Concorde. I got out at Hôtel de Ville, sprinted through the square, down the *quai* and around the outside of St Gervais to rue des Barres.

I arrived to see you waiting outside, sitting on the window ledge in your jeans and t-shirt, dangling your legs in a way that was inexplicably appealing.

Out of breath, I offered my hand. You took it.

'You look lovely,' I said.

'Come nearer,' you said. You were undoing the top button of my shirt, still sitting on the ledge. 'You're hot.'

'I didn't want to be late.'

You smiled. And when you'd finished, I kissed your cheek which was cooler, and you kissed mine.

I took off my jacket and you pushed yourself off the ledge with the palms of your hands. I was about to walk with you but you asked me to stay where I was.

You did a strange thing. You walked around me, as if you were inspecting a horse at a market. And I stood there, a dumb, sweating animal, ready to bear my mistress.

You faced me again. You gave me a look of such sexual confidence it threw me for a second.

But here was another test, the next stage of this irresistible examination. Did you think I would lower my eyes? Come on. I gave it back out, all of it from the stinging stare to the soft, enveloping gaze. And it seemed that each look was never quite finished with, but lingered round us like dervishes, urging us on.

I made to kiss you but you stopped me.

'What?'

'I haven't decided whether you're a prick or not.'

'I'm the nicest prick in the world.'

'That's what I'm worried about.' You smiled. 'Are you hungry?'

'Of course,' I said.

'That's good,' you said, looking directly at me.

'If you're hungry,' I smiled back at you, 'yes it is – '

'I'm quite hungry,' you said.

There was a life in your voice, a shine in your eyes, that hadn't been conveyed by your words. And I couldn't get over the way you were.

You sensed that I was about to kiss you and started walking.

'There's an Italian place, I think it's in rue Pastourelle.'

I knew the one you meant. It wasn't the place I was going to suggest, but it was a hundred yards from my flat.

We walked down from the church, then up through rue des Archives. It wasn't late but the men having an argument ahead on our left had clearly taken things outside. I moved to your left without thinking and you looked at me gratefully.

We left the crowds and I felt you move away. We'd put our arms around each other as we'd been walking and I'd hoped it was for more than solidarity.

I reached out for your hand, then put my arm back around you. Felt that place on your waist that my arm was made for and drew you closer. Felt you put your arm back around me. And rashly assumed as we walked arm in arm on that hot night, that I was forgiven.

26

'Train In The Distance'
by Paul Simon

Venus sat in Alex's flat trying to relax. Minute details of the way he lived made an impression on her. The bead on the end of the string that turned the bathroom light on, his razor on a shelf by the basin, a box of soap inside the cupboard. She'd been expecting him to be a different species – everything was disconcertingly familiar.

She took a sip of the glass of wine he'd given her, got up and walked to the sofa at the other end of the room. She knelt on it and looked out of the window. A *Bateau Mouche* slid under the Pont de la Tournelle like a limbo dancer, its lights beginning to show in the early evening.

He called from the kitchen. It wouldn't be much longer.

The walls of the room were covered in red velvety paper. It was comfortingly tasteless. She touched a bit of it, beside the window, and thought of the short hair at the back of his head.

He was wearing worn cord jeans and an indigo t-shirt. Moving about the kitchen.

She sat down on the sofa. There was a stereo on the low cupboard on her left. She hesitated over the iPod and looked through the CDs instead.

And glasses, that was the other thing. They made him

look doubly attractive. He must have worn contact lenses at the wedding.

Maybe she was overdressed, she thought. She undid the second button of her shirt. It was warm in here anyway.

She noticed Tchaikovsky's Pathétique Symphony among the CDs. She picked it up and started humming the surging theme of the first movement.

She was still looking at it when he came out of the kitchen and gave her something to eat – a small piece of toasted bread with lumps of white cheese and bits of fresh fig.

Their hands touched as she took the bread. He went back to the kitchen.

She looked at the food. A bit rough in the assembly, but it smelt fresh.

She began to eat. After the first mouthful, she stopped for a second. More slowly, she took another bite.

The salty cheese with the sweet fig, and something underneath, greenery but it was bitter like watercress, and then oil on it, not too much, just coated, everything fitting together.

She called to him, told him it was incredible, really, she wasn't being polite. He looked surprised and smiled. Then as he turned away from her, back into the kitchen, she noticed him smile again, a private overflow.

She watched him reaching for things, attending to things, absorbed in the cooking. The way his shoulder blades were set, how they moved under his t-shirt.

She could walk up behind him, kiss the small of his back, put a stop to this platonic project before it began. But no.

She'd eaten most of the bread and cheese when she wondered whether he'd had any himself. She knocked on the half open kitchen door.

He turned around, and the intimacy of her thoughts and his unprepared look stilled the air between them.

'Sorry,' she said. 'Can I have a knife?'

'Yeh.' He gave her a sharp looking black handled knife.

She took it to the table, put what was left of the bread and cheese on a plate and sat cutting away her bite marks and eating them so that a small piece of everything remained, looking like the delicacy it was.

They ate pasta, she ate pasta all the time, it should have been normal, but she couldn't stop telling him how good it was. Thinly-cut bacon, courgettes, parsley. Parmesan cheese. Spring onions. Lemon juice. Some kind of cream. Maybe chilli. And then an ingredient, she didn't know what it was, that took everything together and made it taste of something, beyond the taste of each thing separately.

They discussed the food while they ate. He made chicken stock from scratch and kept it in the freezer. She was so stunned she couldn't get the thought out of her head.

So, she said, he really took it seriously, this cooking.

He said he made the stock for soup. He liked soup.

Oh right, she said.

Yes, she said, she liked soup.

Oh really, he said, looking up at her.

A strange hysteria was rising in her, each attempt to get her breath like a push on a row of dominos, her composure begging to be toppled.

She pulled back.

'Sorry.' She paused. 'I'm slightly nervous.'

He looked up at her. 'I hope I don't make you feel nervous – '

'No. No – '

She cleared her throat.

They ate again.

She took in the large white plates, the glasses. Bread on the board. Salad in the bowl. The weight of thought he'd put in. And she felt again that his domestic decisions might blind her to the substance of his life.

She met his eyes. They looked like dark honey.

'Thank you,' she said.

'What for?'

'For inviting me, making all this.'

'It's my pleasure.' He looked at her. 'Thank you.'

She grinned. 'What for?'

'I don't know – for coming, for pretending to be nervous.'

'I wasn't pretending.'

But the room seemed to breathe out, as if it had been waiting for his remark.

They went back to their food.

'You know,' she said eventually, 'I'm worried the real me will bore you out of your brain.'

His expression relaxed with affection.

'I'll tell you every detail of the last four years and by the end of it you'll shrivel up into this dried pea – '

He reached around their plates and took her hands.

'It'll be a diet of pure pulses.'

He smiled. 'Pulses and soup.'

'Yeh,' she laughed.

He pressed her hands.

They began to eat again.

They both spoke at the same time. Go on, he said.

She asked him about growing up in the country, and he talked about it with a captivating pleasure, sparked by his own enthusiasm, and then in answer to her stream of questions when she thought he might stop. She built up a picture of him and his sister in a house with fields around it, playing in the woods, camping out in the hay, seeing the lanes get filled with snow.

His parents had both grown up in cities but wanted to live in the country. His father an artist, his mother pregnant with his sister, they'd sold all they had to make a new life.

It was idyllic, he said, at first. Whenever he thought of it, he felt content.

She asked about later. He shrugged. It went wrong. Money problems, his father having an affair, his parents divorcing.

She asked if he was in touch with him.

No, he said, he hadn't been for years, it was as if he didn't exist.

It was too simple an answer. She wanted to speak honestly.

'You loved your father. But he lied to you. And that screwed your ideals up. And you can't love him anymore. That's what happened?'

'Not really, I just don't like being with him. I've still got ideals, because of how it used to be. And it could have worked out, if he hadn't been such an idiot.' He paused for a moment. 'I've seen it in other people. You know, how much they love their wife, how strong it is. I really think it's possible.' He paused again. 'Not that you need me to tell you that.'

'No, it's inspiring.'

He studied the table, then looked at her. 'But you must think like that?'

She didn't know how to answer.

'I mean in that you remember how it was with your husband. Or I suppose you still love him.'

She thought about what he'd told her. Her saga, in all its she-saids and he-saids, seemed revolting in comparison.

'I'd give anything to talk to him.' She was listening to herself speak. 'Perhaps you're taking that for granted. With your father I mean.' But she carried on, compelled to say it. 'One day we'll be dead. You can't forget it. You have to assess yourself, everyone you've ever loved, *knowing* that like it's been branded inside you.'

She stopped. This truth in which hid the source of life's preciousness, the only perspective on petty neuroses, and in which lurked hopeless paralysis.

'What would you say to him?'

She looked up. She had no short answer so she said nothing.

But he didn't speak either. It was as if she was in the

room with a stranger, both of them waiting for something. And it hardly mattered whether she spoke, except that there was a kindness and intelligence about him that made her think honesty was all he deserved and all he'd tolerate.

'It came out of the blue,' she said. 'We argued the night before. I even threatened to leave him for a few days. Not seriously, but he didn't know that. When I woke up the next morning, I could hear him, I knew he was still in the house. I was literally on the point of getting up to talk to him when I heard the front door close. I should have shouted from the window, but I was cross he hadn't said goodbye. I had to go to work, I thought it could wait.

'Later that morning, I got a call from the local hospital. They said he wasn't well, so I went in. He was already dead.

'I thought it was the argument, I felt terrible, I knew I'd panicked him. Then I found out he had this genetic cholesterol condition. My daughter might have inherited it, but it's treatable, she should be all right. The point is, if he'd been treated, he'd still be alive. He'd never mentioned it so I assumed he hadn't known, but then I spoke to his family. His mother – who I didn't really get on with – had been warned about it years ago. She told me he'd had the test and they'd agreed not to discuss it.

'At first I thought that was a complete lie. If he'd had the test, he'd have told me, done something about it. But little things occurred to me, it wasn't inconceivable. And I thought, surely she would have told him he was at risk – he was her son, why wouldn't she?

'Then something else happened. I've never known my father, but soon after my husband died, my mother met this man. It was wonderful for her, but to me it seemed like my daughter was the only one left, and even that wasn't for sure. Without her, I don't think I'd be here.

'And then… ' she saw the sympathy on his face. She took a breath. 'This is the last shit bit. His mother – the one who said he'd had the test – had a nervous breakdown. It was soon after he died but I didn't take it in at first. She's still alive, but she's not well, she can hardly speak.

'And after that, I got fixated. I still am. I come to see her every six months, not out of kindness, just to try to get her to talk. It's shameful. But I can't bear the fact that he might have known and not told me. Not even taken any action. It's like a devil on my shoulder. It calls everything into question. That's what I meant when I said I wasn't free of it.'

He looked at her. She didn't meet his eyes.

'I still can't sleep without being physically exhausted. In the first year, I walked over a thousand miles.' She paused. 'I work ridiculously hard. I look after my daughter. The odd guy invites me for coffee, I say no. And that's it. Loneliness creeps up on you. You get obsessed with yourself, you can't get interested in anyone else. Even my husband – I couldn't remember him properly at the beginning.' She looked down. 'We'd talk about how scared we were that the other would die. I thought that if I worried about him dying, it wouldn't happen. Or if we loved each other enough. Now I just turn into a child and pretend he's still alive. But it's dangerous, not living in the real world, it doesn't work forever.'

She sighed, her voice quiet with talking, Alex still intent, as if he knew she hadn't finished.

'The truth is there's no one you can rely on. People die, however much you love them. I used to be incredibly idealistic about love. But it's impossible – it doesn't last. It's what you see when you're happy – it's a trick of perspective.'

He flinched slightly.

'I don't mean you should let it go, it's too nice. But it's just a trick.'

He didn't say anything.

'So that's why I'm here,' she said, 'to talk to his mother. Give it another chance.' She smiled. 'And feed you pulses.' She blew her nose. 'Maybe now I'm not so – overwrought, it will be easier.'

He was making her babble with his quiet.

'… Sorry, I sound wretched.'

'No. You sound resilient.'

They both sat quietly.

'Before he died,' he said, 'you loved each other?'

'Yes.'

'And then he died and his mother said in effect that he hadn't wanted to live, as if he hadn't wanted to be with you – '

'Yes, exactly.' She couldn't believe he'd understood so well.

He paused. 'I think you love him more than anything.'

She was silent.

'If you didn't, you wouldn't be this preoccupied. So you shouldn't worry about whether he knew or not.'

'What?'

'I mean, your obsession – with finding out what happened – proves your love.'

'No it doesn't, it proves my distrust.'

'But it's a distrust you're constantly trying to turn into trust.'

'Yes, but I can't possibly succeed. Either he knew and didn't get treated, which comes down to suicide. Or he thought it was a possibility and ignored it, which is almost as reckless. Or his mother said nothing, which is appalling.'

She waited for a moment.

He didn't say anything.

'I don't know,' her voice relaxed slightly, 'his father died of the same thing, perhaps his mother couldn't face losing someone again – she pretended he was fine, blanked it out completely – and then when he died, she had to admit what she'd done, at least to herself. I know they had a big argument around the time she found out – about what he was going to do with his life, but it must have been more than that.'

'So in fact you've decided she didn't tell him. You don't actually doubt him.'

'No. Listen to me. I doubt him all the time, for hundreds of reasons. I'm a mother, the last thing I'd do is let my child die, she told me he'd had the test, he routinely deluded himself about pretty much anything, the last time I spoke to him was in anger, and I can't ever speak to him again.' She paused. 'When someone you love – someone you *thought* you loved – dies, you begin to doubt *everything*.'

'But I don't see why you would even talk like this if you didn't love him.'

'Well clearly because I used to love him and now I have no idea.'

'I think you have every idea,' he said. 'You still love him, you miss him and you don't want to stop thinking about him.'

She stared at him, staggered that he was defying her. 'Why do you want me to love him so much?'

'I don't believe what you said about tricks of perspective, not for love.'

'You're arguing with me about my life for the sake of that? An abstract belief?'

Again, he was quiet.

'Okay, so you think we're incapable of self-deceit? You think everything we feel as true in the heat of it is true forever? I'd give anything for that to be the case but it just isn't. You know it's amazing how wrong you can be while being certain you're right.

'Then consider that you're wrong now.'

She stopped herself from replying immediately. She looked at him but his expression gave away nothing.

'I used to be like you,' she said. 'Naive enough to be unforgiving. I'd have said the same things. But life has a habit of stripping you bare. You realise the world isn't how you thought.'

'That's no reason to ditch what you live for.'

'It is if you're living for something that doesn't exist.'

'No, I'm believing in something that not everyone will

experience. You were lucky to love your husband for the time that you did. Some people never do that. Forget what's happened since, think back to when he was alive. You have to realise that true love is possible. That survives anything.'

'But Alex, it's never perfect, you must understand that. In reality, people fight each other, let each other down and die.'

'But they also love each other and live.'

'What are you arguing for? Love that survives death?'

'Why not? You think of your husband as existing still.'

'What, some disembodied soul floating in heaven? Of course I don't.'

'But you talk about him, you remember him. You pretend he's still alive. It's like thinking about someone you love when you're not with them. He exists *in you*.'

'Yes,' she whispered, 'but whatever I do, he doesn't exist *in him*.'

She hesitated. 'It's wrong of you, to talk like this to me. All these fantasies and ideals, they're so attractive but believing in them doesn't make them true. I can fantasise all I like, it won't bring him back. It's the truth that matters. Only the truth.'

'Usually, but not always. Not in this case.'

'Bullshit.'

'I'm not just saying it for the sake of it.'

'Nor am I.'

'I mean, I've thought it through.'

'Yeh I think most of us have.'

They looked at each other. Ashamed of herself, she realised it was a relief to be arguing properly.

He made to get up.

'Wait – ' She held his arm.

'What?'

'Tell me what you think.'

He sighed. 'Let's calm down for a second.'

'Why?'

'I don't want to fight.'

'We're not fighting, we're having a reasoned argument about abstract ideas.' Then she whispered, 'It's a substitute for sex.'

He stared at her. 'I disagree with you already.'

'Good,' she smiled. And she wondered what had made her say that and began to laugh. 'You think I'm sick. It's only honesty.'

'No,' he said, an edge to his voice, 'I've never once thought that.'

She felt her thoughts loosen as she watched him. 'Well, that's the foreplay done with.'

He looked away as he smiled. 'I'd better not wait any longer.'

He went into the kitchen. She wondered what on earth he meant.

It was getting dark outside. She could see the cars' headlights on the other side of the river.

He came out with two small bowls and put one down in front of her. Raspberry mousse.

They sat on the carpet as they ate, their backs resting against the sofa, and she brought him back to their conversation.

He said he thought truth was like a city, with science as its palace. It was what she called a trick of perspective that the earth was flat. You got hold of more evidence, the palace was re-built. Then there was moral truth –

'You see I want to live in this city,' she said, 'that's exactly where I want to be, I love that idea.' She was grateful to him. 'You're good to talk to... So science is a palace, what's morality, an empty block of flats?'

He smiled. 'A treehouse that keeps getting blown down.'

'Yeh,' she smiled back. '... And maths is the orangery next to the palace. Or something made of glass.'

'Yeh exactly.'

'Music,' she said, ' – music's the garden. You plant

things, and look after things, but the beauty's too much for a human to claim.'

There was a spark in his eyes as he looked at her, in the way of someone who has had a private thought augmented. She was aware again that she was with him. The way he was, the way they were talking, it was real. It made her feel barely physical but wholly present.

He was no longer smiling, but simply looking back at her.

Almost imperceptibly he touched her fingers. She felt the tips of his fingers on hers. There was the smallest suspicion of a smile on his face, like a faraway star, better seen by glancing away.

She nearly kissed him but stopped herself.

The friends thing, it was a strange idea. But maybe not a bad one.

'Languages,' she came into focus. 'Rivers. Or no, bridges… '

If they were going to break the rule, they'd have to break it together.

'… So,' she cleared her throat, ' – but I don't know about truth in music. I suppose singing can combine truth and beauty. That's the best way to get to people. To their senses and emotions as well as their reason. You know when you see a swan and you realise it can master land and water as well as the air? A song's like that.'

He smiled and again she felt the drifting, over-real sensation.

But it would do, she thought. Someone to talk to freely like this. To be with someone, properly, as herself, to like and understand someone that much, it would do.

He gave a short sigh, then sat up. 'You might not want to hear what I was going to say.'

'Go on.'

'Well I think even in this truth place there are things you have to take on trust.'

'Like what?'

'Like believing the world exists as you see it. Without that, your life doesn't make sense and science wouldn't exist. Or believing other people have inner feelings like you do, otherwise we couldn't live with each other and morality would be a waste of time. And the irony is you believe in those things whether they're true or not. Even if you knew they were false, you'd still believe in them, because if you didn't, you couldn't function.

'What I'm saying is that believing in love is just as essential, even if you don't want to admit it. You're willing to curb your doubt to make your everyday life possible, you do it all the time. You just have to do your emotional life the same favour.'

'But Alex you don't have to believe in love for life to make sense. One, that's sentimental fantasy, and two, why should life make sense anyway? People ask what's the point of life, why should there even be one?'

'Because we're human, that's what we crave.' He paused. 'There's more to life than the things you can prove to be true, you have to accept that. Take music. You said the beauty's too much for a human to claim. That's unlikely to be true from a scientific point of view. But even if there's nothing more than people making sound, you can't ignore the fact that you *feel* as if there is. Ignoring that, it's like being a tree without leaves – you die from the inside.'

She didn't answer.

Then she said, 'What do you mean by love? Tell me that.'

'Caring for someone else intensely, as if that person were yourself, acknowledging their inner life as you acknowledge your own, for as long as you are conscious.'

Silently she thought about what he'd said, its scope and its limit.

'I think,' she said finally, 'you believe in God. That's the term for your essential beliefs. The world exists, love exists, thanks be to God.'

'Maybe, I hadn't thought of it like that… My grandmother

had this Greek saying, 'Trying to prove God exists is like trying to eat soup with a fork'.'

'Right, because we made God up.'

'But so what if we did? There's so much we'll never know for sure. In a finite life, you have to find an answer.'

'By living in a dreamworld.'

'No. By using your common sense.'

She smiled. He smiled back.

'No surrender?' she whispered.

He blinked slowly, like a clock winding down. 'Never.'

She kissed the air in front of him, liking everything about him. She saw him blush and felt herself do the same.

Breathily, she started to sing.

'… Our lips shouldn't touch… Move over darling… '

'You're a Siren,' he whispered. He got up and went towards the kitchen.

'That's not nice.'

Alone in the room again, a thought struck her.

'Alex?'

He poked his head around the door. 'See, you can sing after all.'

'You still haven't told me the answer,' she said to his shoulders.

'What?'

'Well why you want me to love him so much.'

He looked at her. 'You know the answer.'

'No I don't.'

He turned back into the kitchen. 'If you can't love him, you won't be able to love anyone else.'

27

'Our Love Is Here To Stay'
by George and Ira Gershwin and Vernon Duke

I couldn't speak Italian, but I'd been cursed with the urge to keep trying. Sitting in the restaurant after supper, me making it up, you laughing at my incompetence, the words *mozzarella di bufala* slipped from your lips in an accent that made the waiter stop in his tracks.

I asked you to say it again. *Mozzarella di bufala.* Like a girl on a garden swing, the Italian you floated into my mind. I had to hear it again. *Mozzarella di bufala.* I was addicted to you saying *mozzarella di bufala. Mozzarella di bufala. Mozzarella di bufala.*

Of course you could speak Italian. Verdi, Puccini, it was obvious.

'*Mozzarella di bufala*,' I said, wanting you to say it again.

'*Bravo*,' you smiled.

'*Grazie professore*.'

Your eyes sparkled. '*Professoressa*,' you whispered.

Yes, how stupid of me. *Professoressa*, of course.

The waiter approached our table. He began talking to you in Italian. You said something Italian in reply and he oozed all over you like a wanton oil slick.

If there was an Olympic sport of keeping a conversation

with an attractive woman going for as long as possible, whatever the situation, whoever else may suffer, there would be no point any other nation sending a team. Damn them and damn my incurable admiration.

But hang on Gilles, wake up for God's sake, you're cheering this pest on.

I told him in French that you, Vee, were the woman of my dreams, and suggested he leave us alone.

He'd gone before I'd finished. You'd apparently already asked him to leave.

'Sorry,' you said.

'What did he say?'

'Just,' you whispered, 'something about my chest. I told him to go shit in the woods.'

I looked at the little masturbite standing against the bar in the distance.

We finished and I paid the bill.

On our way out, I unbuttoned my shirt and gave him a flash of my assets. Beautiful, weren't they? He could look, I said, but he couldn't touch.

He laughed in an unamused way and told me, on translation, that I should go shit in the woods.

You were chuckling as we stopped on the pavement. 'I can't believe you did that.'

'I don't want him thinking about you all night.' I was going to say something crass about that being my job, but you'd started buttoning up my shirt. And I thought, tread softly.

We walked hand in hand.

When we came to my street, I said, 'My flat's just up here on the left.'

I felt you tense.

'The one with the face,' I pointed it out as we walked past, 'funny isn't it?'

'Oh yeh.' You relaxed the further away we walked.

For all my furious fantasising, I was relieved. The me

with you by my side was in danger of becoming incomprehensible to the me alone.

Vee, you were twenty-one, I was twenty-seven. You lived in Walton-on-Thames with your mother, I had a flat in Earlsfield. I didn't say it but I was pleased you lived with your mother.

I'd never heard of Walton-on-Thames. It was a wealthy suburb in Surrey, you said, where people drank gin and tonic and competed about where they went on holiday. You hated the place, you couldn't understand why your mother had stayed there so long.

Why hate, I asked.

No one questioned the formula, you said, there was no nobler, more imaginative ideal.

And I thought what a strange thing age can do. How if you're not careful it can make you stop being the next generation and sink back into being the last. And I felt invigorated by your youth.

One brother you had.

Me? No brothers, no sisters.

Together we asked questions. How old was he – ? Did I miss not having – ?

Yes. I did miss it.

His name was Matthew. Four years older than you.

He was married, you said. He had a baby. You'd see him this weekend, at the christening, they were doing it at Easter –

This weekend. I seized up.

You said you'd get the ferry on Friday, it was all happening in Kent.

Friday? But it was Wednesday now. And the weekend, Friday night, Saturday, Sunday, the pearls I spent my life diving for, swept away.

Then the lightning struck. I was a felled tree, split down the middle. *Easter*. This was a *BANK HOLIDAY WEEKEND*.

I tried to speak calmly. 'So you're away for the whole weekend?'

'Yeh.'

Shit.

'Sorry,' you said sweetly.

'When are you coming back?'

'Monday.'

God above.

'Morning?'

You paused. 'Lunchtime.'

'I'll miss you,' I said quickly.

You looked at me.

'*Mozzarella*,' you said.

Oh luscious sound.

'*Mozzarella*,' you smiled.

I went to kiss you but you stopped me again. I couldn't understand it.

'I'm not a prick,' I said.

You were chuckling again. 'I just said I hadn't decided.' You looked up. 'You know, even when you're serious you make me laugh.'

'Yeh well I'm serious all right.'

I held your gaze, saw you take it in. The street was quiet.

I took your hand and kissed your cheek, that was acceptable. And then you sighed, and I kissed your hand, slowly and lovingly, and the smell of your skin, the way you breathed and moved, were injected into me.

I asked you if you'd ever been in love.

You said no. At least, you were in love with music. It made you feel alive. Perhaps that was similar. But not with a man. You thought you had been once, but you hadn't. You paused. You sometimes wondered if your name was a joke – the goddess of love.

I told you never to think that. Your name was perfect.

I asked you whether you wanted to know what my name meant.

Gilles, you said. Farmer on whose land are many hedges?

No.

Wait. You had it. Carpenter with special aptitude in the construction of beds.

I laughed. I wished it were true.

Small goat, I said. SMALL goat. From the Greek word *aigidios* meaning not just goat, but small goat. I made a bleating noise as proof.

You giggled, you said goats had a sense of humour.

I said you didn't have to make the best of it. Anyway it got worse – did you know that tragedy literally meant *goat-song*? The chorus in the old Greek plays used to dress up in goat-skins. Didn't they realise there'd be a man named Gilles who wished they'd resolved their fetish off stage?

You were laughing.

You said listen, it was okay – the chorus wouldn't have fitted into *small* goat skins – they would have had to use obscenely large goats surely, to get enough skin.

Yes, I hadn't thought of that before. What a good point.

Darling, you wanted to know all about the women I'd been to bed with, how many there were, who they were, why we'd split up, everything. You were so interested in the subject I knew the truth was pointless. I told you about the four that came into my head first. Armed with data, you asked more questions.

I said I didn't want to dwell on other people. I wanted to dwell on you. You didn't know how much I thought about you.

'Oh dear,' you sounded like a concerned nurse. You touched my forehead. 'With this?' you asked, 'or… ' You gently touched my right hand.

It was as if you were gliding towards me, like a water-bird fresh from its nest, frankness and modesty all at once, getting away with both.

I glanced down, the embarrassed patient. 'I'm rather worried,' I whispered solemnly, 'that my head might fall off.'

'Oh God – ' You stifled a laugh.

And then you lifted my right hand and kissed my palm, your tongue hot and light on my skin for a shiver of a second.

Vee to think about it. Your inexhaustible supply of erotic occasions. Could the holiest saint fail to rise?

But you didn't let me loose. More details about the fourth. Not you was it? After all, we hadn't slept together had we? *No Miss Venus we hadn't.*

I had no idea how thoroughly you'd remember that conversation. One thoughtless remark after our first spellbinding summer and you were on your way out.

When we'd screamed and cried, when I felt sure you'd understood that I'd only lied because I loved you, still and calm you said you would go home, to your mother. You were sorry, you said, but you had to trust me, that was all that mattered.

I was so shocked I had to catch my breath. How could we let this happen? Two people who loved each other, it was insane. I'd do anything to show you I loved you.

'I want to believe you,' you said. 'But how can I when you lie?'

'But if I hadn't, that would have been it. I lied *because I love you* – '

'No Gilles, listen. I want you to tell me the truth more than I want you to love me. Of course I want you to love me,' you said. 'And I love you, I know that. But if I had to choose between you loving me and you telling me the truth, I'd choose the truth.'

I felt both forsaken and honoured. But so cold Vee. I wished you hadn't said it.

We hadn't got there yet. And if I'd told the truth back on that spring evening down by the Seine, we wouldn't have got anywhere.

We left the girlfriend discussion on the right bank and crossed the Pont Louis Philippe, the river surging underneath, the reflected moon almost full above us. We walked down the steps on the other side of the island and strolled along the cobbled *quai* by the water. There were more steps, set into the edge of the bank, that lead right into the water. We walked down to the last dry step. The crests and pools were picked out by the city lights. We stretched a hand into the current and minutely diverted the rush. And it seemed that if we watched the river long enough it would run through us.

'What are you thinking?'

'Oh,' you said, 'nothing much.'

We sat on the steps higher up.

'… I used to walk by the Seine a lot when I was little.'

'… We'd always walk along the Thames to Hampton Court. My mother would make us traipse around the whole thing.' You looked askance. 'That's what happens when you have a teacher for a parent.'

I smiled, I could have guessed it. 'What does she teach?'

'Oh, she's a headmistress now, but languages, and piano.'

'I had piano lessons,' I said proudly.

'Seriously?' You began to laugh. 'You practised and everything?'

'Of course. I might even be better than you.'

'Oh you think so?' Your eyes were two diamonds of self-assurance. 'Let me see your hands.'

You measured them against yours, flexed my fingers.

'What was your teacher like?'

'She was the only pretty woman within a hundred miles of my school… ' You were testing each finger incredibly delicately. '… Nothing like you though.'

'So you only skipped one or two lessons?'

'… Correct.'

'Well,' you said, putting my hands together, 'you've got

nice fingers.' You looked away. 'Maybe she liked to watch them, touching her piano keys.'

'It's possible,' I said, 'that she did.'

I was beginning to see how you played your game. I wondered, if I could restrain myself, how dizzying it might become.

The river lapped.

'It's funny,' you said, 'there was this guy who came for piano lessons who I'm sure liked my mother. He'd come in the evening after work. He always stayed late. Sometimes he even had supper.'

'Wasn't your father annoyed?'

'No.' You paused. 'My father's... missing,' you said quietly. 'He left before I was born, I have to think of him as dead.'

'Oh God – ' I took your hand. I ached to tell you. 'My father died when I was six.'

And we understood then, even if we could later forget it, that it was unlikely we'd be apart.

I don't know how long we stayed on the steps. Animated and still, animated and still, like the river, letting it sink in.

We'd both looked for him, a more reasonable thing for you to do than me. But your mother had done everything, followed every clue.

What you told me – Vee, it broke my heart. How could anyone do that?

You said he knew you were a girl, it had been his idea to call you Venus. Perhaps it was the responsibility. He was afraid, your mother had said, of becoming emotional. Things would overwhelm him. It was hard to understand if you'd never experienced it.

He'd had to go to a special hospital, a few years before. He'd started lecturing again, he taught maths. Everyone thought he was better. But obviously he wasn't.

Still by the river we were. Not noticing the evening cooling.

Not speaking much. My thoughts flooding around our conversation. I wondered if some part of you could hear them.

You said that it was strange – you almost didn't come to Paris. You'd planned to go with a friend but she'd backed out. And then the French lessons, you'd just organised them on a whim. Nothing to do with the Guildhall.

I said I was only here because the first person they'd asked said no. Even then, I'd hesitated.

And when it was raining before the lesson, I'd considered not turning up. But my written French was so bad, I thought I ought to make an effort.

You took my hands.

'Good student,' you said.

It would be better than being in the office at least.

'Was it?'

I smiled. Of course it was.

You glanced at me.

Back on court. Playing it from the baseline. Eye on the ball. Coasting it over, easing it over.

Surely, I thought, I'd earned it by now.

I looked at you, smiled at your wide smile, grinned at your coy grin. Wanted only to kiss you. Anticipated my lips on yours, closing over yours, bent towards you.

Like a piece of elastic you sprang up off the step and ran. You didn't look back, you knew I'd follow. Laughing wildly, racing through the night.

The *quai* narrowed to the width of a person, and sloped down to the height of the river. On the land side was a cliff-like wall that went up to road level. On the river side was a lower wall, built up above the *quai*. I imagined you'd carry on running along the *quai*, it was rarely wet, but as soon as it began to descend – yes, of course.

You were sprinting along the top of the wall. River on one side, drop on the other.

For God's sake, what was I worried about? I could have roller-skated along that crappy wall.

I jumped up. It was easy, you'd be fine. And if you fell in the river, sweet heaven was I eager to save you.

I was gaining on you. I looked at you, running, flying.

A slipway ran up the other side where the wall ended. The river had partly covered it. You could jump from the wall back on to the *quai* but there was hardly any landing space. Or you could jump over I couldn't see how much water, to get to the dry part of the slipway. Or you could stop running, get down slowly off the wall and back on to the *quai*.

I knew what you were going to do. I felt my grip on the world loosen, that pressure in my chest, the physical panic.

You jumped, vanished. Then the sound of spray and you reappeared, running up the slipway, on towards the road. I breathed out.

I caught you on the slipway. Nothing polite about it.

28

'Beauty Boy'
by Suzie Ungerleider

'Shall I turn on another light?' Venus leant forward on the sofa. She was watching Alex look through his CDs in the red-tinged glow.

'It's okay, I think I know where it is.'

She undid the buttons on her cuffs and rolled up her sleeves. His flat seemed to be getting warmer.

'What happens when you take your glasses off? Can you still see?'

'Yeh kind of, not at a distance.'

Venus checked her watch. It was half-past eleven.

'Alex, you know I should be going. Aren't you working tomorrow?'

'Wait, no, don't go.'

'I still don't know what you do,' she smiled.

Sighing, he looked through the last few CDs. 'It's not here… I can't find it.'

She'd give it five minutes then go, she thought.

He stood up. She thought he'd sit with her, but he took a folded contraption from behind the sofa which turned into a sort of sun-lounger.

'It's not difficult is it?' he was asking. 'Staying a bit longer?'

'No,' she said. 'Of course not.'

'Good,' he smiled.

When he sat down on it, he pushed himself back and the whole seat tilted so that it was as if he was lying in a hammock.

'What an amazing thing,' she said.

'Yeh. I got it for sunbathing on the *quai* but I can never be bothered to take it down.'

She lay back on the sofa and looked sideways at him, but he didn't see.

'I like the thought of you sunbathing,' she said quietly.

'... You have to know where to avoid.'

She looked over at him, wondering what he meant.

'I went to the bit by the park at the end of the island when I first moved in. These two men came down the steps calling and whistling. I had no idea it was a gay hang out. There was no access other than those steps. They kind of had me cornered.'

'Really? God, what did you do?'

'Got my keys and dived into the river.'

Venus turned her head to look at him. 'No way.'

'Yeh.'

She was laughing.

She imagined him gliding through the water, leaving his pursuers on the bank.

'It was hot anyway, so... ' He looked at her. 'Do you like swimming?'

'Yeh. In the sea more... So wait, how did you get out?'

'Up the steps, just after Pont de la Tournelle.'

'Right out here?'

'Yeh.'

She smiled. 'Quicker than walking?'

'Yeh,' he smiled back.

She stretched for his hand.

'How was the water?' She laughed.

'Not bad.'

She imagined him swimming in the river, and then under the arch of a bridge.

'God what about the boats? You could have got squashed.' She pressed his hand. 'Don't do that again.'

She felt him look at her. She took her hand away. '… D'you know that story about the man who swam the Hellespont every night?'

'Hero and Leander?' he asked.

'What happens again? He swims to see her – '

'Yeh. Then one night it's stormy, she holds up a lantern to guide him but the wind blows the flame out. So he gets lost and drowns. And then she finds his body and drowns herself.'

'Mm.'

They were quiet.

'But,' she said, 'better brief happiness… '

'Yeh,' he said.

'So he'd swim to her and then swim all the way back again, the same night. That must have been tiring.'

'Yeh,' he said, as if it hadn't occurred to him before. 'They don't make much of the return journey.'

Venus stretched.

'Do you speak Greek, you know with your grandmother?'

'No… just a few words.' He paused. 'I should really improve my French.'

She thought for a second. 'You don't use it at work?'

'A bit.'

'So come on, what is it?' she asked. 'Drugs, guns?'

He looked over at her. 'Bonds.'

'Working for a bank?'

'Well, different banks, as clients.'

She laughed. 'Why didn't you want to tell me that?'

He shrugged. 'It's only money. Once you've got the hang of how everything works.'

'You mean, you find it boring? Or you don't like the aim of it?'

'Both.'

He sounded oddly accepting. Like he needed to dive into the river but couldn't.

'Why don't you do something else?'

'I don't know. Habit. No good reason.' Then he added, 'It's okay until you stop and think, you know, it's not terrible, just limited.'

She could hear Gilles saying the same thing, the way he'd submit to this loop of dissatisfaction and inertia. As if life would sit and wait.

'What about you?'

And she'd got pregnant and there was an excuse. And his childhood dreams drifted, like plankton waiting for a fish…

'I mean other than sing.'

… He didn't know what he hoped for. Like that it could be anything. Its vague perfection guaranteeing disappointment. Was that supposed to be virtue? To be alive, to be on the right side of the most insane piece of generosity ever devised, and play it *small*?

'For God's sake,' she breathed impatiently. People were like this, life drifting, letting it go when it was there for the taking.

'What?' Alex seemed slighted.

She sat up, tried to hide her anger. 'I can't understand it. I mean why not do what you want?'

'That's the stupid thing, I don't know what else to do.'

'Please don't say that.'

'What?'

'You're telling me you have absolutely *no idea* what you want to do?'

'Sorry but it's true.'

'That's pathetic.'

He was speechless for a second. 'Everyone questions themselves,' he began, 'you can't pretend it's easy.'

'Easy? Look at you, how could it get easier?'

He made a tired noise. 'Why do you have to argue?'

Years of rage spilled over inside her. 'You want me to

accept it? For what, for convenience? Live like you're dead, it's so much less effort, so manageable.'

'And you've never had a moment of self-doubt?'

'Can't you see how trivial that is?' she breathed. 'You have to *want life*.'

With a sigh he closed his eyes. 'It's not a big deal.'

He hadn't felt the force of what she'd said. He was lying down, fight-less, retired from the conversation and the fact she was there.

The shock hit her like a fist in the chest: it was up to her to teach him. She got up, a sense in her head of playing a part, went to the table and picked up the black-handled knife she'd used to cut the bread. She went back, saw his eyes still closed, knelt down beside him and, someone else now surely, brought the knife to an inch above his throat.

Aware of her there, he opened his eyes, caught the glint at the edge of his vision.

'Venus – ' He was tilting the sun-lounger back upright.

But this was real.

He stared at her. 'What are you doing?'

She didn't react.

'Venus.' He pushed at her arm.

She pushed back, breathing hard.

'*Ugh*.' He clenched his teeth.

She set her jaw, her heart pounding.

He shoved her arm back, the blade flying out of her hand, catching the side of his own arm before hitting the floor, the blood falling in small drips.

She was shaking, her fingers were shaking.

There was blood – on the floor, on his shirt.

She couldn't catch her breath.

'Venus?'

She couldn't slow her breaths. She hid her face.

'Look at me.'

Tears behind it.

'Look at me.'

'I'll – I'll help you,' she whispered, 'then I'll go.'

He grabbed her hands.

Overcome, she looked up as he kissed her. Then behaving as if he hadn't, he told her to sit down while he got some water. But she picked up the knife, went to the kitchen and dropped it into the sink.

He filled a glass with water and gave it to her.

She drank some, her hand shaking. She put down the glass.

' – Sorry,' she breathed.

'It's fine, it's hardly bleeding.' He drank the rest then filled it again.

She scanned the room for a bowl, gathering things she could use to clean it.

She got tissues, pressed them against his arm, replacing the tissues with new ones and pressing again, watching the tissues for blood.

Sighing, she clamped her eyes closed. '... God I'm sorry... ' She wiped the tears off her cheek. 'I like you beyond anything – '

She put on a new set of tissues and pressed harder.

'It doesn't hurt?'

'No,' he said, 'thanks.'

She looked at him. 'Sorry, I mean it – ' she faltered. 'I get this awful, intense emotion, I'd never have – '

'I like you too,' he said.

They were quiet.

When she next took the tissues off, the bleeding had stopped. She found a plaster in her bag and put it on the cut. There was nothing more to do.

'I'll leave you alone.'

She took her bag into the bathroom. She went to the loo, washed her face, drank more water, then put the lid of the loo down and sat on it. She couldn't stay.

Her phone was flashing. She checked her messages.

Charlotte, an hour ago: *Caught Max in bed w f-ing fone.*

He swore he wouldn't take it. No talent, hotel crawling w devout capitalists. F-ing livid. Over.

She replied: *Leave him then. V x*

She made the message alert noise louder and tossed her phone back into her bag.

What was wrong with her? It was as if she wanted to be unhappy, and when life wouldn't conspire against her, she would.

She'd just have to leave.

She opened the bathroom door.

'How are you feeling?' Alex called.

'Like a complete fucking lunatic.'

But he laughed.

'No, Alex. I did a terrible thing.'

'Here.' He handed her a plate of fruit.

'You can't be nice. What if I'm a lunatic?'

'You've still got to eat.'

Confused, she looked at him as they ate.

He told her about a man he'd worked with who'd died suddenly. How much he'd liked him. How it had made him think.

'He knew what mattered,' he said. 'Like you.'

Why was he being kind?

'You didn't need a knife.'

'I know – sorry, God I – '

'No, listen,' he looked straight at her. 'You make me feel alive. You're enough on your own.'

'Wait Alex, no, you really don't have to be like that.'

'Don't tell me what to do. – I feel I can say anything to you.'

'But – only because you make me feel like that.'

'Well that's even better.'

Disorientation, fear and happiness bundled together inside her.

'I'm falling in love with you. And if you don't want that, please say now.'

She froze for a moment, then saw the frankness on his face.

'I know what I want to do before I die – in this aspect at least.' He studied her, then looked away. 'We only met on Saturday. You just nearly killed me. I must sound stupid – '

Her eyes watered. How she longed to love him back.

She tried to put her feelings into words, then startled, felt him touch her hand. Sensing it, he swallowed. She put her hand over his, and could only think of lying with him as their hands were.

His lips opened, as if he could see into her head.

She looked at him, his expression without shyness or presumption. And her stomach felt like it was hollowing out with longing.

But there was a noise coming from somewhere. An insistent beeping noise. She stayed still. It was her phone.

'*God*.'

It continued.

She sighed. 'It might be about my daughter.'

He looked down, smiling. 'Go on.'

She went to the table and checked her messages. '… For Christ's sake.'

'What?' He was leaning over the side of the sofa, looking in the cupboard under the stereo.

Another text from Charlotte: *Lush Yank on tennis court. New balls please*.

'It's nothing, it's Charlotte. I shouldn't have checked.'

She put her phone down on the table. He seemed to be looking for something.

'What's she say?'

'She found Max in bed with his phone. Working I suppose. Now she's chasing some American.'

'Oh,' Alex smiled.

She picked up her phone, switched it off and put it down.

He opened the window and she came back to the sofa, kneeling on it like she'd done before supper. He knelt down next to her and they rested on the window sill, looking out at the river, the bridge and the lights shining in the dark.

She closed her eyes and breathed in. The air was like water.

'I found it by the way – the Lark Ascending.'

'Oh well done.'

She smiled to herself.

She opened her eyes a very little and in the blur made out his arms on the window sill next to hers. She closed them again.

'Has Charlotte gone yet?'

'Nearly,' she smiled. '... Sorry,' she whispered, 'about everything.'

'It's okay, it's nothing.'

'Well, it's not.'

'In comparison I mean.'

She listened to his voice again in her head.

'You're so... good to be with,' she said.

The window moved softly against the catch, then settled as the breeze died down.

'I'm thinking of you swimming in the river,' she whispered.

You could go out there now, she thought. And she wondered whether if she were very still, she could hear the river, and the sound of him in it. And the sound of her going into it, the sound of them both in the water.

'Venus,' he whispered.

She opened her eyes and saw him looking at her. And then his face was full with it, a complete openness, so in need of its companion that her expression couldn't fail to answer his.

'Wait there – ' he breathed.

He got up and went towards the kitchen. He switched off the lights, and turned back to her in the dark.

She rested her forearms on the window sill, lay her head down sideways and listened to him come towards her. She sensed him behind her, then felt him lift her hair away from the back of her neck and kiss it, her breath in her throat.

She turned around thinking he would be in front of her but he put his hands on her shoulders, and turned her further so that it was her back that faced him.

Delicately he touched her neck, his fingers hesitant, the nerves in her skin fusing with his. He reached into her hair, behind her ears, and then his fingers were back on her bare skin, feeling for the line of her jaw, his little fingers stretching to her lips, her breath shaking as she licked his fingers, stroking his hands to bring them closer to her mouth, kissing his fingers at his broken breath, both of them so light with it, and then one of his hands feeling down to her right side, to the start of the swell of her breast as she leant closer to him, and the axis becoming fainter, the where and when of anything more remote, the quiet and his hands most of what there was.

He was undoing the buttons of her shirt. Carefully he moved her bra straps to the edges of her shoulders, kissing her skin.

Her mind was turning in on itself, half of her wanting to stay like this, half of her wanting to face him. But she didn't move. Just felt the quickening of her breath as his hands lifted her breasts. Swallowed as he let his fingers brush over the material that covered her nipples, his breath warm on her neck as their shape defined the material from underneath.

She felt his hand move down to her stomach, and put her hand over his, his hand moving under hers. Sighing to feel it, she spread her fingers between his.

They got up and went into the bedroom. It was warm and it smelt more of him. There was a high window but the curtains were open, letting in the light from the street lamps.

His expression was like a heat haze. Quickly, so as not to show she cried to see him, she kissed his lips. And he sighed with pleasure, as if it was something he hadn't expected.

She lifted her hand to his glasses, and when he'd taken

them off, they kissed again. And then he kissed her more strongly, bringing her closer, his kisses getting more and more passionate, so that she became subdued.

'Sorry – ' He caught his breath.

'No – ' she whispered. She felt for his fingers, gently taking them into her hand.

He hugged her to him, making a sound like an animal that was both wanting and contented. And with a wave of gladness and gratitude, she felt how right he was, how utterly right; that he seemed to have an instinct for her, that he could see the underneath of her no matter what she said or did.

She brushed her lips over the corner of his, kissing him slowly, her tongue on his lips, his lips kissing hers, kiss over kiss in overlaid desire.

She loved it that he could let her do it, kissed him more ardently, felt his hands move up to her breasts as her tongue met his.

The smell of him, the taste of him, her rushing pulse as she pushed up his t-shirt, her stomach tightening with anticipation.

He pulled his shirt off over his head.

And then his mouth was back on hers, each breathing the other's breath, his fingers unhooking the clasp of her bra, hers moving down his back, his holding her breasts, cupping them, squeezing them, feeling down her sides, in with her waist and out over her hips. She imagined them between her legs, the way his finger would slip, willed him to touch her there, but he was feeling up her body, kissing her mouth as if he were kissing between her hips.

The million things she could do with him blazed in her brain. She moved her hand below his waist, felt his cock set hard through his trousers.

He sighed, his breath in her mouth.

They took off their clothes and came back together, he running his fingers down from her back, along the insides of her legs, making her shudder as he touched the wet between.

Then she took his hand and drew his forefinger to her

mouth, rocking the tip of it on her lip, the finger of her other hand gliding over the top of his cock.

'Shh – ' he whispered, his breath quickening.

And as his eyes closed, she kissed his finger with her tongue and sucked it into her mouth.

'Uh – ' He tensed. ' – God – '

Bringing his finger to her lips again she stood on her toes, let his cock press against the outside of her cunt.

'Ah – ' he shivered, 'ah, stop – '

He grabbed her hands. Their eyes met for a second, her heart in a race. And close against her, he felt down her sides to her buttocks, squeezing them as he eased them apart, the wet spreading between her legs as he kissed down the front of her, crouching down, kissing her hips, kissing the inside of her thighs. She felt him tip her to him, the thought of what he might do in all of her mind, until his tongue touched her clitoris and cunt and she couldn't keep standing. His mouth, caressing her, making waiting any longer unbearable.

She brought them both onto the bed, pulling him on top of her, sliding her finger over her clitoris at the feel of his cock coming into her, aching with wanting him. She wrapped her legs around him, pushed him, couldn't hold on. And he moved up inside her, pressing up against her like he already knew her, until finally he was deep inside her.

They came almost immediately, barely moving. And with him lying partly over her, her with her arms around him, they stayed together for a while. Then lay down side by side, pulled the cover over them and fell asleep.

Higher the lark went, still there but always leaving. The strings became fuller, like the wind changing in the trees. They enveloped the lark, then softened and released it. It was breathtaking to hear it come back.

The orchestra was soaring, then falling away. Surging,

then gradually becoming quieter, waiting for the lark to return.

Until there it was again, no orchestra, flying alone on the warm air. Up, beyond everything, until it was almost gone. Almost but not quite, that high note still held.

And then there but not there, like an echo. And then gone.

When Venus woke up, there were tears caught in her eyelashes. Gilles and Leo, she couldn't find them, she'd looked everywhere.

But no, just a dream. God the saddest dream…

She was sweating. She closed her eyes. Just a dream, back to sleep.

Stunned, she opened them again. Realised it again. Scrambled for it in her mind like a beetle on its back. He is dead he is dead he is dead.

She breathed in, the tears falling down her face.

She wiped her eyes and tried to calm down. She looked around at the unfamiliar room and felt dazed, but then remembered she was in Paris. Gone to see Hélène in Paris. It was okay, ssh. Back to sleep.

Her heart jolted. Alex.

She turned and saw him sleeping beside her.

Quietly, she got up.

Her watch? It was still on her wrist. Ten past five. Shit.

She rushed about finding her clothes, got dressed, put on her sandals, collected her bag.

She went back into the bedroom. He was sleeping on his side, his face serenely beautiful. She looked in her bag for a piece of paper and a pen. All she could find was an intricate colouring book of Leonie's and some coloured pencils.

She looked around the living room for paper. Turned the kitchen light on. Nothing.

She flicked through the colouring book, then saw a page which was slightly ripped and carefully tore it out. On the back she wrote:

Dear Alex,

Sorry not to say goodbye. I had to go back.

Thank you, for a

She stopped. She crossed out the *a* and put *everything.*

See you soon I hope.

She hesitated, then wrote:

Love, Venus/Madeleine

ps excuse the paper – I will get a telling off from my daughter

She put the message on the table where they'd eaten, then wrote her mobile number on the bottom. Then also wrote down the Place des Vosges number. She put the paper on the middle of the table, picked up her things and left.

Outside, it was cold and dark. She started to run, then slowed back to a walk.

She turned down rue des Deux Ponts.

There was no point faking guilt. She'd wanted him so much she could still feel it.

She crossed the bridge to the right bank, the dark river underneath, the sky between black and blue, the cold on her skin.

He was dead, he no longer existed, that was the plain fact.

And how simple it could be.

She'd told Alex everything. It had only gone wrong before because she hadn't told him.

She turned right down rue Charlemagne.

How she liked him. It wasn't only… It was his care, such incredible care, she'd never met anyone like it.

And he liked her. No, he loved her.

Oh poor man.

Why was she crying? Why did she *keep* crying?

Left along rue St Paul.

But she could love him, his goodness, his thoughtfulness, his honesty, his way of being… His face, his hands…

There was a woman ahead, walking her dog, coming towards her. Venus pushed back her hair.

They smiled.

She walked on, brought up close to herself, trying not to cry.

Alex's niceness, Gilles' duplicity, her chants were getting swamped, her head saturated with Gilles' absence.

What did she have but the way she survived? He, with her, loving her whether he was loved back or not, whether he was alive or not. And now she held the two of them tight in her hand, like squeezing a glass, waiting for it to shatter.

She turned right down rue des Francs Bourgeois. There was a sound of a far away argument; a car's wheels screeched in the effort to leave. She walked faster.

She came to the square, back to the order of things, and stopped in her tracks.

'No,' she breathed.

Oh how *stupid*.

She felt her heart shrink, her pride fall. Hadn't done it for so long that she could actually *forget*.

What about him? What was he thinking? That she had it all sorted out?

Older woman, had a baby, ought to know.

Must have known.

She sighed.

Morning after pill. Doctor later.

Should she ring him? Tell him?

She started to walk. Ovulation two weeks from start of period. Last period – when? She tried to work it out. Ages ago surely?

She came to the door.

Four weeks ago surely? She turned the key.

29

'Sweet Nothin's'
by Dub Allbritten and Ronnie Self

Vee, if I hadn't tried it on by the river, you wouldn't have had the chance to refuse point blank. The answer was no. I was crazy about you.

By half-past five on Thursday, I was back in the *lycée*. Right on time, but there were already people sitting next to you. I went for the closest desk: two to the left in the same row.

I watched you open your purple folder. Two biros and a ruler. Your mother was a headmistress. It was in the blood.

Back to school I went. French teacher? Or no, Italian. And private extra lessons for boys named Gilles. Hmm, yes. And all around me the other boys would sweat with jealousy.

I noticed your shoes under the desk. Dark pink suede high-heeled sandals. For a French lesson? I felt a renewed confidence in the language of women.

Vee, during that lesson you were a model pupil. It brought out the worst in me. I stared at you distractedly. When the teacher asked me a question, I improvised; when she lectured, I fantasised. When she wrote on the board, I composed *billets-doux* on the firm's headed paper, folded them and when again she wasn't looking, skimmed them along the floor to you. My greatest work went something like this:

Venus
you tease
my penis
I deemed it worthy of your attention and sent it across.

I watched you. You unfolded it, read it, scrutinised me briefly, then looked ahead.

I waited for your smile but it didn't come. You didn't even look at me.

Oh, how childish had I been? Hadn't a twenty-seven-year-old man anything better in his head than this filthy smut? I sought out your gaze, hoping to re-establish relations.

You carried on looking ahead, but you had a wilful air about you, as if you were considering exposing me to the whole class.

And then you half closed your eyes. And your tongue crept to the corner of your mouth, licked round your upper lip as if you'd come out of the sea and needed to taste each particle of drying salt, and idled down to the other side. Like a frantic *papparazzo* I clicked my mental camera, scanned the image into my brain and played and replayed.

Six-thirty and we were out. Catching the odd glance from fellow students wondering what had gone on between us, talking and laughing in the warm spring evening.

We went down to rue Vieille du Temple, a beautiful, narrow street that purred with the tread of its *habitués* – elegant women, orthodox Jews, bookish men, long-nailed Indians and antique sellers, boyish girls and girlish boys. And their trophies – a paper, a bag, a carpet, a parrot, dog after dog, or just the clothes they stood in. People walking unencumbered, nothing to transport but themselves.

The place took us in. Be at home here, it said. Stay all night, do anything you like.

We sat down at an outside table and ordered tea and cakes. You watched a young man cycle shoulders back, no hands, wheels gliding along the tarmac. But oh cruel Venus, don't look at him, look at me.

Could I do that? No, I said, honestly. You neither.

Could I wolf whistle? No. You neither. But your friend Charlotte could.

Could you ski? No.

I could. Hahahaha.

Could I dive? As in with oxygen tanks? No.

You could. I didn't believe you.

But I could snorkel. I was good at snorkelling.

And I was excellent at ping pong. World class demon player.

Chess? No, I couldn't be bothered with that. You could.

Drive? Of course I could, what a question. Racing legend Gilles Villeneuve, my inspiration.

Well, you said, I was older.

'Wait,' you looked at me intently, 'have you got a car?'

'Of course.' It was my duty to rouse my mother's Citroën.

'Here?'

'Paris plates.' Mary would wangle it.

You smiled.

One to me, fruity shoes.

You wanted to know something. You paused for the question. 'Has it got a stereo?'

I knew that no was the wrong answer. I told you that yes, the car had the benefit of a portable stereo.

I gave my mother's Citroën more thought in that moment than it'd had in the previous five years. You going away for the weekend was bad enough, but at some point you'd go home properly and that would be doom itself. A lantern had been lit in my darkness. Driving North on a Friday, meeting you in Calais, scuttling away to Honfleur, walks by the sea, surging tides, galloping horses…

Cook? No, not really. Neither could you really, you said.

In fact you could and I couldn't.

Ride a horse? No.

I could. We could ride along the beach together?

But you were impressed. Those childhood lessons I was forced into were paying off.

Ice skate? No.

I could. Not gracefully, but fast.

Blow smoke rings? No. You neither.

Blow kisses? Yes. Yes. Yes.

Blow jobs? Oh now come on.

That strange land under the table-top. Your heat-seeking hand. Your ability to continue a conversation while I could feel the blood draining out of my brain.

A dangerous… uprising, I said.

Oh, you said innocently. And what was my favourite film? Your hand on my thigh, not breaking protocol, just making me think you might.

There'd be – an overwhelming – insurrection –

Anything you like, the street said. Anything at all.

After moments that seemed like minutes, your two hands and ten fingers lifted your tea cup to your lips. You looked at me over it. Another successful manoeuvre.

You were left-handed and I was right-handed. That meant you could be a genius.

Did I still have my school books? My mother had kept them. You? You'd kept them.

For reference?

You pinched me.

So I did law at university? Yes. It was thrilling.

What A-levels did I do? I racked my brain. English. French… History, yes.

You? They rolled off your tongue. French, Italian, music, double maths.

Double? Good God.

What was wrong with maths? Didn't I do any?

As little as possible. But I remembered, your father the

lecturer. And I could see it suiting you, a fortress of truth from which bullshitters were banned.

Then, you said, you'd teach me.

Hmm. I wanted to be taught *professoressa*, but maths?

You told me that not learning it was like deliberately blinding yourself. That it was second only to music. It shaped the way your mind worked, like learning a new language. But more so because there were so many new concepts.

Thoughtful conversation. I asked you to elaborate.

'Well,' your eyes met those of your student, 'take *esprit d'escalier*.'

Luckily I'd heard of this obscure expression.

'There isn't an English equivalent.'

I nodded sagely. *Not thinking of a riposte until you've left the room and gone downstairs* was long-winded.

'So when you learn the phrase it makes the concept take shape and allows you to refer to it more easily. It saves you from forgetting how it feels, to think of things too late. It diminishes your isolation, from other people and from your former self.'

Poor little Gilles at the table there. Do you see him? Getting more than he bargained for.

I took your hand and I thanked you.

'For what?' you smiled.

'Diminishing my isolation.'

You looked down shyly. And I reckoned that, while there were galaxies to which you could introduce me, there was also a world out there you didn't know about. A world of less rigorous magic. A world of instinct. No words, no maths, no staves, no scores. And its companion world, a world of ease. Of quietly being. A world where we'd be like two trees growing next to one another, together underground.

I asked you whether you'd tried the madeleines here. You said you didn't know what madeleines were. Little cakes I said. Did you want to try one? Yes, you said, you did.

Back I came with five on a plate.

You asked me why I was doing law now if I didn't like it at university.

I said it wasn't so bad.

You liked the madeleines.

You said you'd thought about doing law. You liked arguing.

I told you about my run-in with Cecil Pitt. You didn't find the joke of his name particularly funny. Then you didn't believe the *jouissance* story. But you were outraged on my behalf, which was the main thing.

I asked you what you wanted to do after the Guildhall. You said you were enjoying jazz more than you'd thought. I pictured you as a serious musician, being tempted into spontaneity.

You started eating another madeleine.

I wondered how to get beneath the wordy talk like we had on the *quai* the night before.

'Can I ask you something?'

'Yes,' you smiled.

'Do you daydream about things?'

You were eating madeleine crumbs. 'As in?'

'I don't know, what you want to do in life?'

'Yeh definitely. My father had a good voice. I never heard it, but my mum talks about it a lot. That's something I want to live up to.'

'Yeh,' I said. I could understand that.

I thought about how to ask you.

'... What about meeting someone, falling in love with someone?'

'Oh,' you said archly, 'like you dream of your Leicester Square woman?'

'I've found her. I'm not looking any more.'

You shook your head in disbelief. 'Why won't you accept that I'm not her?'

'Because you're my dream woman.'

'But what's wrong with admitting that I'm not the Leicester Square woman?'

'Well how can I do that,' I smiled, 'when you *are*?'

'No I'm not.' You stared at me.

'That's what you think. I think something different.'

'You're being deliberately annoying.'

'No, lucky coincidence.'

You simmered, a hint of a smile on your face.

Vee I couldn't abide upsetting you. 'Let's pretend I never mentioned it.'

'That's not how my mind works.'

Too right. And I loved that about you, I loved you.

'The thing is,' I had to make you understand, 'it's not just that you're her. It's like looking at the cover versus reading the book, I can't believe it, I can't believe the pages.'

I caught your smile before you looked away.

'How about,' I said, 'we call it a mystery. I'm Catholic, I'm content with mystery.'

'Well I'm not,' you said, 'but I suppose I could try to make an exception.'

Then you stunned me. Your hand was making its way up my thigh again. 'And by the way, hello Mr Holy Catholic, maybe I should kneel down and pray.'

God the power of suggestion. My theory was Aladdin didn't actually touch his lamp at all.

'... Mistress Venus,' I was murmuring in an Eastern accent, already half drunk, '... I am the genie of the penis.'

You threw your head back and laughed.

We kissed full on the lips. It was at least a minute's worth of pure paradise.

'... *Uh*,' I sighed, 'what am I going to do without you?'

You looked tenderly back at me. 'It's only one weekend.'

I focused on the pavement, trying to hide how I felt. On one level, mounting the peak of my excitement so eagerly I was giving myself altitude sickness, on the other, willing to give up making any move at all if it meant I could be with you.

What did this mean?

Only one thing.

'Venus?' I whispered.

'Yeh?'

'I love you.'

You blushed and looked away.

'You know that don't you?' Your soft eyes darted up to me. 'Everything about you.'

And you looked a bit sad and said, 'Thank you.'

'You don't have to say anything back.'

It sounded as false as it was. What I meant was that you could wait, and a few minutes later tell me you loved me. Above all you couldn't say that you didn't love me.

Anyway, you didn't need telling. You didn't say it for months.

Whether or not I saw you at Leicester Square, my inaccurate tally of ex-girlfriends – they were convenient excuses, they weren't what it was about.

But I couldn't have kept it to myself any longer.

30

'Can't Keep It In'
by Cat Stevens

'Venus love,' Mary knocked softly on the door of Leonie's room. 'It's your mum on the phone.'

Venus opened the door. 'Can you tell her I'll ring back?' she whispered. 'We're nearly at the end of the chapter.'

''Course. You finish off, love. I'll keep her talking.'

Venus finished reading, kissed Leonie goodnight and switched off the light.

'Mummy?' Leonie was using her stay-with-me voice.

'Yes?'

'Why's the girl called Fern?'

Venus thought for a second. 'Because her parents liked the name.'

'But a fern's a plant.'

'I know but they just liked it. Leonie's a lion, so it's not that different.'

'I suppose so.'

'Goodnight my love.'

'Mummy?'

'Yes?'

'What are we going to do tomorrow?'

'Well, in the morning we can do whatever we want and

then in the afternoon Mary's going to look after you while I see *Mémé* in hospital.'

'Why can't I come?'

'Leo, she's not very well. She can't talk properly.'

'Why not?'

'Because she's old. Now I've got to speak to Grandma – '

'Is *Mémé* older than Grandma?'

'Yes she is.' Venus bent down and kissed her. 'But you're the eldest aren't you my love? You're the eldest of everyone aren't you?'

'Yes.' Leonie said.

'Mummy?' Leonie whispered.

'Yes?'

'I'm not older than Daddy.'

Venus snuggled up and hugged her. And Leonie held her arms round Venus's neck and hugged her tightly, with a passion that was irrefutable.

'I love you so much,' Venus whispered.

'I know… ' Leonie whispered.

She stroked Leonie's hair away from her face.

'So does Daddy. He does, I know it for sure.'

'… Did he do something wrong?' Leonie murmured.

Venus took a breath. Leonie's eyes were hooded with sleepiness.

'… Don't think about it now my love.'

Curling her legs up under the duvet, she turned to her side to sleep.

Venus kissed her cheek. 'We both love you very much, we can't believe how much, that's what matters.' Her eyes were closing.

Venus waited until Leonie's breathing had softened, then pulled the bedroom door to, leaving a crack of light from the hall. She walked into the sitting room, carefully closed the door behind her and picked up the phone.

'Mum?' she whispered.

'Hi Vee.'

'Oh there you are love.' Mary was on the kitchen extension. 'Your mum and me were having a lovely talk, weren't we Pat?'

'Yes, we were. – Vee, Mary's been kind enough to ask me and David over to Paris.'

'No, be a pleasure to have you Pat, brighten the place up. Having Venus and Leo always does me a power of good. Had Leo making fairy cakes last night didn't I love? Took me right back.'

'You should start a bed and breakfast.'

'Now it's funny you say that Pat, I did think of taking people in, you know, but then I thought, what about Hélène? Strangers in the flat and that. I mean I'd have to ask her wouldn't I? She's ever so fragile at the moment. But, well, you don't ask you don't get do you? After I've given her an update on the cleaning, that usually perks her up.' She paused for breath and then seemed to stop herself. 'Well I'll get off the line then, leave you two ducks be.'

'Bye Mary. Thanks again.'

'My pleasure, Pat. You just pick up the phone, whenever it suits like I said.'

The receiver made a clicking sound.

Venus waited for a second. 'Are you going to come over?'

'We might well do, it's sweet of her to ask.'

'She'll demand payment in conversation.'

'Oh Vee.'

'No, she's wonderful – it's worth it just for the food, she's an excellent cook.' Her thoughts span off. 'I've been eating so well here.'

'Good, darling.'

'And she's fantastic with Leo. I think they've both really enjoyed it.'

'You sound well.'

'Oh – thanks. How are you?'

'Well the reason I'm ringing – Vee, this might upset you – '

'What?'

'Particularly with… ' she paused. 'Well, Matt told me what happened at Charlotte's wedding.'

Venus tensed.

'Sarissa Clarke, head of English, her daughter's getting married in September – she just wanted me to ask – '

'Oh.' She relaxed slightly. She wondered what else Matt had said.

'She's always kept a look out for you. She came to Carmen, you know that time when the toreador tripped up. She'd love you to sing but she'll understand if you'd prefer not to – '

'When is it?'

'September.'

'When in September?'

'I'll get the diary. Hang on a sec.'

She came back to the phone. 'Darling it's the 25th, don't worry. I'll say it's too soon after Gilles' anniversary. Sorry, it slipped my mind when I was talking to her.'

'No, I'll think about it. What does she want? Ave Maria?'

'You don't have to, she'd more than understand.'

'What does she want?' She felt impatient.

'Well I don't think it's happening in a church, but they'd like you to do something at the reception.'

'Right, so anything.'

'Well, obviously something, you know, *happy* – '

'Yeh I'd grasped that.'

Patricia didn't react.

'Why don't you tell her I'll think about it and give her a call next week?'

'All right I will.'

There was a small silence.

Venus took a breath. 'How's David?'

'Oh, fine thanks. Very well.'

'Mum, Matt said something about your party for the wedding anniversary. You know I'll come – '

'Oh darling!' She sounded hugely relieved. 'That is good news.'

'Why did you think I wouldn't?'

'I just wasn't sure, that's all.'

'So why didn't you ask me straight out?'

She sighed. 'Maybe I should have done. I just didn't want you to get cross.'

'You've got to stop being polite with me. I can't stand all this pissing around, you asking Matt, Matt asking me, it's ridiculous.'

'Okay, okay.'

'Don't be so careful.'

'Well if you were slightly less aggressive it would make it easier.'

They were both quiet.

'Okay,' Venus said eventually. 'Sorry.'

'How was your day?' Patricia asked.

'Good thanks. Took Leo to the Musée d'Orsay. She loved it, I was quite surprised.'

'Oh wonderful.'

'We got another one of those geometric colouring books in the shop, she's obsessed with them.'

'She's got a good eye.'

'She notices things I don't even see.'

'I bet.' She sounded moved. 'You know I'm so glad you did that Vee, were you there quite a while?'

'Well if this damn receptionist had told me the doc... ' Venus stopped herself. 'Anyway, we can go again.'

'The doctor?' Patricia was anxious. 'What's wrong?'

'Oh nothing.'

'Vee, what?'

'No, it was for me, it's nothing.'

'Well why can't you tell me?'

Venus sighed. 'Just the morning after pill.'

'What?'

'Mum – '

'What happened?'

'Nothing, nothing bad. Nothing to worry about.'

'But who on earth do you know in Paris?'

Venus paused. 'I met someone… at Charlotte's wedding.'

'Oh, I see.' She seemed too quickly pacified. 'So he lives in Paris? Matt didn't say.'

Venus raised her eyes. 'What did Matt say?'

'Darling don't get cross. It was perfectly natural for Matt to tell me.'

They were quiet.

'I'm not going to disapprove, you must do what you think is right. I just don't want you to get hurt.' She paused. 'You know you really should have got him to use a condom, it's not just contraception.'

'I forgot.'

'What?'

'I – kind of forgot about it.'

'Oh Vee.' She sounded resigned to Venus's hopelessness.

There was another silence.

Her mother hesitated. '… Do you – like him?'

'Of course I do – '

'Good.'

But she felt false, the conversation too cut and dried. Did she like him? Did she love him? What paucity of language.

'One minute I think of him, the next Gilles might as well be in the room – ' She stopped, embarrassed. 'I just, God, I don't know what I'm doing.'

'It's bound to be like that. You'll be more certain once the shock wears off.'

Venus shut her eyes. She found herself not wanting the sympathy she'd asked for.

'… Vee?'

'Well what d'you mean, the shock?'

'It's a shock, meeting someone new.'

The words 'someone new' rang in her head. As if Gilles were replaceable and she distractible.

'… Vee?'

She swallowed. 'Yeh?'

'Have you told him about Gilles?'

'... Yes.'

'And what does he think?'

'He thinks – ' She could hear Alex's voice, the kindness of it. 'He thinks I have to – love Gilles. Before I can love anyone else.'

'Then,' her mother said quietly, 'he's a rare person.'

A tear trickled down Venus's cheek.

'I know... I know.' She wiped it away. Venus took a breath. She had to say more. 'I just don't know what to do. I seem to be talking about Gilles all the time – Leo mentioned it again tonight, I'm going to have to answer her.' She thought for a moment. 'I'd do anything – to stop plaguing myself and everyone around me. So much of me loves him. But he's dead, Mum. I'll never know what happened, and I can't see how I'll ever forget it.'

'You can and you will. Because I did. I just waited far too long to do it.'

Venus didn't reply.

'Vee, think how lucky you were. I've never seen two people more in love.' She paused. 'I'd watch you sometimes at home, I'd see the way you looked at each other.' She sighed. 'I'd feel so envious.'

'Oh Mum – '

'It's awful but it's true. And I know you had arguments. But you never *tired* of each other. You never took each other for granted.'

Venus blinked the tears out of her eyes.

'All he did was die.' Her mother's voice shook. 'That's all he did.'

Alex walked into the crowded bar. He pushed through the people to the room at the back. Ray was eating at a small table in the corner.

'Took your fucking time.'

'Sorry,' Alex said.

'Don't order the *canard*.' Ray was holding the bone and eating off it. 'Tastes like shoes.' He pushed a plate of chips towards Alex.

Alex took off his jacket and tie. 'No thanks.'

Ray nodded his head at a glass on the next table. Everyone was standing around them. Alex took the glass, inspected it, poured himself some wine and sat down.

'What's going on? I thought you were kicking your heels.'

He drank. 'Just an assessment. I got in late, forgot about it. Then Pitt caught me on the way out.'

'Cess?' Ray laughed. 'That man needs a medal.'

'He's an idiot.'

Ray sprinkled salt on his chips. 'What did he want?'

'None of the trainees were around. Translation.'

'What?'

'Some marketing crap. I told him I'd do it by the weekend. He said he needed it tonight. Then he said he makes all his assistants cry at least once and he hasn't seen me cry yet.'

'Jesus, what a gobshite.'

Ray took hold of his glass. 'So you did it?'

Alex looked faintly disgusted. 'Of course not.'

'AACH,' Ray crashed his glass against Alex's. 'Well done man.'

Alex smiled. He drank some more.

Ray started eating his chips. 'You bring the formula?'

'Yeh, thanks – half the department's away.' Alex took out some papers from his bag, put them on the table and pointed to the maths. Ray picked up the sheet.

He went to the bar to get another bottle. He'd go, he thought, once they'd gone through it. He'd ring Venus from home. They could eat at least…

'Okay.' Alex sat down, poured them both more wine. 'I just – '

'Pen?'

Alex handed him the pen from his jacket.

'Can I write on here?'

'Wait – use the back of this.'

Ray copied out the formula.

'Okay. So it's what the guy with the bond gets when he's paid back.'

He'd ask her. She might come.

'… the N*, you get that, that's why the 1's there. You get that, *plus* that times the rest of the shit… '

It was unbelievable, what had happened.

'… the maximum of two numbers, which are? Okay one is *zero*, and the other is the *minimum* of the fraction and the A%... '

Sex, and her…

'… example. Say A is 6 and the index goes up 5%. The Min says *take the 5%*. Got that?'

Alex came to, staring at the formula for a moment. 'What's the sigma for?'

Ray looked at him like he'd asked something irrelevant. 'That's just summing it up over n years.'

'What?'

'Okay, this is where the fraction comes in. So $Index_i$ is defined as the average of the Relevant Prices on the first three exchange business days – '

'Wait, wait. Maybe it's best if you don't explain the details.'

'Alex it's piss easy, give it a chance.'

'Yeh, I just want to know what it means.'

'You're losing the best of it seriously.'

'Please.'

Ray sighed. 'Every year, if the index goes down, you get nothing, so you don't lose. If the index goes up, you get the money you put in times whatever it goes up by, up to A%. Then at the end, everything you've got over the n years is added up and you get that plus the money you first put in.'

'So it's guaranteed, and capped at A%, whatever A is?'

'Spot on.'

'Okay, great. Thanks.'

'*Mon plaisir*.'

Ray put down the pen and went back to eating his chips. Alex picked up the pen and wiped the grease from Ray's fingers off it with a napkin.

'*Don't* remind me,' Ray said melodramatically.

'What?'

'Cucumbers.' Ray ate some more chips.

Alex didn't understand.

'Lotta's got these cucumbers. I saw them with my own eyes.'

'So?'

'Alex, do I have to spell it out?' Ray put more chips into his mouth. 'How'm I supposed to compete? I'm animal, they're vegetable.'

Alex rubbed his forehead. 'No one in their right mind eats them.'

'Exactly.'

Ray ate more chips then looked up at Alex.

Alex began to laugh.

'What's wrong with you?'

'Nothing.'

Ray looked at him suspiciously.

'Where's she keep them?' Alex asked.

'Fridge.'

'Body temperature's thirty-seven degrees, fridge is less than five.'

Ray stopped eating. 'Now that is information.'

Ray turned sharply to Alex. 'Freezer?'

'Minus twenty.'

His eyes widened. 'No mercy. No fucking mercy. Hey – ' He raised his glass. '*Santé* my friend.' They drank.

Ray adopted a kung fu pose. '*Sayonara cucumba*.' He drank again and slammed his glass on the table.

Alex poured out more wine and sat back.

It was better when Ray wasn't talking. His thoughts were

like a shoal of fish, rising to the water's surface as soon as it was calm, gleaming in the light, each one directed at Venus.

He'd ring her tonight, he thought. She might come tomorrow as well. If she stayed – they'd have the morning. The day even.

So much had happened. The whole thing with her husband. Something that had seemed impossible was possible… Anything was possible.

'… Turnip, now that's a real vegetable.'

It had overtaken him. Friends, work, books, they were nothing in comparison.

'… Alex?'

To be interested in her, and to be attracted to her…

'ALEX.'

Ray was speaking.

'… Yeah, so what's on the agenda?'

He thought about it. He couldn't remember. He should ring her, before it got too late…

'After carrying out extensive tests,' Ray put on a BBC accent, 'experts now doubt there is life on planet Alexander.'

Alex looked at Ray.

'Focus man, come on.'

He sighed. 'I've forgotten.'

'What the hell is wrong with you?'

'Sorry.' Alex breathed out. 'I'm pretty tired.' He smiled slightly. 'I think I might… '

Ray peered at him. 'You been drinking before you got here?'

Alex began to laugh.

Ray nodded. 'Something's twinkled your toes hasn't it?'

But Alex didn't answer.

'Shit.' Ray sat up violently. 'The woman. It's the woman isn't it?' Ray began to smile. 'You little bastard. You rang her like I told you?' He took a swig.

'She's over here – '

'What?' He almost choked. 'Christ, well done man.'

'She had to come anyway. She was over here before I spoke to her.'

'Nice. So she's after you, perfect.'

'She came round last night.'

Ray looked at Alex open-mouthed.

Alex blushed slightly.

'Mother of God.' Ray nodded his head. 'You got laid,' he breathed. Ray stared at Alex, his tongue lodged between his teeth in concentration. He nodded. 'You did, didn't you?' He began to laugh. 'God man couldn't you at least have told me that?' Ray was shaking his head. 'I don't believe it. I don't bloody believe it.'

He put his tongue between his teeth again for a moment.

'Hey.' Ray poured them more wine. They toasted, drank and sat back.

'Fuck me.'

They were quiet for a second, the hum of other people's conversation around them.

'So,' Ray began, 'was it pretty – you know – terrible?'

Alex smiled.

'Shit on ice.' He took it in. 'What are we talking, two years?'

Alex didn't reply.

'God not three?' Ray closed his eyes. 'Holy fucking Christmas.' He began to laugh. 'NASA better stop the testing then, eh?' He shook with laughter. 'So,' he said, settling in, 'okay, so this was last night?'

'Yeh. I made her supper.'

'Nice touch. Yeah, role reversal, they love it.' Ray pointed. 'But not too often. Sensitive but strong believe me. Now look, call her tonight whatever you do.' Ray looked at Alex. 'So hang on, what about her husband?'

Alex met Ray's eye then paused. 'He's dead.'

'Oh shit. Emotional. So wait, you're the first since… ?' Ray glanced at Alex, stroked his chin, then stopped abruptly. 'When did he die?'

'About four years ago I think.'

'My God – '

'What?'

Ray's voice had almost disappeared. 'We're talking choirs of angels.'

Alex raised his eyes.

'Seven years, total. *Seven years*. I mean we're talking hosanna in bloody excelsis.'

Alex began to smile despite himself.

'He's smiling, Toddie's smiling. Now that's a sight.' Ray sighed and looked into the distance. 'No man is an island. No man is a fucking island.'

Alex was still smiling.

'She's the one then?'

He looked down. 'I really like her.'

'She must be something.'

'Yeh.'

'She's – principled and that? Kinda straight?'

'Yeh, I think so.'

Ray was nodding. 'A good, simple, honest woman.'

'Well – '

'She a country girl?'

Alex paused. '… I don't think so.'

'You mean you shagged her without knowing? That was rash wasn't it?' Ray was chuckling. 'God Alex, what else don't you know about her? Shoe size? Voting history? I was expecting a fuller, you know – what d'yamacallit.' Ray clicked his fingers.

'Due diligence.'

Ray began to laugh. 'Due fucking diligence… So, wait a minute, is she here? In Paris?'

'Place des Vosges.'

'Bloody hell. Is she rolling in it?'

'I don't think so. It's not her flat.'

'Still… ' But Ray paused. 'So Alex, I mean the night is young. What are you waiting for? Get her over here for Christ's sake.'

Alex felt his head swim. 'No, I don't think so. It could be difficult, she's got a child – '

'Oh come on. Give it a try. I'd love to meet her.'

'It's sensitive because of her husband, I don't think – '

'I won't put my foot in it.'

Alex blinked his eyes closed.

'Well don't you want to see her?'

'Of course.'

'So what the hell are you waiting for?' He offered his phone.

Alex fiddled with the biro on the table.

'Go on, she'll say no if she doesn't want to.'

He looked at his watch. He didn't want to leave it too late. He could call now…

'Go on mate.'

He got up. 'I need to call her anyway.' They wouldn't have to stay long. He'd say he was tired, they could go back to the flat… 'I might not ask her. I don't know.' Ray would be impressed. He would.

'Okay, fine. Fine.' Ray held out his phone again.

'I'll use mine.'

'Easy tiger.' Ray reported into his fist. 'And in a surprise move here in Paris, Alexander Todd has abandoned a solemn oath not to touch his phone outside office hours… '

Mary knocked on the bathroom door. 'Venus love,' she whispered.

Venus dried her hair and put the towel round her. She opened the door.

'Sorry, love. Oh… ' Mary fanned the steamy air with her hand. 'Phone for you. Like Piccadilly Circus tonight.'

'Who is it?'

'Young man, said his name was Alex.'

Venus's heart started to race.

'Well spoken.'

'I'll go into the sitting room.'

She felt dizzy.

Mary walked back towards the kitchen. 'Don't catch cold love – '

Venus rushed into the sitting room and shut the door.

'Alex?'

'Oh hi.'

She smiled. He sounded good.

'… How are you?' she asked.

'Very well… A bit… tired.'

Mary had put the phone down. Venus leaned back.

'How about you?' he asked.

'Yeh, the same.' She liked his slow voice. 'It's good to hear you.'

'You too,' he said. 'I could smell your skin, on the sheets, when I woke up… '

She breathed in as she smiled. Just to be talking to him…

Tomorrow was Friday. Perhaps she could see Hélène in the morning, Mary could take Leonie for the whole day.

'Did you get my message?' she asked.

'Yeh, thanks. I hope your daughter – '

'No, that's okay. I meant the phone message.'

'Oh, no. No. I haven't been back.'

'Ah. Okay… ' She pulled up her towel.

'Sorry, I know it's a bit late, but would you like to come out tonight?'

'Alex, there's just something I have to tell you.'

'What?'

'I'm… I'm not on the pill. Last night – '

'Oh.' He'd woken up.

'I totally forgot. I'm sorry.'

'No, no, so did I.'

'You forgot?'

'Of course. I mean I would have said.'

'Well at least we were both as stupid as each other.'

'I'm not in the habit – '

'Yeh, nor am I – '

He was quiet. She could hear people talking in the background.

'Well, look, anyway. I've got this other pill. I have to take it within seventy-two hours.'

'But you don't know you're pregnant?'

'No, I couldn't find that out yet. Anyway it's unlikely. The thing is I haven't taken it so far, because I wanted to ask you… ' She wasn't sure what she was asking him.

'What?'

'Well the likelihood of me being pregnant is about 1%, because I'm – I'm just about to have a period. The pill's around 75% effective. So there's a 1% chance if I don't take it, versus a 0.25% chance – '

'Why are you giving me all these figures?'

'So that we know enough to make a decision.'

'But what we've got to decide is whether to have a baby.'

She was shocked.

'Alex, look, having a baby, it's a huge, massive… '

'I know that.'

But the assumption she'd made was deflating almost pleasingly, like a soft pillow. She hadn't considered the possibility.

'What do you want to do?' he asked.

She breathed in. 'I like you Alex. So much. But we've only just met.'

He didn't say anything. She wondered why she'd brought it up if she'd already made the decision.

'Well, look, it's such a low likelihood, I probably don't need to take it. But if it turns out I'm pregnant… ' She sighed, stopped herself, became slightly excited by the thought. 'Do you want to have a child?' she asked.

'No, no. I mean yes, one day, but… ' Then he said, 'If you want to take it, please take it.' He sounded further away.

'Well, I may know soon anyway. That I'm not pregnant. They say 1% but I think it's pretty much impossible.'

'Okay. Thanks – for asking my opinion.'

'That's okay.'

He paused. 'Look, why don't you come down to the bar. Ray, this guy I know, he'll be here, but we don't have to stay long. Or I could meet you somewhere else.'

'I'd like to see you,' she said.

'But?' he suggested.

'No, no but. I've just got out of the bath.'

'Oh.'

She looked down at her bare feet.

'Are you – naked?'

The word distracted her.

'No, no. I've got a towel – '

'Oh.'

' – Not naked,' she smiled.

'Venus… ' he said.

It came out dreamily, as if he was just saying her name and didn't intend to catch her attention.

She stood up, holding the towel round her. 'Tell me where you are. I'll get dressed.'

31

'Son Of A Preacher Man'
by John Hurley and Ronnie Wilkins

I took your hand. 'It's just down here.' We were almost within touching distance of your hostel on the other side of Rue des Barres. I opened the back door of St Gervais church and watched you walk inside.

Your eyes widened. We'd arrived three-quarters of the way through the Holy Thursday Mass, the monks and nuns singing without accompaniment, the light of the candles shining on the bare walls. It felt entirely alive.

'I love it,' you whispered.

I felt euphoric. We stayed until the end, then made our way to Ile Saint Louis.

'Thank you,' you said, less sadly this time.

We crossed the bridge back after supper, laughing about a fellow student with a lisp and a compulsion for saying 'past participle' who I was sure, like every sentient being, fancied you uncontrollably.

Suddenly you cried out.

Your toe was bleeding, there was blood running over your sandal. Some idiot had left broken glass all over the pavement. I gave you my handkerchief and stopped a taxi.

As if suffering from a special form of alcoholism, I said I had a bottle of Dettol back at the flat.

Okay, you said.

We arrived. I unlocked the front door. The staircase looked steep and narrow.

Did you want me to carry you? No, you laughed. It wasn't that bad.

So up the first flight of stairs you leaned on my shoulder. Then up the second and third you held your pink shoes and I gave you a piggyback.

I carried you in, settled you on the sofa, filled a plastic bowl with warm water and poured in the Dettol. We watched as it clouded the water, the smell of it evoking maternal attention. And among the many types of attention I wanted to show to you, I realised with an odd sensation that that was one.

I started to wash your cut.

'Stay still,' I said.

You flinched as I took out a flat, sharp piece of glass. I held it up for your inspection.

'Woo. Thank you.'

I continued, unnecessarily, to wash the rest of your foot, the small splashes sounding louder the quieter we became. And when I touched you right, I could hear you breathe in, and I thought of washing more of you, and hearing you sigh while I did.

Out of nothing, you asked me how come if I was such a holy Catholic I'd shagged four women.

I looked up at you and felt the liar's cheap relief.

You smiled down on me, regally.

I laughed.

You stretched your toes and waited.

I said that Catholicism was all about sinning. The more you sin, the better you are when you repent.

'Have you repented yet?'

'No,' I whispered, 'not quite yet.'

You pushed your hair out of your eyes as you smiled. 'So you think sex is a sin?'

You were just getting started. 'No, of course I don't.'

'But, isn't that what Catholics think?'

'I don't care what anyone thinks.'

And then you said it was too weird just having one foot washed, the other one felt odd somehow. So I washed that foot too.

'But then, why do you call yourself a Catholic?'

I said I thought religion was mainly an accident of birth.

I asked you if you'd like to have a bath – I had a big bath – with a large supply of hot water.

You laughed. No, you said.

'But, don't you believe in it? If you go to church?'

Yes, I said, I did.

'But why should you, if it's just an accident?'

What I meant, I said, was that you couldn't believe it in a doubt-defying way.

'But what kind of religion's that?'

I looked up at you, your handsome, furrowed brow.

I said I thought a religion was like a person. The moral system part was like a human body – almost the same everywhere. The rest was just clothes, haircut, accessories. Different gods, holy days, rituals –

'Right,' you said, 'so you don't believe in the clothes?'

Yes, I did. I went to church. But I didn't expect other people to, because that came down to faith.

'But – ' you looked at me, 'I don't understand how going to a particular place every week can make you a better person.'

I said it didn't. It was more that I needed it. To be quiet and remember people. But what could make me a better person was loving other people, just for the fact that they were human. I believed in that, and I'd preach it and live it... if I were a better person.

You stared at me studiously, as if you were interested in

my answer but the words I'd used were foreign. And then a detached look came over your face, and I took it to mean you'd had enough, but it wasn't quite that. Because in a deep whispered voice, you began to sing.

'… Being good isn't always easy… ' And after a deluxe pause, your eyes roaming over me like soft-gloved hands, '… No matter how hard I try… '

In the middle of knocking up. The devil of a backhand lob.

'Son of a Preacher Man,' you said.

I knew it, or I thought I did. Your version arched over me then landed at my heels. There was no doubt about it, the ball was in, the chalk flew up.

My God Vee did you need to be caught. But if I chased you hard I'd never see you again, and if I played it softly I'd go insane with lust. The secret was unpredictability.

'So tell me,' I sat down next to you, solemn as a vicar, 'are you a religious person?'

'No,' you said. 'I don't think so. I liked the singing in the church.'

'Yes,' I said, seriously. 'It's striking how sensual choral music can be.'

You looked at me.

'And of course,' I continued, 'some of the greatest musical works were inspired by religious devotion.'

Baffled, you tried to catch my eye, but I was lost in sacred contemplation.

You started to dry your feet. I went to my bedroom and found a clean handkerchief, then remembered there was some Sellotape in the kitchen.

I handed both to you. 'You might like to make yourself a bandage,' I suggested.

'Thanks,' you said. 'I'll give the handkerchief back.'

'Keep it,' I said, 'if it would be useful to you. Is your foot feeling better now?'

'Yes,' you smiled nicely at me, 'much better, thank you.'

'Good,' I clasped my hands, 'in that case, I think it's time for me to walk you home.'

You glanced at me in sweetest, most edible disappointment.

I got my keys.

You stood up, but yelped as you put your weight on your foot. 'I'm not sure I can walk all the way – '

'Don't worry, I'll hail a taxi if your foot starts hurting.'

'Well, it's hurting now.'

'Perhaps there's a bit of glass left in it.'

'Perhaps,' you said.

I asked you to sit down, undid the bandage and examined your foot for as long as a vicar decently could.

'No,' I pronounced finally. 'No glass at all.'

I looked at you. Unmistakable impatience. I re-taped the bandage.

'Well then,' I said, 'we'd better be going.'

You picked up your things and we went to the door.

I pushed down the handle and stopped short. 'Oh goodness.'

You stood still. 'What?'

'I almost forgot.'

'What?' you asked innocently.

'Well, there's an important ritual I ought to perform before we leave. I'll need your help you see, there must be two people.'

You looked bemused.

'I suppose it can wait, I don't want to hold you up.'

'Well you might as well do it now. What is it?'

I smiled at you as the vicar left us to it.

'... What?' you smiled back.

And slowly I kissed you. And the satisfaction of it sounded in your throat. And you began to kiss me. And then I couldn't get enough of you.

Back on the sofa, kissing kissing, you sitting on my lap, you with your legs either side of me, my hands on your waist, your breasts, kissing kissing, never enough.

'*Dottore*,' you whispered.

We could be making love in this position.

'*Signorina…* '

God I wanted you Vee.

'Do you mind,' you whispered, 'being a university doctor?'

Did I mind? Did I mind? Kissing, kissing.

'*Dottore*?' You stopped my mouth.

I looked at you, smiled at you. You wanted an answer.

'It… would depend on my subject, *Professoressa*.'

You sat beside me on the sofa. 'What subject would you like, *Dottore*?'

'The subject, I like… ' I put my arm around you, brought you nearer to me. '… *Professoressa*, I believe you are a unique authority on it.'

'Oh?' Your hand was on the inside of my thigh.

'You see,' I lifted you back onto my lap, 'I need extra lessons – '

We were kissing again.

You laughed. You said I got so kinked up about teachers.

Oh but Miss Rees, I got kinked up about you. I started to undo your shirt.

'Wait,' you said. 'Let's wait – '

I put my head to yours. 'I only want to touch you.'

'I want to *touch* you too,' you whispered.

'You have my full, immediate, enduring permission.'

You smiled.

I crept my hand underneath your shirt but you took it away.

'… I just want to wait. Sorry.'

'We don't have to make love.'

'I know,' you said definitely. 'But if you start to touch me, I won't be able to stop myself – sleeping with you.'

Holy shit. 'Then don't, for God's sake don't. – God,' I whispered, 'you don't understand how much that turns me on, everything you do – '

'Gilles, I don't want to sleep with you yet.'

I looked at you. It was our last night together.

'But you're leaving tomorrow.'

'I'll be back on Monday.'

I sighed.

You smiled. 'It's not that bad.'

'You know, you telling me to wait – you're probably right, but all it does is make me more attracted to you.'

'It's not that I think it would be wrong, I just know how it affects things. It's not to do with honour.'

So earnestly you clarified Vee, so loath you were to be misunderstood.

Then as if I'd find it unwelcome news, you said, 'I don't plan to abstain forever.'

And your face so anxious, I didn't understand. 'Thank goodness for that,' I smiled.

'No. You like me because we haven't slept together – like your dream woman, but one day we'll do it. Then what'll be left? I'll just be one on the list.'

'*What?*' I was incensed. 'Can't you feel it between us? I'll love you more every day. We won't believe it. It'll never stop.' I gripped your hand in mine. 'Whatever we do, whatever happens, it'll *never* stop.'

32

'I'll Be Seeing You'
by Irving Kahal and Sammy Fain

The bar was hot. Venus pulled off the sweater from around her shoulders and caught the smell of perfume in her hair. She hadn't worn perfume in her hair for years.

She went to the back room. Smiling, she recognised Alex in the distance. He was wearing a pale blue shirt with the top button undone. He was sitting with a brown-haired thin-faced man who looked like a weasel. The weasel was talking animatedly.

'Hi,' she came up to their table.

'Oh hi,' Alex got up and they kissed each other on the cheek. 'Ray, this is – '

'Hey,' Ray stood up and smiled, 'Madeleine isn't it?'

Alex and Venus both started talking.

Venus explained that her name was actually Venus. She'd sat at the wrong place at the wedding and the Madeleine thing had taken off.

'Aah.' Ray turned from one to the other as if he'd divined the name's significance.

'So, Venus,' he looked her up and down and smiled, 'as in the heavenly body…?'

Alex pulled up a chair.

'Yup,' she said crisply, sitting down. 'Afraid so.'

'Don't be,' Ray smiled. 'I hadn't heard it as a name.' His eyes darted over her. 'I'm a rural Irishman.'

She smiled at Alex. 'I suppose I should be grateful it wasn't Uranus.'

Ray cackled. Alex laughed.

'Or one of its moons,' Ray raised his eyebrows.

Ray and Venus laughed. Alex looked at Ray.

'So,' Ray said quickly, 'I hear the wedding was… quite something.'

Alex stared at Ray.

'Yeh… ' Venus smiled. 'It was pretty eventful.'

She looked at him. He wasn't so unattractive.

'Do you want a glass of wine?' Alex asked.

'Yes, thanks.' Venus thought. 'No. Actually, *citron pressé*. Thanks.' Alex went off to the bar.

'So it was a good day then?' Ray asked.

'Yeh. Yeh it was.' Ray was looking heavily at her. She cleared her throat. 'There were a few fuck ups but Charlotte was in charge so… Have you met her?'

'No, I've not had that pleasure,' he said. 'To be honest Venus, he doesn't tell me much. But if she's a friend of yours, I'm sure she's an interesting woman.'

'She is,' Venus said.

She found herself wanting to change the subject. Her eyes fell on the black motorbike helmet on the floor beside him. She looked back at the table, the papers spread over it. A mathematical expression was written in a scrawl of biro. She supposed it was Alex's work.

'You're from Ireland?' she asked.

'Yeah, Kilkenny,' he said. 'Not far from Dublin.'

'Oh right,' she nodded. 'What's it like?'

'Irish, you know. Rain, booze, lots of liquid. The thing with Ireland, the more shitty it is, the more you love it. It got decent a while back, everyone got traumatised. They called me up, they said, 'Hey Ray, come on home, we need a Minister of Shite – ''

She laughed. He winked at her.

Alex came back with the lemon juice and water and sat down.

'Thanks,' she smiled at him. 'So how do you know each other?'

'University,' Alex said.

'Okay, announcement,' Ray cleared his throat, 'Venus, I'd just like to say, in my capacity as Alex's friend, that I can see you're a very special woman, and I'm very happy he's met you.'

'That's kind of you,' Venus smiled.

'Yeh,' Alex studied Ray dubiously.

'… Did you both do the same subject, at university?'

'Nah,' Ray was defiant, 'I'd sooner have boiled my own head. He did philosophy, you know, touchy-feely, wind chimes… '

'Be quiet… '

'Whereas I did maths, I'm a maths teacher… Beauty, concision, precision… '

'So what's all this?' Venus picked up the pad of paper with the maths on.

'Oh,' Alex said, 'it's not very interesting.'

'Well,' she looked at Alex, 'I didn't tell you I teach maths.'

Alex's face paled.

'No way,' said Ray. He seemed stunned. 'School,' he paused, staring at her, 'or university?'

'Sixth form.'

'Hey,' Ray smiled. 'Just like me. Isn't that something?' His voice was lighter. 'So wait, complex numbers, de Moivre, all that?'

'Sure, e to the i pi plus one.'

'God, that's such a result. It's one of those Pelé results. I teach in terms of football – '

'I often use music – '

Aware of Alex, she cut herself short.

'He's not interested Venus, take it from me.'

Alex looked hard at Ray. 'I didn't say that.'

'I mean how can you not be interested? All that philosophy, history, it's all crap, it's not in the zone. Maths is pure naked pleasure.'

Alex sighed. 'Can't you have one conversation without mentioning sex?'

Ray's mouth gaped in mock affront. 'When did I mention sex?' He smiled at Venus. 'Alex, listen mate, you've just got to let me prove to you, I don't know, that √2 is irrational. It's like someone handing you the best poetry you're ever going to read and you just telling them to fuck off. But it's even better than that, because it's not about words. I mean the inevitability of a proof – you feel it coming before you know it.' He looked at Venus. 'You know that time just before you come when you know you're going to – '

'When did I mention sex?' Alex imitated Ray. 'When would I ever let a ting like dat escape me lips?'

'Shut it.'

Venus was laughing.

'Anyway,' Alex said, 'teaching's obviously worthwhile, especially given I know absolutely nothing about maths.'

Grinning, Ray tipped back on his chair. 'Okay, put it this way, maths gives you a fuck sight more thrills than philosophy ever did.'

'Yeh well I disagree,' Alex stared at him. 'What's the good of a thrill divorced from people or life? It's abstract, you've got to accept that.'

'Course it's abstract, it's liberating you from your own fucking navel. You stay in your navel, you get no bloody answers. I mean it's so obvious. Maths is *unassailable*.'

'Except Gödel's theorem blew a hole in it.'

'See that is typical philosophy trash – '

'*No*. He *proved* even maths comes down to faith. Who said, 'God exists since mathematics is consistent, and the Devil exists since we can't prove it'? *André Weil, mathematician* – '

'Woo,' Venus said. 'You can love one thing without hating another.'

'Right,' Alex said, 'of course you can love both.'

She stood up. 'Anyway music wins hands down.' She picked up her purse, went to the bar and came back with plates of bread and *saucisson* and olives. She took a piece of bread herself and offered the food to them. Ray declined. Alex took a handful of everything and tucked in.

'Look at that,' Ray was smiling at her. 'Eating like a puppy… You know Venus, I think he likes you.'

Alex took more olives.

'Why?' she smiled.

'Eats your food. Wouldn't touch mine.'

Alex peeked up from the table.

Ray laughed. 'Look at him, he's half starved.'

Ray ate an olive and spat the stone out at Alex. Alex caught it in his right hand and put it in the ashtray. Ray drained his glass and put it down.

'He's been taking life too seriously Venus, you've got to sort that out. God knows I've tried. I mean I'm a living example to him, I accept the pointless comedy of life, go with it. I think of myself as a frisky young dolphin, playing in the waves… '

Alex took an olive stone out of his mouth with his left hand. 'Don't get lyrical.'

'But it'll take a woman. You know, to get him to lighten up. Pay less attention to those dickshits at work.' Ray made to leave. 'You told Venus about Pitt? Can't get over that name… there's this bloke in his office called cesspit. Absurd.'

It felt like a spot of rain had hit her cheek. That name, she'd heard it before.

'So, Lotta's off tomorrow. Three days of rest.'

Something to do with Paris, when Gilles had worked there – when they'd first met –

'Jet lag.'

Floodlit, her mind shrank in the glare. Gilles' trainee – Alex, his name was Alex – good-looking, serious, philosophy, wanted to work in Paris, *Lapin* –

'Yeah, good point. Thanks mate.'

He said bank. But no, Cecil Pitt. It had to be.

His friend, his friend who died. Her stomach twisted. It was him. Beyond any doubt. That bloody philosophy –

She took a breath. She could just ignore it, not give it a thought –

The letter. Alex Todd. He'd written the letter she'd imprinted on her brain.

'Hi,' Alex looked fondly at her. 'I'm glad Ray's gone.'

Always something more.

… Never forget that I love you. Never forget that, Vee.

We won't believe it. It'll never stop. Whatever happens, it'll never stop.

33

'In The Still Of The Night'
by Cole Porter

Late that night Vee, after you'd gone to my bed and I'd folded out the sofa, I woke up. And I couldn't get back to sleep.

I went to the window and watched the orange dark begin to lighten. I wondered what would happen between us.

I knew I loved you. I was overcome with wanting you to feel the same way. For my sake, and for yours. I couldn't make you feel it, but I could inspire you that it was worth the risk and reassure you that I risked the same.

I had a responsible job and now I had a reason for doing it. I thought about what we'd do, where we'd live, the children we'd have. You'd be in London for the next year, and I was going back in September. So that was perfect. We'd get a house. We'd come back to Paris, get married in St Gervais. Then we'd go somewhere, for the honeymoon. Not France. Italy? No, too many men. Greece? Maybe Greece. We'd hire a house on the beach, on one of those islands with ten people and a *papas* and so many goats I'd be sure to feel at home.

And I knew that whatever life threw at us, if I felt at home, you would do too. We were one in the same person. I was convinced of it, I just had to convince you.

Every idea took on that night-time urgency. I was an

unstoppable genius, each new thought of more greatness than the last. I had to tell you. I had to tell you everything.

I tapped gently on the bedroom door. No sound. Slowly, I eased open the door.

You were sleeping. On your back, your head to the side. The sheets up over your shoulders, your hair on the pillow. I could hear the slow rhythm of your breathing, each breath like a wave washing over a stretch of sand. And it seemed that I was looking at you, and inside you, dreaming your dreams while I dreamt my own. And I felt that I shouldn't be looking, but I wanted to keep looking forever.

To be in love is not to be mad. To hold life in the palm of your hand and know that it is sweet – Vee, you could let distaste deny you that, but not fear. To be in love is to conquer fear, to kill madness. It is to be overwhelmingly and finally sane.

IV

'There can be no philosophic interest in disguising the animal basis of love or in denying its spiritual sublimations, since all life is animal in origin and all spiritual in its possible fruits.'

George Santayana

34

'Shelter From The Storm'
by Bob Dylan

There were wine glasses dotted around the table, a half-drunk lemon juice and the water that came with it, and grouped to one side, an ashtray, an empty bottle and a pile of plates.

A waitress came and picked up the plates, the bottle and the glasses. Two people were sitting in silence at the table. Emptying the ashtray onto the top plate, she took everything with her, winding her way through the other people in the bar, drinking, flirting, giggling, while the two sat like stones.

He'd recoiled when she'd told him. Closed his eyes, covered his face with his hands.

Nice, Gilles had said, they must ask him to dinner. Good-looking. You'd like him, Vee. A bit serious. Keen. Intelligent.

And with all this earnest talk they'd had, she'd been jealous enough to think that at least it wasn't a woman. And then jealous of it as it was, a friendship. But a real friendship. Not a drinking acquaintance, not a passing-the-time colleague, not someone to whom a favour was owed.

How had that *Lapin* name come about? They'd called him that, as if he'd been their child. And when Gilles got another trainee, *Lapin* survived, his name a cover for Gilles' fondness, both continuing to seek each other out.

And sitting in Alex's flat, she had told him that she doubted her dead husband – she doubted this friend of his – and as if he had a sixth sense, he'd told her that she was wrong, that she'd loved him and that she still did.

He took a deep breath. 'Let's get out of here.'

They pushed through the people in the bar and went outside. But the atmosphere was still chaotic. They went down a busy side street, then turned right down rue des Guillemites. It was quiet but narrow, the buildings overbearing on both sides. They walked to the end, turned left back into the noise, then quickly left down rue Aubriot to get away from it. They walked around and around the circuit formed by the two quiet parallel streets, passing through the crowd and then back into silence.

In the quiet, Alex stopped walking. He asked Venus whether she'd already known.

No, she said, of course she hadn't. Why would he think that?

He said he just wondered, that was all.

They walked through the noisy street, she containing herself until they came back to the quiet.

'Why would I lie to you?'

He shrugged.

'Alex I don't lie. *I do not lie*.'

'You lied to me at the wedding.'

'I made a mistake.'

'You didn't. You said you wanted to be someone else.'

'That wasn't scheming, it was pitiful. – I can't believe this, of course I didn't know, how can you not understand that?'

'You never even said his name – '

'Don't you see I could say the same to you? Your bloody name, your job – '

'But I never tried to hide anything.'

'But after I explained everything on the phone *nor did I*. God you're paranoid.'

He looked at her, then looked away.

'What I can't believe – ' He breathed out. 'You gave me that crap about not being sure of him, not loving him – '

'IT WASN'T CRAP.'

'He loved you more than anything. He utterly adored you. It inspired me just to see it.'

From up above there was a sudden noise, a window being opened on the first floor, a man in a t-shirt.

'*Vous ne pouvez pas la mettre en sourdine?*'

'*Excusez-nous*,' Venus said.

Muttering to himself, he closed the window.

They carried on walking, through the noisy street and then back to the quiet.

'Wait. I told you in that letter. I wrote it in that letter – '

'You think I don't remember?'

'But when it's staring you in the face you can't see it. I don't understand what you need. How could you love anyone?'

'Listen to me. You think every day I remind myself of what his mother said in case my life is too good? You think I haven't spent the whole time since he died half dead myself with wanting to love him?' Her hands shook. 'I make one mistake with you, I put it right, I do everything I can do, and you have the *nerve* to act like this whole thing is *my fault*.'

They were silent for a second.

He sighed. 'I shouldn't have asked you whether you knew, I don't think that. But what I can't bear is that you're determined to think the worst, against all the evidence – '

'How can you say that? When I've told you all that happened, how can you possibly say that?'

'What about everything you haven't told me? How you met, how you fell in love? You're doubting something that I know for sure you have no basis to doubt.'

'Well, lucky you… '

'Don't, *don't* be sarcastic.'

'Oh so precious.'

'It *is* precious.'

'Well then there's no way out, is there? If I love Gilles, I don't love you. And if I don't love him, you don't love me. So come on Alex, let's just get it over with.'

'What are you saying?'

'Well what are *you* saying?'

His eyes seemed to be searching her out.

'If he were here now, how would he convince you? If he told you he loved you, how would you know he meant it? You can't know.'

She didn't answer.

'It's nothing to do with whether he told the truth.' His voice weakened as if he'd come to a realisation. 'It's just that you're not him.'

'Look, if I could love him again… I swear to you I would.'

'But from one stupid thing his mother said, you lose all faith? Why? I can't understand it.'

'What are you doing? Acting for him?'

The street was quiet. He was looking at her, without anger, sorrow welling in his face, his expression beginning to break. And as if they were slowly sinking, something seemed to loosen between them.

'Sorry… ' he breathed unevenly. 'Sorry.'

They held each other.

And then she felt his whole frame breathe out. 'It did seem… like I already knew you.'

The air was hot and dense. They walked towards the river, not speaking, moving with weary momentum.

The wind began to pick up, chasing people through the streets like leaves, the night quickly growing darker.

Just before they reached the river, Venus recognised the hostel she'd stayed at years before, and as they walked past it, the heavy door of St Gervais church opposite. It was all completely unchanged.

The street broadened and the river came into view in front of them. With one gust, the wind swept out the dry air and made room for the rain. Thirty yards beyond it, rain stinging their skin, they rushed back to the church, pushed the door open and ran inside, the hammering outside making it suddenly quiet.

She sighed, wiping her face.

Hearing her, an elderly man turned around, focused on her briefly then walked towards the chapel behind the altar.

They went to the row of wooden chairs nearest the door and sat down.

She cast her eyes around the barely lit building, drawn by the pillars to the high arches between them, the huge arch-shaped windows and vaulted ceiling.

She hadn't been into a church for years. Hadn't taken Leonie. Couldn't understand why she felt guilty.

She sensed Alex look at her, but waited before looking back at him, and by the time she did, he'd looked away.

Here, in her husband's church. His wife sitting with his friend. She in Paris to see his mother, his friend no doubt established at work through his connections. Nowhere to hide.

After nearly four years, on the point of starting again, daring herself to believe it might happen –

It was an impossible thought. They would have no life. Gilles shrinking them into nothing, Alex revering him for it. She and Gilles and their great lost love. Was that what it had been? This vice-like passion that she longed to be crushed by and that incited her to crush back. So that no one could get between them. So that the two of them were condemned to be together and condemned to be alone. So that life, time, other people were shadows in the face of them.

The rain dwindled, then returned more steadily.

She felt Alex look towards her again.

'I think it's stopped,' he said.

She listened for a moment. She couldn't hear anything.

'Look,' he said, 'why don't I walk to Place des Vosges with you?'

'It's okay,' she got up from her chair. 'I'll stay for a bit. You go home and sleep.'

They held each other briefly.

Then he walked a few steps towards the door before turning back.

'Don't go home without telling me will you?'

She blinked with tiredness. 'I've got to tell you about… ' She touched her stomach.

He was quiet.

'I'm not sure what's worse,' she said. 'Knowing what you'll miss, or missing what you'll never know.'

'We don't have to come to a decision like that.'

'There's,' she said, afraid to say it, 'there's something wrong with me, to do with Gilles.' She started slightly at hearing herself. 'I think I'll have to make it better on my own.'

She listened to the words again, the starkness of them.

'You can't mean that. Not forever.'

She glanced at him and wished she knew what to say.

'Don't give up,' he whispered.

They looked at each other, unsure what to do next.

'Goodnight,' he said eventually.

'Goodnight,' she said.

He walked a few steps, then turned around. He smiled at her. And as she looked back at him, it felt like the rain had become her tears.

He started walking.

'Alex – '

He turned around again. She smiled.

He blew her a kiss. As if he were going away for the weekend. And he left.

There was a small cushion hanging on a hook in front of her chair. Tired, she put it on the floor and sat on it, resting her head on the seat of the chair in front.

… She'd get a taxi home, she thought. Visit Hélène tomorrow, see how that went.

She closed her eyes.

Abruptly she had a sense of waking up. She checked her watch. She couldn't have been asleep for long, five minutes maybe.

It occurred to her to take Leonie here before they left. Sometime anyway.

She hung the cushion back on its hook and decided to walk.

On her way out, she saw a stray sheet of paper on a pew. She picked it up. Just the readings for the day. But something caught her eye, and seeing it properly, she did a double take.

Sainte Marie Madeleine

Mémoire

She looked down, scanning the words.

J'ai cherché celui que mon coeur aime.

Lecture du Cantique des Cantiques 3, 1-4

Toute la nuit j'ai cherché celui que mon coeur aime.

Étendue sur mon lit, je l'ai cherché, je ne l'ai pas trouvé!

Quickly she read on: the woman looked all night, all through the town, not finding him. She asked the guards whether they'd seen him. And then, just after she'd asked them, she found him! The one her heart loved.

She folded the piece of paper, pushed it into her pocket, walked out of the church and into the street.

35

'The Joker'
by Steve Miller, Ahmet Ertegun and Eddie Curtis

At three o'clock on Good Friday afternoon, my jacket hanging convincingly on my chair, I walked the couple of steps from my desk to the door that led to the back stairs of the office. I went down three flights, quiet as a cloud, tapped in the caretaker's code on the locked door at the bottom, strolled into an advertising agency with a completely different set of lifts and landed in the street entirely undetected.

Good Friday wasn't a bank holiday in France, so continuing my quest for pointless adventure, I ran to the Madeleine like an escaped convict. And although I made no claim to piety, I aspired to it, and if anyone could understand that, I felt sure it was the woman the church was named after.

I switched on at school when Mary Magdalen came up. They made it clear she was a sinner, but the exact nature of her sin wasn't described. I wondered what she could have done. Murder? That was the best sin I knew, but it didn't fit. She had long, beautiful hair and she cried on Christ's feet and used her hair to wipe away her tears. And her sin didn't matter, because she loved so much. And she mistook the risen Christ for the gardener, which made me think she had a sense of humour.

There was a large cross on the left side of the church

made of red and white cut flowers. People were adding flowers to it themselves, white where the head would have been, red for the rest. I went back to the entrance and bought a red carnation and a white lily and put them in. Then I walked further up the church, knelt down and thought of you.

After the priest had said the stations of the cross, I joined the people queuing to kiss the wooden cross by the altar. I often felt like a fraud at Mass, which was fair enough because I was a fraud. But this time the experience was heightened by the fact that I couldn't get you out of my mind.

You asleep in my bed, me kissing you, kissing every part of you, you kissing every part of me. And I tell myself no. Control yourself. For God's sake. But the nearer I got in the queue, the more impure my thoughts became, until my imagination began to emit a nuclear glow of lust, the mental activity becoming so frenzied that words wouldn't come fast or strong enough to contain it.

Only two people in front. I could hear lips touching the crucifix.

Venus.

Must I step aside? Before it's too late?

Oh Venus.

Does everyone do this? Am I beyond redemption?

But oh God Venus Venus Venus.

Of course I didn't think sex was a sin. I didn't think that Vee. Which is lucky, given bona fide Catholic sex has always been beyond me. I have never qualified. As we know contraception isn't always reliable, thank goodness for that. But even when you were pregnant, you could hardly claim the purpose was procreation.

There's always the confession tactic. Sin and then ask forgiveness. The problem with that is you have to want to be forgiven, and who in their heart of hearts wants to be forgiven every time they do it?

So you come to the obvious solution. Renounce your religion.

To be honest, I've no idea why I believe in God. Of course it's made-up. It's complete balls. Do I believe in talking hedgehogs? They may be charming in concept, but that doesn't make them real.

But this brings its own inconvenience. I'm addicted to my religion. I'm a practising hypocrite, I can't give it up.

Whether it's a failure of courage or an extravagance of sentiment, I don't know. I only know that having something to aspire to is better than having nothing. The will to believe, the perverse glory taken in its exercise, will always distort my reason. I believe. I am a believer. Churches just corrupt my vision.

… The Eternal City, forty degrees and I, papal legate, pace the perimeter of St Peter's Square.

'Father Gilles,' say the ladies who sell the light-up shrines, 'you look anxious.'

Anxious? I pound the Vatican pavements day and night. Damn it, I'm falling apart.

This cannot wait, I must speak with the Holy Father. I conceal my identity with a simple moustache and beard set and, passing myself off as the legate's lay cousin, procure an audience.

I enter a large gilded chamber in the Vatican. John Paul II sits on a throne at the other end of the room. I walk slowly towards him. I notice there is a small television by his side. And I remember the cardinal's words of caution: 'Be quick; his Holiness does not like to be disturbed during the football.'

I kneel down in front of the Holy Father. I must use all powers at my disposal.

'Contraception,' I mutter nervously.

The Pope looks down on me kindly, placing a bookmark in his TV guide.

'My son,' he says, 'a conjugal act that is detrimental to the faculty of propagating life contradicts God's design.'

'But,' I stammer, 'but if contraception contradicts God's design, then – then so do knives and forks.'

The Pope changes channels. Still pre-match discussion on the other side.

'Human life is sacred,' he says, 'from its inception it reveals the creating hand of God.'

'Yes,' I say, 'yes. But,' I rush, 'but contraception only prevents life from starting – '

The cardinal comes in with a cup of tea and hands it to the Pope. I must make use of this diversion.

'Sex before marriage,' I whisper hoarsely.

The cardinal glances at me warily. He places a high table next to the Pope's throne, whispers something to him and departs. The Pope blows on his tea, and puts the cup down on the table.

'My dear Gilles.' No! He sees into my heart! 'Premature relations cannot ensure, in sincerity and fidelity, the interpersonal relationship between a man and a woman.'

'But,' I splutter, my defences collapsing, 'but I love her, and I want to marry her – and God made us with feelings and urges – '

The Pope takes a sip of tea and puts down his cup.

The cardinal enters again.

'Your Holiness,' he whispers, 'the game has now started.'

It is time for me to leave.

I look up at the Pope.

'Nice beard,' he nods.

'Thanks,' I swallow.

I withdraw from the gilded chamber. Sister Venus has departed for England, and I must face my God alone.

Except not entirely alone. There is one rather unusual technique left at my disposal: in pale imitation of the Trinity, I will split myself into two persons. And I will take myself in hand.

I, Wised-up Gilles, go back to the Madeleine that Good Friday afternoon and kneel down beside my younger self.

Young Gilles budges up. He knows I see his hidden guilt.

I shoot him a nice point about the resurrection straight off.

'Come on,' I say, 'how can bodies be bad if Christ got his back? He was totally reheated, that's what Easter's all about. And in the end, that's supposed to happen to everyone.'

'Yeh,' he says.

But he's still fighting, that's the power of religion.

'All right,' I tell him, 'out with it, why do you secretly think sex is a sin?'

He sighs. 'Well for a start,' he says, 'it gives you a great excuse not to be a saint. If your whole existence condemns you, why bother?'

'Okay,' I say, 'but the truth is you're not condemned. All it takes to be God is to love everyone – sexual love of one person needn't stop you doing that, not if you're good enough.'

'Yeh,' he replies, 'but I don't want to be a saint. Original sin's handy cover. Anyway, it's not just that,' he continues, 'Venus isn't sure about me, that's why she doesn't want to do it. And I admire her for that, despite myself. And I'm hoping that one day she'll love me, and that when she does, I'll at least graduate to a different league.'

The poor man. A bank holiday weekend alone, it will remain conjecture.

Now he's on the right lines, but he needs some extra fire-power. And I've got just the thing. A demented piece of Christian genius.

I lean in close. 'Listen to this,' I whisper.

'What?' he whispers back.

'*Christ was made man*. Not God, *human*. He breathed, he ate, he slept, he had urges. What if he really did do it with Mary Magdalen? She regretted her past, they fell in love and they did it.'

He looks at me like he hasn't seriously considered it before.

'The Christian world relieved of two thousand years of nervous tension, what a mind-bending thought that is.'

He stares at the altar, he's not objecting to the idea.

'Get on and believe it,' I say. 'Live it out.'

'Perhaps there's nothing holier… ' he wonders.

I nod, he's getting it. 'Nothing holier.'

36

'Bookends'
by Paul Simon

It took fifteen minutes on the train out of Gare du Nord for the railway sidings and high-rise flats to give way to fields. Venus looked out of the window.

She wished she'd bought a newspaper.

She'd already phoned the hospital. She'd apologised, she was going to be ten minutes late, her train had been delayed. In a soft accent whose origin Venus couldn't place, the nurse had told her not to worry, Hélène would still be there.

On her own, no child to entertain, nothing to read. She watched a young woman in the seat opposite playing a game on her phone, then looked out again.

Flat field after flat field.

What was she after? To sit in silence with a woman whose last words had haunted her for years. And if the woman spoke, if she answered Venus's question, then what? Gilles would still be dead.

She'd hated Hélène. She'd hated almost everyone, for almost anything. Her mother, the wholesome couple she and David made. Matt and Isobel and their overextended sympathy. Colleagues and friends, either stifling or unaware.

He'd just let it happen, her own husband. He hadn't even fought. She could hate him for *not* knowing.

Alex seemed to think she did it deliberately. It was infuriating of him.

Time only healed by making things less simple. It layered life up, so that the moments of clear sight got fewer, and the hate and love were blurred until your eyes could take it.

You didn't love someone, not after a week. He'd said that because it was what he'd wanted – not that that wasn't a lovable thing to do.

He was lovable. And what was she going to do, stop thinking about him? She fancied the fuck out of him. She could fly to his flat, soar across the fields.

He'd brought the outside world back into view. His kindness, his beauty, like soft lights. Looking, in his company, had been bearable again.

Pity wasn't it, that he was the one person in the world who took her husband more seriously than she did.

At the station Venus got a taxi to the hospital. She walked inside, through another set of doors and the smell hit her. Bodies too close, windows unopened, urine that had dried in the heat.

She found the nurse she'd spoken to on the phone. Her name was Anne-Maie. Together they went to look for Hélène. Venus asked in French where she was from. Mauritius, she said. She'd been here four months now. She often looked after Hélène.

The nurse stopped at the television room, scanned the grey heads and continued to walk down the corridor. She said Hélène hadn't been well lately. She was more confused than usual. The doctors still didn't think it was Alzheimer's – but of course she hardly ate which didn't help.

At least, the nurse added, she was talking more.

Venus was astounded. She asked the nurse what sort of thing Hélène had said. The nurse asked Venus whether she was a relative of Hélène's. Venus had assumed someone would have explained. She told her briefly about Gilles.

The nurse poked her head into another room. Venus looked.

There among the white plastic tables and chairs was Hélène. She was alone, sitting with her side to them at a table at the far end. The nurse whispered that it was a good sign that Hélène was here and not in her bedroom. She stood with Venus on the threshold for a moment, then excused herself and left.

Venus went into the room, stopping a clear distance from where Hélène sat.

'Hélène?' she said softly.

Hélène turned towards her. Her face had thinned further.

'Hello,' Venus said.

Hélène turned back to the table.

Venus couldn't tell whether she'd seen her or not. She walked a little nearer.

Hélène didn't look up. She was folding a piece of white material with pale blue flowers on it. Once it was folded, she took it in her hands, got up out of her chair and started to walk between the tables towards the door. Venus followed her.

Like a remote control toy, Hélène changed direction. She headed to the right side of the room. Then, apparently noticing she was walking towards the wall, she turned sharply back in the direction of the table. After a few steps, she came to a halt.

For a second Venus didn't move. She couldn't understand how Hélène could have declined this much.

Although, she thought, perhaps restlessness could be seen as progress. It was better than sitting surely, her mind might be more stimulated as a result.

Slowly she went to her and offered her hand.

Hélène looked at her as if she hadn't realised there'd been anyone in the room.

'Would you like to sit down?' Venus asked quietly.

She looked at Venus again, taking her in.

'Hélène?'

Hélène started to whisper almost silently in French. Venus couldn't make it out.

Childishly, she whispered back, 'Hélène, Hélène, Hélène.'

Then with a jolt, she heard the words, '*j'étais méchante, j'étais méchante, j'étais méchante*,' repeated over and over again.

I was a bad person. That was what she was saying.

She must have recognised her. She was saying sorry. She must be trying to say sorry.

'No,' Venus whispered.

Hélène stared at her.

Venus stared back. '*Vous n'étiez pas méchante*.'

You weren't a bad person.

Hélène looked agitated.

'*Qui êtes-vous?*' she said, hoarsely.

Who are you?

Venus's grasp of reality slipped for a second.

She urged Hélène's eyes to come to life, desperately searching her out. She needed someone to look for her, wasn't that it? Someone who had to get her to talk.

Venus said in French that her name was Venus, that she was Gilles' wife, that Gilles was Hélène's son.

Hélène seemed to be concentrating. His name. That was it.

But she pointed to a nearby table. Venus looked. There was some spilt jam on the edge. Two flies were buzzing around it.

Venus got a tissue from her bag and wiped the table, but some jam remained, smeared. She folded the tissue in half and spat into it. She wiped the edge of the table again. All the jam came off. She screwed the tissue up and put it back in her bag.

They went to Hélène's original table and sat down.

Hélène kept the material in her hands. Venus noticed that there was a finely embroidered H in one corner. A scarf perhaps. She imagined Hélène as a young girl, the scarf tied under her chin, walking down the street with her nose in the air.

She smiled at her.

Hélène rested the material on the table, still holding it in both hands.

Venus said that it was pretty.

Hélène replied that she'd made it at school.

Her heart in her mouth, Venus asked whether it had taken a long time to make.

Hélène said no, it hadn't.

A conversation. A real conversation.

They sat for a moment without talking.

'*Hélène*?' Venus whispered.

But Hélène asked again who Venus was.

Venus told her her name.

Hélène said, like the plant, the flytrap.

Venus laughed in amazement. Yes, she smiled, Venus flytrap. Just like that. Again she wanted to believe that the woman she'd known was inside, trying to clear a way through.

'*Hélène*?'

Hélène asked whether she was checking on the nurses.

No, said Venus.

Hélène said that she ought to be. Her eyes darted with life. She said that some of them had done terrible things. They were wicked.

The word rang in Venus's head. *Méchantes*.

Hélène said that it wasn't clean here. There were germs. Venus should mention that to her superiors.

Venus didn't reply. She waited a while and smiled at Hélène.

She asked Hélène how she was feeling.

Hélène looked down and became coy. Quietly she said that she was going to have a baby.

For a crazed second Venus thought that Hélène knew somehow, about her and Alex.

But she smiled. She wished Hélène congratulations. Did Hélène know, she asked, whether it was a boy or a girl.

Hélène frowned. She said Venus should tell her which girl it was.

Venus paused.

They did it, they forced her. They are wicked, she said. *Méchantes*.

What did they do, Venus asked.

Hélène looked into Venus's eyes, as if she'd been dreadfully wronged. It was the nurses, she breathed. It wasn't me.

She looked at Venus imploringly. It wasn't me, she said. She started to cry.

Venus got another tissue from her bag and gave it to Hélène. Hélène wiped her eyes.

Venus put her arm around Hélène's shoulder.

But Hélène looked at her accusingly. You're a nurse, she said.

No, Venus said. I'm not a nurse.

I know your name you know, she said. It's Venus.

Yes, said Venus, it is.

They didn't speak. Hélène felt the material of the scarf with her fingers while Venus sat still. Eventually Hélène looked up, and Venus smiled at her.

My best friend… Hélène hesitated. My best friend was the flower-seller.

Who was the flower-seller, Venus asked.

A little girl, Hélène said. And in a wistful voice, she added that the flower-seller sang all the names of the flowers.

How beautiful, said Venus.

Then seemingly out of the blue, Hélène smiled. Venus smiled back, taking her hand.

That must have been lovely, Venus said.

Hélène smiled again.

Their erratic talk continued, punctuated by Venus's delicate attempts at questions, until finally, having at least to say the words, Venus asked Hélène straight out whether Gilles knew he would die.

Hélène replied that the builders came inside and turned things upside down.

When Venus looked at her watch to plan which train to catch, she saw that she'd been with Hélène for forty minutes.

She left her sitting with some others in a room full of armchairs. She asked her whether there was anything she wanted, but Hélène didn't reply.

Venus kissed Hélène on both cheeks and said goodbye.

She found Anne-Maie preparing doses of pills.

She asked her whether Hélène was more lucid at some times than others. The nurse called another woman over, explained to her whose pills were whose and led Venus into an office.

She said that for the last month Hélène had been quite ill. She hadn't been taking her sleeping pills, but had collected them in her purse. She wasn't deemed to be at risk, she'd never done anything like that before – no one had known until another nurse had discovered them four weeks ago. It was the stress of the discovery, bearing in mind that she was already sleep-deprived and confused, that had brought on the agitation.

Shocked, Venus said she hadn't had any idea it had been that serious.

The nurse said that obviously she was being closely monitored now. She had at least become talkative, even if what she was saying didn't make sense.

Venus imagined the nurses forcing her to give the pills up, calling her *méchante*. But she was weak physically, the nurse added, which made everything worse.

Venus confirmed that the hospital had her address and phone number. She asked to be informed if there was any change.

She began to apologise for not coming more often. It was difficult, she lived in London.

Well, Anne-Maie said, everyone had their lives to attend to.

Uneasily Venus said goodbye and left the hospital.

There was nobody in the flat when she got back. It was a muggy day, Mary and Leonie had obviously gone out. She went to the bedroom and dropped her bag on the bed. She sat on the bed herself and took off her shoes.

She closed her eyes, her teeth ground down, sunk with emotion. A conversation with Hélène at last – all she'd wanted, a window to look through – and she'd looked without thinking, hadn't realised there'd be a person inside.

Hélène's utter lack of prospect, frankly acknowledged, had become her own. What more was she? Unhappy, lonely, half mad. Who could tell one from the other?

Hélène's fate twisted in her head. The nurses couldn't let her die, but they couldn't offer more than a managed falling apart. It was death by another name.

The key of her thoughts shifted for a moment.

If Hélène could come home, if Mary were willing to look after her – she'd offered to do it, she'd said that –

Was it unfair, to ask Mary when she'd balk at the task herself?

Hélène was functioning. Enough to decide she couldn't go on, enough to make the nurses pay attention. Which they'd paid. And she was talking. But they didn't need her to make sense. And Venus did. Because that was her trashy angle. Be kind until she tells you, then what?

Sick with herself, she wished Leonie were there, thought she would have been waiting, longed to hold her, love her without question.

She thought of Alex, her brain like damp paper. She began to cry quietly, trying to stop herself. Then, unable to believe the future that had been denied them, she started to sob.

She heard the door of the flat click open. She ran to the bathroom and locked the bolt. She filled the basin with cold water and sunk her head into it. She coughed from the shock and washed the water over her eyes instead.

She decided to have a shower. Taking off her pants she saw the sludge of blood. For a moment her brain shut down.

So, that was good. That was one less thing to worry about. That made things simpler, didn't it.

The tears flowed into her face.

37

'Little Wing'
by Jimi Hendrix

I woke up pointlessly early on Saturday. You were lost to me in rural England for fifty-three more hours, and I'd spent half the night with Georges Costel and his men, toasting bank holidays. My bed felt like a motorboat, at least one of the curried kebabs I'd had for supper had been poisoned and I doubted all possibility of future survival.

Vee, I missed you.

Where would you be? Having breakfast with your brother?

No, not food, I couldn't think about it.

Maybe you hadn't got dressed yet. Still warm in bed in a nightdress that was on the short side...

But I was powerless against the listing sick-green haze.

Swirling, I walked twenty yards to the nearest *pharmacie*, got hold of the salty fizzy stuff, drank it and went back to bed.

The chemist had pink fingernails. Venus watched them as they moved around the Tampax box. She was wrapping the box in brown paper, as if it was going to be given at a dinner party. She explained that she only had white bags left – the packaging tended to show through.

Venus and Leonie went on to the bakery. The queue

stretched outside the shop. Leonie went inside to have a look. A man with red trousers and a baby in a pushchair joined the queue behind Venus. They smiled at each other.

She told herself she ought to phone Alex.

She moved into the heat of the shop, holding the door open for the man. The smell of pastry made her mouth water. Leonie came back from the counter and asked if she could have a *pain au chocolat*.

'No,' said Venus.

'Oh please! Mummy please!'

'But why not?' the man behind smiled. 'One only, it is harmless.'

Leonie looked at her mother. Venus replied in French to the man that unfortunately her daughter was on a diet for medical reasons – to protect her heart. Hastily the man apologised. Leonie looked at him. She'd understood, his demeanour was translation enough.

Venus came out of the shop with a loaf of wholemeal bread and a small fruit tart.

'Mummy?' Leonie was cross. 'I want to go back to the flat, I'm fed up with shopping.'

'Just wait,' Venus said. 'We've got to get something for Mary. We'll be in the flat for most of the weekend anyway, we've got to pack all Daddy's stuff before Monday.'

Leonie sighed melodramatically.

Venus looked at her sharply.

'Sorreee.'

By the early afternoon, I was cured.

I thought about which restaurant to take you to on Monday evening, had a shower, went out, bought a paper and noticed the blue sky. I walked down to Hôtel de Ville and got off the train at Porte Maillot near the Bois de Boulogne. I stopped in a *boulangerie* for some lunch, went into the park and rented a bike. I cycled around in the sun, found a quiet patch, ate and read the paper. Then I got back on the bike and, when no one was looking, took my hands off the handlebars. If that little bastard on Vieille du Temple could do it, so could I. I later learned that it wasn't all that difficult, if you had the *right kind of bike*. Which only confirmed my suspicions.

When the sun started going down I looked at the cinema listings in the paper. A cinema near the Sorbonne was showing a film called *Un Homme et Une Femme*. I got the *métro* back into the city. The film was whimsical and romantic, and it didn't take long before I was the man driving through the night across France and you were the beautiful woman with the long eyelashes laughing on the sand.

I walked out of the cinema seized with inspiration. I'd drive to England to see you. Get the last boat, race through the night.

It was 9.45. You were staying with your brother. His address was at home. I ran north and got a cab. I arrived at the flat and out of habit, checked my post. Like a naturalist caught unawares by his find, I saw it nestling there, amid the flyers. Your handwriting on a bulging white envelope.

I turned the letter over. Nothing on the back. I looked again at the front. Just my name. No stamp, no address. You must have delivered it before you left on Friday. Had you got in through the front gate? Or no, perhaps you'd just dropped it through, perhaps the concierge…

God, what kind of mooncalf would worry about the postal procedure?

The thing was, it was important. Everything about you was important, especially if it involved me.

Carefully I opened the envelope.

Of course… the handkerchief. Clean and neatly folded. It smelt nice, a little of you. Well that was kind of you Vee.

I looked in the envelope again. Thoroughly. Slightly stuck to the inside was a small piece of white paper. I took it out. I turned it over.

Darling, how I adored you for it. And maybe, on

reflection, invading a family baptism wouldn't have gone down too well.

A print of your lips in rosy lipstick, a slender space between them and at the bottom the words: *Until Monday*.

I'd wait for you until then.

Venus looked around her at the clutter of childhood possessions, cardboard boxes and masking tape.

Leonie began to cry more loudly.

'Leo, for God's sake what is it?'

'IT HURTS,' Leonie shouted.

Venus went over to her. She had a small graze on her finger.

'Okay, sorry.' Venus kissed her forehead. 'Look,' she whispered, 'you can watch telly if you want.'

'I don't want to any more,' Leonie whispered back.

It was going to take ages. There was so much more stuff than she'd thought. Things she'd gone through just after he'd died, deemed useless and then forgotten so firmly it was as if they'd never existed.

'... What about your book?'

Hélène had kept toys, baby clothes, little cardigans...

'It's boring.'

She must have wanted another child, Venus thought – then decided later to keep things in case Gilles had a child, in case they'd had another child. The same longing, transferred.

She'd given Leonie a few toys. But she'd kept things back.

'Mummy?' Leonie said quietly.

'Yeh?'

Leonie looked at her without speaking, as if she was trying to pull Venus into the present.

Venus took her hand. 'Everything will be better once I've done this, I promise. Darling listen,' she said after a moment, 'why don't you help me?'

'No thanks *merci*.'

She packed things into boxes while Leonie lay on the bed.

A few minutes later Venus heard the door.

'Want a cuppa love?' Mary called. She poked her head into the room. 'Venus love, I don't want you feeling you've got to do it all before you go. I mean not for the B&B – I'll just move it into Hélène's – '

'No I should have done it years ago.'

'All right, but don't you rush on my account.'

'… Have you seen the clothes in here?'

'Well that's Hélène for you. Can't stand anything going to waste.' Mary made to go, then turned back. 'Tell you what, there might be some bits in her room, little souvenirs and such.'

'Yeh thanks, I've looked through it all before. I won't take anything that's hers.'

'All right love.'

Mary went out. Venus carried a box over to the far right of the room and started taking the books off the shelves and packing them into it. There was a fat blue one with gold-edged pages which looked like it had never been opened. It was called *The Weekday Missal*.

The pages were so thin you could see the writing on the other side. Readings for Weekdays in Ordinary Time, The Order of Mass, Prefaces. Then nearer the end, Proper of Saints. Venus flicked forwards. Proper of Saints, 21 April. Proper of Saints, 29 June. Proper of Saints, 22 July.

22 July. St Mary Magdalen. There she was, the woman who looked for the one her heart loved.

On my bed, at night, I sought him
Whom my heart loves.
I sought but did not find him.
So I will rise and go through the City;
In the streets and the squares
I will seek him whom my heart loves.
I sought but did not find him.
The watchmen came upon me

On their rounds in the City:
'Have you seen him whom my heart loves?'
Scarcely had I passed them
Than I found him whom my heart loves.

The Holy Week Masses are well designed. They bore you to death with all the histrionics about Barabbas so that by the time you get to Easter Sunday resurrection takes place through liturgical relief alone.

Newly light, I hung around the kitchen, dispensing my lightness to Mary, opening a bag of peanuts, finding the corkscrew, hunting for glasses.

I took my glass back to my room. The doors were open on to the square which was full of children. I wondered what you'd think of it. I doodled some lovesick crap for a while, gave up and strolled back into the kitchen. I could smell the beef roasting. Mary was standing at the sink doing the potatoes. I took one of her peeled carrots and started eating it.

Mary handed me the peeler. She went to get another carrot from the larder and gave it to me. I sat down at the table and worked up to peeling it.

'Good service was it love?' She was standing against the sink looking at me.

'Yeh, not bad.' I couldn't peel and talk at the same time. 'How was the market?'

'Yeh, you know… Françoise – did I tell you she's getting married to this bloke from Bristol?'

'Oh?'

'She's a lovely girl,' Mary smiled. 'Anyway according to her, there's this quiet bloke on *noisettes*, Philippe he's called – she reckons he's up to something with Nicole – I couldn't believe it. That's Nicole on *quiches*. She's got two kids.'

'She liked the look of his nuts.'

She chuckled and pinched my cheek. 'Give him his due though, he's got a lovely stall, Philippe. Not easy, making a living out of nuts, but he's done all right.'

She paused. She was standing looking at me.

'What?'

'You got my bloody peeler haven't you? Come on, give it here.'

Mary peeled the carrot at warp speed and got going with the potatoes again.

'So,' she said, 'what's her name then?'

'Venus.'

'Yeh,' Mary paused, 'your mum did say.'

The potatoes jumbled about against each other.

'Give her time love, she'll come round. With you being here, you know, it's worse in a way. It's a change for her. She only wants what's best for you doesn't she? I mean if you like her, this girl.'

'I like her all right. I've just got to get her to like me.'

'Course she likes you,' Mary tutted, landing another peeled potato on the draining board.

I thought about how much you and I had in common. 'It's weird,' I said. 'She never knew her father. He walked out before she was even born.'

Mary turned round. I looked behind me. My mother was standing in the doorway. She stood there, looking at us, almost smiling.

'So,' she said casually, 'we will have to meet this Venus, won't we Mary?'

Leonie'd caught the sun. Rowing on the lake in the Bois de Vincennes, not a bad way to spend a Sunday afternoon. She and Mary had brought in the breeze of their outdoor activity and taken off with it into the kitchen.

The elastic band in Venus's hair was coming loose. She took it out, pulled her hair back and wound it round tighter.

There were only clothes left now, and the books on the top shelf.

She pushed a chair up against the bookshelves to stand on.

Maybe she was wasting this mood. She could be getting rid of most of it now. Why pay for the clothes to be moved? But no, it all had to go back to London. One of those rules that grew in significance with the slackness of its logic.

She took an armful of books and put them one by one into a box. She stopped at a tattered collection of Edward Lear poems and opened it. In the front was his name, written backwards in unsteady capital letters. Leonie had done that. She put the book down carefully on the bed.

She stopped again at a very thin book. *The Virgin and the Gypsy* by D H Lawrence. She glanced at the blurb on the back …gypsy awakens within her an elemental force… It might be a good one. She threw it over to the bed.

She came to a blue-covered Clairefontaine exercise book. She flicked through it. Nothing but squared paper.

Hilaire Belloc's Cautionary Verses. She'd teased him about it. There was a plate inside which said *PRIZE awarded to Gilles Matheson for Religion and Biology*.

Another exercise book, green-covered, ring bound. She opened it. It was lined, English in style. Ragged stubs of torn-off paper hung from the white metal spiral. She flicked through the few pages left.

A picture and words. An outline in blue biro of lips. There was a suggestive space between them, as if the lips were saying 'oooh'. Some adolescent thing. And the words *Until Monday*, like a title. Until Monday?

That took up the top third of the page. Then underneath his writing – smaller than usual, words crossed out. But not a child's writing, recognisably his.

She pieced it together.

To watch the lips of you sing the sound of you
hear the hands of you touch the skin of you
Kiss the back of your neck's child-scent
Breathe your breath
Be where I'm meant
To be

She closed the book, climbed steadily down from the chair and laid it beside the bed.

Didn't I remember her telling me Mary had washed the sheets? Yes, I remembered that.

And I'd insisted Vee that you take every single phone number I could possibly give you. My flat, my mother's flat, the Earlsfield flat. In case.

And tomorrow was Easter Monday. You were coming back at last.

And it was comfortable here, and it was late now – not that the ten minute walk was arduous but it was further than you thought, quite a way up rue de Turenne, and it's one of those streets that's always windy.

And for God's sake when it came down to it, it pleased my mother.

She'd been in a good mood that day. I'd already booked a restaurant for Monday evening, but I asked her advice as if I hadn't. When I suggested the one I'd chosen, she said it was much too expensive. Amicably I thanked her and changed the subject, like the sea that washes a layer of stone from the cliff and pulls back without the cliff feeling a thing.

I had a bath, huge and hot – her bath was even bigger than mine, I could stretch out in it completely. Only five feet six and slim as a pencil but my mother's never been taken in by all those elfin-sized baths and beds you get everywhere. And the shower could have served a harem, a picture that in my lonely youth I occasionally dwelt on.

But that night I was innocent as a lamb. I got into bed in the dark. I liked the smell of my mother's sheets. I felt content and quiet, as if anxiety hadn't been invented. And I thought that wherever you were, wherever I was, in my mind I'd always be with you.

Venus checked the room. Everything was either in boxes, in one of her bags or beside the bed ready to pack in the morning.

She stretched, then bent down to touch her toes. Her hair hung in front of her. She'd have a shower, she thought, get the dust out.

The mirror in the bathroom was steamed up. She supposed Mary had had a bath.

She took off her clothes and turned on the shower. The water dashed down her back. She angled her head to rinse her hair.

He'd get in with her. She remembered the sound of the door sliding open. Both of them silently giggling. Then at home, when he was brushing his teeth and she was washing her hair, just another day.

But it wasn't, it never was. You'd have to be half-dead…

She wondered what test she could possibly have set, what more there could be than their life together.

She wrapped her towel around her, went into the bedroom and shut the door. She kept the French doors open but closed the curtains. She sat on the bed and dried her hair.

It was too late to ring Alex. She'd ring him tomorrow. It would be better like that anyway.

She put on a t-shirt, took the bedspread off the bed and got in. She felt for the exercise book on the bedside table, and turned off the light.

I had a vivid dream that night. I was in a dark corridor, looking for the back stairs, trying to find my way out of the office. It became a tunnel, with locked doors off it. And I could hear you singing, from far away.

This dream again. She didn't want it. The sea. Nearly dark. Too hot. Cooler by the water.

… I call to you, but you don't reply. I'm worried you can't hear me.

… He's there, by the water. She tries to speak, but no sound comes out.

It's as if everything is covered in petals which take out the noise. I know you can't hear, because I can't either. I retrace my steps, but it makes no difference. I can't find you.

If only he'd wait. If he could just wait for her to think of what to do.

A breeze comes and the air clears. I feel serene. I think you must be turning around because I can hear you as if you're next to me.

'Vee?' I call laughing, 'Vee?'

Gilles! He was looking! He'd heard her, he must have!

You're there. Oh my love. Oh thank heaven.

38

'There Is A Light That Never Goes Out'
by Johnny Marr and Morrissey

It was strange, that night at my mother's. The happiness became a memory and in its place came the opposite. I'd fallen out of life, the dead were there waiting, their creed not one of bitterness, no – it was more lethal than that.

Nothing, they say, there is nothing. And the hopeful are nullities. Look at the poor fool, does he not know? Exhausted, they whisper it. All you do is die.

Leo woke up in the night. She was standing by the bed shaking, tears squeezing out of her eyes. And I thought you were still alive. She said she'd had a bad dream, she had things in her teeth and her teeth were broken. Someone was chasing her, they kept running after her.

I thought of my mother and me silent in hospital, my father dead. Perhaps everyone saw their parents' lives as a prophesy. And you, not knowing whether your father was dead or alive, which was infinitely harder to take. And then I thought of us. And I felt that whatever the future held, I could choose hope like a prize at the fair.

She came into bed. And I told her I loved you and I loved her. She fell asleep and the dream came back to me, how patiently you'd waited. I remembered how I'd left you in Paris just after we'd met. Matthew and Isobel were grown up, I had more in common with their baby than with them. I wanted you to come crashing into the church in that car with the Paris plates. You were the one who'd drain life dry. Gi? I loved you, after a week I loved you, but I couldn't tell you what I couldn't tell myself.

That's what I knew. I could die tomorrow. You could walk away, pretend we'd never met. But without hope, the most glorious future was bleak. If I could hope, I'd have a part in it, even if it never went beyond anticipation. And with every minute that passed, anticipation would become reality. If I did right by you, you'd realise I loved you, you'd believe in me. Maybe one day you'd love me.

I crept out of bed while Leo slept, absolutely possessed. I had to get everything arranged, I had it all listed in my head.

There was no time to lose. I was going to drag that bloody Citroën out of its hole and onto the road.

Would you have left her to die? You'd have hated it. Mary didn't want it. I was the one who could stop it.

It puffed up like a bullfrog. There was a mechanic in the first garage I tried. Petrol, a bit of oil, fine. I gave him every note in my pocket and went back to my mother's to get my wallet. And talk to her, I was doing it properly.

Mary was the kindest person in your life. And all I was doing was getting her to salve my conscience. I could hardly bear to bring it up.

I parked right outside, a gift for the nearest *flic*. I looked up and there was Mary, already on guard at the window.

She started to cry when I asked her. I felt terrible. I said there would be full-time nurses – there was the hospital money. She'd done so much.

'Sorry,' I said, 'sorry I mentioned it.'

'Oh love,' she said, 'you've got me all wrong.'

Everything was in place in five minutes. Monday lunchtime. Calais. I'd worked it out in my sleep.

'Having her here's the right thing, I'm sure of that.' She sighed. 'It was just you asking me, what with you getting

ready to go.' She paused, as if there was something holding her back. 'I know they seemed at odds, him and his mum. And I haven't got a clue what happened with his illness, you know I'd have said if I did – '

I came out of my room and there was my mother. She knew I was going to see you. She smiled, and she told me I looked happy.

'I am,' I said, 'I'm extremely happy.'

'But whatever they did, whatever they said, they understood each other. They tried not to, but they did. No argument could change it.'

She had that look about her I loved, as if she'd felt part of what I was feeling herself. I knew she'd say something nostalgic.

'Remember Gi, those fortune-tellers at the races.'

I remembered it. They'd followed us all the way back to the car. I was only a child, I couldn't work out what they wanted. They came up close to me, taking my hand, repeating that they could tell me my fortune and tell it true.

I was scared to death. I thought they'd suck the dreams out of my head.

'He was all excited, off to meet you in Calais, I remember it like it was yesterday. Him and Hélène, they'd been talking, I don't know what on earth they said. But I saw them say goodbye. And they really hugged each other, you know.' Mary wiped her eyes. 'I could see Hélène, I could see her eyes watering. He didn't notice, he was too caught up. Not that she would have wanted him to. But it stuck with me, that. And I thought, he's made an effort. Whoever this girl is, he's serious.'

She had tears in her eyes. She wasn't actually crying, but I knew she didn't want me to see, so I pretended I hadn't. I should never have done that.

But there was Mary, like a second mother to me, staring out of the window, blocking the traffic wardens' radar with all her might.

'He came up to me, and he gave me a proper tight hug. I lived for that. And then he said, 'I'm going to meet her off the boat!' As if I didn't know. And I said, 'You have a good time love.' And he said, 'I bloody well will.' '

Me and the bullfrog. Surely when you saw I'd driven all the way in that scrap heap, you'd get the message.

'Eggs!' Mary called down the hall, then added quietly to herself, 'always the answer.'

Venus and Leonie stopped packing their clothes and ran to the kitchen.

Five minutes later, Mary having finished her scrambled egg, Venus close behind with her poached egg on toast with parsley, chopped tomatoes and shallots, and Leonie still dipping soldiers in her boiled egg, Mary said, 'Right, let's get this sorted.'

The guests would sleep in Mary's flat upstairs. They'd have a view, a separate entrance and a kitchen and bathroom to themselves. Mary would sleep in Gilles' room and they'd use Leo's room for the nurses.

'All we've got to do now,' Mary said, 'is get Hélène home.'

They called Hélène's sister Christelle who'd recommended the hospital in the first place. She'd help in any way she could. They called the hospital, discussed how best to work out what Hélène wanted, how mobile she was, what kind of nursing she'd need.

Each with their list of jobs, Venus reckoned they could get her back before September.

'Oh easy,' Mary agreed. 'Hey,' she added, 'don't forget her stockbroker. He's the one in charge of the detail – legal, money, the works. He knows his own mind that fella.'

'Right,' Venus's jaw set, 'I'll deal with him.'

After breakfast, Venus rang her brother. She asked him if they were still looking for a chef. She said there was someone she knew who might be interested.

Matthew said they had a guy temporarily but they were so busy now they had enough work for someone else until September at least.

When she'd finished talking to him, she went into Gilles' room, closed the door and dialled Alex's number.

'Alex Todd,' he answered.

'Hi Alex, it's Venus.'

'Oh hi. Hi – it's great to hear from you... Hang on a second.' She heard a door close in the background.

'How are you?' He sounded tired, strained.

'Fine, I'm fine. How are you? I'm not interrupting am I?'

'No, no. Of course not. I thought you'd never ring.'

It wasn't right, she thought, talking about it on the phone.

'Well I – I mainly wanted to let you know that I'm not pregnant.'

He paused. 'Oh. Okay.'

She couldn't gauge his reaction.

'My period started. I didn't take the pill.'

The line went quiet. 'Right.'

He didn't sound relieved.

'I don't know what I wanted you to say,' he said.

'Well,' she breathed in. 'I suppose it's for the best.'

For the best?

She changed the subject. 'I also wanted to tell you that – I don't know if you'd be interested in this, or – well anyway, my brother and his wife, they run a restaurant in Cornwall.'

'Where your daughter stayed?'

'Yes – ' She was surprised he remembered. 'Yes, that's right. They have a vacancy for a chef, at least until September... ' She stopped herself. What was she doing? Leaving him by finding him a job? Why was she even bringing this up?

'Right,' he said.

'Sorry... I... it just occurred to me.'

'Okay,' he said. 'Thanks.'

She felt ashamed. She should never have mentioned it.

'So,' he said abruptly. 'What are your plans?'

'I'm... I'm going back to London. This morning. I wanted to ring you before – '

'*What*?'

'Well I've got to get back – '

'You're running away.'

'If I was doing that, I wouldn't have called.'

He didn't say anything.

'I know it sounds sudden, but I've – '

'Don't disappear.'

He'd interrupted, as if there was something he didn't want her to say.

'Well... ' And as she dictated her address in London to him, she knew it wouldn't do.

She wondered how she could possibly finish the conversation.

'Have you got mine?' he asked.

'Yes,' she said. 'Thanks.'

'What time's your train?'

'11:13,' she said. She looked at her watch. It was twenty past ten. 'I'd better go, the taxi's about to arrive. I'll ring you, later today – '

'I'll see you there.'

'What?'

'I'll see you at Gare du Nord.'

'Oh no. No, you needn't – '

'Why not?'

'It's just – my daughter, it would confuse her – '

But she had to get to the point. Full of nerves, she started to speak. 'Alex I like you so much. But he'll always be there. It'll be impossible. He'll follow us like a shadow.'

'Not if we both love him.'

She closed her eyes. For the odd day maybe, but not forever.

'I'll come to the station.' He paused. 'Then it'll be in your hands. I won't ring you, I won't try to get in touch with you.'

She sighed. 'It's in both of our hands. Nothing can change that.'

There was a toot outside.

'Look my taxi's arrived.'

'I'll see you there.'

Within five minutes Venus, Leonie, Mary and the bags were inside the taxi. They sped off towards République. Venus looked at her map of Paris, then again at her watch. She and Leonie were supposed to go through the gates at ten to. It would take him longer, and he'd have to find a cab. So they would have, what, two minutes?

There was still a queue at the gates when she caught sight of him. He was running up the stairs from the main station. Without explanation she left Leonie and Mary sitting on a row of seats and ran down the stairs to meet him. She went as far down the stairs as she could – maybe Leonie wouldn't even notice.

She smiled. It was good after all to see him.

He looked up and, seeing her, smiled back.

He was out of breath from running.

Accidentally his hand brushed against hers. He moved it away. She took it.

'Sorry it was so weird on the phone,' she said.

'No,' he breathed. 'I'm glad I caught you.'

He took her other hand.

'Thanks,' she said, 'for coming.'

He was getting his breath back. He looked drawn.

'Were you working at the weekend?'

'No – no. Why?'

'You look – I don't know – tired.'

'Well. It's so hot.'

The fear that they'd be apart was so clear on his face she felt it herself. He wouldn't see her in London, she wouldn't see him in Paris.

'Alex – '

'Give it a chance,' he breathed, 'don't wait for certainty, it'll never happen.'

She wouldn't see him at all. At her suggestion, as if that was what she wanted –

'Mummy!'

Leonie was standing at the top of the stairs. Venus saw her look at him.

'I'll come here,' she whispered.

'Of course – anywhere – ' He gripped her hand. 'We'd find a way.'

'Mummy! *Come on*! The queue's all gone.'

They went up the stairs.

Alex said hi to Leonie. Venus introduced them as they ran to get the bags. And then there was Mary, beside the bags, close but a little apart, listening and watching. Venus introduced Alex, a friend, to Mary. The four of them carried the bags to the passport checkers' cubicles. Venus found Leonie's passport and Mary kissed her goodbye. Venus found her own and kissed Mary goodbye. She waved goodbye to Alex, and felt it was inadequate.

She and Leonie walked on. Leonie fed her ticket into the machine and went through the barrier. Venus, about to do the same, stopped. She told Leonie to wait. Leonie groaned.

She ran back through to Alex.

She asked him to come to her house on the twenty-first of September – whatever happened. She said she knew it sounded strange, morbid even, but as he wasn't at the funeral.

'Mummy, what are you doing?'

She said it was the anniversary. It might not mean anything to him. But it might make it more real.

She felt she'd been extraordinary.

A train official told her to go to the platform immediately.

Alex took her hand, then she let go.

V

‘I can live no longer by thinking.’

William Shakespeare

39

'Homeward Bound'
by Paul Simon

Venus had sat on the train to London corralling each day until 21 September to the most strong-willed part of her brain. To have anything outside the school calendar in her future was unusual. But to see eight whole weeks forward, fifty-six controllable days, with good in the date to come, was life-changing.

Steaming through France, her new sense of self-determination distracted her completely. But when the train arrived in Kent, she wondered whether she could see Alex sooner and alone, without having to explain anything to Leonie.

That evening, she spoke openly to her mother. Patricia offered to look after Leonie as soon as Venus wanted her to. And for a long weekend in early August, Leonie stayed with Patricia while Venus went to Paris supposedly to see Hélène – four days which, unlike the trip she'd make later in August half justifying the lie, didn't involve Hélène at all.

Returning to Leonie, perspective shifted beyond recognition, she subtly sought atonement, took Leonie out, cast routine aside. She made her phone calls at night, put together songs to send to him, received a food parcel the next morning. She thought back to Gilles in confusion, then imagined a possibility she'd never guessed at before, that she might one day be able to see her life with him as a store of happiness, rather than gone forever.

'Darling, I'm right outside,' Charlotte was on the phone. 'I've got the hound. Why don't we go for a walk?'

She'd get a grip on herself before 21 September. After all she wasn't dead yet.

She and Leo. Definitely not dead yet.

'Venus Rees, *what* are you wearing?'

Venus smiled as she locked the front door, wearing nothing more immodest than wide-legged trousers and a closely cut shirt.

'And where on earth is your daughter?'

'School.' She kissed Charlotte's cheek.

'Just look at this,' Charlotte pinched her waist. 'Where d'you get this outrageous stuff?'

'Internet.'

'Makes sense, two sizes too tight round the bust.'

'Be quiet.'

'Come on Doggo.' The dog ran ahead and they started to walk. 'Honestly you've got five years younger, I'll have to up my game.'

'Ssh. Listen, I've got something to tell you.'

'You've taken up with a Tongan prince.'

'Wow, you know everything.'

'Yes, it's a burden. Go on.'

'Well – ' Venus felt her eyes begin to water. 'Sorry, I'm going to cry.'

'What?'

'It was normal,' she blinked the tears out of her eyes. 'Leo's test results. Every single one – '

'Oh darling come here.'

She'd been thinking the doctor would give them the results at the next appointment. They'd spent the month eating like vegans, done the test, and that was that. Until Friday morning when the nurse called her up the moment she heard. And only then did she know she'd been worried. Because now she was living a different life.

' – you know that's how I remember him. Crying with laughter. Hopping about like a bloody monkey.'

Venus wiped her eyes.

'Imagine his face.' Charlotte squeezed her hand. 'Darling you've done it.'

'Well. It wasn't me.'

'Who's been looking after her for four years?'

'Anyway it's not done yet. There'll be another one.'

'There's always another one – tests, horses, boys – I mean think of all the things you could worry about.'

'Yeh,' Venus smiled.

'When is it?'

'When she's fourteen.'

'Good God… '

'Exactly. She's a force enough already. I told her she was in charge this weekend. The first thing she did was call Matt and Isobel and ask for one of their puppies.'

'That's my girl.'

'I'm not looking after it. It's entirely her domain.'

'My arse. It'll break your steely heart.'

She'd played out Gilles getting his results from the day she'd got the postmortem.

Arguing in the hospital car park, he telling her to forget it, he was fine, it was all crap, she not letting him move until he took it seriously. And then the slower version, imagining she hadn't protested, imagining him asking her eventually, whether she thought maybe – about that heart stuff – maybe they should do something. Both of them, making the case for the life he would have lived.

They got to the Common, walking along a narrow path to join the broader track ahead.

Charlotte's dog careered off to harass a pair of poodles. Venus dashed after it, caught it by the collar, apologised to the poodle owner and walked it back to Charlotte.

'Darling, you're a puma.'

Venus took a breath. 'Aren't you going to put it on a lead?'

'Haven't got one… I tell you what Vee, now's the time. Singing I mean. You're on fantastic form, your mother's nearby – '

'No, not yet.' She got her breath back. 'Leo's too young. I'm singing a lot anyway, at school, at home.'

'Bullshit.'

'No, it's okay.'

'I note Gilles isn't the excuse.'

Venus felt surprised.

'Though why he was in the first place beats me. He wanted you to do it more than anyone.'

'It was him dying that was the problem, not him in himself.'

'Right. In other words it was you.'

Not about to betray her past self, Venus was silent.

'Vee, one of me is worth a million sympathetic mimsers. They love it, they eat misery. I, in contrast, want you to get better.'

Charlotte's dog came bounding up with a stick. She threw it what seemed like miles into the distance. 'Your life is in your hands.' She watched the dog run. 'Realise it.'

'And you don't think I would have done,' Venus said, 'if I'd been able?'

'You know very well what I think. Had Gilles known what was wrong with him, he'd still be here. What happened is sad, but it wasn't his fault. Let it *out* in your voice, don't keep it in.'

Venus wondered whether to declare her conclusion to Charlotte. 'Well, all that's irrelevant now.'

'What?'

'I've realised I'll never be truly certain.'

'Oh come on... ' The dog was already back with the stick. Charlotte hurled it again. '... Why on earth not?'

'I'll never know in the way I thought I could. It's part of how he was, and part of how I was.'

'Then you're impossible.'

'No I'm not, I'm honest. Of course I can believe in him, which is what you're telling me to do. What I can't do is know. Which is an answer in itself.'

Charlotte screwed up her eyes. 'Darling what is your point?'

'That I should stop trying to prove something which is unprovable.'

'And?'

'Start to miss him properly.'

Charlotte sighed.

'You have no idea, it's been like a fly in my head. And when I haven't been obsessing about whether he knew, I've been trying to recreate him, which is just – not real.

'You know something? He went on and on about me. He had to be the one who felt it. Venus, Venus, Venus. Beautiful, sexy, clever. Yeh, he's nuts about her. Fuck it. Enough. I loved him, even when he was being a total idiot. Arguing, sitting there doing nothing, spouting perverted fantasy gossip about the neighbours, answering the phone with a pathetic Japanese accent... '

Charlotte started to smile.

'I'm serious.'

A collie barked in the distance. Charlotte's dog twitched, then bolted, its black body curling and springing with acceleration. The collie barked twice, ran for a moment, then sank its head to the ground, ready.

Charlotte and Venus looked at each other.

'Be my guest darling.'

How often did you become intoxicated by someone who got drunk on you at the same time? It was barely allowed once and yet it had happened. And, despite his death, and her raging uncertainty, she'd kept trying to love him. As if he was right there in front of her. But of all they had, the closeness, the laughter, the passion, there was nothing she could give him. The person in her head was not him. And she didn't understand why no one had told her, or why she hadn't realised it before. But he wasn't there for her to love.

'So, what's the gossip?' Venus handed Charlotte an ice cream and sat down at the picnic table. 'What happened about that tennis guy?'

'Tell me more,' Charlotte licked her ice cream, 'sounds interesting.'

'On your honeymoon… you texted.'

'Aaah yes,' she said, as if they were on an archaeological dig and Venus had just shown her a dinosaur bone. 'Yes, Mason. Or was it Jason. Attractive, in a dense way. Gym body, nice arse. Hints of money-itis, smug, designer gear, shouted at a waitress. I challenged him to a match, he took the sunny end, and as he did it, he said – ' she turned on the accent, ' – '*That's how much I love English women*.' Darling, lick me till I scream.' She took a bite out of her cone. 'We started gently – in that I won every point but made it seem accidental. He realised I was good. I realised he couldn't serve for toffee. Then I'm afraid I lost my patience and absolutely thrashed the man.' She sucked the ice cream off her finger. '… That's one thing about Max, he's got a beast of a backhand.'

'So,' Venus was smiling, 'a rapprochement?'

'We understand each other Vee. Normal people wouldn't put up with either of us.'

Charlotte paused, attending to something under the table.

In the silence, Venus suddenly thought Charlotte might ask her about Alex. On the point of pre-empting her, she stopped herself. She'd hear Charlotte's opinion soon enough.

She hadn't even told Leonie yet. She'd have to do it this afternoon.

Charlotte wiped her hands with a napkin, and Venus realised she'd been feeding the ice cream to her dog.

'Talking goss Vee, remember Jake Ashley – the farmer whose cows came into the marquee? Listen to this. In the run up to the wedding, some charitable neighbour just happened to spot my mother's car continually driving in and out of Jake's farmyard. What was she doing, delivering meals on wheels? No, she was shagging him ragged. To calm herself down apparently. She got all furious and denied it, told her accuser Jake was a savage, he didn't appreciate that later in the pub and sent in the cows. To be honest I wish he'd sent them in sooner, they made the day. Anyway, she's suing him for damages. Probably jumping the lawyer as we speak.'

Chuckling, Venus set off with Charlotte back home.

She thought about the wedding as they walked, how Alex had been sure Jake was pursuing Charlotte, how passionately he'd seen it. Maybe Gilles had inspired even that. And although she knew she couldn't love a dead man, although it contradicted every rational thought she'd ever had, at the same time she felt he was as alive as he'd ever been, that she loved him intensely, that somehow he'd been waiting for her to feel that way and that he would have waited for as long as it took.

They turned out of the Common, discussing the song for the couple Patricia had put Venus in touch with.

'The bride approves,' Venus said excitedly. 'We hit on the right one.'

Heaven, I'm in heaven, And my heart beats so that I can hardly speak; And I seem to find the happiness I seek.

Charlotte would start, going through once but without the *Dance with me*. Then Venus would go through, slow and straight. They'd harmonise on the *Dance with me*, then jazz it up, but not too much.

By the time Charlotte left, Venus felt satisfied. It would sound good. Who knew, it might be worthy of Gilles' Leicester Square love.

Driving Leonie home from school that afternoon, Venus told her about the man who'd been at the Eurostar station that time, that he was nice, that he was coming over tomorrow, that he'd stay for a few days.

'Oh,' Leonie said, 'like when Lucy came for a sleepover?'

'Yeh,' Venus nodded, 'exactly.'

She changed gear, and distractedly began to think of him diving into the Seine.

'... He's good at swimming,' she added with a legitimising tone.

'Oh,' Leonie said.

Then Leonie told Venus how many house points she'd got that day and what they were all for, and how Lydia had faked one but Mrs Harris had caught her and given her a timeout, and they didn't talk about it further.

Shortly after supper, Venus put Leonie to bed. She washed up, then went to the sitting room. She looked through the stacks of sheet music on top of the piano, dug out a photocopied version of *Cheek to Cheek* that Gilles had taped together and put it on the stand. She tried to play it, but couldn't bring it to life.

She stepped away from the piano, expecting to hear him in the distance, reeled in when anyone else began to play.

After a moment, she left the room. Smiling, she started to make it out. The introduction, like a child playing peekaboo, the volume steadily increasing, her voice automatically relaxing, and then all round the house with such elegance of rhythm, such subtlety of touch, the song itself.

Heaven. She sang it as she locked the front door.

I'm in heaven. Looked in on Leonie.

And my heart beats so that I can hardly speak. Moved the duvet back over her legs.

And I seem to find the happiness I seek. Walked up the hall to her bedroom.

When we're out together dancing cheek to cheek. Lay down in her bed and turned off the light.

40

'This Must Be The Place'
by D Byrne, T Weymouth, C Frantz and J Harrison, covered by Shawn Colvin

Hi darling.

Hi my love, Leo's asleep.

It's such good news Vee.

It really is.

How are you feeling?

Happy, sad. What are you thinking about?

Oh – Calais, meeting you off the boat.

You got them to play that announcement when we came in. God I choked laughing.

Yeh, I'd forgotten that, I wish I'd heard it. It was the bit after I was thinking of. Talking in the car.

Like we're doing now.

Yeh exactly. We'd parked under the trees, there were raindrops all over the windscreen. And you looked straight at me and you said, 'I'll give it a go.'

I was being romantic.

You doubted me still, but something was different, you were prepared to shelve your doubts.

I had to tell myself it was an experiment, I was so afraid.

I know my love.

But I knew there was no choice.

I'd never been happier Vee. I felt like it was a new life.

I'd thought about you that whole weekend. The two of us running out of that bloody christening. I just didn't want to be away from you.

God knows what the weather was doing then but in this world the sun was out.

Like it is now.

You see it Vee?

Gi, I need to tell you something.

What?

When we argued, the night before you died, when I said I'd go and stay with my mother – you know I didn't mean it.

Oh my love, I know that now and I knew it then.

But it panicked you, I could tell. I had a sense something was wrong, whenever I said anything like that.

Vee –

I should have worked it out. I knew about your father. I can't understand why I never made the connection –

Vee, you have to believe me –

But hear what I'm saying.

We did everything we could. You said it to Charlotte the day I died – everything was all right. I watched you sleeping, before I left the house. We didn't want to leave each other. Because we loved each other. Like a fire in the dark. Like the sun.

Like we do now –

… Darling? You can see it can't you?

Of course. I'm addicted to looking.

I tell you, in this world, it's as good as it gets. I know it's only a dream…

No, it isn't. It's too good a dream. It's become real.

… which is killing to me, but I can't escape the rightness of it.

No Gi it needn't be. We both do it. It's just as I dream you up. We don't have to stop.

Remember the way we were, the way we loved each

other. The bells of life thud out the facts. I can't be with you, so how can I love you? And if I can't love you, how can I be?

No. I can keep you alive. I can. You're in me.

God what a joke, the cockless wanker argues himself out of existence. You know if Descartes had genuinely thought of himself without a body, he wouldn't have had time for all that philosophy, he'd have just copped it.

Darling, stop.

Oh my love. I want to.

Then stop. Gi, please.

Kiss Leo for me. Ah God. Love her for me my darling, I know you will. Shit. It's going to vanish.

Then don't let it.

Mummy. She might not bear it. Just see that she's all right. Please Vee?

Of course, I know. She'll be home soon – I will, I –

And you. Darling wife. True companion. Oh but tell me it's been worth it.

I love you. Gi, I love you.

Live for me Vee. Live like you made me live.

Listen to me. God I love you so much.

I can hear your voice. Lying in bed. Singing me to sleep.

Telling you I love you.

And hearing me tell you.

Acknowledgements

Thank you to anyone who's helped this book see daylight, by being encouraging, having their ideas stolen, letting me quote from their writing, giving reams of generous, perceptive, much-needed editorial advice, believing that a publisher would say yes, being a publisher who said yes - and a fantastic one at that - and from start to finish, lending me a room, providing financial support, childcare, supper and (near) unflagging kindness and understanding.

Particular thanks to Trevor Greetham who helped with almost all of the above. Thanks also to Sharon Galant, Lauren Parsons, Thomasin Chinnery, Benython Oldfield, Robert Harries, everyone at Legend Press, Anna South, Helen Gordon, The Literary Consultancy, Alan Brooke, Jo Theodoulou, Anne-Sophie Hofmann, Sarah Rumsby, Lizzy Woolf, Sharon Cohen, Melissa Glass, Sheila Espela, Prue and Nicholas Cooper, Lynda Simpson, The Chelsea and Westminster Hospital, Heart UK, Caroline Seymour, Adrian Stanley, Jennifer Johnston, Angela Greene, Isabelle Grey, Rae Langton, Paul Nathan, Molly Trefgarne, Gaby Larios, Annabel Abbs, Lyn Farrell, Sam, Charlie and Alb Greetham, John and Billie Burnett, Laura Burnett, Rob Burnett, George Burnett, Raquel Burnett, Frank and Celia Müller, The A-Team, Pam Smith, Jan Smaczny, Colin and Patrick Deane, Celia Larner, Olivia Rye, Crawford Howie, Paul Reid, Jane Ayers, Kate Watkins, Anne Lepage, The Camus Estate, Éditions Gallimard, Sarah Watling and Amy Rutherford at

The Wylie Agency, Allison Jakobovic at Penguin Random House, Jonathan Law at Market House Books, Nico Evans at the Music Publishers Association, Sarah Baxter at The Society of Authors, George Pearce at Music Sales, Tara at Universal, Kara Darling Kennedy and Lisa Lombardi at Imagem, Lindsay Woppert at Hal Leonard and Leah Mack at Sony/ATV. Literary thanks to Ivan Turgenev's obsession with the singer Pauline Viardot and the writing of Jean-Dominique Bauby, Alain de Botton, Geoff Dyer, Barbara Kingsolver and Theodore Zeldin among many others.

I'm grateful beyond measure to the woman who sang so beautifully in Leicester Square tube station on 1 July 1997.

Most of all, thank you to anyone who reads this book. You bring it to life.

Alice Burnett grew up on a farm in Devon, England. She studied maths at Cambridge University followed by a degree in philosophy, a subject she is still passionate about. She qualified as a lawyer in the City and worked in London and Paris before leaving law to write full-time.

Alice lives in London with her husband and three sons. *Ideal Love* is her first novel.

Follow Alice on Twitter
@BurnettBooks

Visit us at

www.legendpress.co.uk

or on Twitter

@Legend_Press